I0653913

# CAMELIA

*a novel*

## Dianna Dann

Wayward Cat Publishing

While inspired by, and built upon, an historical event, CAMELIA is a work of fiction. All its characters are figments of the author's imagination. Any resemblance to real persons is entirely coincidental.

ISBN 978-1-938999-09-3
Library of Congress Control Number: 2013948976

Wayward Cat Publishing
Palm Bay, Florida
www.waywardcatpublishing.com

Cover art copyright © 2013 Wayward Cat Publishing
Photo of girl on train tracks by SoulOfAutumn via istockphoto
Photo of camellias by dtsuneo via istockphoto

For Camelia

*M*adness dances in the light

*S*olace sleeps in shadow

# 1.

I was drunk, standing on the roof of Three River Terrace ready to jump to my death. You do things like that when you're drunk. You think, maybe I'll drive off the road into that telephone pole, or maybe I'll play with this gun, or maybe I'll take my clothes off and go stand on the roof of Three River Terrace and think about life, and eternity, and non-existence. Philosophical stuff, you know? And there was something about sex. I knew it was absurd, standing there, looking down at the parking lot–should I land on the concrete planter and the ferns, or on that Jaguar illegally parked–to jump to one's death over something as ridiculous as sex. I knew somehow, there was a deeper reason–a better reason. A reason fit for poets and suicide notes. But I couldn't think of it just then. Maybe because I was drunk.

Your mind keeps going before you jump off a building–maybe busier than usual. It's not like you're standing there chanting jump, jump, jump. That's not your job. I thought of Camelia, for some odd reason—hadn't thought of her since I was, maybe, twelve or thirteen. Bacon. Bacon came to mind. I like to think that's because it's one of life's true pleasures and I'd miss it once I was toast—ah, I made a breakfast pun—but it was probably because of the aroma wafting up from the restaurant across the street; *The Wizard of Oz;* rotting seaweed, because you can't escape that smell anywhere near the lagoon; that I'd never have children—and I couldn't decide if that was a good or a bad thing, but no, it was good; and the fact that I hate my name. And that song was running through my head. *Summer of '69.* I can safely say that the days of summer 1969 were not, by any stretch of the imagination, the best days of my life. But I couldn't get the damn thing to stop playing.

I have always, from the moment that little snot girl at the beauty salon when I was, maybe, four, told me mine was an ugly name, hated it. What nerve. The little shit was playing with *my* ponies on the floor and asked me what my name was.

"Eunie," I said.

"Eunie? Like loony?"

"Eunice."

"That's an ugly name."

"Is not."

"Is so."

And then the brat got up, took the palomino with her, and stomped over to the row of women sitting under hair dryers and shouted, "Mommy, isn't Eunice an ugly name?" Her mother nodded and mumbled something like, "Yes, yes it is," never taking her eyes off her *Life* magazine. That was when I knew. First. Never let pretty girls play with your ponies. And second. Eunice is not the name of a pretty girl.

Before then, I suppose I was too young and stupid to realize it was awful. I pity all the Eunice's in the world. I probably would have jumped off the building in honor of them, had I my wits about me at the time. Instead, I thought it was because of sex...or something equally stupid. Anyway, since that putrid little girl stole my pony, I've wanted to be Aurora or Delphinia–someone special.

When I was fifteen, I told my mother that one day I would write a book and make her a murderer. She told me I couldn't keep my underwear off the floor of my bedroom, how was I going to write a book? But I meant it. I had the plot all worked out. My mother's name would be Ethyl Bart, rhymes with fart, and she would kill her daughter, the precocious Rose, and her little dog, too, and chop up their bodies and bury them in a hole in her back yard.

I didn't know what precocious meant at the time and I've used the word a lot since then, without knowing, and miraculously being correct. But sometimes words are like that. And it didn't occur to me that maybe letting the vile mother murder her adorable daughter wouldn't make for good reading. But what do I know from writing books?

And then there's the fact that women named Ethyl would be unlikely to have enough self-esteem to name their daughters Rose and Aurora and Camelia. Which is, I'm sure, exactly why I called my invisible friend Camelia. Precisely because I knew that girls named Eunice could not grow up to name their own daughters Camelia. Look, it makes sense if you think about it.

My mother claims she named me after her favorite person in the world: her Grammy Eunice Gurnsey Holder. And I asked her why she didn't call me Gurnsey and she said don't be ridiculous. The problem was Grammy Eunice's mother–I doubt it began with her but she was as far back as I knew, so she gets all the blame. Her name was Bertha Mae Abernathy and she wanted to stick it to her daughter for the pain she endured being called Bertha through childhood. Big Bertha Butt. Not that I know anything about my Great Great Grandma Bertha. But it appears we have a thin line of big butts in the family–and I'm on it. Those svelte dark-haired beauties splashing around in their string bikinis over in the good gene pool had the luck of inheriting Pop Willie's little butt.

Bertha Mae named her daughters Eunice, Bernice, Waynice, and Clarice. Then she finally had a Gabe who the girls dressed up in frilly lace until someone beat him to death up on Lake Lure when he was nineteen. Eunice, the First, named her daughters Prudence, Gertrude, and Mildred, but was blessed with a Clifford, a Harford, and a William after each one. I come from the Gertrude line. Gert had the sense to change her name to Grace, after Grace Kelly, and name her daughters Aubrey, Darlene, and Mary Jean, which she apparently thought were lovely names and would break the cycle. Alas.

The truth is the Abernathy's were Southern strong and there were traditions to honor. The tradition to name your daughter after someone up the tree was sacred, just as was the tradition to stand idly by while your baby cried, to have your child choose a twig with which you would strike them across the legs if they talked back, to frown and scowl and ridicule. They were much like genes of ugliness, the memes of failing to love. And the names they chose reflected it.

There were the middle names, of course. Lillian, Bella, Willa, Dove, and Summer. Tossed in as afterthoughts in case maybe one of the girls might have a brazen streak, like Gert, and take up the challenge. The yearning of our nettled branches was the hope that sometime, some Abernathy woman would be the catalyst for change–you know, she'd actually love someone. There must have been, long ago in the family tree, a woman with a perfect name who became a prostitute in Old South Louisiana, shaming the family, and so for generations a beautiful name became a curse–struck onto the birth certificate, desired in an unhealthy, lustful way, and finally forgotten under the heavy burden of a chaste and wholesome ugly name.

"I named you in remembrance of her," my mother said long ago, getting all teary-eyed.

So, hang a god-damned picture, why don't you? "Who names their kid Eunice?"

"It's a family name," she said.

And that answered it, didn't it? Crazy people, that's who.

It was around the time my mother tried to kill me that I started writing letters to Camelia. I was only eight years old. I don't think I knew that a camellia was a flower. I didn't know where I got the name. But my mother acted like I'd stolen it.

"You can't write to someone you've never met," she said.

"She's my friend."

"She's not your friend. You don't even know her."

Clearly my mother had no understanding of the difficulties involved in fake friend relationships. Of course I didn't *know* her. I had to make the stuff up. So, for me, instead of inviting her over for dinner, say, or having her sleep over, and letting my parents and Sausage make fun of me and tell me I was talking like a crazy person, or as my mother put it, seeing ghosts, I chose to make Camelia a pen pal. A, shall we say, questionably existent, never writing back, pen pal.

I could have had her write back. Once, in the seventh grade, I wrote letters to myself from Jason Prescott and showed them to the other girls at school. Jason loved me and could not wait until we were together again. Jason was so sorry he couldn't meet me at school and walk me home or take me to the school dances. He was too old to be seen at the middle school, after all. But in every letter, he reminded me of the great times we enjoyed on our car dates and how mature we both were. Not one of those girls believed that Jason Prescott wrote me those letters, a fact that continues to bother me to this day.

"So that's why," I told Dr. Crazy, "I wrote her letters."

What was it to the doctor, anyway? Was there some kind of make-believe friend code that said they must sit with you at dinner and say prayers with you at night or else you were crazy? Had no one in her entire two and one-half years of experience counseling lunatics ever had an invisible pen pal for an invisible friend? I was perturbed at her insinuation that Camelia wasn't real, in the pretend sense.

Ah, what the hell am I saying? It's not like I could pull off a Lilly or a Summer anyway–certainly not an Aurora. It wasn't until my eighth birthday party that I even knew I had a middle name. My father and mother, Sausage and some older friend of his, Aunt Aubrey and her then-husband Whatshisname, all gathered around the cake with eight candles stuck in it and sang and Aunt Aubrey belted out April instead of Eunie and then there was a huge fight.

Was that some kind of sick joke, my mother screamed at her. She was crying and telling Aunt Aubrey she'd confuse me and April wasn't a very good month, anyway. I remember Aunt Aubrey smiling, but then, she was always smiling in one way or another. I didn't know what the hell was going on so I asked Sausage and he told me my name was April.

"Is not," I said.

"Is so. It's your middle name–probably because you were born in April."

The sheer vulgarity of sticking the name of her birth month in your child's name didn't occur to me until much later, probably not until I was on the roof of Three River Terrace.

"What's a middle name?"

His friend, Pinky? Squat? I can't remember his name, laughed and punched Sausage in the arm.

"You know," Sausage said, shoving Dufus away.

"Like Jesus H. Christ. The H stands for Holy; it's his middle name. And your name is Eunice A. MacMillan."

"The A stands for April?"

"How do you know the H doesn't stand for Henry or Hank?" Ditzboy said.

Sausage rolled his eyes. "Don't be stupid. Gods aren't named Henry."

I didn't believe him of course–about my name, he was completely correct about the gods–and was too afraid to ask my mother about it for a few weeks and when I finally did, she sighed and said, "Yes, it's true. Your middle name is April."

She was so sad about it. And it all happened so fast that I thought maybe that was why she'd decided to have me killed. Having a name like April must be awful. And it actually was. For one thing, once I'd got used to it and Sausage and my friends started calling me April, every time someone said April I thought they were talking to me. People who pronounce apricot as ape-ricot freak me out. And as I got older I realized that April was not the name of an old person.

There I was, at twenty-five, after all, standing on the roof of Three River Terrace knowing full well that when I was seventy, no one could call me April; it would be absurd. I was trapped by Eunice–nowhere to go, but back to Eunice. And after I'd fought so hard every year in school to train the teachers and the new bullies. All for naught. Anyway, everybody knows just by looking at me that I'm a Eunice or an Ethyl, or a Big Bertha Butt. Aprils are sweet and charming with dimples. Like Cindy Brady from *The Brady Bunch*. She could be an April all her life.

But not round-faced, round-eyed, funky-nosed people with straw blonde hair. We're Eunices.

The important thing is that when I was twenty-five, I tried to jump off a building, right? That's what I mean to be getting at. The trick was to find something worth living for and I had failed. It's apparently an unspoken rule. In fact, it's more like an unconscious pact with biology that most people are born understanding. *The thing worth living for is life itself.* But it wasn't working for me. Like a lever was supposed to be switched on at some point and nobody had bothered. I couldn't figure out what it was all for, what it was all about, and why everyone was so happy. Didn't they see what was happening all around them? People watched the news; I just didn't understand why none of them ran screaming from their houses into traffic afterwards.

Stay positive, they kept saying. Focus on the good stuff. Stop and smell the god-damned roses. Well, you know what? If you can smell roses while climbing over a pile of corpses—well, that's beside the point. And you know, my mother wouldn't have set a place for Camelia at the table, anyway. And she was never one to point to a bare spot next to you and say, "And has Camelia said her prayers?" She'd never be caught dead tucking in my Teddy bear at night, much less my invisible friend.

It was morning, maybe eight thirty and already hot. My god, it was only June and the summer was still to be got through. Reason enough to step off the edge and count. How many seconds to the ground? A moist wind from the lagoon behind the building sent my hair into my face, tickling me. I hated that. Hair in my face. Hair anywhere it didn't belong. I never understood the lure of the convertible. In Florida no less. Not to mention the prospect of eating bugs. It's not like in the movies, you know. That's all done with stops and takes, and the makeup and hair people running in to fix things. The reality is that your hair is in your mouth—with the bugs—and whipping against your face and when the car is finally stopped you're battered and crazed-looking. Who wants that?

And I mean any hair, really. The hair on my arms is a constant irritation. What the hell is it doing there? I took to tweezing it off when I was about seventeen. I'd sit for hours in my room with my little black-and-white television airing old films where they dance and sing for no apparent reason—and ride in convertibles without losing their hats—yanking the long blonde hairs out of my arms. It's almost like the pretty girls clipping off split ends in their hair, but weirder. It's hard to sit and look dainty or sophisticated tweezing off your arm hair.

Downtown sprawled below me like someone spit it out. Ugly city. Southward drifted off into swamps until you found yourself in a more civilized area—Melbourne, Fort Lauderdale, Miami. West was old, ratty, unplanned, and unprepared Sandy Point. Beyond that, Orlando where intelligent people lived. North was the way out. Out of Sandy Point, out of Florida, out—where any sane person would want to be. And east, behind me, the lagoon and beyond, the VAB, or Vehicle Assembly Building, where they made rockets, and the ocean. Salt from the Atlantic seasoned the air, with a little lagoon rot added in.

10

I know what you're thinking. Why would anyone recall *The Wizard of Oz* when she's about to jump off a building? It was the flying monkeys. My childhood was dominated by a brutal recurring dream about hiding in our family room peering out the window, watching the flying monkeys carry my mother away. They were really after me; and they'd catch up with me sooner or later.

I was drunk. Yes, it was eight in the morning and I was still drunk. I climbed onto the low ledge and looked down. The world spun and I struggled for balance. Walked a few paces this way and turned to walk back, my arms outstretched, see-sawing up and down. It was a pretty wide ledge–I could have danced on it if I wasn't mind-numbingly plastered.

I stopped the pacing and turned to the street. My whole life was supposed to pass before my eyes, and I wondered which parts I'd get to see–because it was going to be a short drop. (It was the tallest building in Sandy Point at the time, mind you, but still only seven stories.) Which parts of my life would be so important they'd come to mind in that brief time in the air?

And then I remembered Camelia, which is strange, don't you think? I stood for the longest time with an empty pain in my belly, staring at the ground. Sirens sounded in the distance. People gathered on the sidewalk across the street in front of that little cafe I'd always wanted to go to. The smell of their cinnamon buns drifted up to the roof and I watched as this guy in a baseball cap took a big bite of what looked like a bagel. Looking up at me. Chewing and smiling. Everything seemed to have come to its momentary conclusion, so I hopped down from the ledge and dug through my purse, pulled out my little journal and wrote her a letter.

*Dear Camelia, All I hear is screaming. Screaming in my head. It's been there since I made you up and I thought forgetting you would make it stop. I was on the ledge, I swear. I stood with my toes at the precipice and I wasn't sure what was next. When you think of a precipice you don't figure that after leaping you'll be dead. You think you'll have begun a new journey, set off on a new path. I don't think dead can be considered a path, no matter what my Aunt Aubrey might say. I'm sorry Camelia. I'm so sorry. But I have to make the screaming stop.*

# 2.

It's not like I didn't try to jump. I ripped the note out of my journal thinking it didn't belong there and shoved them both back in my purse. Then I got back up on the ledge and whirled a bit looking down at the street below. Police cars pulled into the parking lot and people emerged from the building, stood on the asphalt in the building's shadow and looked up at me. Hairdressers and the dentist's staff who had businesses on the first floor; old ladies in their bathrobes who lived in the condominiums, and a few kids.

I yelled at them. "You should all be in bed." I stretched out my arms and looked to the sky, like an Olympic diver. A woman screamed.

The year started out all right. Same old, same old. I spent New Year's at a bar and got kissed by some perverted drunk at midnight and probably let him drive me somewhere. I withdrew from all my classes again at the community college and muddled my way through the first few months avoiding my mother as best I could, which wasn't easy since we lived together.

And then April came and I was dumped into the worst dark pit ever. April was always hard. For one thing, everywhere I turned my name came up. Almost made me want to go back to Eunie the Loony. April was always, always dark. And I thought maybe it was worse that year because I was twenty-five, and no one said anything—no cake, no candles. But honestly, I got up early, left the house, spent the entire day and into the next morning in bars, so it's no one's fault but my own. I must have spent May drunker than usual because I couldn't fathom how I'd made it to June.

I think I was surprised by April—surprised I'd lived so long. I'd been expecting death for seventeen years. So, climbing up on the roof of Three River Terrace made perfect sense. But, I don't know...writing the letter to Camelia sobered me up or made me feel stupid. So, I got back down and coming at me were these two office guys with their arms reaching out for me like they wanted to grab me but were afraid they'd be infected...with what? Suicidal tendencies?

I had my clothes back on and was smoking a cigarette by the time the wheezing cops arrived. I could have told them how hard the elevator was to find, if maybe they'd taken the time to shout up at me from the street. But it was agonizingly slow, so it was probably best that they climbed the eight flights.

I wasn't completely naked, mind you. That would have been crazy. I was cuffed for my own protection, and quickly found myself at the Lakeview Psychiatric Treatment Facility out in the middle of the state where there was nowhere to run if you managed to escape. Nice place. It was on a lake, at least.

When they led me into Dr. Reginaldi's office late that afternoon, I first noticed the cigarette smell. It wasn't at all like the smell in the bisexual inmate lounge–stale burritos and urine. No, this was fresh cigarette. I gathered they cleaned the doctors' offices regular. And then I saw my note to Camelia on Reginaldi's desk. It was crumpled, but I knew I didn't wad it up or anything. I was clutching at it, I guess, that morning when they followed me into my little room and took it from me; they took everything I had, including my clothes–all of them this time. I was completely naked when I got the body cavity search. Is there another way to do that? If I'd have just left it in the damned journal, I couldn't have gotten to it, and nobody would have seen it–assuming they didn't obsessively leaf through every page of people's notebooks.

Dr. Reginaldi came in, a tall skinny sort with spiky, black hair--reminded me of a dancer in an off Broadway, new age kind of way. And she wore tight jeans, to show off her lack of thighs. She smiled at me and gestured toward the couch.

"Am I supposed to lie down?"

"If you like."

Well, I didn't like and from her tone she didn't like the idea much either. That was too theatrical–perfectly theatrical. In the movies the patients are always lying down, and the therapists pick at their teeth and do crossword puzzles behind their backs, while they ramble on about their mothers.

And I do mean bi-sexual, by the way, as in, both sexes use the common room. But we were split between men's and women's dorms at night. I considered asking Dr. Reginaldi about homosexuals, but I thought better of it. So I curled myself up in a corner of the sofa. There was an open pack of Salem menthols on the end table and an ashtray. I lit up and breathed in. Calm washed over me from head to toe. I was just a little dizzy by that time, fed, and a bit nauseated. My eyelids were puffy and scraped against my dry eyeballs every time I blinked.

Reginaldi took her time pretending to read a file on me. How much could they have?

"Eunice MacMillan?"

I shuddered. "It's April. Eunice April MacMillan." I emphasized the April.

"Did you try to jump off a building this morning?"

Well, that was blunt. "I thought you were supposed to ask open-ended questions."

She smiled. "Who's Camelia?"

I took a long drag from my Salem and flicked a bit of ash. She waited in that psychiatric pause they get into. It's very uncomfortable. I think they intend it to be.

"The policeman was rifling through my purse," I said. "He took my letter."

She nodded. "And you took it back."

"That's right."

I did take it back and almost got myself a charge of resisting arrest. I could stand before the judge and explain that I was not, in fact, resisting arrest. They could arrest me all they wanted. What I was resisting was the taking of my property. Even I could see I didn't have a case.

"Can I get you something to drink?" She said.

I nodded. She got up and went to a little porta-fridge

and pulled out a Diet Coke, looking at me hopefully. I nodded again and took it from her.

"Diet Coke is popular here," she said.

She was trying to be friendly and that struck me weird. Why would she want to get friendly with crazy people? Because I can tell you, after a half day in there, even though I slept through the first hour or so of it, it was pretty clear to me that I was among lunatics. The doors were very heavy, for one thing, and bolted with too many locks. People, hunched and sickly, paced in circles or along patterns they imagined on the floor; one guy smacked himself on the face every time I looked at him. And they were all in their pajamas. They made me wear pajamas, too, which I have to admit, I didn't mind. I never thought about wearing pajamas for a job before, but all the nurses and orderlies wore them. That first day, I decided to be a nurse so I could wear pajamas all day. When I walked to the cafeteria, some of the crazies stared at me and one guy barked. I was just a drunk, I tried to tell one of the guards–they acted like they were nurse orderlies but I knew better–he smiled at me like I was insane.

"That must be some thick glass," I remember saying to the orderlies and cops who brought me in. "If I ram it, will it crack my head open?"

And then I understood the cavity search.

"Would you like to talk about Camelia?" Reginaldi asked.

I dragged on Salem again. The tiniest bit of a silly smile hit my lips and I blushed.

"Camelia is my imaginary friend."

Reginaldi said nothing—just stared back at me. When you say something like that out loud, as an adult, it sounds a little bizarre.

"From when I was little."

"She's not a real person?"

I shook my head.

"Then I'm curious as to why you would say—" and here she looked over my crumpled letter. "Go on without me; I'm done here."

I dragged on Salem and eyed Reginaldi like an outlaw. Then I took a long drink of the cold Coke and wiped my lips off on the back of my hand. I shook my head.

"I didn't write that."

She leaned forward and held out the crumpled piece of paper. I took it and pulled at the corners trying to smooth it out. It was my handwriting, all right. Messy. Drunken. Scribbles, really. All it said was, "Dear Camelia. This place sucks balls. Go on without me. I'm done here."

I let out a dry chuckle and tears wet my tired eyeballs, finally.

"That's not what I wrote," I said and laughed a little more. "It was a real nice letter. Real nice. I think I used the word precipice. It could have been in a novel it was so nice."

I looked to Reginaldi, her crisp black hair poking up at odd spots on her head like she was an evil sprite with a soft heart. She nodded.

"And you say Camelia is imaginary?"

"When I was little, I invented her and I decided to live her life instead of mine. That's all. I lived for her.

Drove my mother nuts. I'd forgotten about her until I was on the roof."

"You were going to jump and you remembered your imaginary friend?"

"That's right. I was going to jump. Maybe. In that half-hearted way people think about doing drastic and stupid things. I was drunk."

She glared at me. No one ever appreciated my excuses. But why would she? I was her bread and butter, better crazy than not.

"I'm serious," I said. "She's not real. But if she shows up on visiting day you can call me certified." I laughed. She nodded. Do psychiatrists have senses of humor?

"Have you had any visitors?" Oh, that was a low blow. Very low indeed. "Have you called your family?"

"No."

"Why not?"

"The cops told me they called my mother. They said she knew where I was going."

She nodded.

"Have you spoken to my mother?" I said.

"I'll make sure she's been notified."

"It's no problem. She won't care."

She wrote something in her notebook.

"How long do I have to stay in here?"

"Seventy-two hours."

"Seventy-two hours? How long is that?"

She looked up at me. She knew what I meant. I could almost see the synapses firing. Should she be an intellectual snot and tell me that it's seventy-two hours? That's what I would do. Or should she tell me how long it is in days? Or worse, maybe she was trying to figure out how long it was in days.

"How long do you think it is?"

I laughed. "Good one."

I didn't want to talk to Reginaldi. I did. But I didn't. I can't say why. She'd probably have known. She'd say it was something to do with not feeling like I deserved to be heard. Maybe something about how my overly critical mother and distant, ghostly father, combined to create in me some kind of disorder, where I stuffed feelings way down into a black pit of horror and worked constantly to keep the door shut. Maybe something like that. But instead she let me ramble about ordinary, everyday stuff. She was trying to figure out if I was insane or not and I wanted her to think I wasn't. I probably was, mind you. But I didn't want to stay there in that place.

"The police report says that witnesses heard you screaming. What can you tell me about that?"

"I don't know what you're talking about."

She picked up some papers and looked at them. "It says you were on the ledge. Then you got down from the ledge and disappeared for a short while. They heard screaming, so several of them went into the building to find someone who knew how to get up to the roof. They found an open office and asked a couple of men for help. The men went up to the roof. Witnesses returned outside and at that point you were on the ledge again."

"Well, that's odd," I said.

"You don't recollect screaming?" She started writing again.

"Where do homosexuals sleep?"

She looked up from her notebook, letting on a bit of astonishment. "What?"

"Where do homosexuals sleep?" Nothing. She just stared at me. "Which dorm? Do you put a lesbian in with the women? And if so, can a straight woman be in with the men?"

"Are you a lesbian?"

"No. I'm just wondering."

"Would you prefer to sleep in the men's dorm?"

I shook my head and furrowed the brows like, is she stupid? "No."

That was the end of our first meeting.

In the bisexual urine room all the good seats facing the window, bathed in afternoon sunshine, were taken by crumpled, drawn and gray figures, shaking their heads and mumbling. I figured I deserved one of the good seats, by the window, in the sunshine. *I* wasn't crazy. They couldn't possibly appreciate the view of the lake like I could. I stood beside the green puffy chair with the anorexic in it. She smiled up at me briefly and then went back to her somber gazing. She was beige. Hair, eyes, skin. Blah brown, like her flat expression. No wonder she stopped eating. I stood some more, thinking I could easily overpower her and take her lounger. She was next to nothing–half-starved. Probably on her way out–in the permanent way. There was a bandage wrapped around her left arm and she was unconsciously pulling at stray threads with her right hand.

"Jumper?" She said.

Great. Good news travels fast. Even in the loony bin. "Almost," I said.

"Were you scared?"

"I was drunk."

"Ah," she smiled bigger this time, her thin, wan skin pulled taut against her face and the circles under her eyes deepened into ashy gray. "We do strange things when we're drunk. You should talk to Reginaldi about it. She can get to what's eating you."

"Nothing's eating me." Leave it to the anorexic to make everything about food.

The man in the purple lounger on the other side of me started barking. Anorexia acted like he didn't exist and turned back to her bandage, pulling at the threads. She was maybe thirty, maybe fifty, it was hard to tell. Not a good mother figure. Too near to extinction to do anyone any good.

"I'm Sue," Anorexia said without looking up.

"April. What are you in for?"

She held up her bandaged wrist. Nice. I winced.

"Were you scared?" It seemed like the appropriate question. She was probably not interested in whether or not I was scared standing on the roof of Three River Terrace. She was just projecting her fear into my actions. And I didn't really care if she was scared when she slit her wrist. I was only being polite. I could be Dr. Reginaldi.

She shook her head. "It felt good." She inspected her wrist and tugged slightly at the bandage as if it were on too tight. "You want to hang around with us," she looked over to the barker next to me. "The suicides."

I laughed. Out loud. And it was like everything stopped, for a split second, and all the crazy people looked my way; then they went back to their psychoses.

22

"Is it like a clique?" I said.

Sue looked up at me and smiled. Skinny people shouldn't smile so much. A smile requires a bit of fat to the face to make it warm instead of terrifying.

"You might say that," she said. "We'll all be in group together."

Dog barked again and I turned to him. The old man grinned. "Think I'm insane, don't you?"

I nodded as imperceptibly as I could. He was wearing an oversized scrubs top–our pajama uniform; he'd rolled the bottom up and somehow managed to create a tie, thus designing for himself a midriff. Very cute, except it showed off his bulging, white-haired belly with its cavernous button.

He laughed and hauled himself out of the lounger. "Go on and sit." He laughed again and walked away, his hospital pants slung low on his hips showing off his hairy crack.

"It's all right," Sue said. "He likes to play insane in here."

"Just in here?"

I considered, only for the briefest moment, that dog man might have left something contagious...or fecal, behind, before relaxing in the soft chair. Soon the sun would be below the eaves and we'd have to have an orderly pull the shade–no rods or strings allowed in the loony bin–or move to the other side of the room.

Barking is probably insane; I mean, unless you've got Tourrettes and then you can't help it. But, even if you don't actually think you're a dog, barking is just not right. In probably every culture on earth, acting not right can get you locked up. People want to be comfortable and safe. Barking doesn't get them there.

"He'll bark at you until you call him Rover," Sue said.

"Well, I'm not going to call him Rover."

She shook her head again. The bell sounded.

"What's that one for?"

"Visiting time."

It was a shame. I was hoping for another meal. The mound of instant mashed potatoes covered in watery brown gravy sitting on top of the gravy-covered mystery meat they'd woken me up for earlier was heavenly—salty and warm. Soft buttery corn, and a wedge of lettuce with a tomato slice and mushy, syrup-covered apples. I could only hope for a repeat at dinner.

I heard the swishing of thigh caressing thigh behind me and turned to see a dark woman poured tight into pale orange scrubs approaching. She was all lips. Bright red happy lips.

"Eunice MacMillan?"

I sucked in a breath. "My name is April."

Lord. It was elementary school all over again. Every god-damned year. Eunice MacMillan? It's April. Sure it's April. You think anyone's going to call you April after they hear Eunice? Not to mention the fact that my family refused to call me by my good name. I was Eunie the Unicorn forever.

"You have a visitor. Your brother. Sue, you too. Your husband is here again."

We both sat. I didn't want to give up my good seat; I didn't know about Sue. Maybe her husband drove her mad. Or maybe he slit her wrist himself and smeared her blood all over the mirror in their bathroom. Maybe he drew a heart. Or maybe when he visited he cried and she couldn't stand another hour of it.

"Well?" Scrubs said.

We both forced ourselves out of our preferred seating in the sun and followed her through the lobby into the hallway between two windowed rooms from where they sat and watched us, and probably got to watch cable while we were stuck with soap operas all day. The soaps were what all the crazy people wanted to watch. Maybe because crazy was a staple in daytime television. Granted, I'd only been there the one day so could hardly make such assumptions at the time. But I was certain, anyway.

Three of us waited for Scrubs to unlock the door to the main room where we were allowed to visit. None of us bounced with excitement. It could have been the drugs, brought to us in tiny paper cups–we all swallowed them without question. Or it could be that crazy people don't get excited about visitors from the outside, barging in on their mental disorders. I decided that if I was crazy, I liked it, and I didn't want anyone bothering me about it.

There was James Dean MacMillan, Sausage, sitting at one of the little makeshift meeting spaces. A few chairs around a coffee table. He was his happy, chatty self, holding a foam cup, talking to a blond male nurse. He saw me and smiled, waved. Yes, just like he was visiting me at camp or something.

"Hey," he said.

I sat in one of the chairs and waited for him to finish socializing.

"That was Tom Perry. I ran track with him at SPHS."

25

Nice. Small world.

He sat and sipped and stared at me. "So what happened?"

"Didn't they tell you?"

"They said you tried to jump off a building."

"Only sort of."

"Were you drinking?"

What kind of idiotic question was that? I'd been either drinking, drunk, or hung over for the past five years and he wanted to know if I was under the influence when I tried to jump off a building?

"Mom's too upset to come."

I could only imagine. I was surprised that Sausage was able to leave her in her state of misery to visit. "So, why are you here?" I asked.

"I had to find out what was going on."

"What's going on?"

He rolled his eyes. I have to admit that I enjoyed being clueless when the moment merited. But I didn't know what he was perturbed about. He'd driven halfway across the state to find out what he already knew; I didn't invite him.

"Look, it's like this. Mom doesn't want you to come back home. She wants you to stay in here and get help."

"This isn't the kind of place you go to get help, Jimmy. It's a loony bin."

"You tried to kill yourself; so maybe this is the right kind of place."

"Well, I'm getting out in seventy-two hours, minus twelve, whatever that is."

"No, you're not."

"What's that supposed to mean?"

"I mean you have to commit yourself."

I balked. "I'm not staying in here."

"You either commit yourself, or we're going to Baker Act you."

"What's that?"

"We go to court and tell a judge that you're a danger to yourself and need to stay in here."

My mouth fell open slightly. "But there's crazy people in here."

He shook his head. "Maybe you're crazy."

No. He didn't look like a sausage. He was tall, lean, sure, and handsome with those almond-shaped black eyes, like our mother's. So completely different from me that if I didn't have my father's face, I'd have sworn I was adopted. Sausage inherited parts of my father's face too, but they looked better on him. I called him Sausage in my head all the time, maybe from the first time I saw a roll of Jimmy Dean, wrapped in plastic, at Publix. I said it out loud, "Look mom, Jimmy has a sausage." I laughed and laughed. "Jimmy's sausage." And she slapped the shit out of me. She waited until we were out by the car to do it.

For most of my life I thought she'd smacked me because I was calling James names. That was a bad thing to do—that's what the teachers tell you, anyway. But we called each other names all the time. James called me Priss Pants and Eunie Unicorn and Flubber Butt. I called him Butt Head and Skinny Bones. I wasn't quite as creative. Dad even called our mother Waddle and Duck. So what was the big deal about me calling James Sausage? I didn't get it until I was, maybe, seventeen. I matured slower than the other girls. And when I got it, I guess I understood the slap. But, you really ought to explain to a person why you're hitting her.

When I was six or seven and we were a family, we camped in the Keys. All my memories of the Keys are yellow white and stifling hot with a noncommital breeze that's too mild to suck in and make anything of. You can taste the salt on your tongue just thinking about it; and I always see myself bright red, white blonde, shielding my eyes from the sun—miserable.

That trip, we drove down in the monster. A white utility van with a roaring engine and a metal floor. I vomited white spoiled milk and Mylanta the whole journey and arrived pale, weak, and embittered. I'd have liked to complain—about the lack of air conditioning in the van, about the uncomfortable seat, the smell of gasoline, and the way my father drove—speeding up like he'd stashed a body in the trunk and the police were chasing him, then slowing behind Florida retiree traffic, weaving to a different lane and speeding up again—but I was too tired and shaky from vomiting and emptiness to do anything but moan.

"We're here now; stop whining," she said.

And I lay down on the white hot sand and bits of shell, working on a nice red burn, while they set up the tent near a picnic table on Bahia Honda Key. Finally, I got up and sat at the table while they made the final touches to camp. I said, in my best baby voice, "Daddy, come shit down by me."

I'd reeled off the back of the bench and hit the ground before realizing what had happened. Mom had smacked the shit out of me again. Dad pulled me up by one arm, and I could tell by the look on his face he was pissed off. I didn't even realize I'd said the word shit until the dual, simultaneous lectures repeated it, with Sausage staring back and forth at our parents probably wondering what the hell they were going on about. They cursed all the time. But everybody knows that parents are allowed to curse and smoke and drink and have a whole bunch of sex and go to strip clubs. But just try it when you're a kid and see what you get.

Anyway, that's how you do it. You tell the person what they did wrong. You don't smack them, and then let them keep thinking about sausages whenever they think of their brother. It's vulgar, really–not when you're ten and you don't know what the hell you're doing–but when you're seventeen and suddenly put two and two together and still can't stop doing it.

I used to stand in front of the mirror cursing my round eyes. I stole a charcoal black eyeliner pencil from my mother's vanity cabinet once and drew heavy lines to make my eyes almond-shaped, like the women in the romance novels. But, of course, their eyes were also violet, which I suspected was not a real eye color. There was nothing I could do about the dull hazel brown of my own. And, when I saw the results of my thirteen-year-old liner job, I knew there was nothing I could do about their shape, either.

Cursing at my reflection every time I saw it helped for a little while.

# 3.

I want to go home," I said to James.

He sighed and shook his head. "Don't you think you need to be someplace like this? Someplace you can get help?"

No such place existed.

For a while, I'd been living in an upstairs apartment in a little complex of twelve in the shape of a "u" with a pool in the middle. I pulled up one day, my little red Datsun stuffed full with all my possessions from my latest attempt to run away from home, and found the landlord standing out by the pool in a one-piece and a swimming cap. The color of her suit, juicy green, was an unfortunate choice as she looked very much like a pear on twigs. Her fists were balled and pressed hard on her non-existent hips as she pursed her lips at me.

I liked the place right away. Children laughing and splashing in the pool. A poodle chasing butterflies near the shrubs. Tables with umbrellas stuck through holes in their middles. And a warden-like mother figure for a landlord. Perfect.

"No dogs, no kids," she barked.

I turned to the pool.

"Yes," she said. "Those are children and that's a dog."

Okay, then. One of those no questions no lies deals. I could handle that. I handed her the cash my father had given me and she gave me a key. But my stay was short lived. I had no vacuum cleaner and two cats. The cats barfed on the top of the refrigerator, all over the butterscotch shag carpet, and even on my bed. No doubt the landlady didn't give a crap about my bed. They did this because I was drunk all the time and spent my nights in bars. Cats need attention like any other creature.

Little sticky notes started showing up in my apartment each afternoon as I'd awaken from my drunken stupor into a hangover. "Clean this mess!" Sometimes she'd draw arrows and place the note *just so*...as if there was only that particular mess that bothered her when the entire apartment was littered with dirt, trash, used paper plates, newspapers, leftover pizza, and cat vomit.

I could almost laugh about it when my mother came and stood in the middle of the little living room, turning this way and that, looking at my life. The landlady probably thought she'd scored a winner when I pulled up in my little car. Shy, quiet, neat in appearance–not attractive, so no party or late night boyfriend problems looming. A landlord's dream. Well, I taught her a lesson.

My mother brought me home with her that day. I went because I was sick with fever and my throat felt like a balloon. I told her I was sick, but she didn't believe me.

She helped me pack up a few things and drove me to her little duplex north of town. I slept in the guest bedroom all day and still, she didn't believe I was sick.

"Eunie, get up," she kept saying that first morning. "We've got to go feed your cats. Get up."

She started vacuuming in my room. I still didn't get up. But I can't imagine she'd expect me to. When I was a child, on the weekends and during the summers, I'd stay up all night watching movies in black and white on the little twelve-inch my parents bought me one Christmas. And then I'd sleep all morning. She'd talk as if I was awake, which I guess I was because I remember it.

"I've never seen anyone sleep so much in my life," she'd say, as if I'd gone to bed at ten the night before instead of five in the morning. Then she'd bring my folded laundry in and push it hard onto the bed, come in and dust, moving all the crap off my dressers onto the bed and back again, spray Lysol disinfectant all around, and then, her *coup de gras*, vacuum, bumping and banging the machine against the baseboards. That was her revenge, you know—cleaning my room for me. I could sleep through it all.

But this time I was sick. "I'm hot," I'd say. "My throat hurts."

She came to stand by the bed, her hands on her hips like my landlady, rolled her eyes, and finally, lord have mercy, put her hand on my forehead.

"Eunie, you're burning up."

No kidding. She forced me to get dressed and drove me to the clinic where I was vindicated with a bout of tonsilitis. Anyway, I never left. The cats were brought over and the furniture ceremoniously dumped into the dumpster. Is that why they call it a dumpster?

It was awful furniture. Aunt Aubrey had donated it. A plush mustard sedan chair and a brick-red love seat; a warped, brown card table to eat on, with one folding chair. And the bed. That was about it. No doubt the landlady dug it all out of the trash and put it back in the apartment, and now she's getting half again by renting it furnished.

"I can't stay here," I told Sausage. I couldn't help glancing around and saw an orderly watching me. I rubbed at my arms with my hands; why was it always so cold in institutions? "I have to work."

"Toby called," he said. "We know you got fired."

"But I have a job interview next Friday. And I know I'll get it."

"You just got fired yesterday."

"But I was going to leave, anyway. I want to work at the bookstore in the mall."

"Since when?"

"Since a while ago. You don't want me to lose out on getting another job, do you?"

He sat back in his chair and shook his head, his left knee bouncing up and down in a tiny jiggy dance. A warped reflection of his chest and head in the table moved along with him; the surface would be cool and slick and the urge to lay myself across it gnawed at me. But it seemed like something a crazy person would do, so I didn't.

"You can't hold down a job."

"I can so; I was at the Joint for a while." I was

34

whining and almost winced from my history of having whines smacked out of me.

He shook his head again and looked around the visiting room. His gaze stopped on the anorexic sitting with a man, pulling at her bandaged wrist, crying.

"I'll talk to mom."

The puffy chairs were all taken–proving to me that visiting hour was a big fat waste of my time. The sun lit up a hot white patch on the floor and the crazy people were lying back in their chairs with their eyes closed, drinking it up like anti-venom. I went to the window and looked out at the pink and purple sky at the edge of the treetops and one of the loons sitting behind me said, "Don't stare at the sun. Don't stare. We all stared at the sun too long."

After dinner, a small group of us, the suicides, gathered at our own table in the common meeting room where we could get away from the zombies and freaks but still keep an eye on them. The common room was separated by a glass wall from the burrito urine lounge. The pee lounge was better, in that there were large television sets like they have in hospitals that were hung from the ceiling and lots of soft chairs. But the crazy people were in there all the time–walking in circles, shouting obscenities, groping themselves.

Here, folding tables, square and rectangular, and padded folding chairs created a maze. Several small groups of nuts huddled together at tables as far away from the others as they could manage. One group was addicts, Rover told me–we suicides scared the bejeezus out them, he said. Another group was only alcoholics and they liked to stick together to talk AA—it's a language all its own, he said.

"I'm not a suicide," I told him.

Rover sat at the head of our long table and looked past me to wink at Sue. This scrawny kid named Paulie sat across from her and smiled.

"Sure," Rover said. "Technically, none of us are."

Paulie chuckled. "If you want to get technical about it."

Martin and Millie, the frog and the hermit, sat on a sofa in the corner staring at a television set that wasn't turned on. They were all three, Rover told me. Hard drugs, alcohol, and suicide. Triple threats. And he laughed.

An orderly who was really a guard and probably itching to brandish his gun at us, sat in a chair near the door, watching, waiting for us to flip out, go berserk, throw coffee on him, what? All along the walls were posters with pictures of flowers and puppies and sunrises and weird sayings that didn't make any sense, like, "believe and be," and "positive is power."

"You missed group this morning," Sue said without smiling, tapping her hands on the table.

"I was sleeping."

"You better work with them—work the program," Rover said. "Or you'll be asked to commit yourself."

"You don't want to do that," Martin said from the sofa. He got up and wove his way in and around the tables to sit down next to Paulie and across from me. Martin was a thin, starving frog, wide mouth, large pop eyes, a wisp of hair sticking up atop his head. He sat like a coiled piece of wire at the table, his chin nearly resting on it.

"That'll stay with you for the rest of your life," Paulie said and smiled at me.

Paulie was also thin, like a flat line running at the edge of a page with fine, blond hair and a dazed look about him. You realized, looking at Sue and Paulie and Martin, that there were ways to be thin that a person probably shouldn't give much thought to.

"You don't come away from an institution like this whole again," he said.

"But isn't that why you come here?" I looked around at the lunatics in the room, all of them pretending not to listen to us, and Millie who probably wasn't. "To get whole again?"

"This is a housing facility," Rover said. "A farm. And we're the animals. You're in here until your insurance runs out."

"We're not all served in the same way," Sue said.

"You got that right," Rover said and gave up a little howl.

"I didn't mean it that way." Sue turned to me. "It depends on what we expect, and what we're willing to do to get better. Here we learn to focus on the healing power within us. We all have it—we just have to learn to tap into it."

Rover rolled his eyes.

I asked Sue, "How long have you been here?"

"About a week."

"Were you Baker Acted?"

She shook her head. "I committed myself."

"She has great insurance," Rover said. "Came here right out of the hospital."

"Can you leave when you want?"

"Hell no," Paulie said. "Once you're in here, only Reginaldi can let you out."

Rover barked.

"There are other doctors here," Sue said.

An orderly walked into the room with lidded cups of coffee on a tray and handed them around. She smiled at me. But I shook my head. I knew that, by definition, as a suicide and a lunatic, I was supposed to like coffee. But the smell churned up something awful inside me and I couldn't get past it long enough to try the stuff. If I wanted a soda, I'd have to get one out of the machine in the urine lounge.

"Do you see," Paulie said, getting up and taking the empty folding chair on the other side of me. "How they wear their badges on little clips on their shirts like that?"

I nodded. He sipped his coffee and smacked his thin lips. "You know why?"

"They have to show them to get through the door."

"No, no. Why aren't the badges on chains around their necks, eh? It's so nobody can use them to strangle the life out of them and escape."

"Lord, Paulie, this isn't a hospital for the criminally insane," Sue said.

Rover barked again. He stood, turned around three times, showing off his butt crack under his ill-fitting pants and sat back down.

"Why don't you go in the other room with the freaks," Paulie told him.

We were allowed to wear our own underwear. But we all wore scrubs like the orderlies and nurses. Theirs were colorful–sky blue, grape, or cherry red–but always solid color. I was disgusted to find Sausage had brought me a bag with underwear and toiletries in it. It would be just like my mother to let him go through my drawers. But it was nice to have something clean. Rover didn't wear his underwear and I wondered how clean the scrubs could get. He should be asked to mark his so no one had to wear them after he did.

Paulie said patterns on the scrubs make people violent so the staff wore solids. Ours were drab green–the pants tied at the waist with two four-inch pieces of fabric. Paulie said anything longer than that and we could hang ourselves. We got slippers and light jackets. It was very cold in the asylum. The frozen floor chilled the soles of my shoes. No wonder everyone drank warm coffee and sat in the chairs in the sun.

The orderly by the door let us have a lighter and we passed it around the table. Nobody offered it to the hermit on the sofa, Millie. Millie was so forgettable that I'm certain her name wasn't Millie. No one remembers her. No one cares. She sat huddled all the time, her right thumbnail stuck in her teeth, staring at the ground, or her hands, or the television. She never said a word the entire time I was at Lakeview Psychiatric Treatment Facility, which, to be honest, isn't the name of the place. I can't remember the name of the place. Who would remember something like that? And who would remember Millie? It's pretty sad to be as forgettable as a psych ward.

Pepper dude arrived and took a seat–he was the guy

who grabbed up all the pepper packets off the tables at dinner. And Brooke, with the big boobs and tiny waist that all the men were too drugged up to drool over. And Madge. Sure, that's not her name. But she reminded me of a Madge. Older, not a lick of make-up on her wrinkled face except for two gashes of brick-red lipstick. Like a horror movie Madge. I was starting to get worried about the number of suicides at the long table. Were they shipping them in from across the country?

A large redhead stomped through the doorway, flipping off the warden, who duly ignored her. She stole Rover's coffee cup, forced Martin out of his seat and pulled the chair away from the table.

"Circle time," she said.

Everybody got up and moved the table away and we formed a circle with our chairs. We stood, waiting, and I looked at Sue, wanting to ask her what the hell this was all about. Finally, the redhead sat, engulfing the small folding chair, her knees spread wide apart because of her massive thighs. There, I said it. She was enormous. But strong enormous; not the kind of enormous you could run from. And then we were all allowed to sit.

Surprisingly, redheaded Amazon smiled at us and winked at me, probably because my mouth fell open and I trembled like a rabbit. I didn't believe for a minute that the orderlies would save me in time.

"You're new," the woman said. "You go first."

They shouldn't have let us have makeup. But when I thought of Madge and her red gashes, I realized that maybe makeup could be used as a sign we'd gone over the edge and were ready to make a noose out of our bed sheets. In the movies that's what happens. The crazy woman cuts off her hair, jagged, not neatly at all, and then slashes her mouth with bright red lipstick. Then she takes the gun and, just as the camera moves away from her, shoots herself in the head.

I looked around the room at the others. Several loonies, addicts, and alcoholics scraped chairs across the floor to join us.

"This is Pamela," Sue said. "She likes to have group therapy sessions after dinner."

"She's a doctor?"

Rover let out a howl and Paulie gave my back a slap. I turned to him and glared. I knew he'd only done it to touch me. There was something not right about Paulie. Not right at all. But it was no different from what was not right about almost every other man in the world, so I figured I could deal with it.

"Introduce yourself to the group," this Pamela person said.

"They know me already. We all live together in the common room." I almost said urine room. And I almost said, the urine room where I've never seen you before.

"Tell us why you're here," she said.

"They all know that, too."

"Come on," Paulie said. "Play along. It's fun."

"Does Reginaldi know about this?"

"I tell her," Pamela said. "I tell her everything you guys tell me."

"Do not," Sue said and lit up another cigarette, her hands trembling. Someone should tell her to eat. Not only could she light up a cigarette without shaking if she'd eat, if she bulked up a bit, she'd probably be strong enough to successfully slit her wrists.

"I could tell if I wanted," Pamela said.

"Like you could remember," Rover said.

"I remember everything. I've got a mind like a steel trap."

"What did we have for breakfast?"

"I wasn't here at breakfast. I was gone all day."

"That's right," Sue said. "She had a pass."

Paulie winked at me and I couldn't tell if there was a private joke going around or he was just being a man again.

"We have the same fucking thing every day," Froggy guy said.

"So, spill." Pamela ignored them and leaned toward me, her watermelon boobs dropping onto her knees.

"I was caught on the roof of a building."

"A jumper." She licked at her lips. "Would you like to tell us how you felt, standing on the ledge?"

I winced. That hardly seemed like a good idea. Euphoric. Excited. Brilliant. And drunk, of course. Should I share that with people who've slit their wrists or attempted to hang themselves? Though, does little frog guy's attempt count? He did it in the middle of a family get together—in the kitchen. And while I can relate, there was no way he would have succeeded. Other than him, these people really wanted to kill themselves. I didn't plan on telling them how freakishly cool the ground looked from the roof of Three River Terrace.

"Scared," I said and looked around at them all.

One of them actually laughed.

"Come on," Paulie said. "How did it feel?" He was on the edge of his seat, his eyes wide with anticipation.

I looked to Pamela. She was pretending to write something on one of her palms with an invisible pen. This was odd enough, but odder still, I was angry because she was acting like Reginaldi; it was as if she wasn't paying attention to me at all.

"I didn't like the wind," I said.

"Why not?" She still wasn't looking at me. For all I knew she was fake doodling pictures of Gumby.

"I don't like wind."

This she found interesting enough to raise her head.

"You don't like wind?" Rover said.

I pulled my forehead in and shook my head. What was the big deal? What's to like about wind? It's one of the most bothersome aspects of nature. It moves too much. Sun, you can get out of. Sand you can wash off. Same with sea water. But wind, well you have to go inside. And then there's the almost constant breeze from the air conditioning vents that never seems to be blowing on the right spot in the room.

"What don't you like about it?" Reginaldi/Pamela said.

I wrapped my hands around myself and rubbed my arms. "I don't like the way it feels on my skin."

Frog guy sputtered and laughed. Like he should talk. I caught on to his ear pulling obsession ten minutes into meeting him. He was sitting there right then, tugging hard and fast on the left lobe.

"Would you like to say something, Martin?" RegiPam asked.

He laughed again. "Why'd she take off her clothes then?"

Oh, yes. Very funny. And how was it that all of the lunatics in the asylum knew about that?

"Everybody knows," Paulie said, "that crazy people take off their clothes."

Laughter rippled around the circle, but it was a knowing sound, and I couldn't help joining them. Maybe I *was* crazy.

"Well, I didn't get naked. Not completely."

Rover danced his eyebrows up and down at me several times.

"And I have to feel the wind even when I'm dressed. I just don't like it on my arms or my face."

"Can you say why?" RegiPam asked.

"It tickles. Is this important?"

She fake scribbled in her Gumby-notebook hand. I felt like I was in a dream, or trying to have a conversation with a homeless agnostic philosopher under a bridge—I've done that. Nothing made sense. Everything everyone else said was stupid, but they all seemed to understand one another, and agree that I was the crazy one—in a fake group therapy session sort of way.

I proved not to be interesting enough and RegiPam moved on. At some point, when we all got quiet and I couldn't remember who had been talking or about what, Paulie started. He whispered at first.

"I was thinking about it," he said. "And I think I got it figured out."

We all turned to him and RegiPam got her hands ready to take notes.

"It's the screaming. When there's a natural disaster. A flash flood, and you watch on television, the helicopter hovers over the woman in the rushing river, clinging to a tree branch. The water's stripped her naked and she drowns. Right there on live television, the whole world watches her drown. Or tornadoes cut mile-wide swaths through Oklahoma or mud slides in California. Everybody's screaming and begging God to tell them why. Why did this happen? And the crazy ones–people like us–we're not panicked."

Paulie took a sip of his coffee and looked around the circle.

"Don't you get it? It's the screaming. All the people are screaming. But we've seen it before. We don't have the shield. They all wear this shield that keeps them from seeing what's going on around them every day. So, when something happens–when someone murders a bunch of people, or a fire wipes out a family, they act like it's not supposed to happen, like it's unusual. And they scream. But we didn't have our shields up–we don't have them at all. We've seen it already. We remember it. We were..."

"Expecting it," I said.

Paulie smiled at me and nodded. "Our screaming is in our heads. It's always there. Always. We don't have a shield to hide behind."

My father started sending me checks when I was seventeen, about a year after he disappeared; it bothered my mother. He told me I should go to college and get an apartment on my own. Maybe he was trying, in his typically inadequate parenting way, to help me get away from her. Maybe he felt guilty for not taking me with him.

Or maybe he was just a jerk and thought sending me checks would piss her off.

"What did the asshole send you this time?" She'd say. "Is that his idea of love? A check? Does he at least send a letter with it?"

He did, in fact, always send a letter with it. But I never let her know that. His letters were happy. He told me about his adventures surfing in California, riding an ass into the Grand Canyon, seeing the dead alien autopsy in Roswell. And he told me about his new wife and baby and how wonderful life was. It was sick. And I protected her from it. At least that's what I told myself.

RegiPam tossed her hand notebook away and slapped at her thighs. "What business is it of theirs, anyway?" She said. "Whether I live or die? I have the right to do with my body whatever I want. Don't I?"

Paulie snorted. "Libertarian suicides."

I was the only one to laugh with him.

"Why do they care?" Pamela said. Her facade fell away. Her Gumby notebook and play group therapy were just what she did to convince herself it was all working, she was being made whole again—but it was a lie. We all knew it.

"Death," Rover said, sounding like a regular person instead of a crazy dog-man, for a change. "Reminds them of their own mortality. Suicide brings them closer to that objective truth—the horror of the real world—that they've worked so feverishly to blind themselves to. They cling to life like petulant children, demanding you join them in their obsession with it. Anyone who dares to challenge the notion that we must suffer and survive—at all cost—is silenced. Institutionalized."

Paulie snorted out a laugh and said, "Petulant children, clinging to life." We all stared at him and I smiled, but he was looking at something beyond Rover–a spot on the wall. "When I was a child I thought as a child," he said as if he was reading it. "But now that I am awake, I put away childish things."

It turned out Rover was a history professor at some fancy university up north and wrote huge, dry, and depressing volumes on the Civil War and Reconstruction. No wonder he was in the asylum.

Of course, I didn't have an interview at the bookstore, or anywhere else. I'd just lost my job, and I wasn't nearly responsible enough to plan ahead like that.

# 4.

The next morning I was on schedule. Up at 6:30, breakfast at seven. Wonderful mushy yellow scrambled eggs with a hint of salt. Floppy, greasy bacon. Watery grits that I turned into sunshine in a bowl from the unlimited margarine packets available to us. As much salt as I wanted, but no pepper, of course. And a pancake, soggy with syrup.

I saw Reginaldi first thing, I guess because I was the new recruit. I curled up in the corner again and popped open the Diet Coke.

"No cigarette?" She asked.

"Too early."

She nodded big, like she was on stage. I figured on the weekends, she tipped those brunette spikes purple and orange, and went to some nightclub with fluorescent lights or disco balls and picked up sleaze and screwed them in the backseats of unlocked cars; and she always made a point of leaving something behind–something for the owner of the car, or his wife, to find. Her panties, her bra, a used tampon. It was wrong to think of her that way; I knew I was making her evil when she wasn't. But there was something satisfying in it. Something felt right about knowing that no one could be that good. Faces like that, that smile and chatter and help–they hide something that lurks. But they're not covering up for their own personal faults; those faces hide all the ills of humanity. It's thoughts like that, that tell you you're insane and maybe you should stay in the loony bin.

"Smoking is only for alcohol," I said. My voice wavered and I felt the sudden urge to explode with baby tears and beg her to let me out.

"Something's bothering you."

Wow. Maybe she was a psychiatrist, after all. Or psychic. I often got those mixed up. And psychotic. Psychics are probably just psychotic. But not by the real medical definition of course, which no doubt is long and boring and has nothing at all to do with rampaging serial killers.

I grabbed the pack of Salems and lit up.

"My brother said he and my mom are going to Baker Act me if I don't commit myself." I wiped the brimming tears from my eyes.

"April," she said, in this droning, soothing sort of voice that freaked me out. "It was the Baker Act that allowed law enforcement to bring you here against your will. You're on a hold no longer than seventy-two hours, after which you'll be released."

"I will?"

"Unless we felt that you were a danger to yourself or someone else."

"I'm not. I swear I'm not."

She smiled. "Tell me about that morning on the roof. What led you there?"

I dragged from the cigarette. My hand shook. I thought of Sue and how I'd nearly gorged myself on breakfast and eyed her full plate like a ravenous half-starved beast. You know how they tell you that you're stuffing your feelings in when you eat like that? I wondered what that meant for anorexic Sue. If she wasn't stuffing them in, was she trying to give them away?

"I got fired," I said.

"Why were you fired?"

I rolled my eyes.

"It's okay," she said. "From the beginning."

The beginning.

"I was working at The Burger Joint–I've been there for two years," I said.

It was close to the lagoon and the road out to the beach. The cool place to work. I remember the surprise I felt at getting hired. Toby, large, round and gray-headed, with rimless glasses–he was my new father figure; he believed in me–thought I could handle the sandwich line, the drink station, maybe even the drive thru. And I did. I handled them all. It was my life's ambition to be the best Joint employee they'd ever seen. And they gave me money to do it.

On my first day, Mr. Toby–that's what he asked all the young girls call to him–taught me how to make the burgers. There was an order to it; it had to be just so. Each burger had a funky name and that name meant precisely these or those ingredients. The Sandy Dune: lettuce, tomato, ketchup, and onion. The Beach: Mayo, lettuce, onion, and one slice of white American cheese. I had to memorize them all. I went home with my list and got out my crafting supplies and cut out pieces from construction paper: buns, top and bottom, ketchup, mayo, mustard, lettuce, all of it. And then I practiced slapping those burgers together for hours.

I was the best Joint Girl ever.

"A few weeks ago, they hired on this new girl. Amanda. She's weird. Uses that fake orange tanning cream. Plump, and has her hair cut in this way that circles her face, making it look round. She's like an orange ball wearing a black wig."

Reginaldi smiled.

"But we hit it off. We started hanging out after work. We'd go to bars mostly. But I always had to have her back to her car at the Joint by ten. It was a pain. Anyway, school got out on Wednesday for the summer and so we figured, I don't know, it was an excuse to go out, but this time I picked her up from her aunt and uncle's house. She's living with them because she had problems at home, back in Wisconsin or somewhere like that. She told her aunt and uncle we were going to the movies, but really we were going to Harold's up north of town."

"Harold's?"

"Bar. Pool hall," I said. "When I picked her up, she told me she was going to run away and asked me to take her to a hotel. So I drove her out by I95 to what I thought was the Red Roof, but I guess I wasn't paying much attention. She got a room and then we went out to Harold's. We weren't there more than an hour when she hooked up with this backwoods type. Cowboy hat, short cut hair. Redneck, basically. I'm not saying he wasn't cute. But at closing time she told me she was going off with him. So, that was that. I got home around five. My mother was sitting up in her bed with the lights on. Royally pissed. Apparently, Amanda's aunt had been calling every half hour since midnight."

And I told her, why didn't you tell her to stop.

"Do you think I'm stupid or something? I told her if she didn't stop, I was going to report her to the police for harassment. But she told me she was the police."

My mother had this way of looking angry all the time. Her hair was usually pulled back into a snooty bun and she wore suits with too-tight skirts hemmed just below the knee. When she was in bed, everything was loosed and falling and her face sagged like it was glad not to have to hold itself up for a while. But the brows were always pointed and alarmed and ready to pounce.

"The aunt's retired," I told her. "With some kind of disability."

"Where the hell have you been?"

"Don't start bitching at me," I said. "I'm not the one in trouble. Amanda is."

I went to bed. And the phone rang. My mother forced me to talk to Amanda's aunt. She was not happy.

"I knew," she screamed. "I knew you weren't going to the movies. Not in that glitzy showgirl top."

What the hell? It was my best top, draped low in the front, loose and swingy. Shiny, silver threads were woven through it. It was awesome, especially under a disco ball on the dance floor. An ugly girl has to go with what she's got and I had boobs and shiny tops. Sue me.

"Where is she?"

So I told her: Red Roof Inn, room 512.

"There," I said to my glowering mother. "Go to sleep."

Not half an hour later, the damned phone rang again. This time it was her uncle. He was pissed. She's not there. There's no one in room 512. Well, how do you know? You think she's going to answer the door to you? She's with some hick from Mims. But it turns out he forced the manager to open the room up. I think that's when I started to get a little antsy. I mean, who were these people?

"I don't know where the hell she is." My voice cracked from booze, cigarettes, and lack of sleep. "I took her to the Red Roof Inn. If she's—" and then my mother grabbed the phone from me.

She told this stranger, who might or might not be a cop, to come and get me and drive me around all of Sandy Point looking for that little shit Amanda. It reminded me of how she used to always volunteer me for things. Eunice would be happy to mow your lawn. Eunice is happy to take care of your cat while you're away. Eunice would be happy to babysit. Of course you should take Eunice with you to find your slut niece so I can get some sleep.

He picked me up in a little blue Toyota and we tooled over to the Interstate and as we were getting near the Red Roof, I saw it. I hadn't taken her to the Red Roof at all. I'd taken her to the Best Western.

"Oh, no," I said.

He's like, what? What?

"Amanda told me later that he did believe me when I swore it was a mistake," I told Reginaldi. "I really did think she was at the Red Roof. Anyway, he made me knock on the door to 512 so she'd answer."

And once the door was opened, we both saw the hick back by the bed, pulling up his pants. Amanda waltzed out of the room with a slick grin on her round fat face and got into the front seat of the Toyota. It was a very quiet ride back to my house. And the whole time I was thinking how sleazy Amanda was, all of the sudden. And how sleazy her aunt was. Her uncle wasn't so bad; but, what was I doing with these kinds of people?

"All right," Reginaldi said. "And we're leading up to you being fired?"

I nodded. "By that time it was, maybe, eight? And I went to bed. I was supposed to go in to work at 10:30. But I slept until three. When I showed up–that was it. I was fired. Well, I mean. This wasn't the first time something like that had happened."

I remember standing in Mr. Toby's cramped, filthy little office while he sat in his squeaky chair on wheels getting the paperwork ready for me to sign. I kept waiting for some signal from him. Some gesture should tell me how sorry he was to see me go. I was the best employee they had, maybe the best they *ever* had. Sure I didn't show up that time last fall. But I couldn't help it if I was lost out in Scottsmoor and had to sleep in my car. And sure, I called Wabeth, his assistant manager, a fucking bitch that time and had to apologize to the kids in the restaurant who overheard me. But she was a fucking bitch.

But nothing. And I can still feel the way my hopes

sunk slowly into my gut, standing there looking down at the bald spot on the back of his head as he filled in his reasons for firing me. This little girl in me wanted him to say something. Advice maybe. Good luck. At least, for Christ's sake, hand me a fifty and shake my hand.

So, for me, it was that moment, strangely enough, and not the time he closed the door of the utility closet and ran his hands all over my polyester uniform for a fondle, when I realized Mr. Toby was no better a father figure than my real father.

Reginaldi was nodding at me. Where was I? Right. Unceremoniously dismissed.

"I went over to Harold's and started drinking again. I was like, what the hell am I doing? And the dreary guy came over–"

"Dreary guy?"

"Well, yeah, the guy's dreary–looks like a lost dog. He's more smarmy than dreary but once you give someone a name, it sticks."

Reginaldi smiled a bit and waved her hand. "Okay, go on."

Steve was wiry thin, and thought he was much better looking than he was; his shirt was always unbuttoned down to his navel and you could tell he thought that attracted the ladies. He was like, forty. And I was nineteen when I met him. He picked me up at Spike's Pub the first night and took me to some trailer. It was okay. But after that he counted on me to be his go-to girl when nobody else would sleep with him–which was apparently all the time.

"Anyway, Steve starts trying to pick me up, and I

guess that disgusted me more."

What disgusted me about it was that he didn't care, to be perfectly honest. I told him we could hang out, but I wasn't going to sleep with him. And he didn't believe me.

He said, "Really?"

And I said, "Really."

And he said, "Really. No sex?"

And I said, "No sex."

And he said, "Okay." And then the prick got up and left.

"The more I drank the more disgusted I got," I told Reginaldi. "And it occurred to me that I could jump off the roof of Three River Terrace and all my shitty problems would go away."

"Would you say you were serious?"

"Not really. I mean, the problems would go away, but I'd have to go with them. And I wasn't sure I was all that prepared for nonexistence. Nonexistence lasts quite a long time, you know. So, anyway, I'm standing up there and I remembered about Camelia."

"Camelia who doesn't exist," she said.

# 5.

There was something about the way she said it. My eyes closed up and I glared at her. Of course Camelia didn't exist. But why didn't Reginaldi believe me? Why would I lie about something like that? Why would *anyone* lie about something like that? If I was writing to a real person, I'd say so. Unless, I suppose, I murdered her and buried her body out back by the dog house. But if I'd done that, Camelia wouldn't exist, right? So, I'd still be sane. As much as a murderer who buries people by dog houses can be.

Paulie followed me around the rest of the day asking me bits of trivia and I could never tell if he knew everything or if I just didn't know enough to know he was lying.

"How many people died in the making of the Hoover Dam? Huh? Huh? Do you know?"

"I have no idea." I always said that in a way that would clue the poor kid in that I didn't give a rat's ass, but I had a feeling Paulie was one of those self-absorbed types who couldn't read other people. Was that self-absorption? Or was it that thing serial killers have? Sociopathology. I couldn't tell. Paulie didn't have that serial killer look to him, exactly. He was agitated and excited all the time. Too scrawny and concave to manage to overpower a woman—unless she was anorexic. And he certainly didn't have the child molester vibe. Paulie was a mouse. A mouse addicted to heroin who claimed to have purposely overdosed.

What exactly does a rat's ass have to do with caring anyway? Has anybody ever asked that question? Why do people say things like that all the time without thinking?

Anyway, Paulie's trivia almost always had something to do with death and when it wasn't death it was something gross. Like, "What color is your vomit after eating mint chocolate chip ice cream?" Who would know that? Paulie would.

"Hey, hey," he'd say if he thought I wasn't paying attention to him anymore. "Listen, listen. You know why the nurses wear rubber soled shoes? Huh? It's so when someone electrocutes himself in the shower, they can get in and turn off the water."

And suddenly we're back at death.

Mashed potatoes again and sweet cooked carrots with peas. Groans erupted across the room as people started to dig in, but I was in tv dinner heaven. Everything was warm and mushy. Sure it was bland, but salt packets were readily available—no pepper. I wasn't sure exactly what the meat was this time, but it was good; I could cut it with my fork. And as usual, it was smothered in gravy.

"What did you eat on the outside?" Sue asked me as she sat down with her tray.

At first the question made absolutely no sense to me. She might as well have asked me, what did you grasshopper on the football.

"On the outside?" And then it hit me. Like we were in prison or something. "What do you mean? Food is food."

"You like this stuff so much, I wonder if you've been starved or something."

Look who's talking about starving. Ah ha, the anorexic made another joke.

"No," I said. "I eat a lot of fast food. Burgers and fries. I don't get much home cooking."

Sue and Paulie laughed.

"Well, sure it's not exactly home cooking. But still."

My mother and I did occasionally get drunk and cook up a batch of spaghetti sauce. It was garbage sauce filled with whatever our beer-soaked palates thought might work. Ground beef, sausage, bacon, mushrooms, onions, green pepper, black olives, you name it, we'd put it in the sauce. And it was always good. It was always good because we'd gone all day or all weekend on nothing but beer and peanuts and those little mini pretzels. You could have fed us eggplant and we might have liked it.

"Where do you live at?" Paulie said.

"Sandy Point," I said and Sue gave me a stern look.

"How about you?"

"I'm over on the island." A short laugh escaped him, like it wasn't intended. "We're practically neighbors. I've been to Sandy Point. It's nice."

"Why would anyone go to Sandy Point?" I said.

"It's always good to scout out the bars where they

don't know you so well."

Then Sue gave Paulie a stern look. Maybe this was Sue's problem. Maybe she was too concerned with everyone else. And naturally all that concern took away her appetite. She wasn't fooling me. She picked at the mystery food and put a tad on her tongue, and when it was time to turn in the trays, she took Rover's and he took hers.

Were these people stupid? Could they not see someone committing suicide right in front of them? Sue had figured out the greatest con ever. She slit her wrists so they'd think she was trying to kill herself, not starve to death. Sure, we can see it's the same thing, but when you're looking at someone's file and it says she slit her wrists, you're so freaked out you don't even think about whether or not she's eating. It was the perfect cover.

Our group therapy session was after lunch in the meeting room. We got crayons and drew pictures of our families and made lists, and read them aloud, of what we were going to do right, when we got out. Not things you'd expect, like, get a job, be responsible, stop trying to kill ourselves. No. It was stuff like, see the positive in every situation, stare at ourselves in the mirror and chant stuff like, you're a good person, you are kind, people *like* you. The suggestions were right there on the posters all over the walls—so nobody had to think about it. Did anybody really believe that telling myself things that I knew damn well were lies was going to keep me from jumping off the roof of Three River Terrace? I felt like jumping just sitting there listening to their lists.

Later that evening, Sue and I sat in the comfy chairs

by the window looking out at the lights of the big city. Okay, it was probably a power station all lit up in the distance, but we imagined it was Disney World.

"You shouldn't tell Paulie too much about yourself," she said.

"How come?"

"He can get a little obsessed."

"What? You think he'll go to Sandy Point and stalk me or something?" I laughed.

"I wouldn't put it past him."

"He's harmless. Trust me. If there's one thing I know, it's that cute, young, heroin addicts don't want anything to do with ugly girls like me."

She didn't say anything else about Paulie. He did seem harmless, like a Chihuahua—excitable, but no bigger than a rat. What am I saying? Little dogs are vicious. They can jump higher than you think and they have tiny, razor-sharp teeth. When I was fifteen or so, I walked over to Sunny Dale to some girl's house; I think her name was Kim. To this day I can't for the life of me figure out why I'd go see her; she wasn't my friend or anything. It's possible I blocked all thoughts of friendship with her out of my mind after her dog bit me. Stunted little thing.

The damned puny mutt let me walk up to the house and knock on the door, no problem. But when no one answered and it was time to leave, suddenly the bitch thinks I'm a burglar and won't let me go. You watch those tiny dogs snarl sometime, you'd be scared too. The thing jumped up and bit me on the thigh. I managed to climb onto a decorative wall in front of their house and was trapped there for the longest time until some girl I also never hung out with rode by on her bike and laughed at me.

"Eunie, what are you doing up there?"

"Can you come get this thing away from me so I can go home?" Forget the pleasantries. Can't you see I'm in danger?

She laid her bike down and, still laughing, picked the little sucker up. She started saying something about how you just have to get to know Peaches, but I ran all the way home and never went back into Sunny Dale. Actually that's not true. I rode my bike through there one time and was chased by dogs. Sunny Dale is evil.

"So where do you live?" I asked Sue. "Or do you think I'll come stalk you when we get out?"

She smiled weakly. "I'm on the island, too. But don't tell Paulie—not that he's interested in me."

"Jealous?"

She shook her head. "I don't need any more stress."

What stress could she possibly have? She had a husband to take care of her. Granted, I hadn't decided if he was the culprit or the victim, yet. But how shitty could her life be? Eat a brownie for Christ's sake. Brownies make everything better.

"Come on," I said. "We could all use a little Paulie in our lives."

Finally she laughed. What a total downer Sue was. We sat for, maybe, fifteen minutes, until I'd forgotten she was there and then she moved forward in her seat, stretched a bit, as if she was getting ready to rise, and turned to look at me.

"Maybe you're not in a place where you can hear me,"

she said.

And I thought, wow, crazier than I realized.

"But, I thought I'd say this." She turned to the window as if she was looking out, as if she saw something in the darkness besides the lights. "It's not about what you want, or what you think you need. It turns out," and here she looked at me. "It turns out, it's just about what you can and can't get...what you can and can't do. Once you're to the point where you decide you can't do anything about it, that's when you're lost. Then something has to come around to save you and what are the chances of that? I mean. Once you've let yourself become that lost, it's nearly impossible to let someone find you."

She stood and stretched her arms over her head, her elbows bent and her hands behind her back.

"That's all," she said and shuffled back toward the dorms.

I sat there thinking about what she'd said and couldn't make anything of it; she was clearly much more than a wrist-slitting anorexic; she was bonkers.

That night in bed, probably dreaming about brownies, I found myself waking and as I turned to my left side, I saw Paulie standing in the dimly lit hallway outside my room watching me. Nurse Tom hustled him back to the men's side of the bin.

Sunday morning they held church in the common meeting room before breakfast. This smarmy preacher with slicked back hair and a terrible southern accent kept trying to tell me about my sins and my repentance while I was looking around like, who invited this creep in here? His name was *Thee* Reverend Billy Davies.

"Jaysus luvs ya; it don't matter what you done; it don't matter the drugs or the way you treated nobody. Jaysus luvs ya. If you turn yer laf over to him. All will be forgiven."

It's always that easy. Just chant the magic words and poof, you've got some holy spirit dude living in your heart, ready to make you a better person. If it worked, well, it would work and we'd all be better people.

"They rotate," Sue said. "Last week it was Catholic."

"A mass?"

She nodded. "You'd be surprised who's Catholic when they want to be."

Who would want to be?

Preacher dude approached us on his way out and took my hand. He was sweating all over and smiled too much. Clammy. He gave me a Bible. "God has impressed upon mah hardt that I was to give this to you."

I tried to read the Bible a few times. Every time I got to the begats, they kept going on and on and on. I figured it was God's way of telling me to stop reading. You're not interested in any of this. It's not important. Give up now. I could see how it might be a test. God is saving all the important, good stuff for the people who could manage to get through the begats. I needed to accept the fact that I wasn't one of those good Christian people. I wasn't going to be a saint, like Claire Lindsay.

I wonder, though, if Claire Lindsay ever read the Bible. Claire was the type who ate up everything anybody said. She was the cheerleader with the weird body: long in the waist, short in the legs. But she could jump with those stubby legs. Cute enough, with a heart-shaped face and an enormous mouth, perfect for singing–naturally she was in the choir–and screaming out cheers over the crowd at high school football games. At Sandy Point High, in tenth grade, Claire was born again, and boy did everybody know about it. Of course, that was the year they built the fancy Baptist church up north of town where all the rich people lived. Claire didn't live up there, and neither did I. But we wanted to go to that church because that was where all the rich kids went.

What is it about rich people being more beautiful on average than us ugly people? On average, hell, what am I saying? They're prettier. The poor people have it bad. At least the middle class kids could get their teeth straightened and perm their hair. My Aunt Aubrey, who happened to be wealthy (dead husbands) and beautiful, told me that God smiles on good Christians and that's why you'll find them more attractive. If that's the case, I have to say, though I never told Aunt Aubrey, she should have converted to Mormonism. Have you seen the Mormons? They all look like Osmonds. Either that or they hide the ugly ones somewhere in the Utah mountains in concentration camps.

Still, everybody wanted to go to Sandy Point Baptist. They put on what they called Joy Explosions for the teens where, I guess, joy exploded. Claire invited me along and yes, joy was certainly exploding all over the place. Live bands played Christian music that sounded a lot like pop music to me. Everybody swayed and danced and sang and raised their hands and beamed. They were exploding with a weird glassy-eyed, forced joy.

Claire told me it was the holy spirit. She kept looking

over to me with her huge mouth pulled up into a ridiculous smile. But she never seemed to notice that I wasn't exploding. I didn't get it. I wanted to get it. I did. But no matter how much I wanted it, I couldn't make myself raise my hands toward the ceiling and pretend I had it. It felt wrong.

"You spend too much time with your eyes looking out," Aunt Aubrey told me once. "You'll find God inside."

I suppose she was right. I watched too much, so that by the time the holy spirit got around to my heart, I'd already decided I didn't want to jump around and shudder and speak nonsense. No, thank you. I'll take the prim church where everybody stands still and listens—or pretends to. No one would know if they let their minds wander to other, not necessarily sinful, things. But the holy spirit apparently doesn't visit there.

Then Claire invited me along to a revival at some podunk church out in Mims. The altar was set up like a talk show. Guests came and went and told their stories about how they were stricken with cancer and Preacher Denny smacked them on the heads and they were saved; or how they were crippled and Preacher Denny smacked them on the heads and they could walk again. Then the music shook the room and everybody stood and bounced and danced and sang, while cripples and the cancerous and the blind all walked up the center aisle to the altar to get smacked on the head, and then they danced back through the crowd, probably out the door and onto Preacher Denny's bus. Claire's hand slipped into mine and squeezed it hard. She was eating it up. Then the music slowed and the lights dimmed and Preacher Denny called everyone who wasn't saved up to the steps of the altar to chant the magic words and have their sins washed away. Claire bounded out of her seat and up to the altar to get saved. *Again*. It must have been her fourth time. But whatever is necessary to keep the all-loving God from torturing you for eternity in hell.

So I took the smarmy preacher's Bible; I figured I might as well give it one more go. As *Thee* Reverend Billy Davies waited for the heavy locks to be opened on the thick doors to the loony bin, blessing everyone he laid eyes on, I looked a bit closer at the Bible and saw a stamp in the lower right corner that read, "Placed by The Gideon's."

# 6.

**B**reakfast was wonderful. Yellow rectangles of scrambled egg, a little bowl of grits loaded with butter, butter, butter. Even the toast made me happy, soggy with butter. No pepper.

"You got a Bible from the preacher," Paulie said.

"I did."

"You ever read the Bible?"

"I've tried."

"That Jehovah, now there's a dude who knows how to kill people."

"Oh, Paulie," Sue said. She huddled over her breakfast tray, her shoulders drawn in, her mouth pulled into a deep frown. "Stop with the God bashing."

I laughed and they both looked at me like I was not in on the joke.

"How long have you been in here?" I asked Paulie.

"Three weeks. I get to stay for a while. Maybe three more."

"You've done this before?" I said.

He nodded. "Few times now." He gnawed off a bit of

toast and chewed with his mouth open, smiling widely at me. "I know what you're thinking," he said, and swallowed. "I'm very rich." He poked his piece of toast into his chest.

"Your parents are very rich," Rover said.

"Which is probably why you're here," Sue said. Wow. Sue was especially critical that morning. The circles under her eyes were darker than usual.

"When do you go home?" I asked her.

She shrugged.

"She'll be here a long time," Paulie said. "She came from the hospital. Nearly died."

"You're in here for slashing your wrists," I said.

Sue looked up at me, tired, like her head was very heavy. "I thought you knew that. I told you that."

"Yeah, yeah," I said. "But you're like...anorexic, right?"

Her brow furrowed.

"Anorexic?" Paulie said.

"We should have a policy in here about diagnosing one another," Rover said.

"Come on. It's obvious."

"Are you a doctor?"

"You're one of the seventy-two's," Paulie said, as if that confirmed that I should shut up. "We don't get that many. Most of us are regulars."

"I'm not anorexic," Sue said.

Please. Did she not see herself in the mirror? Skin and bones. Dark shadows under the eyes. Sunken cheeks. Halloween all over her face. She could fool the doctors, the nurses, orderlies, even Paulie. But she wasn't fooling me. And I was pretty sure she wasn't fooling Rover, either–he let her turn in his empty food trays after every meal. I couldn't say what he was getting out of it, but it probably had something to do with him starving one of his dogs to death when he was a kid. Things like that will make you act out in weird ways years later.

Dr. Reginaldi was chirpy for a Sunday.

"You work on Sundays?" I said.

She didn't respond–just smiled at me. I imagined she was there especially for me and I liked it. She wanted to talk about my feelings and my plans for staying sober but I figured I'd pretty much had all the counseling I needed. What was left to say? I got drunk and did something stupid. So what if I hate my mother; everybody hates her mother. It's almost like we're supposed to hate our mothers. It's natural. On Monday morning she would sign the papers so I could go home. Well, at least to a halfway house.

"Your mother has arranged for you to stay at Hope House in Sandy Point for a few months."

"Months?"

"It'll give you an advantage. It's a good thing."

What Reginaldi didn't know was that my mother didn't want me living with her anymore. She was kicking me out, basically. At least this way, I had someplace to go while I figured out what I was going to do. I didn't worry about it; it's not like I hadn't been kicked out before. I could go back when I was ready. Certain things never stuck with my parents and kicking their kids out of the house was one of them. Not that they'd ever done it to Sausage.

When I was sixteen, and we were still a family, I ran away from home. When I called my parents after being away for three days to tell them I needed to come by and pick up a few things, they said fine. I showed up at the house and they glared at me, didn't say a word. My father gave me his I'm-so-disappointed-you're-not-the-pretty-daughter-I-ordered look. And my mother gave me the how-dare-you-hurt-and-embarrass-me-like-this look. I walked past them and into my room to get my stuff and there, sitting on the bed was a fifty-dollar bill and a little note, on a piece of folded notebook paper. It said, "Eunice, we hate you and don't want you to come back." Okay, I don't remember what it said, but it was something along those lines. Verbose and poorly edited and filled with psychobabble about tough love and needing space for all of us and good luck. They said I could have my car and I did the typical eye-rolling thing. Of course I was taking my car; I'd have liked to see them try to stop me.

I was peeved, I admit, that they were trying to get credit for my leaving. I ought to have pinned a note to their bed letting them know that I ran away–they didn't kick me out. But I didn't. I left their note, pocketed the fifty–who wouldn't–and left them with their dirty, pitiful glares. I moved into a shack on a dirt road uptown with this girl named Laurie. Laurie was a friend of my friend Sylvie's older sister. At least I thought so, when they told me I could stay with her.

I'd been living out of my car, for the first few days, parking it outside Sylvie's house, until her parents realized what was going on. They weren't going to have a hobo living in their front yard, they said. I wanted to explain to them the difference between a hobo and a homeless person, but I didn't. So, I left.

Apparently, Sylvie's sister Jennifer had it in her head that she was going to be a social worker. She hung out on the streets with the undesirables and that's where she met Laurie. Don't get me wrong; her intentions were good and no doubt she never expected Laurie to try to kill me. She helped her get a job, and then found this little shack for her to live in. They each paid fifty a month, apparently, and let me move in, with the promise that I would find work and start paying Jennifer's share.

I was sixteen. Barely. I'd only had my car five days. (This, I would later learn, was the real sore point with my parents. I was the most ungrateful child on earth for taking the gift of a car only to use it to run away from home. To them, it was an act of betrayal; to me, it was handing me the keys to the cage door.) I had no idea what sort of work I was going to do. But Laurie told me she'd get me a job at the motel where she was a maid. I went with her that first day—I drove, and as it turned out, was her new chauffeur. Jennifer was finally free of Laurie and we never saw her again.

The motel was a few ramshackle rooms sitting on the side of US1 up north of town. The place was roach infested and smelled of feces and death. Laurie taught me how to steal from the several long-term tenants and told me there would be ample opportunities for extra cash from the nightly renters if I stayed until after ten. After three weeks of driving her to work, cleaning the rooms, and pocketing the money the owner, fat Sal, gave me—

while Laurie had sex with everybody, did their drugs, and robbed them of hard candies and cash—on the way home that last evening, she wanted to know where her take was.

"Your take of what?" I said.

"The wages. The job wages from Sal."

She whistled when she said Sal because she was missing a front tooth. Laurie was bone thin and tanned dark brown, spotted like an overripe banana. Her pale brown hair was falling out and her eyes stayed slightly crossed all the time. Laurie was the kind of person you don't look at. I was slightly astonished that the men who showed up, staggering or vomiting, at the motel would have sex with her.

I was going to tell her, you know, the truth. I was going to say, look you crazy witch, I've done all the work for the past three weeks so I get the money. Didn't your Johns pay you for the sex? But they probably didn't—could you blame them? And anyway, I've never been one to actually say what I mean. So I just shrugged.

"I didn't get any money," I said.

She reached across the front seat of my little car, grabbed the hair on the back of my head with her skeleton hand and shoved my face into the steering wheel. I swerved off the road and stopped and she lunged at me, crawling over the gear stick beating me with her fists.

"You give me the god-damned money," she screamed. "I swear," she whistled, "I'll slap," whistling, "the living shit," spitting, "out of you, you slutty," whistle, "bitch."

Of course *I* was the slutty bitch. But you can't argue with some people. I gave her the god-damned money—at least that last week's take. She got out of the car and I sped off. I went back to the little shack, packed up my stuff and left before she got home. Hell, she was probably going out to celebrate with that fifty bucks, anyway. She'd head to the pier, do some drugs, fuck a bum, and let somebody steal it from her before she managed to find her way back up north to the hut.

It was eleven o'clock by the time I got back to my parents' house. I used my key, went in, walked past my father sitting in the family room watching television, past the master bedroom where my mother sat up in bed with a book, all loose and angry looking, and into my bedroom where that stupid little note was still on my unmade bed.

That's the trick of it. Get back before they get used to you being gone–before they can turn your room into a gym or a guest room, or a cat room. Get back into your space before they even realize what's happened. And then go on as if nothing had. Worked for me once; I had no reason to think it wouldn't work again.

I said good-bye to all the sickos at Lakeview Psychiatric that morning.

"How much longer do you have here?" I asked Sue.

"Few more weeks, maybe," she said.

"Take care of yourself," I said. "You know?"

She nodded. But I didn't think she knew. I wondered if her husband knew. Most people are clueless when someone they love wants to die. You'd think that by slitting her wrists, she'd have sent a pretty clear signal. But I remembered her and her husband in the visitors' lounge. I saw his face. He had no idea; he thought it was a fluke–a morbid, shallow cry for attention. He thought he could use it for his own benefit and be the victim for a while. And he thought this place would cure her of her self-absorption, when all it was for, was to hold on to her for a while until the physical wounds healed.

"Halfway house?" Paulie asked me.

"Yep."

"I didn't think you had it that bad."

"I don't have it at all."

"Why, then?"

"Because my mom wants me out of the house."

"So move out. You don't want to go to the halfway house. They're creeps in there."

"I don't have a job. What else am I supposed to do? Besides, I don't know if Reginaldi would let me leave if I didn't go."

"Well, good luck," he said. Suddenly he seemed much older. "I'll see you on the outside."

Jimmy Dean was in the front lobby waiting for me. We walked silently out into the bright light of the morning. Tears licked the rims of my eyes; I wanted to go back. Damn. I wanted to go back in. All that bitching about not wanting to stay with the crazy people and there I was, one of them. I could imagine what ex-cons felt—the ones who get out and commit a crime right away and go straight back in. My first thought when I closed the car door and the suffocating heat blanketed me was of rum and coke. Tall. Double. Jesus Christ.

"Mom wanted me to make sure they gave you anti-depressants," Jimmy said, starting the engine.

"I'm not depressed," I told him. "Just awake."

# 7.

Jimmy Dean prattled all the way to Sandy Point. A full hour and a half of lectures on my attitude and my drinking, veering off into tales of his new girlfriend and their exploits in Orlando at the university, his major, her major, or maybe something different, you should go back to school, Dad would pay, and we could all ride together, it would be good for you, that's all you need, you need a goal in life, something to work toward, you need to stop smoking and drinking and hanging out in bars and picking up men, what are you thinking anyway, why are you ruining your life, Patricia and I are going on one of those gambling cruises, they take you out beyond the state's boundaries and then open the tables, I'm not much of a gambler, on and on and on. It was nice having a conversation with Sausage; you didn't have to say much of anything.

They'd left my car at Three River Terrace. You'd think the psych hospital would do something about that. Isn't that like taking the lunatic and dropping him off at the scene of the crazy? What was to stop me from going right back up to the roof and jumping to my death? Were they not sensitive to what I'd just been through? When I saw my car parked crooked in its spot, I remembered driving there and sitting in the lot for the longest time, waiting for the sun to rise and thinking about Tory King. We were in middle school—seventh grade. Kevin Adderly lived in an apartment in Three River Terrace, but it wasn't called that then, and it was all apartments, not condos. And no businesses on the first floor.

Anyway, the little dude lived with his mother. Everything about Kevin Adderly was awesome. His parents were divorced. He lived in an apartment, something I'd never heard of. Apartments were for single people and college students, not families. He wore ties to school and didn't care what people thought. He was the class president–one of the popular kids. And I was invited to his birthday party, held in the banquet room on the first floor. That party was the scene of my first romance. It lasted almost the entire night–starting with the first kiss during spin the bottle, lasting through make out sessions in dark corners and out by the pool on a chaise lounge where he asked me to go steady, and ended with me in the bathroom telling one of my friends to go tell Tory King I wanted to break up with him.

He seemed to take it very well. I was pretty upset about the whole thing. I wanted to have a boyfriend–who wouldn't? And I supposed Tory King would do. But at the same time, I didn't think he was all that great. And *I* certainly wasn't going to tell him to go to hell. Not after I'd locked lips with him all night all over the first floor of the apartment complex. It was the right thing to send someone else out to do it. Anyway, she ended up going steady with him the next week in school, so that all worked out well.

Sausage pulled his car up to mine and let the engine idle.

"Mom's at work. She wanted me to tell you to call her later today and let her know you got there okay. You know how to get to this place?"

"No."

"It's on Main Street. You know where Main Street is?"

I nodded.

"Drive up and down it. It's there; you'll find it."

"So I can take my car?"

He looked at me. "Do you think you're not supposed to?"

"I don't know. What do you think?"

"I don't know."

"Do you think the other people get there by prison bus or something?"

Instead of laughing he tilted his head and seemed to consider it. "I don't know."

"Well," I said, and opened the passenger door. "I'll see you later."

"Maybe I'll come visit."

I ignored him and dug the keys out of my purse. I heard him drive away and didn't look to see which way he went. I sat in the parking lot of the Three River Terrace condominiums with my car on and the air conditioning running, remembering that night and realizing I could get up on the roof again and jump.

After I'd left the bathroom at the party, to try to

enjoy the rest of the night without running into Tory King, I ran instead into Kevin Adderly. What a lost sort. He'd done the spin the bottle romance with Terry Lautner and bombed out an hour before I bailed on Tory King. So, Kevin showed me how to take the elevator to the seventh floor and walk the hallway to the very end and make the turn into what most people would see as a dead end. There was a door there and the lock was broken, and we walked up a flight of concrete stairs in an echo chamber and found ourselves on the roof where Kevin Adderly poured his loser heart out to me and tried to stick his hand down my shirt.

I dug through my purse and the little bag Sausage brought my underwear in, and everything was there. I thought someone might have stolen my money, but I didn't remember if I had any to begin with. I found my journal and inside it, folded up, my letter to Camelia. I couldn't help laughing at it. I thought writers were supposed to sit at desks in darkened rooms with bottles of whiskey and write great American novels that everybody picked apart and oohed and aahed over. I always suspected that the symbolism and metaphor were just the subconscious yearning of a drunk trying to focus. I couldn't fathom any kind of symbolism in, "This place sucks balls." Not any that I wanted to think about. But there it was, wasn't it? Right in the middle of my drunken haze. Sex. Always sex.

I found a pen and opened my journal again.

*Dear Camelia. I can't remember exactly what Sue said, but for the last part. It's nagging at me, tugging me away from things. If we go too far in losing ourselves, it becomes too late to let someone find us. What does it mean? I figure if I'm going to be crazy, I might as well let you in on it. Remember how I used to cry at night and write you letters? I think I was letting you save me then. Maybe you'll save me again.*

# 8.

I started for Main Street, but then realized, what the hell. If Mom wasn't home, I should go pack my stuff. It was a halfway house after all, not an institution. I'd need clothes and shampoo and a toothbrush. It only occurred to me that my mother might have had the locks changed as I pulled up to the curb of the duplex. She wouldn't go that far, would she? I sat a little too long in the car, imagining myself walking up to the door and not being able to get in, over and over; the embarrassment was infuriating. But that wasn't helping and the car was getting hot. I sucked in a big breath and got out. Before I reached the porch, Aunt Aubrey was out her front door and on her little grassy lawn hooting at me. Literally.

"Hoot! There you are."

Does that woman have her hair done every day?

My mother and my Aunt Aubrey each owned half a mid-town duplex. Their fenced back yards abut one end of something like a pond. It was more the makings of a ditch in my view. All around the edge of the pond were the back yards of other houses and duplexes on other streets. In the beginning, they happily shared a back yard, entertaining and gardening, when they weren't at each other's throats, during which times when one sauntered into the yard to find the other, a standoff ensued until Aunt Aubrey went inside. Princess Patty Cakes didn't change that.

When my mother brought home the sway-backed, matted, ankle biter from the Humane Society–though one wonders how humane they can be and still unleash such a beast on an unsuspecting, albeit bitchy, old woman–and decided The PPC required a life outdoors during the day, Aunt Aubrey installed a line of chain link running straight down the middle from the duplex, thus carving out her own bit of back yard, separate from my mother's, highly insulting her. But there's something neighborly about hanging out by the fence. Is that what the saying means about fences making good neighbors? I don't think so. Nonetheless, Mom and Aunt Aubrey spent quite a bit of time sitting together on lawn chairs under beach umbrellas separated only by the chain link fence, laughing and gossiping, and Mom's frequent outbursts of, "Princess Patty Cakes do not eat that shit! I said no. God freakin' damnit Patty Cakes!"

The sisters also spent quite a bit of time at the back of the yard at what they called the T, flirting with Fat Orange Jack in exchange for oranges from his trees. Jack was pregnant...with beer apparently...and liked to show off his bulging belly, if not by letting it peek out from below an ill-fitted tee, then by exposing it in its entirety through the summer months. A firm, round, perky belly–

that was Jack's pride.

I joined them once when they tickled each other and walked to the T to meet him. I stayed only long enough to notice the chip in his right front tooth, the "HellRazor" tattoo on his right shoulder, and the glares from the old biddies who clearly did not like the way Orange Jack was leering at the teenager in a bikini. A girl would like to think her aunt and her mother were scowling at Jack for the creepiness, not at me for hogging all the attention and forever, so sad, tarnishing their pear-shaped, slightly wrinkled beauty in his eyes. It was true, though, I have to admit. I let him have it. The strut, the pose, the bending over slightly to scratch at my calf. Men are so easy to manipulate. I could have taken Orange Jack through the wringer right in front of the old biddies if I'd wanted to.

Orange Jack's back yard came to an odd point about three-quarters across my mother's, right about the spot, it turns out, that makes a straight line from my mother's bedroom window, down the hall and through my bedroom doorway. You have to wonder how often that little triangle of land needed Orange Jack's attention. Not nearly as much time as he spent there. One day, a week or so after I'd given him the bikini treatment, I came out of the shower, walked to my room, dropped the towel at my dresser and proceeded to rub lotion all over my naked body. Out of the corner of my eye, I saw Orange Jack at the tiny corner of his lawn, bent over, pretending to weed, his face turned squarely toward me. He didn't move, didn't flinch. Didn't cringe realizing he'd been caught ogling a seventeen-year-old girl.

No doubt, Orange Jack had it in his mind I wanted him to see me. He figured I drew open my mother's curtain, wet myself down in the shower and left my bedroom door wide open on purpose, just for him–for the explicit viewing pleasure of fat, Orange Jack. Turd. When I reached out and pushed my door closed, he was still bent over, his face beet red from the lack of oxygen flow to his fat head. I could only hope he'd keel over with a heart attack, but if he did, he did it somewhere else because he was gone when I opened the door again–fully dressed, of course. I told the biddies all about it. He just stood there looking at me, I said. Didn't even try to pretend he didn't see me, or that it was a mistake.

"When you strut around the house naked, Unicorn, what do you expect?"

"I expect a man to have some decency, to give the woman the benefit of the doubt and turn away. Not just stand there gaping."

"Well, you were naked."

And that explained everything.

Aunt Aubrey stood at my mother's front door with her hands on her hips, and her head shaking. "Well, do we need an intervention?"

"I'm fine. Just a misunderstanding."

"Misunderstandings don't land people in insane asylums."

"It wasn't an insane asylum. It was a holding facility. Attached to a hospital. That sort of thing."

"Well, come on," she said and led me into my mother's side of the duplex. "Let's get you some clothes. This place is no Hilton, but it's just across town. I'm right here if you need me."

Who would ever need Aunt Aubrey? All she knew how to do was simper and smile and talk about church.

"Sit down, sit down," she said, playing hostess in my mother's small kitchen. She put on the kettle and pulled the tea bags from the pantry.

"I don't drink tea," I said.

"But tea is what you drink at a time like this."

"At a time like what?"

She peered at me from the stove, her fingers pulling open the tea bags. "You need help."

"That's why they're sending me to the halfway house."

"You think so?" She waited for the pot to whistle, then poured water into the tea cups. I knew what she was thinking; I knew what she wanted to say. She carried the cups to the little table and sat across from me, stirring with one hand and dipping a bag in and out of her water with the other. "I know how you feel about this," she said. "But maybe it's time to pray."

My cheeks burned as I stared at my cup. Wispy streams of tea flowed from the bag like tentacles invading the clean, clear water, turning it brown.

"You don't have to pray with *me*," she said.

I was relieved. She'd learned her lesson, I suppose, from the last time. I was eleven or so and she'd caught me and this neighborhood girl, Renee, with one of Sausage's *Playboy* magazines in my bedroom. She walked in and this look of confusion fell over her face; her head tilted one way and then the other as she realized what we were looking at. Then she turned beet red and left the room. Renee and I were still giggling when my mother burst into the room, grabbed me by the shirt and dragged me off the bed. I was screaming, Renee was crying, and my mother was shouting, "God-damned perverted little shit."

I didn't know what the big deal was. The thing that stuck with me, and that I noticed as soon as she walked in the room, was that she already had the belt in her hand. She didn't bother to see for herself. She never gave me any benefit of doubt. She got an opportunity to hit me with a belt and she took it. Dr. Crazy would say the incident was pivotal. The arousal of curiosity followed swiftly by brute force punishment forever entwined pleasure with pain in my psyche. But psychiatrists are like that.

Anyway, Aunt Aubrey came into my room after Renee had been sent home, to pray with me. She'd done what was best for me, she said. I was weak. I was hurt and scared. And to be honest, I didn't even know what she was doing. She sat beside me and took my hands in hers and told me to close my eyes and then she started talking in this creepy, sweet voice. To God. And Jesus, his son. Something about sin and washing it away from my little girl head. Taking the images I'd seen and erasing them. Protecting me from the perversions of sexual sin. She went on for some time before my mother caught us. And you would have thought that Aunt Aubrey had introduced me to *Penthouse* and whips and chains. The screaming echoed for miles. The only difference was that my mother chased Aunt Aubrey out of the house without hitting her at all.

90

Aunt Aubrey never prayed with me after that.

"That boy called you again."

"What boy?"

I knew very well who she meant, but I objected to my Aunt Aubrey always calling young men boys. If a boy ever called me in elementary school, which, by the way, never happened, then I could see it. They're boys in elementary school. But I was twenty-five years old. I was a drunk. And I'd almost leapt to my death off the Three River Terrace building where Tory King first kissed me years before—at a party that, by the way, Aunt Aubrey insisted I not be allowed to attend, which is probably why I got to go. Bondurant Kilter was not a boy. He was a man. Well, okay, he was pudgy and wore thick-rimmed glasses, and still had some acne to deal with, and somewhat round baby cheeks. But hardly a boy.

The first time I saw Bondurant, I knew there would be trouble. He was standing in the hallway of Building Two at school with Sylvie Bennett. He had her by the shoulders talking to her. Just standing there like that, connected, talking. And when Sylvie introduced him, like a lost puppy she'd found, he grabbed me by the shoulders and pulled me into a squishy cub hug. I couldn't meet up with him, in any hallway at any time, without him hugging me or draping an arm briefly across my shoulders. And everyone else who happened by was treated to a handshake or an elbow nudge. The guy liked to touch people. It was creepy weird.

But I lived with it. I lived with it because Bondurant Kilter was the only other person in the world besides Sylvie Bennett who made me laugh. And we laughed a lot.

But now that Bond was in the picture, the laughing included lots of hugging and petting and grabbing of each other's faces so we could laugh looking into each other's teary eyes. My god, we were weird.

"He sounds like a wonderful boy," Aunt Aubrey said and I rolled my eyes.

Aunt Aubrey thought it was all in the voice: loyalty, good looks, Christian morals, money. She could tell by Bond saying, "Is April there?" that he would make a great husband. Of course, in that instance, she was right. And who knows, maybe if a biker in a murderous gang ever called me, Aunt Aubrey would be able to tell he was no good–as no good as a biker in a murderous gang would be. I mean, I don't want to be prejudiced.

"You should call him. Might be what you need to sort out this mess you're in."

I wished I could tell her I wasn't in a mess. Wished I could say I was fine. I was joking about the jump; I didn't mean it. But she'd counter with the fact that I was drunk out of my gourd and now off to the halfway house with the other addicts. That would be the worst time to call Bondurant. He'd called several times in the last month, after we met up by accident at the mall. I didn't want to start something then, why would I want to do it now?

"Well, I told him where you'd be. So, don't be surprised if he calls you there...at that place."

"You told Bondurant Kilter that I was going to be at Hope House for alcoholics and drug addicts?"

"No, no. I'm sure your father said it was only for alcoholics."

"My father? How did he get into this?"

"How did you think you were going to pay?"

"It's not free?"

"Free?" She shook her head and her frizzy chocolate bob bounced around. "You really have no concept of money, do you?"

Well, that might be true. "How much?"

She lifted her shoulders and stirred her tea. "No idea."

"How did you know my father was paying for it?"

I'd noticed that she wasn't looking at me anymore, but staring into her teacup with her lips squinching this way and that–It's the Abernathy runaround.

"Don't tell your mother," she said. "I've been talking to him. On the phone. Since this happened."

"You mean since I tried to jump?"

"Mm hm."

Holy shit. The ramifications. The screaming and yelling. It could be fabulous to watch from a distance, but I certainly wouldn't want to be around when it happened.

"I won't say a thing."

My mother had names for my father: chicken shit, shithead, freak head, the freak, ass hat. You get the picture. No one is allowed to like him. If he called and you had to talk to him, you were not to laugh or act like you enjoyed it. And if he came to town, you could only meet him at a cheap restaurant and accept money from him. You were not to make like he was your father, even though he was. If you did, the histrionics you would endure would make your life a living hell for several weeks until she got over your betrayal and got back to hating him with as much venom as she'd just spent hating you.

It was then that I realized that my Aunt Aubrey was a sly bitch. She told me that bit about my father to distract me from the fact that she told Bondurant Kilter that I was going to be staying at a halfway house for addicts. What do you take with you to a halfway house? As I unpacked my purse onto the bed in my room, Aunt Aubrey grabbed the Bible, laid down across my mattress and balanced her head on her fist.

"Did you steal the Bible from the room?" She didn't sound nearly as shocked as she ought to, being holier-than-thou moral and all.

"It wasn't a hotel. They had a visiting preacher; he gave it to me."

"Why'd he give it to you?"

"God laid it on his heart or something like that."

"Hmm. Well, take it with you."

"No thanks."

"It can't hurt."

"I might try to read it again. Just not right now. And besides, it could get stolen."

"That's true."

I laughed. Who would steal a Bible? Besides a smarmy preacher, and I wasn't sure that counted. What does a person need at a halfway house? Would I get to sit around in my robe all day? Would they make me clean toilets? I imagined there wouldn't be parties or anything, so that meant no nice clothes.

"You'll remember what we talked about, won't you?"

I knew she was talking about praying. "Of course." Like I could forget. Just looking at Aunt Aubrey was enough to remind a person he wasn't right with God. Jesus oozed out of her eyeballs. Glassy-eyed smiles, high-pitched, patronizing concerns over your health—when you knew she really meant your spiritual health. Aunt Aubrey could ask after your colon cancer and make it sound like you'd better repent or burn in hell.

Aunt Aubrey was beautiful. Like all the other women in my family. Slender, square in the face, high-cheeked, tanned lovely. There was a rumor going around that our family had Cherokee in it—that one of our ancestors who came from England before the Revolution was kidnaped by Cherokee warriors and became one of them and that's why they all looked so gorgeous. Nobody ever confirmed the rumor, but my family wasn't much into confirmations. The point being, if God's going to give all the good looks to that side of the family—and use the heathens to do it—the other side might feel a tad slighted and forget to, you know, worship him.

"Do you want me to come and visit you?" She said it with a grimace. As Christian as she was, it was hard to picture petite Aunt Aubrey surrounded by addicts and convicts. She ought to keep her charity at the Head Start and SPCA. She sometimes fed the homeless from behind a wall at the local shelter.

"No. I'd rather not have visitors."

"True. You should spend this time thinking about your life, you know? Figure out what you can do to get back on the right path."

I zipped up my duffle and slung it over my left shoulder. "What about money? You think I'll need any?"

"It'll get stolen. But you should have a few dollars, at

least."

I grabbed a few bucks off my dresser. Even if I wanted to take more, I couldn't. I wasn't about to let even Aunt Aubrey know where I hid my stash.

"You sure you won't bring the Bible?"

"They'll have Bibles there."

She picked it up again and looked at it. "But they might not have this translation."

I smiled down at her. "It'll be okay, Aunt Aubrey."

I meant to say that I would be okay, but maybe I didn't know for sure. I suddenly felt the way I did when I was sent off south to visit with the Kingston family when I was twelve. The Kingstons had three daughters—two rather cute, if not bland, who looked like their mother. And the other who had her father's face. I sympathized, as I had mine. But Janet Kingston's father's face was that of the devil—that's right, nemesis of God. Too long, gray, and bumpy; wide, crooked mouth and long, bent and pointy nose. All Mr. Kingston and Janet lacked was the wart on the nose and they'd be witches. It was desperately sad. And yet, it was no doubt the reason she was my friend.

Girls like me couldn't have just any friend. Sure, there were the neighborhood kids who played with me in a large group, because you need a good number for jailbreak or tag football—even if I pretty much just stood around trying not to get too involved. But friends who came over to your house, or invited you to spend the night, took you along on trips to the beach—I didn't have friends like that. Unless you counted Janet Kingston, which I didn't.

I suppose I learned how to put up with dating guys I didn't like by hanging out with Janet. I didn't like her. She was weird. She laughed, short and scattered, at things that weren't funny. She chewed aspirin, screwing up her face in disgust, foam drizzling down her chin—because she refused to swallow pills. An odd stork of a person. My only friend in elementary school.

The summer they moved away, my parents sent me south to visit them. They'd purchased a rat-infested, efficiency motel on Cocoa Beach and lived in two of the rooms next to the office; they'd knocked out a wall between them—no door, just a big, ragged hole in the wall. Janet followed me around all evening that first night reaching out and touching me. Constantly. There wasn't enough space to get away from her; she followed me from one room back to the other for hours. When I stepped behind her in one of the little efficiency kitchens and she reached out her foot and touched my leg with it, I started crying and couldn't stop. My parents drove all the way to Cocoa Beach and collected me at four in the morning because Mr. Kingston couldn't sleep with me crying all night.

That morning, all I wanted to do was to get home, curl up in my closet, and write to Camelia. I told her nobody liked me. Even my parents were trying to get rid of me so they could go to the beach with Sausage. I told her I was sorry; she would have been a much better person—cuter and with friends—than I could ever be. It was sad she had to live through me.

What I wanted to do as I left for Hope House, too, was find a quiet place to sit and write a long letter to

Camelia. I wanted to apologize for neglecting her. I'd always believed that invisible friends only exist as long as we pretend them. I'd promised I would never forget her, but I did. If there was a place you could send your imaginary friends where they could be picked up and cared for by better people–an invisible friend clearing house of sorts–I'd have sent Camelia there. She'd have been better off without me.

"Oh, I forgot," Aubrey said, locking my mother's front door behind us. "They've got you set up with a therapist."

"They who?"

"Your mom and dad. It's downtown. In that office building by the mall. You're to call your mother tonight to find out the details."

So, Sausage didn't tell the whole truth. My mother didn't want to hear from me to find out I was okay. She just needed to tell me about the therapist. It was nice of him, to lie. Maybe they would have Bibles at that place–I could use some wrath of God to put things into perspective.

# 9.

At the corner of Main and Whispering Pine was an old, wood-frame house hidden by moss-draped oaks straining against the heaviness of the stringy gray parasite. But they were proud and shaded the little oasis for alcoholics like a protective mother. It was the women's dormitory; I was going to get a room there. I could only hope it had a window overlooking that little front yard. Across Whispering Pine Road was the men's dormitory and the main building. It was squat and unhappy with no oaks or pines in its front yard, only shrubs. It boasted a swing, set up on an A-frame, shaded somewhat by a bottlebrush struggling for survival. Maybe too many drunks spit on it.

I crossed Main and pulled my car up to the curb in front of the mossy yard. I sat there, not sure what to do. That's the worst thing, not knowing what to do. Should I knock on the door of the women's dormitory? Was I supposed to go to the main building? Were they expecting me? Reginaldi said they were.

Do you imagine that psychiatrists live in a crazy

people network where all the doctors know one another and they know all the loons? Maybe they have picnics and game nights and they talk about us, tell funny stories about us, share crazy anecdotes. Do you suppose?

The door to the dormitory opened and a skinny old woman came out onto the drive. Her cotton print dress hung loose on her bony frame. When she turned her head toward me, the helmet of dirty frizzy hair bounced a bit and she pulled it away from the red-framed glasses on her face. She smiled and approached the car. I opened the door and got out.

"Are you Eunice?" She said.

"No." I'd decided I wasn't going to be Eunice anymore, not even by accident.

She was disappointed. "Can I help you, then? The office is in the main building."

"I'm April. I'm supposed to live here for a while."

"Really? We were expecting someone else. Maybe there are two new people."

She sucked at her teeth for a moment, her brow furrowed deeply. She was a nut; you could tell. She started in on wringing her hands together and looking around the yard. I told you that not knowing what to do was the worst thing. And though I was glad not to be the only one to know that, this woman was clearly overdoing it. She wasn't as old as I thought. She looked it, but her face lied. Her skin was taut, but lined and rough. She'd lived more than her years in places I didn't think I wanted to visit.

"It's okay," I said. "Sometimes they call me Eunice. But it's April."

She was relieved and smiled again. "Did you pack a bag?"

I nodded and dug my duffel out of the back seat.

"Well, come on then." She led me into the house. Just inside was a tiny front room remade into a bedroom; she was pleased to offer it to me. But the one window overlooked the drive and the main building across the street. When she showed me around the tiny house, a living room behind my room and two other bedrooms behind it that did overlook the oaks, I realized that much older women than myself got the good rooms. Beverly and Gladys. Longtime drunks. They sat surrounded by a thick fog of cigarette smoke, in their pajamas, in the tiny living room on a battered, plaid sofa watching television. They shared the room on the left, while a Mrs. Dougherty, not present, hogged the room on the right. Tina, the skinny frizz, was stuffed into a tiny closet of a room in the back by the bathroom.

Sure it smelled like stale cigarettes, coffee, and grease. There was a bit of mold in the air, but that might have come from Beverly and Gladys–I was almost sure it did. But it was better than home. It was neat. Ordered. The kitchenette outside my room scrubbed clean. And quiet.

The ladies talked with scratchy smoke-laden voices, and said little. They were my new mother figures. I'd have hugged them, as they sat on the old sofa beaming at me. But they weren't wearing bras. Their sagging, tubular breasts dangled loosely underneath the thin, worn cotton of their jammies. You don't hug braless old ladies. Even crazy people know that.

There was a schedule–a neat, organized routine. And

a chore chart, which unfortunately reminded me of real home. But everyone was on it, apparently, even the men, and even the people in charge, who I found out later were drunks, too. Like trusties in prisons. You hang out in Hope House long enough and they trust you with the keys.

I was introduced at the main building like an oddity, surrounded by gawking men. Chuck was tall and scrawny and beaten down by life. He was old–well, he looked old; his mouth ached for its missing teeth–unshaven, but not exactly bearded, and looked like a lost dog. Talked a bit like one, too. Like a sad, lazy hound. A permanent cigarette had worn stained grooves between the first two fingers of his right hand. Kip looked like he belonged in church and sounded like it, too. North Carolina twanged in his voice and he smiled too much. He was heavier, healthy, and made you wonder why he was there. Skeeter–I swear to holy god, Skeeter–looked like he was twelve with a crop of wheat hanging straight off his head. And John was dark and would have been good looking except for the one eyelid that drooped lower than the other and that drugged-up look about him.

My first day was like boot camp. Apparently it was their regular day for walking into town to look for jobs. They were insane. Why don't you drive? I asked them. Somehow I was the only one with a car. I was relieved that the six of us–the older women were apparently excused from job hunting–wouldn't fit in it. The last thing I wanted was to be chauffeur to a bunch of drunks.

"Maybe I'll meet you there," I protested. "Where are you going?"

"You ain't supposed to have a car," John said. "They won't like it."

"Don't tell them about it down at the housing office."

"She's a paid," Tina said.

I didn't know what the hell they were talking about. "A paid what?" I said.

"Paid in full," she said. "You don't have to go down to the social services and apply for money."

"Money for what?"

Kip rolled his eyes. "Rich people."

I wasn't rich. Even my rich Aunt Aubrey wasn't really rich, so much as rich compared to me and my mother. Just because I didn't think about money didn't mean I had too much of it.

"Come on," Tina said. "Walk with us."

"You can have a car," Kip said. "They won't refuse you for having a car."

But nobody responded to him. So I changed into my sneakers and we walked.

It wasn't as if Hope House was out in the middle of nowhere, but it was north of old downtown in something of a business district. Abandoned buildings and low-rent apartments, where people sat outside as if air conditioning and television hadn't yet been invented, mingled with garages, pawn shops, and junk-littered empty lots.

I walked. It must have been ten miles. In the Florida heat. In June. All the way east to US1, and then south all the way to the mall and the Taco Bell, where they asked about jobs. We looked like hobos coming in off the train. Well, they looked like hobos. I looked like their trainer. Or more likely their captive.

I stood at the counter of the Taco Bell, feeling inadequate. I was the best Joint Girl ever, and there I was thinking Taco Bell was too good for me. My Aunt Aubrey was always singing out sayings and she was in my head at that moment ringing out her favorite, "The apple doesn't fall far from the tree." My tree was alcoholics and I was wearing the same clothes I had on, and off, when I stood on the roof of Three River Terrace. They hadn't been laundered. Staring down at the little girl in charge of Taco Bell, I was suddenly conscious of the odor of stale cigarettes and old beer. Was that why the alcoholics were standing so close to me?

"You didn't check this box." She smiled at me, her teeth covered in silver. A red pimple angered the tip of her nose.

Could I lift more than twenty-five pounds without trouble? I told her I had no idea. I lifted boxes all the time at the Joint but I never weighed them. She looked me up and down and smiled again. "Thanks," she squeaked and spit at me. "I'll give your application to the manager."

As we left the cold restaurant and were hit by the humidity and heat, I balked. "She wasn't even the manager. You'll never get jobs."

"Who says we want jobs?" Chuck said and laughed, then coughed.

"We just have to go and put in applications or ask about positions every week," Tina said.

"You walk to town every week?"

"Every Monday," Kip said.

"And every Monday, little Brianna lets the manager know we stopped by."

"You always go to the Taco Bell?"

"Sometimes we go to Dunkin' Donuts."

"If you don't want jobs, why bother?"

"It's for the government," Kip said. "We have to show we're looking for work. And as soon as we find some, we have to pay for our stay at the House."

"Even John has to pay," Chuck said and laughed and coughed again.

I looked at John and he smiled. His teeth were clean and white, like new. He was good looking once, but ruined himself, probably with booze and drugs. Could have been fighting. He didn't look exactly symmetrical.

By the time we made it back to the House I was exhausted, but they forced me to help Tina cook until I got my own chore assignments. The meal wasn't too bad, but it was not up to institution standards. Tina broiled chicken pieces in a glass dish with only oil, salt, carrots and celery. I told her she needed sausage and green peppers and better spices. She acted like I was from Mars. After dinner we were in charge of neatening up the meeting room in the main house. It was almost eight o'clock and I thought I could find my bed across the street and lie down, but it wasn't over. We had to walk another mile to attend an AA meeting in a run-down plaza on Goldenrod Street. Apparently, the theory of Hope House and the treating of drunks was to keep them as busy as possible until they were too worn out to drink. Those people were sick.

Tina and I went over to the women's dorms to pee and Gladys and Beverly were sitting in their places on the sofa watching the evening news, a haze of cigarette smoke hanging over their heads. I grabbed my purse out from under the bed–I figured if anyone stole it, I would know it was Tina. The old biddies could never get down on the floor and scoot under the bed like that, the men didn't know where I'd hid it, so she would be the likely suspect.

"You can't take that," Tina said combing out her hair.

"Why not?"

She looked at me like I was an idiot. "It'll be dark soon. We're going past the park. No purses."

"But what about money?"

"What do you need money for?"

Now it was my turn to stare at her. Was she out of her mind? A girl must always have money on her unless she was going to a bar, and even then it's always good to have back up. I mean, there could be nothing but creeps. Not that I wouldn't let creeps buy me a few beers. Their money is just as good as anyone else's. But you always had money on you. Still, while I was trying to imagine the idea of a person walking around without money, I could see her point. So, I took my last four dollars and seventy-five cents out of my wallet and shoved it in my back pants pocket.

"There'll be doughnuts and coffee. You won't need money."

"Okay," I said. "But suppose on the way there we get mugged by a goon. You want him to shoot you because you don't have any money for him?"

She opened the front door and held it for me. "He's going to shoot you when he finds out you only have four bucks, trust me."

We all hiked down the sidewalk west on Main Street. Kip and Tina hung back. I tried to stick with them because I didn't know where I was going and I didn't want Chuck walking with me; he was a close walker. He liked it when our hands and elbows knocked together. John walked in the street and I wanted to join him. There was more room in the street but I was afraid Chuck would follow me and I'd spend the whole time moving away from him until we were all the way on the other side at the gutter and then what would I do? Skeeter jogged up ahead and then turned and walked backward until we caught up. We walked past the park where hooligans were shouting and shooting baskets and I wished I could play. None of them seemed the type to mug me for my four dollars. Skeeter tripped on an uneven part of the sidewalk, but that's what you get for walking backwards.

"Why are we having an AA meeting at eight-thirty at night?" I wanted to know.

"Sometimes they're late; sometimes they're early." Kip said.

"It's an after meeting," Tina said. "This group wanted more than one."

"What for?"

"Mondays are hard for alcoholics," Kip said.

"It keeps them from not drinking," Chuck said.

"You mean it keeps them from drinking?" I said.

"What did I say?"

"You said it keeps them from *not* drinking."

He laughed. "Freudian slip."

I looked at him with my eyes wide open. You don't expect to hear something like that out of someone with a

Chuck face. "You know Freud?"

"Freud?"

"Of the Freudian slip. Sigmund Freud."

"What kind of a name is Sigmund?" He said.

"I think it's German. Sigmund Freud, the psychiatrist."

He shook his head and shoved his hands in his pockets.

"You know," I said. "Father of psychotherapy and all?"

"So, you're saying he invented the Freudian slip?"

"Sure," Tina said. "That must be where they got the name."

"So," I said, giving up on that subject, "you just go to meetings all night until you're too tired to go out and get drunk. Is that the plan?"

"We could go to three meetings a day, if we wanted to," Kip said.

"We'd have to take the bus," Tina said.

"I'm just saying."

"But do you know how long that would take? You have to do a whole circuit. You'd be on the bus all day."

"I was just saying," Kip said. He let go of Tina's hand and rubbed his own against his shirt like she was dirty.

"Well, if you're on the bus all day, you're not drinking." Chuck smiled, very pleased with himself.

The sky was fading into gray and we turned down some dark street, spooky with mossy trees and at least one homeless drunk moving in the shadows. When we came up behind the old plaza, I remembered the building; it had been there forever. We were on Goldenrod Street, in the northwest corner of Sandy Point. If you kept on northwest, you'd find the rich people and the rich high school. But on Goldenrod, where there were no goldenrods—ever—was the poorest of the poor.

As we rounded the corner to the front of the building, I was surprised at the darkness. The owners of Sandy Point Plaza had to be desperate. Their sixties-era roach palace housed a veterinarian on one end—we passed it, peering at our reflections in the darkened glass—and a liquor store on the other, distant, where the glow of the booze sign lit up the parking lot. The two anchors jutted out from the rest of the building by about six feet, creating shadowy corners. The seven spots between the anchor stores were empty. Except for the bright lights at the other end, beckoning we drunks with spirits, we had approached a ghost of a building. The others walked toward the liquor store and I got this wild idea that, as an apology of sorts, the store owners invited local drunks to hold their sobriety meetings in the back room, where all the cases and cases of whiskey and vodka were stored. My hopes were dashed when I saw dim lights in one of the store fronts in the middle and Kip held the door open for me.

I was in the saddest AA meeting available, even by Sandy Point standards. Warped, bare, tables formed a rectangle in the middle of the room. The cold folding chairs were rusted in spots, some covered with ratty towels. The set up screamed discomfort. But at the back of the room, like an altar, beckoned a table covered in a green and brown striped cloth. True to Tina's word, coffee urns sat on one end and plates of doughnuts and pastries covered the other. My fellow House drunks stacked their tiny paper plates and poured themselves coffee.

Chuck looked hopefully at me with a steaming foam cup in hand.

"No, thank you," I said.

"Soda machine's down the way."

I nodded.

"I'll come with you. It's almost dark," he said.

Ah, the drunk knight in shining armor with a toothless smile. I shivered. "No thanks. Just save me a seat."

It was better to have to sit next to him than walk alone with him in the dark in the deserted scary part of town. I mean, seriously, I didn't know any of these people. I knew nothing about them except that they were drunks. And had quite a bit of heat and hiking endurance. And liked pastry and coffee. But other than that, who could tell, right?

As I left the storefront I pulled my money from my back pocket. I could get a soda from a machine if it was fifty or seventy-five cents. I should have brought more cash. A few dollars wasn't going to last me very long if I had to buy a soda every time I went to an AA meeting—and from the sounds of it, I was going to be attending quite a lot of them. I'd have to get back home to my stash, if my mother hadn't found it and stolen it all.

I walked toward the liquor store; in the dark corner created by part of its wall, the soda machine sat like a forgotten dinosaur; I couldn't tell if it was even working. If I kept on past it, I could go into the liquor store and get a Diet Coke. There was probably a rule about that. So far, no one had mentioned anything about rules, but there had to be some, and not going into a liquor store would be on the list.

There was something spooky about the dead plaza and the empty parking lot and the Goldenrod Street stop light a hundred yards away–red, no cars waiting. Two cars sat parked out front of the liquor store and I walked toward the light streaming from its neon sign starting to get the feeling I was being followed.

The soda machine was lit up only slightly, but I caught a low hum and figured I was in luck. As I peered at it, realizing it was a dreaded Pepsi machine, something next to it, in the cubby between the machine and the liquor store, moved. I must have jumped ten feet. Curled up against the wall, huddled a crumpled man. I was on Goldenrod freaking Street in Sandy Point after dark trying to get a Diet Coke out of Pepsi machine disturbing a possible serial killing homeless man's sleep. And it was only Monday.

"Sorry," I said and tried to catch my breath.

He was still for a moment, the outline of his lumpy body barely discernable in the dim light; then he reached up toward me with his arm, and for some reason I moved forward, toward him, instead of away. Even as I was doing it I was thinking zombies, or Ted Bundy, and what kind of person steps forward instead of running away shrieking? The slightest smell of urine and feces floated about and he whispered, "Sorry."

"I didn't mean to scare you." I chuckled. He scared the living shit out of me and I was apologizing for scaring *him*. It was like I'd created an opposite world in my head where I was kind and helpful instead of aloof and afraid.

His hand dropped and I stood there for a few seconds waiting to see if he would move again. Jesus, I thought. Maybe the man's dead. I'd killed him.

"Are you all right?" I stepped closer but couldn't make out much. He was thin, bearded and dirty. Well he was a homeless man, so there you have it.

"Could use some water," he said.

I nodded. "Okay, okay. I'll be right back."

As I walked toward the liquor store, I chastised myself. A person shouldn't be making friends with homeless people—I knew this from experience. Now he was expecting me to come back. He could be ready for me; he could grab me and haul me around the back of the plaza and rape me and bash my head in with a rock and they wouldn't find me until morning, if then. I could keep going. I didn't have to go into the store, didn't have to go back to the meeting. I could just keep going, back down the street and past the park and to the women's dorm and to my purse and my car keys.

I was shaking when I got back to the storefront and the meeting was getting started. Tina had saved me a seat between her and Chuck. He eyed me knowingly. I wore the air of someone who had been in a liquor store within the last forty-eight hours. Blasphemy crept onto my face and snickered at him.

"Machine empty?" He said.

I nodded.

I never bought my beer in liquor stores, as a general rule. Liquor stores are large and well-lit and filled with all sorts of breakable things. Going in one was like going to Walmart when all you needed was milk. Senseless. I preferred convenience stores. That's what they're for, after all. Convenience. But, liquor stores know their purpose–selling booze—and they must know a lot of their customers are drunks. Convenience stores sell all kinds of stuff. They're not used to drunks; I learned this.

I shopped at seven different stores for beer. Nine really, but I used seven most often. One store for each day of the week. I wasn't embarrassed about buying beer all the time. Not at all. I didn't care. But when one of the employees at Harley's Bait and Tackle, on the corner a few blocks from my mom's duplex, thought it would be funny to make a big deal about me arriving to purchase a six-pack for the third day in a row by blocking the door so I couldn't get in, well, I took the hint. I didn't buy beer at Harley's Bait and Tackle after that. I didn't shop there at all–it wasn't a burden, I never needed bait or tackle. The point is, it was nobody's business how much beer I bought or how often or why. The last thing an employee should be doing is making comments on what I'm purchasing, much less acting like I can't come in, even if they do think it's a joke. I should have complained to Harley. But for all I knew he was a recovering drunk and told the little shit to do it.

"It was a Pepsi machine," I said.

He shook his head. Why were we drinking caffeine at eight thirty at night anyway?

All the voices were hoarse and a cloud of cigarette smoke hovered over us as we ran through the meeting agenda. I hate meetings. I hate meetings where everyone is asked to say his name and why he's there and tell a little bit about himself. Why do they always do that at meetings? The only thing I hate more is teams. Let's team up in groups of four and brainstorm a new burger. What was Mr. Toby thinking? We went around the room saying our names and admitting we were drunks and telling everyone how long we'd been sober. When it was my turn, I stared around at all the tired, worn drunks wondering what the hell I was doing there. The faces of the older sots were drawn and disapproving–but resigned. I got the feeling they didn't like us Hope House nuts invading their meeting. Turns out recovering drunks just look like that: drawn and disapproving. They're not happy people. Happiness is probably too reminiscent of their glory days sucking at the teat of Jack Daniels.

"My name is April," I said. "And I'm an alcoholic. I've been sober now for...since Thursday, I guess."

There was an audible gasp but I didn't catch which old biddy let it out. What? New drunks never attended their meetings? I wasn't though; I was not an alcoholic. I knew this because they told me at that meeting that alcoholism is a disease–a progressive, debilitating disease from which you can't even begin your eternal recovery until you've hit what they call rock bottom. Until you are lower than the curb, crawling out of the gutter, urine-stained and feces-smeared, can you possibly be ready to go into recovery. And don't even think you'll recover one day. Alcoholism is a disease for which there is no cure. You will be in recovery for the rest of your life. And you can never, ever so much as take a sip of wine ever again, or the next thing you know, you're back in the gutter covered in shit. Well, no thank you, Mary. I wanted none of that. Forget it. I wasn't going to be an alcoholic.

No matter, the old man who led the meeting coughed and said, "It's genetic. You got the demon rum gene and you're an alcoholic. Nothing you can do. The fact that you're here means you're a drunk."

"But I haven't ever peed myself, or laid in the gutter." I protested, mouth slightly open as if to say you people are nuts. I had, actually, peed myself before, but it was completely unrelated. Still, that made me think it was possible that I'd laid in a gutter and forgot.

"You will." The dead lady in the bright, frog green, frilly top said—her lips were powdered in white from her constant gorging on doughnuts. "You'll hit rock bottom before you're ready for sobriety."

"So, you're telling me," I said. Tina shook her head, as if to tell me to shut the hell up. "That there's nothing I can do about it. I'm going to have to be a rock-bottom drunk."

"That's right," the fat lady said. Her name was Weasel or something like that. A wilted hibiscus flower hung loosely in her hair and she sipped coffee with one pinky sticking out. Those old farts were nothing like the drunks at Hope House. They were tailored and primped. They were in recovery!

"You smirk now," fat lady continued. "And after a while of meetings, you'll disappear because you're not there yet."

"But you'll be back," the old dude said. "You'll be back." He smiled at me, showing off his large yellow teeth. He was happy that I was going to hit rock bottom, the feces-filled gutter. I guess it was his only consolation for his own time there.

But no thank you. I was not going to have any of that. And I think even Claire Lindsay would agree with me. "There's no point in going over," she said once when we were looking for a lunch table in the senior cafeteria. The only open seats were at the loadie table—where the pot heads ate lunch. "We don't want to become associated with that." Claire knew all about the bad infecting the good.

# 10.

Finally we were back at the House and I wanted to lie down, but instead we all loitered out front of the main building. Tina and I sat in the swing and glided back and forth for hours while she and Kip flirted and one-eyed John leered at me and Skeeter snorted at everything funny and Chuck tried to say interesting and not uneducated things all night. He wasn't very good at it.

The next morning I helped with breakfast. I was shown to the chore chart and saw what I was supposed to do that week: empty and wipe out all of the ash trays; make the iced tea every morning; help cook breakfast and dinner; and carry the trash to the curb on Saturday morning. It was like being at home, except I didn't mind so much.

"We're walking downtown today." Tina was frying eggs for Chuck, Skeeter, and Kip who stood in a line behind her with their plates ready.

"Again?"

"Just downtown," Chuck said and winked at me. "For fun."

It was June. Did these people not understand heat? "Can't," I said. "I have to run home and get something."

They all stared at me for a few seconds, like they were waiting for me to explain. The toast popped up and I grabbed it and started buttering like mad and by the time I was tossing it onto their plates, they were all back to normal. Sometimes the drunks did that. It was as if they were all connected; they shared a language and manner and whenever I deviated from the script, they stopped and in unison gave me the drunk eye, the what-did-you-say eye, or the oh-that's-right-you-haven't-crawled-in-the-gutter-yet eye. They were like the crazies over at the psychiatric facility and it occurred to me that when you put crazy people together they fall into a crazy synchrony—they move together and think together and talk together and when someone steps out of line, they have to stop and reconfigure.

"I could go with you," Tina said, finally sliding two fried eggs off the spatula onto my plate. I added toast to hers and we sat at the kitchen table with the others.

"Where's John?" I said.

And again, they stopped and looked at me, chewing. Kip's head wobbled a bit on his neck. "He was gone this morning."

"Where did he go?"

Tina smiled at me and Chuck glared.

"I was just asking."

"He's looking for work," Kip said.

"So you want me to come with you?" Tina said.

"I thought we were going to look in that bookshop," Kip said.

118

"We can do that another time."

"She wants to see where you live," Chuck said.

"Do not. I just thought, you know. Well," she turned to me. "You haven't been sober very long."

"I'll be fine. I just need to go home and get something."

Jesus it was like extricating yourself from Silly String. They were weak from sobriety, and clingy. Chuck and John were supposed to clean up after breakfast and Chuck whined so much about John shirking his duties that I stayed and helped him, and then I went back to the women's dorm and got my purse. Beverly and Gladys were finished with their plates so I carried them back over and Chuck started whining again about how he was already finished and it wasn't fair to have more dishes. I told him I couldn't help it and left the dishes in the sink. It was like leaving the aftermath of a tornado. As I drove away, I could breathe again, and hadn't realized I wasn't breathing. I could listen to music and sing and smoke a cigarette alone.

"It's only Tuesday," I told the radio. "Fucking Tuesday. I don't know how much more of this shit I can take."

Aunt Aubrey didn't come out when I pulled up at the duplex and I was relieved. There was something not right about being surrounded by people all the time. I needed to be alone. I pulled open the front door to all the smells of home, and dog shit. Princess Patty Cakes had taken a dump by the back sliding door so I opened it up and let her out. I turned down the AC at the thermostat in the hall on my way to my room. I fell onto my bed and laid

119

there for a while. I might have slept but didn't feel like I had when I got up. It was lunchtime by then, so I made myself a sandwich and grabbed a Diet Coke and watched television. At two, I got out the step stool from the kitchen and took it to my room and put it in front of the closet. I climbed it and stood there. The shoe box where I kept my money was hidden behind a folded blanket and as I reached out to move it, I remembered my letters to Camelia.

It was years ago and my mother was forcing me to clean my room. She tore through my desk drawers, tossing their contents onto the floor–pulled dirty dishes from the bookshelves and scattered them on the bed.

"Filthy mess," she said. "You're not leaving this room until it's spotless."

We'd been through it many times. I could predict the weekend she'd have her tantrum by the amount of junk I'd accumulated under my bed. It was in the old house, where we lived when we were a family.

Next she was on her hands and knees attacking my closet, her head inside, her big butt up in the air, flinging dirty socks and books out behind her. Suddenly everything stopped. It took me a while to notice because I was half under my bed gathering up pieces of stale bread from a half-eaten peanut butter sandwich.

"What's this?" She said.

I popped my head up over my bed and stared, gaping, at my mother. She held up my shoe box full of letters to Camelia. My knees dug into the deep shag of my Donny-Osmond-purple carpet, my heart was a pounding hammer in my chest. An eerie animal sound erupted in my throat.

120

"Put it back," I said.

She climbed to her feet and carried the box out of the room.

As I found my stash box and pulled open the lid, my ankles were weak and wobbly. I grabbed a few twenties and replaced the box behind the blanket and climbed gingerly down from the stool. I couldn't remember what happened after my mother left the room that day. I thought there was screaming. I thought she held the door closed and I couldn't get out, but that could have been another memory. I only knew that the box was gone; the letters were gone. And over time, I'd forgotten about them altogether.

The first week at Hope House was all hustle and very little fun. I can't imagine what I'd been expecting. Counseling, maybe. A lot of talking about how we were drunks and how terrible that was–how terrible we were– our favorite drinks, maybe. Our favorite bars. All the awful things we did when we were drunk. There wasn't much of that, really. Mostly there was a lot of walking, swinging, chatting, and laughing.

At the AA meetings, the drunks talked about how booze ruined their lives, the awful things they'd done; but their stories were bland and noncommittal. They wouldn't dare share the real juice. It didn't surprise me. From the looks of them, every last one, the sleazy details would be all over Sandy Point by morning. I could tell them a story or two but I wasn't opening my yap, that was for sure.

Every night there was one AA meeting or another– even if we'd gone to one in the morning, we attended one that evening, too. It was like a rule that we had to attend every AA meeting within a five mile radius. And what was with that, anyway? Why were there so many? In dumpy Sandy Point?

There were open meetings where anybody in town could just walk in and see us sitting there being drunks. There were closed meetings where supposedly only admitted drunks were allowed, but I didn't see anyone checking papers. There were meetings with guest speakers and meetings with families and oh, my, god, could the mothers or the wives look any more put upon? And Big Book Study meetings. Every meeting had only one thing in common: doughnuts and coffee. Okay that's two things, but according to AA drunks, they're one thing.

Was it Sandy Point? Was that shit hole of a city breeding drunks? I could see it. Sandy Point was beautifully named, but that was it, so far as attributes went. It was flat, ugly, old, depressed. Stagnant. There was one movie theater. Sixteen restaurants. Two malls, but one didn't count as it was sinking into oblivion fast. Four car dealerships and seven hundred churches. It had one fabulous thing: a long road out–out–across the estuary, away from Sandy Point, to Beauty Beach. You get there, the end of the road, and you turn left down a tiny dirt path just wide enough for one car. Along the right are spots where you park, hike the dunes, and play on the most beautiful white sands in the world. And if you drive far enough, you find the nude beach that everybody talked about and probably nobody ever saw. I know I never did.

I'm probably exaggerating about the churches.

On Friday night, Hope House hosted its own AA

meeting. Nobody else was invited. We popped popcorn, Beverly and Gladys made brownies, and we all crowded into the living room of the main building to talk about what lousy drunks we were. I had the privilege of the recliner. I thought it was because I was new, but Tina said it was because I was the youngest girl and all the guys liked me. Tina and Kip took the couch where they could scrunch against one another with their thighs touching and none of the trustees would realize what was going on. John ended up on the floor because he came in late, his droopy eye quite a bit droopier than usual.

There were readings going on when I realized that Chuck was watching me from across the room. When I looked at him, he winked at me. Kip was reading from the Big Book, the alcoholics Bible, the book that would change your life, if you'd do everything it said to do. He was going on about how we should shout it from the rooftops, our sobriety, our plan. We should let everybody know what we were doing. And there Chuck sat with his goofy, toothless grin, winking at me. What the hell?

Kip's voice purred like a preacher's, but softer, smoother, much better than the preacher at the facility. I couldn't picture Kip drunk, much less *a* drunk. Couldn't picture him reeling or vomiting or certainly not standing on the roof of Three River Terrace threatening to jump. His sweet round face looked like it was still plumped with baby fat. And he smiled much too often to be a hit-the-bottom addict. He read with such ease and passion, it occurred to me he was there for the girls. At that I laughed out loud and Kip stopped reading; all eyes turned to me.

"Sorry," I said.

"Did you want to say something?" Bossy Bridget said. Bridget was in charge. I hadn't figured out yet if she was a former drunk, but she looked it. Stern. A person who likes rules a lot.

"What?" I said.

Her head danced on her neck and she closed her eyes for a second or two. "I said...did you want to add something to the reading?"

You mean, something like, I pictured Kip offering braless Gladys a chocolate covered strawberry, wearing nothing but his heart-dotted briefs?

"No, it's nothing."

Chuck was reading next, from a pamphlet that looked a lot like a religious tract. His reading skills were god-awful compared with Kip's. Stuttering, mispronouncing, halting his way through. No one could possibly be listening. Tina's and Kip's feet nudged each other under the coffee table over at the sofa. Tina's big toe stuck out of her sandal, rubbing against Kip's tennis shoe. That would drive me nuts. My foot started to itch thinking about it. I had to look away. I caught Bridget's stare and she smiled at me and turned to glare at someone else. Chuck was going on about how we should keep it to ourselves, not be boastful. This was our journey, ours alone; we shouldn't brag about our successes.

Bridget turned back to me as Chuck was finishing.

"Did you have a question?" She asked me.

"Huh?"

"You look confused."

"Well, it just seemed a little contradictory."

"What do you mean?"

"Well, the first thing we read said to shout it from the rooftops and the second thing said to keep it to ourselves."

Before I stopped talking Kip was flipping the pages of his book comparing notes with the pamphlet.

"It's about the process," Bridget said.

That was meant to end the discussion, before it started. Nobody else said anything. Nobody explained. Nobody cared.

"You ask too many questions," Tina said once we were perched on the swing out front. Chuck, Kip, and John sat on the damp ground smoking cigarettes while Skeeter walked around us, wearing a large circle rut in the grass.

"What's wrong with questions?"

"If you question the process, it won't work. You'll be drunk again before you know it. Just accept everything that's given to you."

"I can't help it if there was a contradiction."

"There was no contradiction," he said.

"There wasn't?"

"No. It seemed like a contradiction to you because you're fighting the process."

"I'm not fighting the process."

"You are so," Tina said. "You're fighting right now."

"Not the process."

"Fighting us is fighting the process," Kip said.

What was this, some kind of cult?

"If you accept it, you'll see that it all makes sense. There was no contradiction."

"So, if I just believe whatever I'm told, I'll believe it makes sense."

"Exactly."

I sat there with my mouth slightly open, swinging forward and back, forward and back, Kip's thick head rising up and sinking down in my view. I realized he wasn't there for the girls at all.

"April, we got a favor to ask," Chuck said. "You can say no. Honestly. You can say no." Of course, that meant that I could not say no. "We was wondering if you'd drive me and Kip and Tina over to Palm Bay tomorrow. Kip's got to get his ex-wife to sign some papers before a deadline."

"What about Skeeter?"

"He ain't allowed to leave town."

At that, Skeeter stopped his circle, shoved his hands into his pants pockets and grinned at me.

"We'll take you to lunch for your trouble," Kip said.

At least we didn't have to walk. I tossed and turned all that night worrying about it. I didn't want to drive the drunks anywhere, much less all the way to Palm Bay. I'd never even been there. I had to figure out a way to get out of it. I could be sick. I thought I *might be* sick. I felt like the world was swinging back and forth all night and I dreamt that I was on the swing in the darkness with Tina and my mother drove up the road and missed the stop sign; she swerved the car and the headlights came at us. I startled awake and the rush of the swinging, back and forth, dazed my head and turned my stomach. Beads of sweat popped out on my upper lip.

The next morning after the breakfast dishes were

dried and put away and everyone else's chores were done, Tina and I went to the girls' dormitory to get our purses for the trip. There was nothing I could do. I was too hungry when I got up to pretend to be sick and I knew I wasn't that good of an actress, anyway. I wished I could stop saying yes all the time.

As we left the building, Bondurant Kilter walked up the drive toward us.

"Bond," I practically shouted. "What are you doing here?" It was really meant to be, "What in the hell are you doing here at the drunk house uninvited?"

He smiled that lazy smile of his–I'd almost forgotten it. Bond looked the same as he did in high school: cute. Not cuddly cute–nerd cute. His hair was parted on the left and there was a flip to the bang. He wore round glasses; had pudgy cheeks. And he wore mom jeans. But you wanted to hug him all the time, even if you weren't the hugging sort.

"I came to see you. See how you're doing. See if you're all right." He practically stuttered.

I glanced at Tina and she was grinning ear to ear. "Are you going to introduce me?"

I did, and Tina had the decency to head across the street to where the other drunks stood outside waiting. They looked over at me curiously, and then down to the ground, nervous, like meerkats when there's an eagle overhead.

"Your Aunt Aubrey told me you were here. Sorry I didn't come sooner. I work days and I didn't think it'd be cool to come over at night." He turned to see the drunks standing stupidly in the front yard of the main building staring at us. "So, you okay?"

"I'm fine. Really." And then I looked at him squarely. "Really, I'm okay."

"You didn't try to jump off a building?"

"Of course not."

"But the police took you to a crisis facility."

"Yeah, well, they didn't understand."

"You were drunk."

I laughed. "A little." He put this irritating look of concern on his face. "Look, I'd like to talk and all," I said. "But I promised the drunks I'd take them to Palm Bay."

"Palm Bay?"

"Kip has to have a paper signed. I don't know."

"You think you should be driving to Palm Bay?"

"I'm not drunk *now*."

"Well..."

"You think alcohol stays in the body for more than a week?"

"Maybe."

"They say it kills brain cells. That's it. I'm brain dead. I'll never drive again."

"You should be careful, that's all."

"I've driven a car before."

"But...getting drunk, going to the roof..."

"You're saying I can't be trusted to drive the drunks around."

He blushed. "I didn't mean that," he said.

Of course that's what he meant. Once, in tenth grade, I ate lunch with Cricket Swanson. Cricket was no small bug. I was yattering on and on about Wally Boner and how he'd lost so much weight and was so much happier, so smart, and attractive, and just seemed to be an all-round better person. As soon as it came out of my mouth, I knew it was wrong. So, I said, "I'm sorry; I didn't mean that."

Cricket said, "What are talking about?"

"Nothing." I didn't want to make things worse by explaining it.

"Really, what are you apologizing for?"

"Nothing."

"Tell me."

"I didn't mean to say Wally wasn't a good person when he was fat."

"What's wrong with that?"

"You're saying fat people are bad?"

Fat-cheeked, barely fit in the chair, couldn't get closer than fifteen inches from the damn table, Cricket said, "How should I know? Anyway, you're the one who said it."

She knew I meant it. We always mean the things that just pop out, the things we don't get to edit. Maybe if we all spoke without thinking the world would be a more honest place—or a war zone. Either way, I always held out hope that if I could edit my words before speaking them, I'd change my mind and be a better person, but I struggle with the first step.

"I'll take you guys," Bond said.

"What? Like you don't have anything better to do on a Saturday?"

He looked to the ground and I felt stupid. But seriously, why would Bondurant Kilter want to drive a bunch of drunks to Palm Bay?

"It's a long way," he said. "You shouldn't drive it with them in the car."

I looked to the drunks. "They're not wild teenagers, Bond. They're pretty subdued, actually."

"How well do you know them?"

Chuck waved at me and grinned wildly.

"Okay, you can drive. Your car's bigger, anyway."

Of course his name wasn't Wally Boner, and everybody knew it. That's what we called him behind his back. I don't think I ever knew his real name. It was probably something normal like Wally Brown and he had the unfortunate accident of having a boner once. There are things in life you never get over.

My car had bucket seats and I'd been kept up most of the night before worrying about Chuck sitting up front with me and reaching over the gear shift to touch me. But in Bond's car, I got to sit up front with him while Chuck and Kip had Tina happily wedged between them in the back seat. They smoked constantly, the windows cracked open. I abstained. Bondurant had enough smoke to deal with. He took it like a real trouper. I wondered if Aunt Aubrey put him up to it. But how could Aunt Aubrey have known I was taking the drunks on a road trip?

We stopped for lunch at a Mexican restaurant where Tina and Kip ate fiery chili and laughed at each other's tears. Bondurant didn't let them pay for my lunch; instead he insisted on treating me. I couldn't help wondering if he might think this was a date. Our first date...with the drunks. Then we drove forever in a neighborhood that never ended to a house where Kip ran in and ran back out and that was it. Business done. On the way back,

130

Chuck said there was one more stop to make.

"Kip and I need to see our former boss," he said.

He gave Bond directions and we ended up at Tequila's Lounge, a hole in the wall joint in Cocoa on US1, right there in the middle of the world where anybody could see you going in and coming out. Bars look god-awful in daylight—old, rotting, paint-chipped, the parking lots with faded lines littered with trash and bottles. If you went in sober, at least you got to come out drunk and not recognize what you'd lowered yourself to.

"Come on in," Chuck said. He lifted himself out of the back seat with a grunt.

"We'll wait for you," Bond said.

"We're going to be a while. You should come in."

And so we went in. Most of the time, music pulsated around a bar before I got to the door and excitement buzzed through me, but not at Tequila's. Tequila's was one of those dark lounges where old men went to get drunk. Hardcore geezers aren't interested so much in underage girls in high heels gyrating all over the place. If they were, they'd be at a strip club in the middle of the afternoon on a Saturday.

The place was dark and smokey, smelled like urine and beer, and while I swore it was far below my standards, there was so much about it that was familiar. Chuck led us to a big booth in the corner and we all sat while he and Kip went behind the bar to talk to the bartender. He was a thick man with tattoos on his bald head. Maybe he was Tequila.

"They used to work with him," Tina said.

"Here?"

"Building houses."

"Are they wanting their jobs back?" Bond said.

"I think they just came to see him."

A waitress came to the table. I'd never been in a bar where someone came to the table so I thought we were pretty classy. Bond and I ordered sodas and Tina shrugged it off.

"My treat," I said. But she shook her frizzy head.

Kip and Chuck came back to the table with mixed drinks and Kip handed an extra one to Tina.

"You can have a drink," Kip told me. "It's okay."

How the hell was it okay? We were drunks at a halfway house; weren't we supposed to be getting sober? There was probably a rule about staying two hundred yards from bars at all times–going inside one was blasphemy and buying a drink was selling your soul to devil rum.

When we left the bar the sunlight hit our eyes and made us turn away. It reminded me of why I never liked getting drunk in the afternoons and stumbling out and not being able to find my car and laughing at being lost in the light instead of the dark. I usually vomited those days.

"What?" Bond said as he opened the passenger side door for me.

"Nothing." He didn't need to know about it.

Bondurant was one of the good people. The sorts I tended to avoid for some reason. Oh, wait, that's right, it's because they're boring and judgmental. They don't have to say anything. They just have to stand there being good, not drinking, not smoking, not cursing, not doing anything at all really, and just by doing that nothing, you

132

realize they're judging you. Or you're judging yourself by comparing yourself to them. Good people ought to at least give bad things a try. Either that or leave the rest of us alone and stop coming by or calling and then standing there or sitting there on the phone judging us.

"Aren't you going to open the door for me?" Tina asked Kip.

He smiled and did so. It didn't seem out of character for him. But he was blushing. Maybe he was drunk. All in all, it looked like Chuck had three drinks and Kip and Tina each had two. It was nearly five when we got back to the House and we all had our chores to get to. Dinner still had to be made.

"I guess I have to get going," I told Bond, standing by his car.

"Are you allowed to go out or anything, while you're here?"

"What do you mean?"

"We could go to the movies or something."

"I don't think so. I don't know."

I could have asked, but I didn't want to. I didn't know what Bond wanted. We were best friends, along with Sylvie Bennett, in high school. They were band nerds and I was antisocial. We were together all the time; I followed them to football games, we went to the movies and out to eat, went to school dances and always danced with one another, trying to pretend that it wasn't weird for three people to do that. We called ourselves Three Beans, after the salad, and read to one another from *The Happy Hooker*, and there was always something askew, something off, that set me apart from them. Maybe Bond wanted that friendship back, but I wondered if there was anything to recover. Anyway, we couldn't do it then, not after I'd tried to jump of the Three River Terrace building. What sort of catalyst to renewing a friendship is that?

"So, are you going to stop drinking now, or what?"

I laughed. "What kind of question is that?"

"Well, you got drunk and tried to jump off a roof and now you're here."

"I didn't try to jump off a roof. I told you, it was a misunderstanding."

"You're still here."

"They're making me be here."

"Who?"

"Everybody."

He smiled at me. Bondurant was always cute when he smiled.

"I don't have a problem with drinking," I said.

"Why didn't you have a drink today?"

"It was just wrong."

"You're a rule follower, aren't you?"

"Maybe. But I could have had a drink if I wanted."

"You didn't want?"

"It's the middle of the day. I've been drunk in the middle of the day before; it's not pleasant."

"No?"

"Haven't you?"

"No, I can't say I have."

"Not even at a party?"

"I don't drink, really."

"What does *really* mean?"

"I don't know."

I had a lot of trouble with people who didn't drink. I mean, what was there to do? How did they spend their time? Twenty-four hours a day, seven days a week sober? Say we went on a date. What were we supposed to do if not go to a bar and get drunk? Sure, there are movies, and then maybe dinner. But after that. Go home and watch television? It just didn't make any sense.

"April," Tina called from across the street. "You're supposed to be cooking with me."

"Well, I have to go, I guess."

"So, no on the movies, then?"

"I don't know. Maybe when I find an apartment."

"An apartment?"

"Yeah, I don't think I'm going back home. Course, I need a job, too."

"You should probably get the job first."

"Probably." I laughed. "They all walk down to Taco Bell once a week and pretend to look for work."

"You don't want to work there."

"Tell me about it. I'd go back to the Joint first."

"Did you quit, or what?"

"I sort of got fired. I guess I'll start looking next week."

He nodded. "Remember that time after Sylvie and I quit the marching band and she drove us over to Merritt Island for the game?"

"You mean the time she disappeared and we ended up having to get a ride from Tim Grant's mom?"

"Yeah."

Of course I remembered that. Bond and I wanted to go to the concession and then over to the other side to

135

meet some of the kids from Merritt Island during the bands' third quarter break. I figured Bond wanted to talk to one of the Mustang clarinetists. He was always talking about this clarinetist or that clarinetist until I figured he indulged in one of those fetishes or something. But Sylvie wouldn't come with us.

"No, let's not do that," she said.

Sylvie wasn't a sweet sort of blonde. Her hair was straight and thin and hung down her back like a silk blanket. Her face was pointed and hard and her eyes were dark brown; she always looked like she was ready to scream about something. And she always got her way.

"Come on," Bond said. "My butt's sore from sitting. Let's walk around."

"No," she said. "You go on without me."

Bond and I both knew that this didn't mean we should go on without her. This meant that we should sit the fuck down and watch the rest of the game with her. Sylvie was always doing things like that. Little tests of our loyalty. She called me once on a Friday night and asked me if I was busy and I said I was. I was getting ready to go out with Lee Harper and what did she want.

"Sorry to bother you," she said and hung up.

I was supposed to call her back; that's what friends did. Friends of Sylvie Bennett, anyway. I was supposed to call and ask her what was wrong and what did she want and of course I had time to listen to her. But I didn't. And we were never the same after that.

I'd already sat back down beside Sylvie when Bond said, "No. I want to go walk around."

"Suit yourself," she said.

Bond looked at me. And, well, I guess things were starting to unravel already. I mean, I'd told Sylvie about Lee flirting with me and asking me to a party and she was already pissed off and I was starting to not care. So I got up and went with him.

We had a great time, eating hot dogs and chewing the ice out of our empty soda cups and spending the whole third quarter with the bands from both teams. And when it was the fourth quarter, we made our way slowly back to the stands and she was gone. Just gone. We ended up begging rides from people we sort of knew and were lucky to find Mrs. Grant who didn't want to drive home alone, anyway. Bless her. It was too bad about the drowning.

"What made you remember that?" I asked him.

"I don't know. Maybe I feel like that. You remember, when we were standing around, asking everybody if they'd seen her? We walked around the whole park and she was nowhere. And finally we looked for the car and it was gone and by that time there were hardly any people left."

"You feel like what?"

He stared at me for a long time and it wasn't like that psychiatrist pause, you know? It wasn't like he wanted anything from me. He just needed me to wait. And I waited.

"Like I'm missing something," he said.

I turned away and pulled my hair back and held it with my hands to keep the summer breeze from using it to tickle my face.

"Okay," he said. "Here." He pulled his wallet out of

his back pocket and slid a business card from it. "Keep in touch."

"Okay."

"Seriously. If you ever need anything, call me."

As he got into his car something occurred to me. I walked to his window and he rolled it down.

"Why did you come by today, anyway?" I asked. "My Aunt Aubrey said you called before. Was there something you wanted?"

"Nah," he said. "I heard what happened. Well, people said you got arrested."

"How did everybody find out?"

"I heard from Kim Walton."

"Who's that?"

"I work with her. You don't know her?"

"Jeez. What nosey busy-bodies."

He laughed. "Well, good news travels...you know."

"So everybody thinks I'm a loser. What else is new?"

"It's not so bad. Now you're mysterious."

"Tell everybody I'm okay." Having everyone think you're okay is almost as good as being okay.

"I will."

When he left, a far away empty sort of spot crawled up inside me and it made it hard to breathe. I thought I might cry but I couldn't figure out exactly what I'd be crying about. It had been a long time since I'd spoken to anyone from school. I couldn't remember what exactly happened between Bond and Sylvie and me, but I knew that we weren't supposed to like one another anymore. Bond was never able to keep those kinds of commitments.

138

Before I made it to the door of the main building, Tina opened it.

"There's a phone call for you; she sounds pissed."

My mother. I'd conveniently forgotten to call her the entire week.

# 11.

"W here the hell have you been?" She screamed at me as I stood in the kitchen at the wall phone. They stared at me: Kip setting the table; Tina with oven mitts on her hands; and Chuck frying potatoes at the stove.

"I'm at Hope House," I said.

"Don't mouth off to me; I know perfectly well where you are. Where have you been? I've called every day for a week trying to get hold of you."

"I don't know," I said. I was shrinking, my shoulders hunching forward, trying to fill as little space as possible; and my voice went wobbly and baby-ish. God, I hated that. The front screen door slammed and John walked into the kitchen. He stared at the others staring at me.

"You've got an appointment with a therapist at the County Health Center on Monday at two. Do you know where that is?"

"It's that building near the other mall, right?"

"You're supposed to get there early to fill out paperwork. Don't forget."

I heard a loud pop and realized she'd hung up. "Okay, thanks, bye. I'll see you soon." I had to say something. I couldn't let them think my mother hung up on me. What kind of mother hangs up on her kid? But they must have heard the click; she'd slammed it pretty hard.

"What's for dinner?" John said. "Chicken again?"

And suddenly everybody started moving. They'd got over the glitch. Tina pulled open the oven door and looked at her chicken pieces.

"There's nothing left for you to do but the salad," she told me.

I nodded at the familiar exasperation in her voice. Like my mother, and every boss I ever had, she couldn't tell me what she was mad about, but she made it clear I should have gotten my ass inside and helped sooner, when there was real work to be done.

"So, is he your boyfriend, or what?"

My cheeks flamed up over the cutting board and I had to be careful slicing carrots. "I knew him in high school."

"He must like you," Chuck said. Grease spit and popped at him from the potatoes.

"Why do you say that?"

"He drove us all the way to Palm Bay."

"He's nice like that. Too nice, really."

"Typical," Kip said. He took a seat at the table and admired his work and John, who never seemed to work at all, joined him.

"Typical what?"

"Typical drunk behavior. Always going after the bad guys. You know, the dark, criminal types. Women drunks don't want nice guys."

"What about men drunks? What kind of women do they go for?"

"It's different for men," Tina said.

"Oh, really? How's that?"

"It's just different," Kip said.

I looked at the both of them. What hypocrites. Then I looked over at John and raised my brows at him. I thought he might have a thing or two to say about women and drunks and all that; he was the drunk most likely to score, sober or wasted. But he lit up a cigarette and looked off into the next room like he wasn't listening.

Finally everyone gathered around the table where we all joined hands and said the Serenity Prayer. Change what you can; accept what you can't. At least it was just that–nobody started in about Jesus. Maybe there was a rule about prayers and they stuck to the serenity one because it was bland and noncommital. Once you start getting into Jesus and sins and salvation and all that, you're bound to offend someone.

"Your turn to take trays over to the women's dorm," Tina told me.

She helped me fill plates for Beverly and Gladys and put them on trays with covers. Beverly and Gladys never ate with the House drunks. They got all sorts of perks. They didn't have to go job hunting. They didn't have to go to AA meetings. They didn't have any chores. Maybe they were dying of cancer or something, so they were excused.

It was still warm, and the sun was hidden behind the house across the street. The odor of cigarette smoke hit me before I got to the door. I managed to transfer the trays to open it. Beverly and Gladys were waiting for me at the little folding table in the kitchen.

"About time," Gladys said, her voice hoarse and rough. "What is it today?"

"Broiled chicken again, but with fried potatoes, peas, and salad."

"Who made the chicken?" Beverly said.

"Tina."

"Oh, good. Chuck never puts any seasoning on it at all. It's so bland."

And Tina's was tasty? Hardly. Maybe there wasn't much budget for spices and sausage. Or maybe spicy food made you want to drink, to, you know, squelch the fire. It occurred to me then that I hadn't really wanted a drink the whole week. I didn't even think twice about it at Tequila's. I knew I wasn't a drunk. I just knew it.

"Chuck thinks old people like bland food," Gladys said. "I think he used to cook in prison."

"He was in prison?" I asked.

"Sit down," Beverly said. "Where's your plate?"

"Was I supposed to bring food for me?"

"Nobody else does," Gladys said. "Nobody ever wants to eat with us."

"Why don't you go across the street and eat with everyone else?"

"We have our reasons," Beverly said and laughed.

"Well, we give them reasons," Gladys said.

"Like what?"

Beverly smiled and cut up her chicken. "We tell them we're incontinent. We have to get to the bathroom quick

144

sometimes, you know."

"They have bathrooms over there."

"Men's rooms," Gladys said. "They can't expect us to use those."

"Heavens no," Beverly added. "So, sit. You can have my salad."

I took a chair at the little table with them and watched them eat.

"How long have you guys been here?" I said.

"Two months," Beverly said.

"How long do you get to stay?"

"I know what you're thinking," Gladys said. "It's a halfway house after all. It's supposed to be in the middle of two places. Rehab or jail on one side, and the real world on the other."

"True," Beverly said. "But we're inclined to stay here a while."

"What about Mrs. Dougherty, what's her story?"

Beverly rolled her eyes and stuck a fork full of chicken in her mouth.

"She's a pip, that one." Gladys said.

"Hush, she'll hear you."

"Why doesn't she eat?"

"You'll see." Gladys said. "Here we are, eating our poorly cooked chicken. Mrs. Hoity Toity gets her meals special delivered."

And at that there was a knock at the door and a young woman opened it and came into the house. "Delivery," she called out. She stood at the foot of my bed smiling at us. A purple scarf covered her teased hair, tied under her chin, and she wore a tan, belted raincoat that hit her just below the knee. Her legs were stockinged in white and she wore ugly white sneakers. Nurse.

"Is it raining again?" Gladys said, and Beverly punched her arm.

"Evening," Beverly said.

"Why you must be new," the woman walked forward, carrying a heavy plastic bag over her left wrist. She held out her right hand to me and I took it for a mild shake. My hand smelled like perfume after and I wiped it on my pants. She had a shiny, pointy nose and wide lips, painted red. "How's Ma?" She said.

Beverly looked toward the wall, behind which was the living room and Mrs. Dougherty's room. "Haven't seen her all day. Thought you were going to take her."

The woman shook her head. "Not today. But I'll be here in the morning to take her to church."

We all sat, and she stood, quiet, looking around for a second or two before the woman thanked us for god knows what and left. I heard her knock on Mrs. Dougherty's door and it opened.

"It's her daughter. Brings her dinner. Comes and gets her in the a.m. Takes her out all day shopping and visiting. She may as well be at home."

"Why isn't she?"

"Because she's a drunk, of course," Beverly said.

"Ain't we all," said Gladys.

"What about you?" Beverly asked me.

"I'm not a drunk."

"Oh is that right?"

"That's right."

"Then what are you doing here?"

"It's a long story."

"We've got plenty of time."

I shook my head and watched them poke at their potatoes.

"Go on," Beverly said.

"I drink. I'm not denying that. And I've gotten drunk. Who hasn't?"

"Who hasn't," Gladys said.

"Don't interrupt the girl."

"I was drunk and I was on the roof of this building."

"What building?"

"Three River Terrace."

"Where's that?"

"The condominiums downtown. On the river."

"Gladys, stop interrupting. So you were on the roof. Did you try to jump?"

"No. I was just up there. And the police came and took me to this place."

"Holding facility, yes. I've been there. Once, when I guess I went outside naked."

"That's something I will never understand," Beverly said. "Why do some drunks take off their clothes?"

"Did you take off your clothes?" Gladys asked me.

"Well, some of them."

"Why on earth? I'm of the mind," Beverly said, "that you people aren't just drunks. There's something else going on there."

"You don't think it's the inhibitions?" I said.

"So, you're saying that as soon as you loosen up a bit the first thing you want to do is disrobe? Have some decency, people."

"What's indecent about the human body?" Gladys said. "Prude."

I couldn't help laughing and that made them laugh, too. I'd been very wise to make these two my new mother figures.

"So, Chuck was in prison?"

"Long time ago," Beverly said. "At least that's the story he tells. But chuck tells an awful lot of stories."

"Too true," Gladys said. "He claims he lost his wife and two children in a car accident out on I95."

"And you don't believe him?" I said.

"He was almost smiling when he said it," Beverly said. "Who smiles when they say something like that?"

"Maybe it was a defense mechanism."

"What are you, some kind of psychotherapist?"

I could be, couldn't I? Clearly I had all the right words and skills necessary. "You know how people laugh when they're nervous? It's the same thing."

"Who laughs about their family being killed?" Beverly said, agitated now, spitting out a few peas onto her plate.

"Well, he didn't laugh, now did he?" Gladys said.

"Right. He sort of smiled. Not even a full smile."

"It was almost like a smirk," Gladys said. "I think he was making fun of us."

"Making fun of you?"

"Mm hm. Because we're old, you know. And we like to take care of the younger ones. I think he was trying to give us something to worry about him over."

"Heartless," Beverly said. "That's what it was."

"But you don't know for sure that he was lying." It felt strange to be defending Chuck. He did come across disingenuous and odd. He watched me at meetings, not leering, like a lech or anything, just watching me–almost sad, like wishful thinking. Maybe I reminded him of his wife, or his kid. Suddenly I felt better toward him.

"So what was he in prison for?"

"Drunk driving, of course," Gladys said.

"He was the one driving. Hit a pole or a tree, something like that. Killed his family."

"No, no." Gladys said. "He ran a stop sign, slammed into another car, killing the people in that, and then skidded across the road and hit a utility pole."

"Oh, yes, that's right. That sounds right."

"There aren't any stop signs on I95," I said.

"Well, there you have it."

I sat and stared at them, watching them chewing, wondering what I had, exactly. Beverly looked at me, smiled and winked.

"Was that your boyfriend here earlier today? He's a looker."

Bondurant a looker? He was above average at best. A normal guy. Normal face, normal hair, normal body. But he was just right for me, if not too good. Not that I thought of him that way. But let's face it, I was no beauty. I'd be lucky to get a Bondurant. I'd be more likely to end up with a Chuck, old and worn, or a Kip even, round and goofy. John, with his droopy eyelid was too good for the likes of me; I knew that.

"He's an old friend."

"An old friend," Gladys said. "Piffle."

"Piffle? Who says piffle?" I said.

"I say piffle. Piffle, piffle. He's your boyfriend."

"Maybe one day."

"Why not today?"

"I have a lot to deal with, you know, what with being a drunken exhibitionist and trying to jump off a building." I smiled at them and they laughed.

"You haven't been listening to Kip, have you?" Gladys said.

"Oh, that Kip," Beverly said. "Thinks he knows all the rules about recovery. He'll tell you how you have to act and what you have to do and say to get sober. He thinks he knows it all."

"He should, it's his third time through the ranks."

"Third time?"

"Yes indeed. He was here when we first got here."

"He got out and came back a few weeks ago. He couldn't stay sober if it killed him."

"Well, that does give him some expertise." I said. And they cackled.

"You're a peach, April," Beverly said.

Picking bits of chicken and potato off their plates, I was warm all over, letting myself be washed in their approval. I couldn't recall an older woman ever thinking I was worth talking to, much less a peach.

"He'll tell you not to start a relationship until you're a year sober. But don't you listen to him." Gladys said.

"And then he runs around the corner to the public park at night, with Tina."

"Yes, but he doesn't see that as a relationship, Bev," Gladys said. She looked at me, touched my arm gently, and whispered, "He's using her for the sex."

"Awful, just awful, isn't it?" Beverly said. She tsked

150

with her tongue and shook her head.

"You don't think he likes her?" I said.

"Oh, I'm sure he likes her well enough," Gladys said, touching her napkin to her lips.

"Funny thing," Beverly said. "I remember bright as day, Kip standing just outside there, by the swing," she leaned across the table and touched my other arm. "We can hear everything you all say on a clear, crisp evening."

"If we turn off the television and get real quiet," Gladys added.

"I heard him tell her all about the one-year rule."

"Two if you can do it," Gladys said.

I smiled. "And what about the two of you? Will you wait a year?"

"Oh, lord, no," Beverly said. "We're married."

"Really? Do your husbands ever visit?"

"No dear," Gladys touched my hand. "To each other."

# 12.

You never can tell about people. I'm not sure how long I sat there with my mouth open making an ass of myself, but Beverly and Gladys laughed. I left not knowing if they were telling the truth or not. It reminded me of the rooming situation at the crisis center. If Beverly and Gladys were lesbians, should they room with the women? You wouldn't want to put them in with the men. Not just because men are men, you know, and would enjoy having lesbians around–they love lesbians; men are so sick–but because they're men and what women in their right minds would want to live with them?

The male drunks at Hope House were dirty–no doubt dirty minded, but also in the literal sense. The living room and dining room over in the men's dorms were kept relatively clean, but I'd had the distinct pleasure of being in Chuck's room and I could attest to the fact that it was filthy. He'd been staring at me for an hour or so while we all watched television on the third evening I was there. I got up and went to the kitchen for a refill of lemonade.

Dear god, lemonade. It was torture being made to drink lemonade, day in and day out. But trying to keep a Diet Coke cold in the community refrigerators was impossible. Those drunks were thieves. And the iced tea was drunk before seven p.m. every evening; I rarely got more than one glass.

Chuck followed me into the kitchen and startled me.

"I want to show you something." And he walked off down the hall.

Hah. Like I hadn't heard that before. Every drunken fool in the city of Sandy Point wanted to show me something at one time or another. Out behind the Pool Pit, by the railroad tracks, out in an abandoned trailer, out on the pier, under the pier, by the dumpsters outside the Joint. I'd seen quite a few somethings in my day. So naturally I followed Chuck down the hall to the room he shared with John.

"Holy crap," I said. "They let you live like this?"

He shrugged and smiled a bit. "It needs work, I'll grant you."

"Is this what you wanted to show me?" Like he was proud of it or something?

He nodded. "I'll give you five bucks to clean up for me. You only have to do my side."

He pointed to the filthiest side of the room. At least on John's side the bed was clear, and made, and the bookshelves were organized. But Chuck's side was chaos.

"Five bucks?" He couldn't be serious.

"Ten?"

"Why don't you clean it yourself?"

He shrugged again and gave me this old, skinny,

wrinkled dog look. Oh, my freaking god. He was one of those men who think women are supposed to do the cleaning. He probably thought we enjoyed it.

"Tina will help. She's done it for me before."

"Why don't you get her to do it again?"

"I thought you might like the chance to make some money."

Did I look like I needed money? I was the only one with a car. The only one who changed clothes daily; and the only one with a clean toothbrush. And I needed ten bucks to clean that filth?

"Okay," I said. "If Tina helps."

Kip's hair sat on his head like a smooth plastic helmet. He liked to comb his bangs forward over his forehead into something like a shark fin in the middle of his unibrow. He eyed me suspiciously while the four of us stood out front by the swing waiting for the church bus Sunday morning.

"Doesn't John go to church?" I asked.

Tina and Kip exchanged a look.

"What?" I said. "I'm just asking."

"They think you like him," Chuck said.

I rolled my eyes. "Well, I was going to ask about Beverly and Gladys, too."

"Sure you were," Tina said with a playful smile.

"And Mrs. Dougherty. Are you sure there really is a Mrs. Dougherty? I haven't seen her." Of course, I knew damn well Mrs. Dougherty was going to church with her daughter, but when you're out to prove a point, you use whatever you have at your disposal.

"She's over there all right," Tina said. "Thank your

lucky stars you haven't seen her."

"She's a total phony," Chuck said. "Using this place to vacation."

"Vacation?" I said. "What kind of vacation is this?"

"It gets her away from her husband and kids," Tina said. "She can't stand them. Gladys said her husband beats her and her kids don't care; they just want her money."

Sandy Point Baptist church sent over a bus every Sunday morning to pick up the drunks and take them over to the better side of town for services. Tina said the bus was always late, always delivering them after service started, forcing them to take seats in the back, over to the far left, where the losers sat.

I'd told Tina I had no interest in church, told her I had that Bible *Thee* Reverend Billy Davies gave me at the crisis center. If I needed God I could find him in there. But she urged me. Told me she didn't want to go by herself with the boys. She wanted to wear a dress and not have anybody make fun of her. So, I put on my dress and joined them out front. It wasn't a church dress, mind you. I wore it to the beach with my flip flops most of the time. It was purple, made of terry cloth, with what they call spaghetti straps, for obvious reasons. You couldn't very well wear a bra with it without looking like a skank. So, not to be skanked, I was braless. I couldn't tell if that was why Kip was casting demons my way or not. I didn't bounce all that much, not like Tina.

The bus turned out to be a van with a picture of a pair of praying hands on its side. We all climbed in and were forced to listen to choir music while the driver took us over to Palmetto Avenue. We got to watch the pretty neighborhood pass by as we neared the church. Church music–organs and choirs–trembled in the air before the doors were opened, and I followed the others as they walked to the left.

People turned to watch us and I kept my head down; I was no fool. I knew who went to that church. I sat at the end of the row and, once the congregation forgot about us, looked over to my right, scanning the crowd. They were all so beautiful and polished and made up. A lot like Kip's plastic hair. There was way too much bright lipstick and too many suit jackets. Some of the women even wore hats, like they were in the big city. Reminded me of the time my mother and I were told to move out of the reserved seating at the high school football game because the mayor had arrived unexpectedly. Who the hell did he think he was, Ed Koch? Sandy Point is a blip on the east coast. It's nothing. It's bright and sandy and dry and it smells like the rot of lagoon seaweed. The mayor of Sandy Point pisses in the nasty restroom at the pier just like everybody else.

Nobody looked back at me. They all faced the choir and when the choir stopped singing everybody stood and bowed their heads, closed their eyes. Tina's hand prodded at my shoulder. I stood, but still watched them all praying. The preacher up front closed his eyes and lifted his hands, some people rocked and said amens loud enough to be heard. A few didn't close their eyes or bow their heads and I watched them. Even when the preacher opened his eyes, they still didn't cower. I wondered who they were.

I didn't close my eyes or bow my head because I was watching. These people weren't watching anything–just staring straight ahead. Maybe they were blind; but I figured the odds of having two blind people near enough in the congregation for me to see, and neither wearing those glasses blind people are supposed to wear so we know they're blind, were too great. They were both young men. Maybe they were rebellious husbands who agreed to go to church for the sake of the children but who refused to toe the line when it came to believing all that religious nonsense.

And who couldn't admit that some of it was non-sense? Virgin births, talking snakes, a god becoming himself in human form and sacrificing himself so that he could save everybody from his own wrath. I don't know, it seemed to me he could have eliminated the middle man, which was himself after all, and forgiven everybody straight out. But maybe God knew that people needed something, or someone, to believe in. People aren't very good at handling things by themselves. That's why they have gods, and prophets, and leaders; and that's why they insist you get out of your seat so the mayor can sit down.

Kip was noticeably quiet on the van ride home while Tina chattered about the service. She talked about the hats and how one day, when she got better, she'd find a real church to go to and wear an old-fashioned pillbox.

"A real church?" I said.

"A Catholic church."

"There's a Catholic church in Sandy Point. Saint Bert's. They have the fair every year."

"They don't send a bus," Chuck said.

"I'll take you, next week, if you want to go."

I heard myself saying this before I could stop it coming out. I was always offering to do things I didn't really want to do. That's not completely true. I wanted to do them when I offered. I meant it always in the true spirit of being helpful or nice. But the thing is, I just wasn't really helpful or nice, because when I realized later what it meant I would have to do, or to give up, I regretted the offer.

"What's wrong with Sandy Point Baptist?" Kip said. He was irritated. But then, Kip was clearly the Baptist type. That's always the way with the round-faced innocent looking ones who gaze at you with those pseudo-forgiving eyes. The smarmy, sweet-faced ones always liked the damnation, the fire and brimstone of evangelical churches.

"You come to mass next week and see what real church is like," Tina said.

"How is that real church?" Kip said. "All that chanting and getting up and kneeling and the little parade to the altar for your piece of cracker."

"Piece of cracker?" Tina was hurt. "Even the Baptists believe in the last supper. Even the Baptists have communion sometimes."

"Sure, but they don't have to do it every week. It's sacred. It's not a snack."

"It's sacred all right. And you shouldn't be badmouthing it."

"I didn't know you were Catholic."

"I'm not, but that's not the point."

Chuck cut in, "You ain't supposed to take the host if

you ain't Catholic."

"Don't be stupid," Tina said. "I can take the host if I want."

"How would they know?" I said. "I mean, it's a big church. Could they know?"

Already I'd pretty much made up my mind that I would be too afraid to take the host if we did end up going the next week. I wouldn't want to upset God. Who was I kidding? I didn't care about upsetting God; I'd practically made it my life's work. I didn't want to be chased out of a church, that's all. I'd been unkindly escorted out of bars, restaurants, public parks, and private parties. Being booted out of a church would just be the last straw on the humiliation camel.

"It's between you and God," Chuck said.

"Are you Catholic?" Tina asked him.

"My ma was. I never made it past baptism."

"Isn't that enough?"

"You got to be confirmed."

"Why weren't you confirmed?" I asked.

Kip turned to look out the window and I caught sight of the amused smile on the van driver's face.

"I'd stopped going to mass by then. Broke my ma's heart. Killed her, it did."

"Really?" Tina said.

Chuck nodded large and slow. "She turned on the gas one morning and never woke up."

"That's awful," Tina moaned, tears brimming her eyes.

I turned to look at Chuck, him and that little smile that lived at the corners of his mouth. What a cad he was.

Unless he was telling the truth. In that case, what a sorry cad.

The van driver pulled up to the curb at Hope House and turned in his seat. "The Catholic Church is Satan's arm. You best be careful visiting."

"Just once won't hurt, will it?" Kip said. His voiced cracked.

"Just once, maybe," the driver said. "I'll come by anyway, next week."

"I'll be here waiting for you," Chuck said. He pushed past me and stuck his ass in my face as he slid open the side door. "It would dishonor my mother's grave was I to set foot in that church again."

"How's that?" I asked him as I jumped out behind him.

"What, after she went and killed herself on my account? Now, after thirty some odd years? Now, I go to mass? That would just turn the poor woman over in her grave. No. I'll remain apostate and burn in hell, thank you very much. It's the least I can do for my ma."

When I laughed he let that glimmer of a smile come full on his lips, they parted, he grinned, showing the spots where his teeth were missing.

"Your mother is up in heaven right now," Tina said with a whimper. "Right now, looking down on you, just praying for your soul. She's saying the rosary and lighting candles, praying to Mother Mary that you save yourself."

"Don't be stupid," Kip said. "She's not in heaven. She was Catholic."

# 13.

That evening, after a Sunday night in-house AA meeting, during which I managed to keep my mouth shut by daydreaming the whole time, we all hung around outside the male house. Tina and I swung again–back and forth. I was getting to the point that I wasn't having swinging nightmares anymore. Skeeter walked his circle. Even John showed up.

"Where were you?" Kip said.

"You ain't my sponsor."

"Do you have a sponsor?"

"Stay out of my business."

"Still," Chuck said. "You ain't supposed to miss meetings while you're here. You'll get reported."

"Bridget wasn't here tonight, was she?"

"What difference does that make?" Kip said.

"So, who's going to tell her I missed the meeting? You?"

John took a step toward Kip and Kip backed up all the way to the swing, as if to get protection from Tina and me.

"He's right, Kip," Chuck said. "This here's the honor system. We work the program as best we can. It's for our own good."

Kip mumbled, "How does his parole officer feel about that."

John rushed toward the swing to get at Kip. I reached out and my arm smacked across his chest. He stopped and looked down at me.

"Leave him alone," I said, sweet as I could. "He's just Kip."

John laughed and winked at me with his open eye, took a long drag on his cigarette and turned to Kip. He nodded at him, then at me, turned and walked to the street, through the glow of the streetlight and into darkness.

"Why do you ask for trouble with him?" Chuck said. "You don't know what he was in for."

"He's a drunk," Kip said, almost spitting. "We're all drunks. They don't send murderers to halfway houses. They send drunks."

"That doesn't mean he isn't a murderer," I said. Another one of those things that just flew out of my head, through my mouth. But the truth was, John looked like a murderer. Not a child murderer, or even a drug-induced panic murderer. He looked like a cold blooded, heartless killer. Rapist too. He could be wrapping a shoelace around your neck, raping you, and he'd be winking at you with his good eye.

"We walking to Taco Bell tomorrow?" Kip said.

Tina nodded.

"Not me," I said.

"Why not?"

"I have more serious job hunting to do."

"Where at?" Chuck said.

"All over. Bookstore, restaurants, Penney's in the mall. Any place that looks nice. Nicer than Taco Bell, anyway."

"Can we go with you?"

I knew it was coming, so I was prepared. My cheeks flamed and my arms shook a bit. But I did it. I said, "Not this time. It doesn't look good, you know, job hunting in packs. I have to look serious. Besides, my mom made me an appointment with a counselor downtown and I can't have you tagging along to that." I breathed again; excuses, for me, always came out breathless and phony and I took a few seconds to recover.

Tina, bless her heart, smiled at me and nodded. "That's true."

"But after I've put in my applications all over," I said. "Like the next day or whatever, I'll drive you guys to places. Wherever you want to go. So long as it's in Sandy Point." Damn it, why couldn't I keep my mouth shut?

"Ah," Chuck said. "There ain't no place going to hire me. Not even Taco Bell."

"That's not true," Tina said.

I almost laughed. Of course it really wasn't true. *I* couldn't think of a place that would hire him, but there had to be *some* place. He clearly wasn't strong enough to lift trash into the back of a truck. He looked like the line cook of a greasy spoon, but I figured even they had higher standards. Chuck looked to be qualified to be a homeless person.

I don't know what it was...force of habit, wishful thinking, reminiscence, whatever, but I found myself pulled into the parking lot of the Joint over at the pier on the lagoon the next morning. Why not? I got out of my car and walked in, trying to look like I wasn't looking for a job.

"Pril," Jacob Stanton called out from the burger line. He was leaning down, peering out into the front room at the registers. "Where you been?"

"Rehab," Janey said, coming through the back doorway. She stood at her register smacking her gum. "What do you want? We're just now turning over for lunch."

I looked at the menu board overhead, like an idiot—like I didn't already know exactly what they served and how. "Give me a medium chocolate."

Janey rolled her eyes and took my money. "You shouldn't have left," she said. "It's been hell around here. You know how hard it is to find good people?"

She took a cup from the stack and pulled at the lever of the chocolate shake machine and I watched as the pretend ice cream poured out in a long poop.

"Toby hired these little snots; they spend all their time doing their god-damned nails and leaning all over the counter rubbing their boobs on it, I swear those little bitches are masturbating themselves against the safe. They go out to lunch and bring back Taco Bell and McDonald's and shit, and sit in the dining room, in their uniforms, eating it."

"Why doesn't Toby do anything about it?"

"Cause he's fucking them, that's why."

My mouth dropped open, but I giggled.

166

"That ain't funny. What's funny about that? It's criminal, that's what it is."

"How old are they?"

"They say they're eighteen, but I ain't biting. You should see these skinny little size-zero bitches. Lord a mercy, they don't do shit around here. And who do you think has to take up the slack? That's right. Me and Nadey and Jake. I even feel sorry for Wabeth. You should see that poor heifer work."

"Be nice." I still felt guilty for screaming at Wabeth all those times. She couldn't help it, after all. I had serious issues. I was a little slack. Sometimes I'd wipe the tables and just wipe the food onto the floor. One time I was too lazy to go back and get the seat cloth and wiped every table and every chair with the same one. Wabeth's head liked to explode. But at least I worked.

"You looking for a job again? I could get Toby to hire you. He always liked you best."

"Yeah, but I'm not sleeping with him. I have my standards."

"Do you?"

She said it with such a face and such a voice, I laughed along with her.

"I'm going to see if I can get a real job this time."

"Waitress?"

"Maybe. Or the bookstore, or record store, or Penney's or something."

She stared at me, one hand resting on the counter grasping a rag, blew a bubble and popped it, smacking the gum back into her mouth. Then she nodded and smiled.

"I could see it. You got the potential to, you know,

move onto something respectable."

I'd never thought of Janey as a sister figure while I was working with her. She was always that older girl who thought she knew how everything was supposed to be done, always ratting me out to management if I gave somebody extra pickle or cheese without charging them.

"Funny isn't it?" She said. "I didn't appreciate you at all when you were here. But now I know. Now I know."

"Thanks for the shake," I said.

"Honey, you paid for it. You paid for it."

I must have been nervous because I had the shake slurped down within a few minutes. It was so hot in my car the Styrofoam cup would have melted, anyway. The shake helped cool me down but once I was at the mall, I started to lose my nerve and I took out a tissue from the glove box and wiped the sweat from my face. Who would want to hire me there? Everybody who worked there was so normal. None of them ever looked hung over and they never smelled of stale cigarettes. I couldn't remember ever seeing anyone in the record store vomit. And nobody ever yelled out "fuck you" in the mall.

The first store on the right was the bookstore. There were two glass display cases on each side of its wide open door. On the right was a summer fun theme with a real grill and a red and white checkered table cloth hanging from the ceiling. Summer cook books and beach reads were stacked on the floor and inside the grill. On the left was a back-to-school theme. Jesus, it was only June and we had to start thinking about school already? SAT books, how to choose a college books, *Sweet Valley High* books.

It occurred to me I ought to think about getting back to school. I wondered if my dad would pay for it, since I dropped out so many times and all. If I got a job, I could pay for it myself. And I decided at that moment I would go back to school. I was going to make something of myself. I didn't know what, but it would be something. And something was better than nothing. I kept saying that over and over in my head as I crossed the threshold and approached the counter. I hadn't really tried to jump from the roof of Three River Terrace, after all. And something was better than nothing. The air thickened with the smell of books–paper, binding, dust, and lust. All energy was absorbed in the pages; the echo of the mall disappeared and every sound was muted. This was something. And it was better than nothing.

The girl behind the counter, on a raised platform, was pretty enough, in a studied and academic sort of way. Her thick black-rimmed glasses said bookstore clerk and her frumpy dress said librarian. It worked. She gave me an application and asked me what sort of work I was looking for. I stammered a bit and said, "I'd like something I would enjoy doing."

"Do you like books?"

I nodded.

"Who's your favorite author?"

I blushed. "I know it's silly, but, Margaret Mitchell, I guess."

She leaned over the counter smiling and said, "How many times have you read it?"

I laughed. "Twice. You?"

"I've read it fifteen times."

"Fifteen?"

"I know, I know. It's crazy. What else do you like to read?"

"I read all sorts of stuff." I was put on the spot and my mind was blank. I couldn't think when I'd stopped reading regularly. It must have been my senior year in high school. First semester, just before homecoming. Because after that, I went to that party and got completely shit faced and lost my two best friends and became a drunk. Suddenly names came to me and I spit them out. "Stephen King, Sidney Sheldon, oh, *The Hitchhiker's Guide to the Galaxy*."

"Eclectic," she said and I pretended I knew what the hell she was talking about by not changing my expression. Damn right I read *Eclectic*.

I told her about my experience at the Joint.

"Why'd you leave there?"

"I had a disagreement with the management."

"About what?"

"He wanted to put his hands on me and I didn't want him to."

She rolled her eyes. "Tell me that story again. I'm Alice, by the way."

"And you're the manager?" I said, after reading it on her badge.

She patted the name tag and smiled down at me. "Glorified bookseller. So, why do you think you'd like to work in a bookstore?"

This was a much more difficult job hunt than I'd expected. I couldn't fathom the purpose of all those questions. I mean, if I had a college degree and was applying for a position with McDonnell Douglas, sure I could see it. There would be an interview and I'd have to answer all those crazy questions that interviewers think are important doors into your employee psyche; but we all know they're utter bullshit. What is your biggest asset? What is your worst fault? Everybody looked the answers up in books like *What Color is Your Parachute*; and they didn't really mean anything. But nobody had a clue what to really ask. They should ask if you planned to come into work drunk and vomit. Would you steal the toilet paper? Do you have a snorting cough? Are you going to sleep with all the men on the floor you're assigned to? These are the things an employer needs to know.

"I like books," I said. "I haven't had a lot of time to read lately, but I'd like to read more." I was babbling, but I couldn't help it. "I like the smell of them." I turned around and took a big whiff.

"Well, that could be mold and dust," she said.

"No, it's books. And I like the way they feel."

"Well, how would you feel about boxes of them being shelved? And going around the whole store every night cleaning them up and putting them back in order after customers make a mockery of your obsessive-compulsive straightening disorder? And vacuuming. Do you like vacuuming?"

"I do, actually."

"You're joking with me now."

"No, I like vacuuming. There's the loud hum, for one thing, you know. Keeps out the distractions while you daydream. And there's something kind of nice about sucking up bits of stuff off the floor. Especially if the floor's really dirty."

"Yes, and you can make tracks."

"Exactly."

"Well, the floor never really gets that dirty here. But every now and then you find a semen-soaked *Playboy* back in automotive."

I grimaced and she laughed at me.

"Where else are you putting in applications?"

"All the stores. Clothing stores."

"Where you stand around all day folding sweaters and raising your nose at fat girls?"

"Well..." What could I say to that? "And the record store."

"Fat chance," she said. "Speaking of fat girls. Not that you're fat. I didn't mean that. But you definitely aren't Bryce's type. He only hires homecoming queens."

Sandy Point boasted two high schools—Sandy Point and Beacon Hills. Beacon Hills was where all the rich kids went, because that was exactly where all the rich people lived. So, it was an all-round better school than the decrepit, rat-infested Sandy Point. Anyway, the point being we only got two homecoming queens a year, but I guess that was enough to staff the puny record store in the mall.

"The bookstore is my first choice," I said, because I thought that counted for something.

She seemed to like that. But she didn't hire me. Instead, she let me fill out the application and said she'd be in touch when she had some extra hours. Sure she would.

Of course, I really had read one Stephen King book.

It was *The Shining*. Scared the living shit out of me. That little kid, running away from the shrubberies. That's some terrifying stuff. And I did read a lot of Sydney Sheldon. But I didn't know if I should have counted that. I should have told her about all the trashy romances I read in high school. *The Wolf and The Dove*, *The Flame and the Flower*, the jar and the bowl, the boobs and the penis. Those sorts of books. They always told the same story, just the hair and eye color of the buxomly heroine changed. She was always raped by the hero, but she fell in love with him, anyway. But if the idea was to impress, it was probably better that I left it where it was and didn't mention my foray into high school porn.

I put in applications all over the mall, but none of the other people I spoke to were nearly as cool as that book lady. I almost tried to act like I didn't really want a job at the clothing stores, or the record store where the guy looked me up and down and sneered at me like I was dog shit, or the J C Penney's. I knew I really wanted to work at the bookstore. Which was funny, if you think about it. Because I'd lied to Sausage and told him I already had an interview there. If I got the job, he'd think I told him the truth, which was enough justification for wanting it.

# 14.

The County Health Center building was old; but everything in Sandy Point was old. The main door was on a suction hinge that closed with a hiss behind me. The receptionist's office was a big box behind a slightly opaque sliding window the size of two cereal boxes. A receptionist hid inside, her upper body warped by the cloudy glass, and I stood, waiting, wondering if I was supposed to knock. Finally, she reached up from her desk and slid the window open.

"April MacMillan," I said.

"Eunice?"

"It's April."

I was given a clipboard with forms to fill out. It had a pen tied to it with string. The chairs were cold, metal folding chairs and the floor was covered in linoleum. I felt mentally ill just sitting down. Two other people were there, waiting. (I thought each person should have a confidential entrance and waiting area. I wouldn't mind sitting in a tiny room with only one chair for me. I liked small spaces. And I liked going to see a shrink in anonymity.) One was a woman staring off into space, but not in a dreamy way, like she had a lot to think about—more like she was too afraid to look anywhere else, certainly not at me or the homeless guy sitting two seats from her. He was watching her. He stopped for a second to nod my way and then went back to staring the old woman down.

Most of the form was standard. Name, address, that sort of thing. But then they wanted to know why I was there. I put down, "I drink too much." What was I supposed to say? Because my mom made me? They wanted to know if I'd been anywhere else or done anything else for my problem. I didn't know if I should put down the crisis center over in the middle of the state or not. I didn't go willingly, after all. I decided to leave most of the form blank.

I took the clipboard to the window and the lady behind the desk said, "You didn't fill out the income portion."

"I don't have any income."

She jotted down some scribbles on my form and said, "That'll be ten dollars."

"I don't have ten dollars."

"The minimum fee is ten dollars per session."

"Well, I don't have ten dollars. Anyway, my dad is supposed to be paying."

Like hell was I going to pay ten dollars for therapy I didn't even want. Well, maybe I wanted it; it could be fun, talking about your problems and having someone actually listen—of course, they could just be practiced at *seeming* to listen. Maybe I could learn something about myself and why I didn't like Bond and why I didn't like saying no even when I didn't want to do things for people. Maybe I could find out why I didn't like people much in the first place. I suppose, if it felt right, I could talk about the roof of Three River Terrace. And maybe about that feeling that sometimes I get–that I'm not supposed to be here and it wouldn't be such a bad idea if I weren't.

"Oh, that's right," she said. "Yes, you're all set."

Damn right I was all set. And they were probably charging my dad a lot more than ten dollars. I should have felt bad about that, but I didn't. I sat back down. A door opened in a hidden hallway and a young man came into the lobby carrying a clipboard.

"Edy," he said.

The homeless man and the old lady stood and followed him down the hall. The place was strange–scary strange. Another door popped open; light footsteps, the swish of clothing. I tingled all over and a flush of heat rose in my cheeks. The door to the reception room gave way, and Dr. Crazy showed up.

"April?"

Who else? I was the only one left.

"I'm Giselle Kirkpatrick."

Crazy wore a paisley print moo moo with sandals. Her hair was piled on top of her head pouring out over a red silk scarf. Her face was wider than it was tall and I did not like the looks of the whole matter...at all. She was a hippie. My therapist was some kind of hippie. But she called me April, so I would learn to live with it.

Her office was nice enough, considering the town we were stuck in, with a couch and a chair and a desk. A lot like Dr. Reginaldi's, but without the refrigerator and free packs of cigarettes.

"So, tell me," she said, adjusting herself and her moo moo into the chair in front of the sofa. "What brings you here today."

Was she kidding? I sucked in a big breath and rolled my eyes and started talking. "I was on the roof of Three River Terrace, drunk, of course, but I wasn't seriously going to jump. I like drama, I suppose, and it was sort of fun scaring people. And I remembered Camelia–my invisible friend from childhood; I used to write her letters, so I wrote to her, but what I wrote wasn't anything like what I thought I wrote. I thought I said all sorts of beautiful things, you know? But it turns out, apparently, I mean, if they didn't somehow fake it, I wrote something really stupid. That's so weird. I ended up over at the psychiatric center with some crazy people and now I'm at Hope House."

"Ah." She looked at my form.

"I just put that about drinking because...well, there wasn't enough room for all of it."

She smiled and nodded. I liked her more than Reginaldi right then and there.

"How much would you say you drink?"

That was clever. She didn't want to know how much I drank, just how much I would say I did. Very clever. I shrugged. "Enough."

She smiled. "And how much is enough?"

"It depends on the event. Or the mood."

"Was the last time you had alcohol when you were brought to the crisis center?"

I nodded.

"How do you like Hope House?"

"There are some pretty weird people there."

"And your AA meetings?"

"They're pretty weird, too."

"Has it been a struggle to avoid alcohol?"

"Not really. I haven't really thought about it."

She nodded her head. "What would you like to tell me about the Three River Terrace building?"

Dr. Crazy was like the lunatic in James Bond films. She never came right out and asked what she wanted to ask, or said what she wanted to say; she weaseled around things to try to get me to say what it was she wanted to hear. But I was on to her.

"Not much." I paused but she just sat there, quiet for once. Waiting. Oh, for Christ's sake, okay. "I wasn't really going to jump. I didn't go there to jump so much as to..."

She tilted her head and her brows perked up. "To what?"

"I don't know. I guess I looked at it as more of starting my life, than ending it. So much." My god, I *was* crazy. If I kept on like that, they'd lock me up for sure. She was quiet for a few seconds, not looking at me, though, chewing on her bottom lip just a bit.

"Tell me about Camelia," she said.

"Why is everyone so obsessed with Camelia? She was just an imaginary friend."

"But you wrote to her when you were–"

"I know, I know. I wrote to her. So what?"

"Aren't you curious why you chose to do that?"

"I felt bad. I screwed up her life."

179

"How's that?"

I must have looked exhausted and peeved. She smiled but said nothing, expecting me to answer. "Maybe that's why I made her up—to live a different life."

"What about your life?"

"My life sucked. It's no wonder to me that I'd want to live someone else's."

"How did your life suck?"

And then it fell out of me, like these things do. "My mother tried to have me killed when I was eight years old."

I'd like to say I planned these outbursts—that I found some sort of personal satisfaction in shocking people; and it's probably true that psychiatrists or psychologists, or whatever Dr. Crazy was, are some of the hardest people to shock, except for homicide cops and obstetricians. But these things just came flying out of my mouth, often without my complete understanding. That, for instance. My mother was trying to kill me? But you know how that happens, when you say something and all of the sudden you realize it's true? You didn't even know it before, consciously? It was, like, in your gut all the time, wheedling you, needling you, teasing at your insides day after day. It's no wonder you're insane. You've got rot in your gut. Mother rot, most likely, least wise that was my problem. And let's face it, mothers are always to blame, aren't they? Even when the father is to blame we still lay most of it at the mother's feet. And rightly so. She's your mother. It's her job to protect you. Trying to have you killed isn't anywhere part of the job description.

Dr. Crazy stared at me in that "go on" kind of way.

Giselle. I wondered if that could possibly be her real name. Giselle Kirkpatrick. She looked like a Giselle. A moo-moo clad, poodle haired, earrings down to her boobs, jangle bracelet tinkling gypsy of a woman, who married a Kirkpatrick. Their offspring would be red-headed spiritualists–that's what you get when you cross a hippie Giselle with a Catholic Kirkpatrick–forced to read palms and hawk wares in Dicago, or Lombago, or what-ever that wacky spiritualist community in the middle of the state was called.

"What makes you feel that way?" She finally said.

"A kid knows when her mother wants her dead."

"Can you give me an example?"

Oh, sure, an example. Of course I didn't have an example.

"What happened when you were eight, that made you think your mother wanted you dead?"

She knew I didn't have an example. But I wasn't making it up. I felt like I'd just made it up, the way it flew out of my mouth. Lies do that for me–just appear out of nowhere. People warn you about lying; they say, the more lies you tell the harder it is to keep them straight. But I never had a problem remembering the alternate realities I created. Maybe because that's just what they were: realities...that were not quite right with the reality the rest of the world was living. But this, I didn't make up.

"Maybe it's more a feeling, than an actual for in-stance."

Dr. Crazy nodded. "Can you reach back into your childhood, to that moment you felt it the first time?"

Reach back in time. Would Reginaldi have ever said

anything that woozy? Reach back in time. And then of course, as if I'd been reaching for a can of tuna on a top shelf with one of those old-people grabber things, it hit me.

"It was the dog," I said. I pulled my pack of Salem's out of my purse and lit up, sucked in. That damn dog.

"Tell me about the dog," she said.

This was all getting too weird. What did the dog have to do with anything, anyway?

"It's a little fuzzy," I said. "But I knew she wanted me dead this one day I went to school. I didn't want to go. I was more scared of it than I'd ever been scared of anything before."

"Scared of going to school?"

I nodded. "It was just that. That was all I needed. I knew she wanted me dead. Oh, my god. I remember it now."

When I was eight, the walk to elementary school was like an obstacle course of danger—miles and miles of possible dog bite, hit-and-run, mugging, kidnaping, and murder. Not only had none of those things ever happened to me or anyone I knew, once I learned to drive, I made the trip, from our family house on Yellow Sands Avenue back through the grid neighborhood, out onto Coquina Drive and down the road to the school, and it was not fifty miles at all. I was sure it would register five at least, but it was barely one. Still, for a little girl, all alone, it was a nightmare walk, morning and afternoon. Some days I got to walk with neighbor kids, but most days their mother worked early and dropped them off and I had to make the trek alone. It was one of those mornings and I knew I shouldn't go. I tried to pretend I was sick, but she wouldn't have any of it.

"Like riding a horse." She put a hand to my back and pushed me out the back door. "Like riding a horse."

"I was crying," I told Crazy. "Standing on the back porch, willing myself to move across the back yard, through the back gate. But I couldn't get my feet to work. And that's when she said it."

Dr. Crazy leaned forward, curiosity on her face, bringing me out of my past for a second. Psychiatrists aren't supposed to be that interested are they? Suddenly I felt self-conscious.

"What did she say?"

"The dog. She said–she asked me if I'd like Puddles to walk along with me for a short way. He'd come back, she said. He'd find his way back home."

A shudder rippled through me. I shivered. Goose bumps sprouted up all over my arms and my mouth fell open. I thought I might scream. And then I thought I might vomit. I dragged on the Salem and my hand trembled when I pulled it from my lips to put it on the ash tray.

"That's when I knew for certain she wanted me dead."

Dr. Crazy leaned back into her chair and jotted notes on her stenographer's pad. "Any idea why?"

I shook my head. Of course it didn't make any sense. Of course it was just the bizarre, disconnected rambling of a lunatic. I was crazy. Here was proof.

"Was Puddles a big dog?" She said. "What was your relationship with him?"

"He was a poodle. I don't think I thought Puddles was going to kill me. But I knew his going with me would be the end of me. I just knew it."

So at that point, I'd rightly upset myself and laughed. "That's ridiculous, isn't it?"

She tilted her head. "Do you think so?"

"I wonder if it's even true."

"You're shaken, clearly," she said.

"Does that mean it's true?"

"The feelings are true, even if the memory isn't accurate."

Thinking about it, I figured the feelings were probably true, like she said. My mother always wanted me dead. She never came right out and said so, and though she never hired a hit man, so far as I knew, it was pretty obvious to me—despite the fact that I'd completely forgotten about it. But what did Puddles have to do with it? For the rest of the afternoon, visiting restaurants and hotels—maid work? That didn't turn out well for me the last time—putting in applications, I kept picturing my mother on hidden camera in the front seat of a car in her meeting with a hit man who was really an undercover cop. She was saying things that were just this side of legal, like, "Teach her a lesson," and, "I want her out of my life." And the cop tried and tried to get her to use the magic word: murder. But she wouldn't. She was a sly potato, that one.

When I'd decided I'd applied at every worthwhile spot in Sandy Point, other than the bars—of course I couldn't work in a bar, I'd be drunk the whole time—I took a quick drive back to my mother's duplex, before she would be home from work, snuck in and dug the shoe box from the top shelf of my closet to raid my stash for a few more twenties.

I thought again about my box of letters to Camelia. I wasn't sure how old I was when I started writing to her. She was no more than a vision in my head. A little girl wearing a print dress, white socks that turned down with lace at the edges, dainty sneakers. Her hair was short, blonde like mine, but she never had a complete face. Sometimes, when I thought of her, I only saw parts. Eyes, mouth, a nose. But I couldn't put those parts together to form a whole girl. That was the problem with imaginary friends, after all. They weren't real. If anything, they're ourselves disguised as something better. Sometimes I imagined her almost whole, but I always felt like I'd created her, like a Frankenstein monster, and all she could do was sleep; I couldn't get the pretend Camelia to live, to smile, or chat, or laugh, or walk with me. Maybe I just wasn't good at the whole imaginary friend thing. You probably needed a lot of experience with real friends to make up a good one.

I wrote her letters whenever my mother yelled at me. After I wasn't invited to Renee Wilkins' slumber party and everyone else was. After I was invited to Shauna Wood's party but got in a fight and stalked home all by myself. After I was punished for vomiting on the carpet. After I refused to eat my dinner even after sitting at my place at the table until ten o'clock at night. I always wrote to Camelia, complaining about how hard it was and how sorry I was. I couldn't remember exactly what I was sorry about, except living, which would explain some things.

I took my seat at the dinner table that night after my mother stole my letters and asked her where they were.

"You just forget about those letters," she said. "And stop writing them. It's embarrassing to have an imaginary friend at your age."

"What's this all about?" My father said.

"Never mind. And stop being so sensitive. A person can't look at you sideways without you crying. The world doesn't need you to cry for every dead squirrel on the road, you know."

It was true. I knew it. But it's not like a person can help crying. Can they? Somewhere in the world, I thought, there must be other people like me. People who cared that animals were being slaughtered by the millions on our nation's highways. But I wasn't allowed to cry about it. And there must be other people who cried watching the nightly news. I mean, there was always some awful murder, or some little kid hit by a car, or missing. But I wasn't allowed to cry about that. And there must be other people who cry when they see other people cry. Like, if you're walking into the grocery store and you see someone sitting at the door, with his arm outstretched and tears rolling down his cheeks and the store manager is yelling at him to get off the premises. I used to cry about things like that. But I wasn't allowed to.

I kept writing to Camelia—my mother couldn't stop me—and I slipped my letters under the mattress of my bed. At some point, the letter writing stopped. I didn't remember when. Or why.

A twinge of guilt trickled through my chest as I replaced the old shoe box and climbed down from the step stool. I walked over to my bed and knelt beside it. It wasn't possible, of course. My parents divorced and they sold the house and my mother took my bedroom furniture to her duplex because Sausage had already taken his stuff. His was better, she said, but mine would have to do. She would have taken the bed apart to move it. The letters wouldn't still be there but I lifted the edge of the mattress anyway and looked.

I remembered then, my mother's face. I'd chased her down the hall and she was in her bedroom with my box of letters, closing the door. And she was smiling.

My mother wasn't Satan's minion, but she liked death. Not in a searching, fulfilling kind of way–more as a hobby. She craved the act of mourning, it seemed. For as long as I can remember, a couple of Saturdays a month, she would deck herself out in black, from head to toe, with a black pearl necklace even–black hat with a lace veil, or just a block of lace covering her head and face–and go to funerals. She'd lay the last few days' worth of obituaries on the kitchen table, and circle the ones she planned to sit in on, like a garage sale fanatic.

I wanted to go, when I was too young to understand it, and she took me once. I got to wear a fancy, black dress–unlike anything I ever got to wear before or since–a hat, short black gloves, and shiny patent leather shoes. I sat next to my mother in a mostly empty church uneasy, trying not to look at her as she wept for a dead person she never knew. But when I did look, she was smiling– just like when she stole my letters. A sly smirk of a sort, like she was getting away with something. I wasn't allowed to go to funerals with her after that; I was deemed fidgety and disrespectful.

# 15.

Thursday afternoon, there was nothing to do but sit around waiting for time to go to the AA meeting at the plaza down the road. Gladys and Beverly were sitting in the living room watching television, Tina was off somewhere with Kip, and I didn't want to sit outside, or on my bed, or certainly not hang out with Chuck who would probably just find something for me to clean.

Dr. Crazy gave me homework. I'd told her that I wrote to Camelia again, after being on the roof of Three River Terrace, and she said I should write to her regularly, as an exercise. It was a stupid idea, but she said I should explore my feelings that way. When I got back to Hope House that Monday afternoon after job hunting, I was a bit upset from thinking about my shoe box and the way my mother smiled when she stole it, so I went straight to my bed in the front room, dug out a notebook from my duffle and started, "Dear Camelia," but I couldn't finish. I was shaking and nauseated and my head ached. I forced myself not to cry. The last thing I needed was for scrawny, busybody Tina to come in and see me. I stared at the paper for a few minutes until the emptiness of it blurred and put the notebook back. I had a whole week to do the assignment, after all.

By Thursday, I realized I'd been avoiding it. But I couldn't make myself get the notebook out. So, instead, I got in my car and decided to drive around. I didn't know where I was going, but I didn't care. As I drove down Main Street, when I got to the park, I saw John walking back toward Hope House and I stopped when he saw me and waved. I rolled down the passenger side window and he leaned in.

"Where are you going?" He said.

"Just driving around."

"Want some company?"

Well, sure. What was I going to say, anyway? And maybe I didn't mind. Maybe I wanted company. John was good looking, except for the closing eye, and the haggard, drug-addicted look about him. If I was going to have company, his was the kind I'd want.

"Were you on your way back?" I said as he slid into the passenger seat and closed the door.

"I guess. I don't really like it there."

"What's to like?"

He laughed at that. I drove us around the neighborhood and then out onto Goldenrod.

"Do you have to stay there?" I asked him.

"I guess."

"Chuck or Kip or somebody said you were there by court order. I'm not even sure what that means."

"It means some asshole judge thought it would be

good for me."

"Oh, so what did you do?"

"Drunk driving."

"You have a car?"

"Not anymore." At that he laughed loud and coughed for a while. Then he pulled a pack of Winston's out of his shirt pocket and asked me if I wanted one. I shook it off. Non-menthols were pretty disgusting. I knew this made me less of a real smoker. Like a poser.

"Why don't we stop and get a six-pack or something," he said.

"What about your DUIs?"

"I ain't driving."

"I guess not." And just like that I pulled the car into the convenience store on Goldenrod Street. I turned off the engine and looked at him. "Who's buying?"

"I ain't got no money."

"All right then," I said, and just like that I went into the store and came out with a six-pack of talls. "You like Bud Light?"

"I like beer."

"Where do you want to drink them?"

"Somewhere we won't be seen by any of the drunks. They walk this street plenty when they're bored."

"Kip and Tina are already out walking around."

"Walking around, my ass."

I drove over to Palmetto Avenue and wound around to Sandy Point Baptist. I pulled into their parking lot and to the right of the building where the church had set up a small park nestled against a ditch, and on the other side sat a row of back yards with swing sets and orange trees.

There were five picnic tables and a few of those grills stuck in the ground on metal poles.

"This belong to the church?" John asked.

"I think so. Why? You afraid it'll upset the big guy?"

He seemed to think about that for a bit. "I guess religious people drink beer."

"Religious people do everything everybody else does. They just think they're forgiven for it."

We headed to the farthest table, shaded and hidden among large oaks. As I pulled the pop top on the can and smelled the bitter, hollow odor of my beer, I realized it had been exactly two weeks since I'd had any alcohol. I sucked the drink from the can and guzzled four swallows. I burped. Relaxation poured over me, wafting through my body, from my middle, to my arms, down my legs to my feet, up my neck to my head. I was awash in gentle comfort. I guzzled several more swallows.

"You think God will forgive us?" He said.

Something inside me, in my stomach, I think, sunk. There's this weight of sorts inside us, like a brick. It can float, when we're happy, when we're pleased and satisfied. And it can roll over and dance when we're hopeful, expectant. And then it can drop on you when you're disappointed. And something about John saddened me.

I shrugged. "I have trouble imagining a god who gives a shit." He frowned at me. "I know," I said. "That's what they all say. That he knows every hair on your head or something."

"He formed you in the womb," he said.

"Exactly. But I have trouble imagining a god who cares that I got drunk and shoplifted a charm bracelet from the Belk Lindsey, when there are kids all over the world dying of starvation."

"But see, that's just it." He pulled himself up to sit on the table and took a long swallow of his beer. "God gives us the opportunity to help people. And we waste ourselves like this." He pointed to his beer.

"Well, if you're worried about it, why don't you join the Peace Corps or something?"

He shrugged again. "I'm too far gone. It's too late for me."

I laughed. "It's not like you're in jail for murder or anything. You're stuck in a halfway house is all. Maybe this is your chance."

"And here we sit, getting drunk."

"Who said anything about getting drunk? We're just having a few beers."

"It is a halfway house," he said. "We're halfway there."

"It's pretty relaxed there, at the House," I said after he popped open another beer. "I don't see that it's really doing anybody any good."

"Well." He lit up another cigarette. This time I took one when he offered. "For one thing, they operate under the philosophy that the people there *want* to be there. So their recovery, as they like to call it, is up to them."

"But if the courts are going to order people there, it seems to me they'd want somebody checking up on you, you know, to make sure you're following the program."

"The program. It's bullshit."

"And second?"

"Second?"

"You said, first of all."

"Oh, yeah, right. Second of all..." He seemed to search around for his brain. "Oh, right." He guzzled beer and wiped his mouth with his sleeve. "They get money. And as long as they get money, they're happy."

"Who gets money?"

"I don't know," he said. "Whoever runs the place."

"Yeah," I said. "Whoever runs the place."

When we'd finished the six pack, he suggested we get another.

"Let me drive your car," he said. For some reason, against my better judgment, I let him. But my better judgment was always suppressed when I drank. Maybe that's one of the problems with alcohol. But if we really had better judgment, we wouldn't start drinking to begin with.

When I worked at The Burger Joint, Toby hired this girl who looked like she was twelve. Her name was Nina and she had a curly mop of blonde hair and a loud laugh; she was always smiling. Nothing at all like the brooding, bottle-tanned Amanda. One night, she wanted to go out with me. I'd told her I was going to a party out in Scottsmoor. So, naturally, I said, sure. I never really liked going to parties or bars by myself; I knew it made me look like a loser. I had to get a drink and stand around or sit at the bar looking lonely, hoping some guy would start talking to me. It usually worked. Sometimes I sat on a stool letting myself get lost in the jukebox–*Total Eclipse of the Heart* or *Sister Christian*–songs that you think are deep and meaningful even when you know all the words. But when you wake up and think about it–I get the feeling

194

we're not supposed to do that–they make no sense at all. Then I'd slink home depressed after two o'clock by myself. But most often, some drunk would start buying me drinks and I wouldn't be alone all night. The funny thing about drunk guys is that, when one drunk guy is talking to a girl, she suddenly becomes more attractive to the other drunk guys, especially as the night wears on and the more respectable girls start leaving.

Parties were even harder than bars. You were supposed to be invited to a party; you knew people there. I don't know how I ever managed to find out about them, probably from the drunk guys who bought me drinks at the bar. But I'd have a few drinks to loosen myself up and show up like I belonged there. It rarely took long for some guy to latch on to me.

I knew I wasn't beautiful. I looked better to them because they were drunk and I was alone–desperate. The sober, responsible, pretty girls wouldn't talk to them. And if this little flat-chested perky squirrel Nina wanted to go along and break the ice for me, that was fine. She had personality, but no looks at all. I could at least boast an above average score. Nina was like a two, on a scale of one to ten; maybe one to forty. A hawk nose dominated her face and her brown eyes were set too close together. She was skinny, but in a scrawny way. She looked like a girl with no interest in guys at all. Still, I took Nina up to Scottsmoor for a keg party and we got pretty drunk. I was never fond of keg beer, so after an hour or so, when none of the good-looking guys would pay us any attention and all the girls snubbed us, I suggested we go to Spike's Pub.

Spike's Pub was a hole in the wall with pool tables in

the back. I rarely went in the back, only if a guy who was buying my drinks wanted me to watch him play. Guys like to show girls how good they are at things—pool, dancing, peeing, driving really fast, that sort of thing. I was surprised they let Nina in the place, she looked like a twelve-year-old boy; but she apparently had an ID. Not that I saw anyone check it; and no one ever checked mine, but I was what you call a regular. I didn't have my own bar stool or anything and nobody ever called me by name. In fact, now that I think about it, the bartenders seemed to avoid that friendly sort of thing altogether. Probably so it would be easier to toss me out on my ass when I got a little unruly.

One Saturday night, Spike's was packed with every bar rat in three counties. I was squeezed up to the bar trying to order another beer when this creepy hick in a baseball cap pinched me on the ass. I turned around and slapped him in the face. That was it. Problem over.

I took my beer into the bathroom. At Spike's, the bathroom was two closets, each about two feet by two feet. In the first closet was the sink, and in the second, behind a door you couldn't open if anyone was by the sink, was the toilet. I came out of the toilet to find this big breasted, brunette bitch with her sour face pinched up tight. She lit into me. Before I knew it, three of her friends were in there with us, all pressed together. My back was pushed against the sink as brunette bitch screamed at me. Why? Because I'd slapped her boyfriend in the face.

"He pinched me on the ass," I kept shouting. I thought I was defending myself. I thought she would be horrified that her hick boyfriend was going around the bar pinching other girls on the ass. But she didn't seem to care. I kept thinking she didn't hear me so I kept screaming, "He pinched me on the ass. You should be mad at him."

Finally, I'd wedged myself around the little room to the doorknob. I pulled the door ajar and screamed at her, "He pinched me on the ass and if he does it again, I'll smack the living shit out of him."

I thought I'd made it, trembling, from the confrontation and out of the bathroom alive when somebody jumped on me from behind. We both fell to the floor surrounded by feet. She was punching me and I was trying to crawl through the shoes toward the door. When the bouncer grabbed me by the shoulders and dragged me out, that bitch was still on my back. Of course, by then I was screaming that it wasn't my fault. It was all her fault. "He pinched me on the ass. I'd smack him again. You should be throwing them out."

I found myself on the sidewalk out front, crowded with other drunks, and I turned to see her standing there, too. She was not happy to have been thrown out and now separated from her wonderful ass-pinching boyfriend. Lucky for me I was a regular, so a few of the guys held her off and escorted me to my car.

Nina and I sat at the bar and drank a few beers and finally these two guys joined us. Eventually, we were all in a booth at the wall and they were buying us a pitcher. At some point, they invited us to their apartment. Nina thought it was a great idea, so we went. They turned on their stereo and we all sat around in their little living room, drinking bottled beer and staring at the walls–I'd never been so bored. When Nina followed me into the bathroom, I was hoping she would agree to leave, but instead, she hatched what seemed to be a brilliant plan at the time. She wanted us to return to the living room and dance for them. She really must have been twelve. When you're drunk out of your skull, these seem like very good ideas. So, we went back to the living room and started dancing. There I am, jumping around, doing my best disco spins, and I see, out of the corner of my eye, Nina doing some kind of slow and steady stripper moves, rubbing her hands all over her body. I slowed to something of a step touch and watched as she twirled her thumbs around her nipples and I started laughing.

After thirty seconds of this, what I can now clearly see as, bizarre behavior by both Nina and me, the guys got up and left the room. She stopped massaging herself and turned to me and we both started giggling. I couldn't imagine what the guys thought of Nina and her prostitution dance, but she said, "Where'd they go? Do you think we scared them?" Well, I certainly didn't.

They were either back in the bedroom deciding which one of them got which one of us, probably fighting over Nina, of all things, because she was clearly a stripper, or they were hiding, hoping we'd leave. And strangely enough, that was Nina's next great idea, let's leave. So we ran out the door and all the way back to my car laughing like we'd pulled off the greatest trick ever. And as we got to the car, Nina said, "Can I drive?"

And I let her. I can't for the life of me remember where we thought we were going. I don't know how we got onto Fiddlewood Highway. But I remember her having trouble making a turn. I remember pressing my foot against the floor board's imaginary break and holding tight to the door handle saying, stop, stop. But apparently she couldn't find the break, either. I woke up with some guy outside the passenger door telling me to unlock it. The windshield in front of me was an exploding star with a hole in the center. The glass from that hole lodged in my head. I unlocked the door and started crying.

# 16.

The next thing I knew, my car was totaled, stitches raged across my already imperfect forehead; and Nina found Jesus and thought it would be the coolest idea if I'd find him, too. My mother dragged me from my hospital room to hers and stood there trying to look concerned and doting while I listened to her mother say, "Nina has some news for you."

Her mother was so unlike Nina that it took me several seconds, and the introduction to Nina's I-found-Jesus speech to wrap my head around her not being adopted. Quite the lump of gray coal, with this straight hair that hung stiff and lifeless all around her face. Dark circles under her eyes, she had the same hawk nose as her daughter. I thought maybe she was a cancer patient, but I always thought the chemotherapy made you vomit yourself thin and Nina's mom was far from thin. She was healthy ugly. She kept beaming at me, in a lifeless sort of way, as Nina told me, "I got saved."

But something was missing in Nina's eyes. I saw it; clearly her mother did not. It wasn't that she was lying. I think Nina really did say the prayer she wanted me to copy. And I think she really thought that she'd turned her life over to Jesus. But she wasn't changed. And that's the way it was supposed to happen. I knew; I'd tried several times, but the holy spirit never filled my heart up like everybody promised me. I didn't feel changed at all. Nothing happened. And in Nina's eyes, it was clear; nothing happened for her either, beyond making her possibly dying-from-cancer mother happy.

Unfortunately, at that time, I'd decided I was done doing what Nina wanted to do, so, even though everyone was standing expectant, waiting for me to drop to my knees and pray with her, in a rather defining moment, I shrugged and said, "Maybe later."

Anyway, I have to wonder why, after that, I'd let John have my keys. I mean, his sleepy eye was all the way closed by that point and he said, "Fuck my license," and drove us to the convenience store down the road. We made it back alive, thank god. But I ended up having to say stop, stop anyway. I don't know how it happened, exactly.

I'd bought myself a pack of menthols and could only hope they'd remove the foul taste of his Winston from my mouth; and I was smoking my third, when the second six-pack of talls was empty, smashed, and littering the ground around our picnic table. I was reeling, no longer in that happy drunk phase, already well into the I-need-to-drink-more-to-go-completely-numb phase. I was counting mine and his. I thought I'd had five and he'd had seven. Or I'd had four and he'd had eight. But I couldn't keep my addled mind on the math. I didn't feel as drunk as I could get, but I was too drunk to add.

People were amazed at how much I could drink. They

thought I should die of alcohol poisoning. But the human body is an amazing thing; and it's funny the things you feel proud of. Many nights I'd get off work at the Joint at five, head home and buy a six-pack of talls from one of my stores on the way. I'd drink all six of them sitting in front of the little television in my room, avoiding my mother. Sometimes, if I didn't see plenty of her Pabst Blue Ribbons in the fridge, I'd take mine into my room and drink them because if I left them in the fridge, no matter how fast I could drink them, she'd manage to steal at least one. It didn't matter if they sat in my room; they never got the chance to grow warm. I finished with them by about nine or ten. That's not too bad. Four or five hours, six talls. Not too bad at all.

And then I'd get in my car and go out to a bar where I'd drink some more, and when that bar closed, I'd drive out past the county line to Harold's and drink some more until four in the morning. I'd come home, crash, wake up at eleven or twelve, shower, head to work, eat burgers and fries and drink a shake, and start my shift. And then I could do it all over again that night. I was either drinking, drunk, or hung over for years. I considered my time at Hope House as something of a betrayal of my record. But I was making up for it.

I finally settled on five for me and seven for him when somehow, John was all over me. He'd leaned over and started kissing me. His wide open mouth covered mine and sucked on it. I pulled away and I'm pretty sure I said, gross, which is probably not a good thing to say. He pulled at me and we were on the ground next to the picnic table. He was grabbing at me and kissing me and I

203

was saying stop, stop, stop, through gritted teeth and pawing at him trying to keep his hands out of my shirt.

I heard a button rip off and inside my head I was saying, scream. Scream. Scream. But for some reason I wouldn't do it. His full weight was on my bottom half while his right arm forced its way under my back where he managed to unhook my bra. My shirt was over my face and his hands and mouth were all over my breasts.

"Stop," I was whining, but clearly he took this, and my squirming to get away, as pleasure. Why wouldn't I scream? Where was my voice?

Suddenly I was eight years old, running across a thick, damp lawn, my screams echoing through the neighborhood behind my house. And then, finally, I started screaming at John. He jumped nearly three feet to get off me it was so loud. He stood over me with this weird look in his open eye and I stopped screaming. Across the ditch, over my panting for breath, I heard the metallic snap of a screened door banging shut.

"Do I need to call the police?" Someone shouted.

"We're all right," John called to the man. "She saw a snake." He looked down at me and reached out a hand to help me up. "Come on," he said. "Let's get out of here."

"I'm not going anywhere with you."

"Aw come on. We were just wrestling. You know you wanted it."

I fumed, infuriated, but too drunk really to understand why. I scrambled to my feet, reached behind my back and tried to re-fasten my bra.

"Turn around," he said like a doting mother. I did so and he raised my shirt and fastened it for me. I wiggled myself back into the cups.

"Come on, let's go," he said.

I glared at him. He pulled my keys out of his pocket and dangled them at me. Great. I'd let him drive and now he had my keys.

"I'll drive," I said. But he pulled the keys away when I reached for them. "Give me my keys."

He smiled. "Come on, get in the car. I'll drive us back to the House."

He walked to my little Datsun and eased himself into the driver's seat, closed the door and rolled down the window.

"I'm not going anywhere until you give me my keys," I called to him.

"Suit yourself," he said. The engine purred to life. He reached down and pulled my purse from the floor, dangled it out the window, and said, "Are you coming or not?"

Folding my arms across my waist, I stomped a bit and shook my head. He tossed my purse to the ground, backed the car up, and drove away. I stood there, gaping, for a few minutes, frozen in completely pissed-off shock, waiting for him to come back; but it didn't happen, so I picked up my purse and started walking. I could call the police, I figured. But I was so drunk, I didn't know if they'd believe me. And even so, I imagined I could get arrested for public drunkenness or something. Urinating on church property maybe, which I'd done a few times. So did John, but that was hardly a defense.

I could call my mother, but the idea made me nearly vomit. The lecture would be mind-numbing, followed by a lot of pouting and whining about how all this made her look. She wouldn't come to get me, anyway. I could call Sausage. But he wouldn't come either. Why bother with those two? I wouldn't dare call Aunt Aubrey. She wouldn't be able to find the place and then we'd both be in trouble. Only me more so when it was discovered I was the one who sent aunt Aubrey out into the world to get lost and die a lonely death in her car on the side of the road up in South Carolina or somewhere, which is where she'd end up once she got on the Interstate. Why does Aunt Aubrey always try to get on the Interstate when she just needs to go down the road to the grocery store?

Then I thought of Bondurant. I dug in my purse to get the card he'd given me with his number on it. I didn't want to walk farther south to the convenience store, so I headed down the road to ask someone if I could use his phone. This was a brilliant idea that I didn't even need Nina for. Heading back the way I'd need to go to get to Hope House, I stopped at the first little house on the corner. A stooped old man answered the door. Perfect. Here was a young, sweet girl on his porch who just needed to use his phone. Of course he didn't mind and he let me in.

You really ought to give men some credit. They recognize an opportunity when it presents itself, and they seize it, shall we say. I called Bond and he said he'd come and get me at the church. I thanked little old gray-haired guy and he said you're welcome by reaching out both his wrinkled old hands and grabbing my breasts. He gave them each a squeeze like they were bike horns. I was disgusted, more than shocked; but if I hadn't just been assaulted by a one-eyed drunk guy who tasted like Winston's I might have found the old guy amusing. I staggered backwards toward his door and made a quick escape.

I paced back and forth in front of Sandy Point Baptist for I don't know how long waiting for Bond. I was a combination of shaken and drunk. I didn't know if I'd been assaulted or was a tease. And who knows what I might have said to the old man to make him think he could touch me? Even though I knew I hadn't really done anything to provoke them, I couldn't blame John or the old guy completely. That might have been what shook me up.

Bondurant finally showed up and I fought back the tears getting into his car. "Thank you," I said.

He pulled onto the street and headed to Hope House. "How did you get out here?" He asked.

"It's a long story."

"Where's your car?"

"Same story."

"How much have you had?"

I shrugged. "I guess I'm pretty drunk."

"So, when you go to another AA meeting, you'll have to start back at day one?"

"If I go back."

"You don't think you will?"

"I don't belong there. It's not for me."

He was silent and I knew what he was thinking. He'd picked me up all the way over on the other side of town. I was drunk, smelled of cigarettes and booze, probably disheveled from nearly being raped, my car was gone, and

I had nothing to say about it except that it was a long story. Long story, indeed. He was thinking I needed AA.

"You have leaves in your hair." He reached over to pull one out.

But Bond didn't know about AA. He didn't know about addiction. And victimhood. And the groveling self-debasing nature of the whole twelve-step proposition. It only took one meeting for me to see it. But I didn't think I could convince Bond of anything, seeing as I was the epitome of the alcoholic just then. I pulled the leaves from my hair and remembered old Bernie who ran the meetings at the plaza telling me about rock bottom; and I supposed I still hadn't hit it, because I wasn't covered in my own shit.

"You're shaking," he said. "Are you okay?"

I nodded. "Probably just the beer."

When we pulled up to Hope House my car was sitting at the curb outside the women's dorm like it had never been moved.

"Well, there's one question answered," Bond said. He turned the engine off and looked at me, smiling. "Why did we stop being friends? I don't remember."

This was how you knew your friends didn't drink. They had no concept of drunkenness. Oh, sure, they'd seen people stagger, they'd seen them puke, and do crazy shit like fall off the back of the bleachers at football games. But they didn't understand that just because you weren't puking, or staggering, or falling down, you could still be too drunk to hold a proper conversation—one that you'd fully remember the next day, anyway.

"You don't remember me telling you and Sylvie I was

going to that party out in Beacon Hills without you, and Sylvie called me a stuck up bitch and said we weren't friends anymore?"

"You make us sound like thirteen-year olds."

"That's about right." My words slurred; couldn't he hear it? "Sylvie kept telling me I was trying to be better than I was. And you two broke up with me."

"I didn't break up with you."

"It was a package deal."

He nodded a little bit and looked over across the street to the main house where Tina came out and stood on the lawn looking at us.

"I was her friend first. Maybe I felt loyalty or something. But..."

"But what?" I said.

He winced. "I liked you better. I wanted to be your friend."

"Sylvie was such a bitch, wasn't she? She was pushy. She pushed you away from me."

"It was more you."

"Me what?"

"You pushed me away. Remember how we used to sit in the hallway near our first class and talk? We weren't the cool kids. We didn't hang out in the amphitheater or the main lobby outside the lunchrooms. We hid in the hallway."

"Were we hiding?"

He nodded. "I thought we were. But you stopped. And Sylvie and I kept hiding."

"Maybe you're right."

Bondurant left me at Hope House and told me to call

him whenever I needed him. Any time, he said. But I was pretty sure I wouldn't. I had some self-respect–it might show up too late, but at least it arrived. Tina followed me to the women's dorm and into my little nook where I took off my clothes and crawled into bed.

"John left you this note," she said.

It was a folded piece of lined notebook paper and inside he'd scrawled, "Sorry about your car. I tried to go back and get you but you were gone."

"Give me a fucking break," I said.

"What happened? You're both drunk."

"Is he still here?"

She shook her head. "He gave me the note and walked off. I don't think he's coming back. Kip already told Bridget he came back drunk in your car."

"Nice. Now she knows I was drinking."

"No," she said. "Kip told her John might have stolen it."

"He did steal it."

"Did he carjack you?"

I turned away from her and nestled my head into the pillow. "No."

"Well, that's the story we're telling."

"Whatever."

"You get some sleep. I'll cover for you."

And she did. I wondered, as I drifted off to sleep, why Tina was so nice to me. She didn't seem to want anything. She didn't want anything from anybody. She was just nice. I couldn't remember ever knowing anyone that nice except for Claire Lindsay and she ruined it completely when she found Jesus and kept trying to give him to everybody else.

I remembered the day she came into the locker room crying, before P.E. class. I was so concerned. I thought something awful must have happened. Somebody must have hit her, or called her a whore or something.

"What is it?"

"I'm scared."

"Of what?" Now I was panicked. Was a killer on the loose in the school?

"I'm afraid God is mad at me."

Oh, is that all? "Why?"

And she told me the story about how she was in line at lunch and saw Larry Halverston take a cookie and put it in his pocket without paying. And God laid it on her heart to tell the cashier. But she was too afraid to say anything. And anyway, she knew Larry was hungry and didn't have much money and his free lunch card couldn't be used on the *a la carte* cookies, and now her god was royally pissed at her. Probably. Because, let's face it, how do you tell? There's no lightning. There's no smiting. No scorpions or anything. Just Claire, crying and thinking God is going to send her to hell for disobeying orders. I really don't think Claire was nice because of God or Jesus. She was just nice. Except when she tried to tell everybody about God and Jesus.

Tina was nice like Claire, without the guilt and fear. I couldn't help thinking there must be something else to her and as I nodded off to a drunken sleep, I tried to imagine what awful thing I would discover about Tina that would make her not so nice after all. A body in her back yard? Maybe she was a racist. Or tortured animals.

Something. It was inevitable.

# 17.

By Sunday, all was back to normal. Tina kept her eyes on me for a while, waiting for that one-drink-drunk thing to happen, but I managed to stay out of the shit-filled gutter of Main Street, so she reminded me that I said I'd take her to the Catholic Church. We waved good-bye to Chuck as he got on the Baptist bus and Tina and Kip got in the backseat of my car to make out on the way.

We sat in the back and sang, and pulled out the kneelers and knelt and followed along with the chants as best we could. It was very ritualistic–no time to think, really. We tried not to laugh too loudly during the handshaking and peace be unto yous, and then we all walked up the aisle to get a cracker. I stood before the priest as he held the piece of Jesus up in front of my face and whispered something in Latin. I held out my hands, as I'd seen the others do, and he put God on my palms, then he quickly slid his fingers to the tips of mine and gave them a bit of a squeeze. I looked into his face and he was smiling at me. He nodded. He knew that I wasn't a

Catholic. I was just a curious twenty-something, experimenting, exploring. Hell, I might have even still smelled of beer. I imagined him as a great father figure, which was really funny and I giggled my way back to the pew. You know, because he's a Father and all. If I were going to go to church, I decided as I drove Kip and Tina back to Hope House, I'd be a Catholic. If they let me in. There must be a way to get in.

At my next appointment with Dr. Crazy, I wanted to tell her about the vision I had while nearly being raped by one-eyed John, but I didn't want to mention the nearly being raped part.

"Okay," I said as soon as I sat down. "I broke the rules and drank, this week, but I went to AA meetings every night. Well, except the night I got drunk." She raised her eyebrows a bit but didn't register any disappointment. Before she could ask me anything, I said, "I remembered something. I don't know if it was real."

"But it's important to you?"

"I think it had to do with Camelia. And my mother wanting to kill me."

She gave me that psychological "go on" look.

"I got this picture in my head, of me running across someone's front lawn, screaming. And then after I got some rest, well, after I sobered up, I started to remember it."

"Tell me," she said.

"I was eight years old, I'm sure of it, and walking home from school, and this car pulled up along the curb beside me and the driver-side door opened."

In my memory, I could see that he meant me no

harm. He was leaning out a bit, not even looking at me, with a soda bottle in his hand; he was pouring brown fluid out onto the curb. But I didn't see that as a child. As soon as the car slowed beside me and the door opened I screamed and ran. Thinking about it, my heart raced and my breath shortened; my own terrified shrieks echoed through the neighborhood. This was it. This was it, I was thinking. The man slammed the car door shut and sped off as I ran up to the first house I could get to and banged on the door. I'd stopped screaming by that point, but I was shaking and crying. A woman came to the door and her mouth fell open when she saw me.

"Can you take me home?" I cried.

She gathered her children and we all got into her car and I pointed out the way to my house. I tried to tell her someone was after me, but I was crying like a mad woman, as much as an eight year old can cry like a mad woman. We got to my house and she walked me up to the porch and rang the doorbell. I was standing on my own front porch, clinging to a stranger, waiting for someone I knew to let me in. It was as if I didn't actually live there.

"When my mom opened the door," I told Dr. Crazy. "I stood there for a second or two and then started shrieking again. The poor stranger lady explained what happened; she rattled out the story in one loud breath, no doubt hoping my mother wouldn't accuse her of torturing me. After they brought me inside and got me to shut up by feeding me cookies, my mother had an explanation for her–this patronizing story about how some of the other girls at school filled my head with crazy nonsense."

"Was it not true?"

I stared blankly at Dr. Crazy's enormous gold hooped earring, brushing against the bra strap sticking out from under her dress. "It was true. Debbie Clark told me all sorts of stories about rape and murder."

But they were ridiculous. I couldn't have believed them, even as a child. She told me a local woman had been kidnaped and tied to a tree and raped eleven times, after which she proceeded to have eleven babies, while still tied to the tree. It was nonsense. Women don't have babies while they're standing up. How stupid was that?

But that wasn't what scared me. It was more than that.

"And the stories frightened you?"

I shook my head. "I was terrified. That's all I remember. Being terrified."

It was a few weeks later that my mother told me to stand on the toilet in the hall bathroom and I watched my reflection in the mirror, in horror, as she took scissors and cut off my hair. All the while she clipped—and wispy strands of straw-colored hair floated to the ground around me—she chirped about how cute it was going to look. How sweet this was. And no more rat's nests.

Rat's nests were the enemy—knots and tangles mostly at the nape of my neck were my mother's bane. She'd leave me to my own devices most of the time, while hollering at me now and then to brush my hair. But every six months or so, for some reason, she'd get it in her head that she needed to groom me. Maybe it was for a party or a vacation, I couldn't recall. All I knew was at those times, she yanked brushes and combs through my hair, and bitched about my irresponsibility and the rat's nests.

And I would think, we don't have rats in our house and if they built nests in my hair, why were they so small? And where were the baby rats? You think they could have babies in my hair without me realizing it? Not likely. But you don't say things like that to my mother or you get slapped and told to shut the hell up. So I stood there and watched her cut my hair from my butt, all the way up to my head–what she called a pixie.

Once, when I was twenty, I tried to tell my mother about that–about how I had no voice. We were sitting outside on the back porch of her duplex and she turned to look at me like a was a baboon who'd plopped down into the chair beside her.

"No voice?" She said. "Don't you remember that room? That god-awful room of yours? Purple carpet. Purple walls. You think that was my decision? You had plenty of voice."

"You look just like Sandy Duncan," she beamed at my reflection and her handiwork. "It's adorable."

My god, I was her little Crissy doll. But I didn't have a hole in my head from which I could pull the hair back out once I'd made it shorter. I was so disgusted that I wore a hat on my head to school for a week. Thick, chunky girls can't do pixie; it doesn't work.

"The only advantage," I told Dr. Crazy. "Was that I looked like a boy. And I didn't think kidnappers wanted little boys. So when I'd walk home by myself, any time I heard a car coming from behind, I'd look down so they could see that my hair was very short and think I was a boy. They wouldn't want me. But at some point I learned that kidnappers liked to murder little boys, too."

"Murder little boys?" Dr. Crazy said.

"Yes," I said. I was emphatic by this point, angry. "After that, I couldn't do anything but hope and pray that nobody would want me. Maybe they wouldn't want ugly girls."

"So you were afraid of being kidnaped and murdered?"

I nodded. "Wasn't everyone?"

"No," she said. "And you were eight years old?"

"That's right." Something was off at that point. I mean, what did Dr. Crazy mean by "no." No? You don't say "no" to your client like she's crazy, do you?

"And when you were eight, you thought your mother wanted you dead."

"Yes, because she made me walk to school by myself—when there were people out there who wanted to kidnap and murder me. It all makes sense now, doesn't it?"

"I see."

Yes. It did start to make some sense. Maybe that was all there was to it. Debbie Clark, the little bitch, scared the shit out of me with stupid stories about women being raped on trees, and my mother made me go to school by myself. But there was more, on the tip of my tongue, and in my head, just waiting for me to find it.

"I told my mother I didn't want to walk to school alone."

"She made you do it, anyway."

"Yes."

"And you resent her for that?"

218

"I really did think she wanted me killed. Why else would she make me go to school?"

"Because it was normal. She had no reason to think you were in any danger. You weren't the only child to walk to school alone."

"She knew."

"She knew what?"

"I don't know. Stop making this complicated. She just knew. She knew I was in danger but she sent me out there alone, anyway."

Dr. Crazy nodded and scribbled some notes on her pad. "And what made you recall this?"

I stared at her for a moment, at the lines around her lips and how her lipstick bled ever so slightly into them.

"I couldn't get myself to scream," I said. "And I think that was the last time I'd heard myself scream. When I was eight."

"Why were you trying to scream?"

I turned from her. "I don't know. I just needed to scream and I couldn't."

"Were you dreaming?"

I nodded. "Sure."

The battle on the back porch wasn't between my mother and me; it was all inside my own head. I wanted to go to school. I wanted to be caught, and raped, and murdered. I feared it, like a child fears the immunization she knows she has to have. It was right and good that I would be killed and that was why, I suppose, I loved my mother so fiercely, knowing she wanted me dead as much as I did.

*Dear Camelia. I can't see you. I can't imagine your face. Every time I try, I only see my own. I don't want to insult you by making you into me, but there you are with my face, squinting against a white hot sun. We're afraid and crying and I want to help us. But I don't know how, because I'm just a little girl like you. Dr. Crazy made me write this.*

# 18.

The Tuesday night AA meeting droned on and on until I thought I would scream. Who were these people? The old dude and dudette in charge, Bernie and Marguerite, were like prunes, glaring at us all night. Marge even rolled her eyes when Tina tried to talk about the time she got drunk and forgot to pick her kid sister up from school. It sounded like a serious story to me. But what did I know? When the meeting broke up, Bernie approached me at the doughnut table. He smiled a yellow-toothed smile and put his arm across my shoulders.

"You got a sponsor yet?"

I shook my head and took a bite of doughnut, hoping he'd leave me alone. He smelled like old whiskey–maybe booze infused itself into his shirts and no matter how much he washed them, the smell of his alcoholism would always be with him–like a curse

"Well, it just so happens, I'm available, if you're interested."

"I haven't really thought about it," I mumbled, my

mouth full of powdered sugar.

"A sponsor is very important to your progress with the program. And I would be available to you day and night. For whatever you might need." He gave my shoulder a squeeze. I knew that squeeze.

"Hey," Chuck pushed himself between Bernie and me. "It's time to go."

Bernie handed me his card and winked at me. "Just call me, any time."

"You don't want to call him," Chuck said as we started the walk back to Hope House.

It was July and a light breeze did its best to fight off the heat. It was useless; I'd be covered in sweat before we got back to the House. We'd get nothing beyond an imaginary chill until after Halloween.

"Why not?" I said. Not that I was considering the old dude for a sponsor. I wasn't considering a sponsor at all.

"Well, other than the fact that he's still drinking," Tina said.

"We don't know that," Kip said.

"He reeked of liquor tonight. Didn't you see the way old Margie was glaring at him and turning up her nose."

"He didn't act drunk," I said. "He was the same way he always is."

"Exactly," Tina said. "He keeps coming to the meetings drunk. He's trolling for women."

When we got back to the House, Beverly opened the door of the women's dorm and called to me. "You got a message."

It was China from the drugstore in the mall. Don't ask me how you name a kid after a country; apparently it happens. China had very short, dark hair. She wore khakis and button-up shirts, sneakers and black socks. She wasn't pretty–a square sort of woman. She reminded me of the girls in school who played softball. Well not all of them, sure, but the good ones–the ones who were built like men–all shoulders, no hips, and not much boob to get in the way of a good pitch. I decided China was a neither woman nor man, but something in between. So what would that make her, exactly? A mother figure? Or a father figure? I'd have to figure that out.

"She wants you to start on Saturday. Call her back, quick, before she changes her mind."

The drunks were ecstatic that I'd gotten a job, especially one of that caliber. The drugstore in Sandy Point was probably one of the top tier jobs. But Kip had a few problems with my choice and he told me so out by the swing in the dark, while Skeeter walked his circle and Tina and Chuck smoked about a pack of cigarettes each.

"I'm not saying it's a bad place to work for a civilian," he said. "But think of the temptations. They sell beer and wine. And there's a pharmacy."

"You think I'm going to steal drugs?"

"You're still a baby," Chuck said. "Barely two weeks in. You can't know what the disease will make you do."

I snickered and Skeeter stopped his pacing and they all stared at me. "Sorry. I'm not sure I buy into this whole disease thing."

Kip shook his head slowly back and forth while the others seemed to lean away from me, ready to flee. "You know what this is?" He turned to look at the others. "This is what we were talking about, before she showed up. Grandiosity. She thinks she can work the program in her own way." Then he turned to me. "You're already drunk again. Maybe not physically yet, but it's already happened."

I didn't know what the hell he was going on about, but I suspected the AA meeting we went to the next night was his doing—some evil plan to make me realize what a rotten drunk I was, make me see the light and start working the program and fighting the disease the way he thought I should. It was Kip's House, after all. The trustees just made the chore chart. Kip ran everybody—no wonder he kept coming back; that kind of power would be enough to keep a person sober.

The meeting was held at a church near downtown and Kip asked me to drive us all over there, even though it meant we had to leave Skeeter behind. Skeet was glad not to go, which made me even more suspicious. This place had Jesus drunks, staying sober through the love of their lord and savior Jesus Christ. There was singing and praying and preaching and Chuck kept nudging me when I wouldn't bow my head or sing or say Amen.

Dan, a round, short man who wheezed when he spoke, ran the meeting. His skin was shiny, almost translucent, and he kept wiping his clammy forehead and mouth with a cloth. At the end of the meeting, when we'd usually say the Serenity Prayer and be done with it, he insisted on one more. He prayed to the lord Jesus almighty that these young people from the halfway house would be strong in their sobriety, and walk with God always. I watched him speak, watched the sweat bead up on his upper lip, and before he said amen, he opened his eyes and saw me watching him.

"Amen," he said, still staring at me.

I didn't say it. When the meeting was finally over, he stood at the door insisting on shaking each of our hands and patting each of us on the shoulder and telling us to go with God and come back real soon. When I stood in front of him, he squeezed my shoulder and whispered, "God laid it on my heart tonight that you are struggling with your faith, my child."

My child? Who did this guy think he was? And what's with Jesus constantly laying crap on people? If Jesus wanted the cashier at school to know that Larry Halverston stole a cookie, why didn't he tell her himself? Why put poor Claire Lindsay through hell about it? And if he wanted me to know he knew I was struggling with the whole religion thing, why didn't he come down from his hiding place and tell me to my face?

I shook my head.

"Yes, yes, he laid it on my heart." He slipped me a pamphlet and his business card and said, "You come back, you hear. Jesus forgives us. All we have to do is ask him."

I pulled my hand from his slimy grip and left. As I followed the others to my car, I wiped my hand on my jeans in disgust. Laid it on his heart, my ass. He saw my eyes open, that's all. He saw that I watched instead of prayed. The whole meeting. What if I was a Jew? What if I was a Catholic? It's none of his damn business why I didn't pray his prayers and sing his songs.

Chuck hung back and met up with me. "You okay?"

"Fine."

"You should be more respectful when you're in somebody's church."

"That wasn't a church; it was an AA meeting. I don't have to pray and sing in an AA meeting." My cheeks burned hot and I pulled the door of my car open a bit too fast and it flew back closed. I pulled again and climbed in.

"Well, it was at a church," Tina said. "So it was bound to be religious."

"They need some quality control," I said.

Kip laughed. "Grandiosity," he said. "Grandiosity."

That night, I packed up my stuff and told them all I was going home. Tina and I sat on the swing under the sad bottlebrush out front of the main building with Chuck, Kip, and Skeeter watching us. I thought I would be at home at the old house with the moss-covered oaks and the old women and the drunks, but instead, I was always one step ahead or to the right. Something didn't fit.

"You'll be back," Kip said.

"No I won't."

"Yeah, you will."

People are always trying to tell you what you'll do, what you want, who you are. My parents took me once to visit some friends of theirs. There must be seven times, in my memory, when I was whisked off to some other town, to visit a different set of so-called friends I'd never heard them talk about before. These people lived in a small house out in the woods. I was sent off with their seventeen-year-old daughter to make friends. Curled up on her bed against the back wall of her room, her dirty feet crossed–picking at her big toenail–she wore sweat pants

226

with the strings untied and a frayed tank top with no bra underneath–her cylindrical nipples poked through. Even at thirteen, I was disgusted. What kind of teenager walks around a house in front of old men like my dad with her nipples exposed? And what sorts of parents let her get away with it? But there was something free-spirited and hippie about her. Her flat face was pock-marked and flaky, dominated by a bulb nose. Oily, dirty blonde hair, hung below her shoulders and looking at it made me want to shower. I don't know why, but she asked me what my favorite color was. Purple, I said.

"You won't like it when you're older."

"Of course I will." If I liked it then, why wouldn't I like it later?

"No you won't."

"Why wouldn't I?"

"We change when we get older."

"There aren't young colors and old colors."

"But that's the point," she said. "Everything you like now will be different when you're older. You can't stay the same. It's a fact of life."

She was crazy. I could see her becoming another Sally Jessie Raphael. She'd have a show called Spirit Guru where she told everybody to stop thinking or liking or loving or trying, because everything will change one day. No need to get too attached to your feelings.

"Your problem," Kip said, "is that you haven't hit rock bottom yet."

"Oh, really."

"Look at you," he said. "You still have so much. A car, a job."

"I just got the job."

"You'll be back. You won't stop drinking until you've hit the curb."

"You don't get it," I told him. "You spend all your time obsessing over alcohol, you'll never be cured."

"There is no cure, don't you see that?"

"How would you know?"

"You think decades of AA history mean nothing?"

"I think you're looking at it wrong. You're concentrating on the wrong thing."

"Oh, do enlighten us." He rolled his eyes and looked to the others.

"I'm just saying...we drink for a reason. And nobody ever tries to get at what that reason is and fix it."

"That's insanity, right there." He pointed a finger at me, like I was the devil and he was going to cast me out. "Insanity talking. You just keep talking. Keep talking. But one day, you'll see, and you'll come crawling back."

But I wouldn't be back. What was obvious to me, was insanity to him. Kip was addicted to the AA fix. If he couldn't drink, he could talk about drinking. If he couldn't get wasted, he could tell everyone about the times he was wasted. He'd never be free of it, because he wouldn't let it go. None of them would. I was going to have to figure out how to do it myself.

On the way home, I stopped at the store and got a six-pack of Michelobe Light. Of course, Spirit Guru bitch was right. Purple's nice enough, but it's got nothing on hunter green.

# 19.

*Dear Camelia, No one gets you, do they? They think they know you. But they don't. They think you are things that you're not. Like a drunk. Or a whore. Or a liar. And they think you won't succeed, but that's only because they didn't. Because they're drunks and they're whores and they're liars. God, this is too stupid for words. Not you. I know I should want to write to you again. But, and please don't cry, I know you're not real. And I'm too old—the time for invisible friends is past. I'm sorry.*

When I showed up at my mom's door from Hope House, her first words were, "What? Is rehab over already?" Her eyes were on the six-pack in my left hand, so she probably didn't even hear me say yes.

My mother was not the queen of evil. We can get that straight right now. The queen of evil is probably a goddess and bitches worship her. I don't know her name. But that was not my mother. My mother was a short, fat woman. She had the dark hair, the almond-shaped eyes, and the beautiful high cheek bones of the Abernathy's, and she'd passed those beauty genes on to my brother, Jimmy Dean. I got my dad's round face, round eyes, and no cheekbones to speak of. From my mother, I got all the leftover bits of not quite pretty that must have been floating around in the Abernathy helix.

She had a very loud mouth. She said "lord" a lot. And "shoot me I'm dead," whatever that was supposed to mean. One time she tried to say, "butter my butt and call me a biscuit," but she said, "lard my ass and chew on it." I don't think she cared what came out of her mouth any more than she cared what went into it. And yet, she had an impeccable sense of propriety about what I could do, and how what *I* did made *her* look. She wasn't evil. She was just mean.

She stood in the kitchen with one hand on her fat hip and the other on the edge of the sink, glaring at me in that way—with her lips in a pout and her head wobbling back and forth, fast, like the fat head wasn't completely attached at the neck and one jiggle kept it going for hours. I don't know, maybe she had one of those diseases that makes you shake. But her head only shook like that when she wasn't happy with me.

She said, "Drugstore. That's not too bad, I guess."

"So, I'll be staying here for a while until I can get my own place."

She let out a snort. "On minimum wage? Where are you going to live?"

"I used to live alone."

"With your dad paying for it. You don't know what it's like in the real world. You've never had to fend for yourself. It takes responsibility and determination and sobriety." Sober to my mother didn't mean abstinence. It meant being able to drink and still get your paycheck.

"Maybe I'll find a roommate."

She turned back to the sink and rinsed off her dishes. "Good luck with that."

I took that to mean I could stay. Not that I wanted to. I put my stuff in my bedroom and looked around. What a dump. My mother had finished off three of my Michelobes by the time I finished the second. I was going to have to invest in a private cooler for my bedroom.

I started work on Saturday. The night before was the Fourth and, well, it was a holiday, so I had to go out. Everybody at Spike's gathered at the edge of the parking lot to watch the fireworks over the lagoon across the way and then went back in and acted like our Founding Fathers got revolutionarily snot-faced after the signing of the Declaration of Independence and we were paying homage. So, I was just a tad hung over when I started my new, respectable job.

After the first two hours, China put me on the front register, at the mall entrance, so I could watch people come and go. I started at the pharmacy register by the back door. But I got a phone call after thirty minutes and I guess I screwed that up.

I picked up the phone like I was supposed to and said, "Pinkerton's Drugs, how may I help you?"

And this guy said, "Is this Walgreen's."

And I said, "I'm sorry, this is Pinkerton's, in Sandy Point."

"Is this Walgreen's," he said again.

And I made sort of a sound, maybe like, are you

stupid or something, and said, "Look, this is Pinkerton's. I don't know the number for Walgreen's." And I hung up on him.

The jerk had the nerve to call back and ask to speak to the pharmacist. I knew it was him. What did he think? That I wouldn't recognize his voice? Apparently he wasn't asking for Walgreen's, he was the pharmacist from Walgreen's and I was supposed to automatically put him through to our pharmacist. It wasn't in the manual; there was no manual. Not like at the Joint where everything was spelled out exactly how you did it, or made it, or cleaned it. Maybe I wasn't good at innovating.

Anyway, the pharmacist told China to move me up front to the mall. I guess I didn't impress him. But I liked my new spot. There wasn't a phone, for one thing. And all I had to do was ring up purchases and straighten the shelves. The only disadvantage was that China's office was only a few feet away. It was a box on a stage with a throne inside it, and a wrap-around glass window, level with her head when she sat at her desk, so she could supervise her realm.

That meant, when she was in her box, I had to look like I was working. But that was okay. Mr. Toby used to say, "Do something, even if it's wrong." So I kept moving. Shuffling merchandise, dusting, stealing little individual packets of macadamia nuts and eating them. Or M&M's. Or chips. China had this awful habit of leaving her office and walking around the store or working in the back room. She was almost telling me to eat candy on the job.

The only other register was the beauty counter across

from mine. A girl named Hannah worked there and she got to wear a light blue vest that made her look like she knew what she was doing. She gave makeovers; who in her right mind would get a makeover at Pinkerton's in Sandy Point?

On my first day, I heard her calling, "Hey new girl, meet me at the trash bags."

I didn't know what the hell she meant, but I wandered down the aisle and sure enough, the trash bags were between our stations.

"Hey," she said.

Hannah was tall and lean with thick, silky orange hair, and freakish blue eyes. Somehow it all worked magic with her blue vest. It made me want to work the beauty counter.

I used to have these ideas. I'd think everything was the same for everyone. Because Hannah looked so fresh and pretty in the vest, I figured I'd look just as good. If my friend looked great in the marching band uniform, holding a clarinet, if I put one on and joined the band, I'd look just as good. And one person's haircut would be fabulous on me. Or that shirt. Whatever. I was always disappointed. It took me a long time to realize you had to be pretty, to be pretty. And you had to have confidence, to look confident. And of course, you had to know how to play the stupid clarinet.

"Check it out," Hannah said. She reached behind her ear and pulled something out. Earplugs. "See?" Wires ran down her neck under her hair, into her shirt, and attached to a little cassette player in her pants. "I'm listening to music and Chinette doesn't even know."

"I bet that's not allowed."

"Neither is painting my nails at work." And she blew on her nails. I liked Hannah right away. "Let's go out tonight," she said. "Have you been to Brassy's?"

I shook my head. That was all the way over in Cocoa Beach. I'd never drive that far by myself. "Okay."

There is an unspoken understanding among drunks. We go out with anyone who asks us. They're almost never psycho mania killers. Was Hannah too young to be a mother figure?

# 20.

*Dear Camelia, Did your mother love you? I will say that she did; and that makes it true, doesn't it? I've often wondered, theoretically of course, about the invisible friend world. Are you trapped somewhere in some invisible friend dimension? Did I save you from it when I wrote to you? Three River Terrace was just a game—I was only toying with death. Now that I look back at it, I'm wondering if I want to stay here. I think I always felt that way and something in me took me up to the roof to show me, and now I can't forget it. But you saved me up there—when I wrote to you. Would you do it again? Could you?*

The last time my mother hit me, I was sixteen. I rode the bus from the high school, and because the bathrooms there were disgusting, I inevitably had to pee like all get out by the time I walked from the bus stop. One day when I got to the front door, it was locked. This wasn't unusual. Sausage and I were latch-key kids, only our parents weren't nice enough to actually give us keys. When the house was locked on us time and time again, we broke into the garage through the back door using a screw driver Dad left out. We damaged that door so thoroughly, we never had to break it open again. Our parents, undeterred, continued to lock the door from the garage into the kitchen. But the garage held all sorts of tools that enabled us to get in.

This particular day, however, I had to pee so bad I knew I wouldn't make it around to the back of the house to break in. I sat on the porch and clenched every muscle in my body. I was in a pickle. Getting up would make me pee my pants. So, I hunched there, royally pissed off at my parents—my mother in particular, as she was the one who could have been home to let me in. Chances were good she'd left only moments before knowing full well Sausage and I would be home soon. It was as if she were the only living being on earth who mattered. The entire family could be home on a Saturday morning, but when she left the house, she turned the air conditioner up to its holding pattern of eighty degrees, snapped off the television, and locked all the doors.

I decided I'd just have to pee my pants. So I did. I peed. Then I got up, walked around to the back of the house, broke in, took off my wet pants and underwear, and dumped them in the hamper for my mother to deal with. She got home an hour later and wanted to know what the puddle on the porch was. I said I had no idea.

"It smells like pee," she said.

"Does it?"

The next Saturday, she found the pee-soaked pants while sorting the laundry and came after me with a belt. She chased me through the house screaming something about lying to her and purposefully pissing on the porch and what kind of satanic creep was I. You know, it wasn't funny at the time, but thinking back on it makes me laugh. She grabbed my arm and twisted me around, raised the belt and whipped me across the chest and back with it. So, naturally, I hauled off and slapped the shit out of her...right across the face. It's natural, these things. You learn them from your parents. The rest was a scene from a Three Stooges movie with the two of us slapping at each other. I shoved her against a doorknob and she screamed about calling the police and I screamed something about child services and then I was in my room fuming...and smiling. That would be the last time that bitch hit me. And it was.

Things were better between us after that, in that we acted like it never happened. She played the role of doting mother who doesn't actually dote, and I played the role of obedient child who wasn't really obedient. I was at the very least, polite, so, I called her that night from Pinkerton's and told her I was going out with my new co-workers and not to wait up. I wasn't going to tell her I was going to Brassy's. She didn't need to know that much.

She said, "Don't stay out too late."

And I said, "Sure." The last time my mother was allowed to tell me when to come home, I was twelve. I often wonder if I was mis-parented, or if I was just an awful person. As much as I'd like to blame my parents, sometimes it's difficult.

Hannah drove us to Cocoa Beach in her big green Chevy and I was in nightclub heaven. Brassy's was an old grocery store converted into an enormous bar and dance club. It was Saturday night and the place was packed with the exotic beach and island crowd. We got drinks and wandered through the mass, dancing, flirting, gabbing. Before we knew it, more drinks were bought for us. I liked Hannah. She was loud and obnoxious and drew a crew of admirers. I didn't have to wander around by myself hoping some desperate guy would latch onto me; Hannah was surrounded by them, and the ones she wouldn't pay enough attention to, took to me. Another thing about Hannah...she didn't slink off and have sex with anyone, which I found strange. And she didn't get me more smashed than she was by buying me drink after drink, and then take me outside around back and introduce me to some guy who I only ever saw in silhouette. Nothing like that at all. She got wasted. I got wasted. We danced, and then we left and drove over to the all-night burger joint, ate and laughed, and then went home.

It was the best time drunk I ever had. I finally had a real friend. Like a sister figure. Or, hell, maybe she was a best friend figure. I'd never really had one of those before. I was still smiling, with disco fever in my head when I snuck back into my mother's duplex before dawn and fell into bed.

The next morning, at work, I thought I'd die. I was nauseated; my eye lids were red, puffy, and itchy. Even though when I rubbed them it was like sandpaper, I kept doing it. My head throbbed and pulsated with pain. I stole as many packages of peanuts as I could; they seemed to be the only thing keeping me from vomiting. I'd just hidden the last of the empty packages in the trash under my register when China tossed a box of condoms on the counter. I stared at them.

"Those aren't mine," I said.

"I know." She was counting out dollars. "Ring 'em up."

I rang up her condoms. I wanted to ask her what she needed them for but that's not really the sort of thing a person asks her boss. I always thought of the condom buying as the man's job. The pill or the diaphragm, that's the woman's job. I mean, sending your woman into the store to buy condoms for you would be like sending your man to the store for tampons. You just didn't do that.

It was only a couple of years before that I went to my five-year high school reunion. The idea was monstrous, but I'd sat at the reception table for Sausage's five-year and those people knew how to party. If that was high school reminiscing, I was all for it. My class, however, was a bunch of turds who insisted on a sit-down dinner where all the snobs schmoozed together at the cool-kid tables and talked about the rest of us.

Over at our nerd table, Bill Hixley told us that he heard one of our classmates had a sex-change operation. He didn't know if it was a she, who became a he, or a he, who became a she, but it was one or the other. So, I told them all who it was. It was Vonnie Porter, of course. I mean, Vonnie Porter, right? She looked like a boy. She acted like a boy. Clearly, she always wanted to be a boy. They all agreed it must have been Vonnie Porter. And wouldn't you know, two weeks later I saw Vonnie Porter at the mall scarfing down a chili dog at the Orange Julius. And she still had breasts. I could only hope if she heard the rumors that she'd become a man, my name wouldn't be mentioned. Because, let's face it, I didn't mind talking about people, I just didn't want them to know about it.

"Thanks," China said and walked to the back room with her condoms in a bag.

You just never can tell about people, can you?

Near to noon, Bond showed up and wanted to do the lunch thing. I had to ask China if I could go on break, but I had to find her first and I wasn't allowed to leave my area. If I were the manager, I'd have spent all my time up in my little throne booth looking down on people and ordering them around. But she was always somewhere else, running this way and that, acting like managing the drug store in Sandy Point was very important.

Hannah told me she was in the back room and I'd have to wait, so I sent Bond off to the Orange Julius to meet me there. By the time China showed up and acted all surprised—like, why would I want to eat lunch at lunch time—I figured he'd gone home. But he hadn't. He was staring down the mall toward the drug store and when he saw me, he turned away like he hadn't been watching for me. I slid into his booth, opposite him. He'd already eaten and had a half-full Julius. He asked me did I want a chili dog. Did I want a chili dog? Other than McDonald's cheeseburgers, Orange Julius chili dogs with cheese and onions were a godsend to the perpetually hung over and I told him so.

I said, "Please, I'm so god-awful hung over, you have no idea."

I guess I shouldn't have been surprised by the look on his face. But I wasn't at Hope House anymore, so I didn't see the big deal. I told him I didn't have a drinking problem; didn't he remember? He went to the counter and got me a chili dog and an Orange Julius and another dog for himself. He sat down and shoved my food over to me. He ate, while he watched me eat, and I realized that eating while being stared at was not at all good for hang overs.

"What?" I said. "*What?*"

"I thought you were going to give up on the drinking."

"Who are you, my mother?"

"No, no." He shook his head and looked away. "Sorry."

Damn right he was sorry.

"Are you glad to be out of Hope House?"

I nodded and chewed. "The people there were crazy. It was like a cult or something."

"So, the drug store."

"I wanted to work at the bookstore, but," I shrugged. "Maybe one day."

"You could go to school. Get a degree.'

"They're not mutually exclusive."

"You like books?"

"Remember when Sylvie and I read passages to you from Kathleen Woodiwiss before school?"

He blushed and nodded. "What are you reading now?"

"Bible," I said and took another bite of chili dog.

He had the audacity to laugh but then his face froze up and I heard her voice behind me.

"As I live and breathe," she said.

# 21.

*Dear Camelia, Why are you in shadow when I dream about you? Weren't you ever in the light? Have my memories brightened over the years so that the past is lit and the present is darkness? Lately I'm getting light and dark confused.*

I turned to look behind me and there stood Sylvie Bennett, posed with one foot slightly in front of the other, turned out, and one hand on a hip. Chin down, hat at a tilt, low cut top, big boobs hanging out. Sylvie-my-god-Bennett. I turned back to Bond as she slid into the booth next to him and grabbed him around the neck.

"I can't believe it's you," she said and squeezed his face up against her lips. "And you," she turned to me while wiping her crimson lip color off Bond's cheek. "I haven't seen you in ages, either."

Bond moved south with his parents in the second half of our senior year at Sandy Point High. With him out of the way, Sylvie forgave me for going to the party in Beacon Hills with Lee Harper and eating lunch with

Marty Fillingham. But I was done with sitting in the hallway of Building Two every morning and lunchtime like a loser. She sat with me out in the amphitheater in front of the band room and acted like nothing had changed.

Sylvie turned eighteen that January and got me a fake ID so I could go with her to every bar in three counties where she fed me junk food and alcohol, seduced every male within earshot until one took the bait, usually took him out somewhere, got him all hot and bothered and then disappeared, leaving me fat, drunk, and the only vagina within reach. It wasn't until the end of May that I realized she was always hiding somewhere watching me do what she was never willing to. I was glad when school was through. She went off to college or moved away or something. I never bothered to find out.

"How's the job, Mr. Bigshot?" She asked Bond.

He nodded. Bond was working at McDonnell Douglas. He was one of those regular people. Wore a tie and all. It did make you wonder, when Sylvie said it like that, what he was doing at the mall having lunch at the Orange Julius with the likes of me.

"Hey," she said and leaned her big boobs onto the table to reach out and grab my hand. "Let's all go to the Pool Pit tonight. For old time's sake."

"We never went to a bar together," Bond said.

"What difference does that make?"

"If you want to do something for old time's sake, we should go visit the high school."

"Oh, my god, you haven't changed a bit." Sylvie laughed and snorted and I couldn't help smiling, even if

Bond's jaw was set hard.

I met Sylvie at the bar; we had enough of a history for me to know better than let her drive me someplace. The Pool Pit was a hole in the wall in a plaza along Cedars Avenue, backed up against the railroad tracks that ran through town, parallel to US1. It was a big square box with a long bar on the right, booths on the left, and pool tables between. People were packed in like a drunken zombie horde, tumbling in and out the door, floundering around the pool tables and booths, and lurching toward the bar or restrooms. I couldn't hear anything–not the jukebox or the billiard balls or the arcade games along the back wall–nothing but the loud roar of brainless revelry. I squeezed into a spot at the bar, figuring Sylvie would find me, and Bab Reynold's gave up her seat to me so she could play pool. Ricky Jarvis was next to me and winked as he tipped his beer upend and guzzled.

"You heard about Bryan Cleaver, there out back?" He yelled at me over the din.

I shook my head.

"Passed out on the tracks. Train cut his head clean off."

Of course, I didn't believe him. But everybody was nodding like he was telling the truth. I hadn't heard anything about it. That's the sort of thing you hear about, isn't it? I tried to remember Bryan Cleaver.

"Always wore that baseball cap," Ricky said. "Sat right there every Tuesday and Thursday night drinking Budweiser and smoking Winston's."

I had a vague recollection of him. He never paid me any attention, like I was trouble. It's natural to not notice people who don't notice us, right? By the time Sylvie found me I struggled to get Bryan Cleaver's severed head out of my mind. And the sad thing was, I wasn't even sure it was Bryan Cleaver's. It could have been somebody else I didn't know that well, and now I'd be shocked if I saw him alive again sitting at the bar.

Ricky gave Sylvie his bar stool and she chatted everybody up during the entire ladies night special—even let Herb Poole put his hands all over her chest, even though we both knew that Herb Poole was a sexual pervert. We called him Herbert the Pervert. When we were at Sandy Point High, he'd roar across the parking lot after the last bell in his beat up yellow Plymouth Road Runner with the thick black stripe on the hood. That first time he showed up he drove slowly along the walkway out front and stopped when he saw us.

"Hello ladies," he said, pressing on the gas to make the beast roar.

Sylvie and I were waiting for Bond; it was fall, junior year, and we were going to the practice field. Sylvie and Bond were in the marching band and I sat and watched sometimes. Mostly because I didn't have another ride home and would rather sit for a few hours watching the band than ride the bus.

"I'm Herb Poole," he said.

We looked at each other and laughed but he wasn't at all dissuaded. He had a handlebar mustache and wild curly hair; he was smoking a cigarette even though they weren't allowed anywhere on campus and his tanned shoulders were bare.

"I'm looking for my Lolita," he said.

We laughed louder. And then he turned the engine off and got out and leaned against the side of his car in torn jeans and a dirty white tank top. He told us all about the 1970 Plymouth Road Runner. He talked for fifteen minutes about it until Gina Daniels finally showed up. Lolita indeed; she was a freshman and Mr. Herb Poole had to be forty-six or fifty. So he was Herbert the Pervert forever more.

He must not have been forty-six, because there at the Pool Pit, he didn't look much more than thirty-five. Anyway, I like to say I don't remember things when I'm wasted, like everybody else. But I remembered everything. I even remembered the times I passed out. It was a curse, I think, like the hang overs. You get these people who drink themselves into oblivion and they're so sick and vomitous the next day that they swear they'll never drink again, and they pretty much stick to it. But not me. I don't seem to be bothered much by vomiting. You drink, you enjoy, you go home and go to sleep, you wake up, you vomit, you eat a hamburger and go to work, then drink again. It's the way of things.

Anyway, I went to a bar once a few years before and ended up going home with Herbert the Pervert. He lived with his mother up north in this sad, treeless grid of a neighborhood on the other side of I95 from Beacon Hills where the rich people lived. Mansions turned their backs on his front door every day—that's got to mess with a person's self-esteem. He wasn't really all that perverted. No more than any other guy.

"So, you and Bond are friends again?"

Sylvie slid her arm across the bar toward me and laid

her head down on it. The ladies night special was over and the crowd thinned and we could hear ourselves talk. Herbert was playing pool with Ricky and some of the other losers.

"No," I said.

"But you have lunch together."

I raised my eyebrows. I didn't think the Orange Julius counted as a lunch destination–as in, let's do lunch. "I ran into him; that's all."

"You remember that time you pushed him into Mosquito Lake? Right off the pier? Remember?"

Her eyes were shining, as if the past was tears, but it made her happy. I remembered it, sure. I remembered Bond standing at the end of the pier and Sylvie and I were behind him gabbing about something or other. She pointed at his back and I thought she was going to make fun of him–about how sometimes he got all mopey, especially out in nature, and would stare at things, like trees, or anthills, or the water, for a long time–but instead she went to push him and I stopped her. I stopped her by throwing myself against her; she pushed me back, smacking me into Bond and he went into the water.

She laughed so hard she had to sit down while I tried to help Bond out. She told him I'd pushed him–that it was me. Bond didn't say anything; he climbed onto the pier and dripped all the way back to the car. And Sylvie refused to drive us home for two hours while he dried off.

"You remember when you got caught having sex with that guy out in no-man's land? Remember how the cop pointed his gun at me when I came out from the bushes?"

248

I'm not making excuses. Really, I'm not. It's not like Sylvie made me do any of those things. I let her lead me up to them. I let her take me places and buy me booze and cigarettes. I let her pick up guys. And when she would get things going and then walk away, I didn't stop. For the longest time I thought I was the moral one–I was the one willing to finish what we'd started. It took me almost forever to figure out that neither one of us was good.

She was disappointed somehow, when I didn't say I remembered, when I didn't want to walk back with her.

"I'm visiting my sister," she said. "She just got a divorce. I'm going back home tomorrow."

"Where do you live?"

"Baltimore; didn't you know?"

"No." I drank some more of my beer and put on an uninterested look.

"I'm a paralegal with Bunns, Bozo, and Bonobo."

She could have said exactly that, but she probably didn't; she was trying to impress me, not make me laugh. I didn't know what a paralegal was, so I had to believe she was telling the truth. Who would make up something so obscure?

"Married?"

"No," she said. "How about you?"

"No."

"Dating?"

"Mm hm," I said and drank some more.

"Well, tell me all about him." She sat up and drank her beer. "I want to know everything."

"He's a doctor," I said. "Name's Paul Whittingham."

She was impressed by that. "What's his specialty?"

"Pediatrics."

"Nice." She said. "You think you'll marry him?"

I shook my head. "I don't think so."

"Why not?"

"I'm not finished with school yet. I'm working on my masters in psychology."

"Well, you'll make quite a team."

Herbert came back. Sylvie looked around the bar and said, "My god, this place is shit. I'd forgotten how putrid this little town is."

When Sylvie was locking lips with the Pervert, I figured that was my cue to leave. The last thing I wanted to do was sleep with him again, and certainly not for her viewing pleasure. So, I slipped off my stool and staggered to the door. When the hot, damp Florida night air hit me, combined with the muted sounds of the outdoors, I shivered a bit and decided to take a walk to the end of the plaza and back until my ears stopped ringing. I didn't mind driving drunk, but I'd at least like to hear the sirens when they pulled me over—not that they ever did.

When I hit the end of the plaza, I wandered around back and stood staring at the railroad tracks—raised up just a bit past a shallow ditch. I figured I might as well have a look. The fence was damaged in one spot, and yellow police tape was strewn all about; I climbed over the downed chain-links and up the small hill onto the tracks. I sat in the middle, on the ties and little white rocks, and stared down the rails north—out of town. Roads up that way led away from Sandy Point; I could take any of them and never come back, but I didn't know where they'd end up, and I suppose that's what kept me where I was.

I couldn't make out a blood stain and I thought for a few seconds of walking the tracks looking for the spot Bryan Cleaver got hit, but instead, I lay down and dropped my head over the rail. It was an awkward position. How drunk would Bryan have had to be to pass out like that? Unless he did it on purpose. It would be easier than jumping off Three River Terrace. Up on the roof, you actually had to do it. You had to take that step off the edge. You could stand there all day and not be able to do it. But on the tracks, all you had to do was lie still and let the train do it for you.

I closed my eyes and thought I heard the ding ding of the crossing at the intersection down the road. The rail beneath my head vibrated and the wind picked up in the trees overhead. A train thundered in the distance, the horn blasting–a person couldn't just lie there. How wasted would you have to be to not hear it, not feel it, until you were headless toast? There was no way Bryan did it on purpose.

I passed out at that party in Beacon Hills–the one that Sylvie got all pissed about. I drank all kinds of stuff and smoked whatever was handed to me. I wandered around this enormous house, looking for the kids I'd come with, Lee Harper and his best friend Roger and his girlfriend Sammy. The truth is, I broke up with Lee Harper after the party. I didn't tell anyone about it for weeks. But it didn't matter. By that time, my friendship with Sylvie and Bond was over. My life was over. I didn't break up with him so much as he never called me again.

I remember walking out the front door into the dark;

people were shadows, carrying drinks, talking, watching me; I couldn't make them out except in silhouette. I stumbled across the lawn and fell onto the thick, cold grass. It was soft and soothing and I thought I might stay there. The next thing I knew someone was carrying me to the curb and laying me on the roof of a car.

"Am I going to die?"

"No," he said. "You passed out."

Like it was nothing. Just passed out. Happens all the time around here. I lay on the car for a long time thinking about how I was going to die and all those people from Beacon Hills weren't paying any attention. It would be down to the guy who owned the car I was on, to find my body and alert someone. I could only hope he wasn't blamed. That worried me, so I managed to slide off to standing, resting my head against the person next to me. At some point, that person put his arm around my shoulders and led me away. He put me in the backseat of a car, drove somewhere, got in the back with me and proceeded to undress my bottom half and have sex with it.

I was drunk as all get out, and here was this guy fucking my lifeless body. I would have laughed if I could have. That was the epitome of ridiculous. It should be the end, I decided. And how wonderful to die right there while this creep from Beacon Hills High was getting off. He'd have to find some way to dispose of my body, and he'd take it on the lam, but end up behind bars anyway, if not for killing me, which I could only hope, then for defiling a dead body—my dead body, which he was defiling at that very moment. How cool would that be?

What a way to screw up your life. So, I held my breath. I seriously believed I could just hold my breath and die. I held it and held it, until he thought I'd died, I guess, because he stopped his humping and put his head to my chest to see if I was still alive; and then I breathed again. It's pretty hard to just stop breathing. I was laughing like mad in my head. I did it again and again and every god-damned time the idiot stopped and checked for a heartbeat. But it didn't deter him. Finally, a light laugh escaped me and I asked him what his name was.

"Ron Brigham," he said, still huffing and puffing, having a hard time with it, apparently.

I knew damn well he wasn't Ron Brigham. Ron Brigham was the football coach at Sandy Point High. What a perfect little ass this creepy fucker was. I felt sorry for him; I really did. The best he could get at a bat-shit-crazy party in Beacon Hills was the drunken lifeless girl who'd passed out. You had to feel sorry for someone like that.

I don't think he ever managed to get off, but he took me back and left me standing against the same car from which he'd taken his prize. Everybody looked like cardboard ghosts in the moonlight. Ghosts of Beacon High students that I didn't know. Nobody said anything to the guy; nobody blinked. It was nice of him to bring me back and not murder me and bury my body in the woods somewhere.

At that point, lying with my head tilted back over the train rail and my eyes closed, I thought of Camelia and sat straight up like I'd been stuck with a pin. I crawled off the railroad tracks and made my way back to the parking lot in front of the Pool Pit. Bryan would have had to be out, dead cold, to let a train take his head like that. Maybe he *was* dead—before it got to him. And I knew him then—a kindred spirit. One of the struggling weary just waiting for a train to come along and do the dirty work for us.

# 22.

*Dear Camelia, Last night I lay down on the railroad tracks and thought of a train. I was perfectly still, my head back, eyes closed. And I remembered that you were always sleeping. I can't figure out how I remember things I never knew, but there it is. I thought about it for a long time and I think maybe you're sleeping because I want to sleep. But for some reason I got off the tracks.*

That wasn't the letter I read to Dr. Crazy on Monday afternoon. The one I read to Dr. Crazy said something like this: "Dear Camelia. I always think of you with your eyes closed like you're sleeping." And Dr. Crazy rambled on in some psychobabble about Camelia representing my childhood, or me as a child, and the child was asleep. Stuff like that.

I think, sometimes I imagined Camelia with short, blonde hair and a dainty, pointed nose and a sharp chin because she's me as I would *like* to be. But then her name should be Summer. And when I imagined that little girl, she moved and danced, she was on the beach. And it turned out I'd imagined someone real, like Sylvie Bennett or Claire Lindsay and I was thrown back to the start, trying to imagine Camelia. I wanted Camelia to be the way *I* wanted to be. That's what Dr. Crazy said. She said Camelia was the essence of my hopes, or something like that. But that's ridiculous, because let's face it, I'm a round sort of person. My nose is never going to be dainty. And I don't even like short hair. I had short hair once. And hated it. It made no sense to hope for impossible things or things I didn't really want.

And why was she sleeping when I pictured her? Because my inner child is dormant, or it's my unconscious self, or because...therapy was like *Choose Your Own Adventure* books. I could say anything and go anywhere with it. Dr. Crazy would tell me that's the process. Where you go with it is where you should go with it, and you'll find your answers in seeking them. I really should have considered going back to school and becoming a Dr. Crazy.

I spent the better part of three years wondering who the fake Ron Brigham was. I might have talked to him at a party or a bar and not even known it. What a turd. I liked to think maybe he felt some guilt, but chances were, he didn't think he'd done anything gross at all. People are evil like that.

Hannah was royally pissed off that China let me take lunch at lunchtime on Sunday. Five people worked that day, she said, and the new girl doesn't get lunch at lunchtime. She ranted for a good ten minutes in the hallway next to the time clock until China opened the door to the back room. At that point she stormed off and China told me I'd be working stock that day. I enjoyed stock. It was like Christmas. There were several huge tables in the back room and the guys, who were stronger than me, put boxes on them. I opened them up, took everything out and priced it, then put it on carts for the stockers to shelve. It was fun, mostly because I got to listen to the radio and have a drink with me. China liked to work stock too, because she was usually in there with whoever was doing it. She was a little weird–a little too familiar, if you know what I mean.

Once when I was working my register at the mall entrance, Hannah went storming past me, crying. I didn't find out until later that China made her take afternoon lunch again and so she'd missed seeing her niece perform in the talent show down in the middle of the mall at the main entrance. I guess she'd promised to be there. Hannah was always pissed off at China.

After I'd been working at Pinkerton's for about three months, I took my break at the Orange Julius and Alice from the bookstore sat down in my booth. I'd seen her from time to time and she'd smile at me–I always imagined her trying to figure out where she knew me from. But apparently, she remembered me just fine.

"How are you liking the drug store?" She said.

I shrugged. I wasn't going to tell her I loved it, right? I mean, I'd still rather work at the bookstore. And I couldn't tell her how much I liked the free food, because it wasn't really free. I don't think it's a good idea to tell the person you want to work for that you're really enjoying stealing from your employer. It's funny, really. When I started taking the packets of peanuts, macadamia nuts, and candy, I was just starving. I couldn't wait until break time. I told myself I'd pay for it all. But then I realized I couldn't admit I'd already eaten the stuff and wanted to pay. I might as well confess to stealing. I'd have to purchase new ones and then sneakily put them back on the shelves. I could get caught doing that. What is that, like, reverse shoplifting? I didn't want to risk it.

"It's okay," I said.

"I might have an opening soon."

My eyes lit up, I knew, and I tried to act nonchalant, not too eager, not drooling.

"Are you still interested?"

"Books are my passion." I turned beet red and she laughed, but I think she liked it, and didn't think I was a complete nerd at all.

When I got back to the drug store, there was another fight. Hannah was threatening to quit and China said just do it then. Apparently, China found out about Hannah's radio earphones and confiscated them.

"That bitch stole my stuff," she said. "She can't do that. This isn't high school." She was standing at the far end of my register counter, acting like she was ready to take off her blue cosmetics coat and walk out.

"Maybe she'll give it back when your shift is done."

"I've had it," she said. "She'll pay for this."

"What are you going to do?"

"I'm going to report her."

"For what?"

"Come on," she said. "You know what."

And I guess I did know what. When the investigator from the home office came to the duplex to interview me, I was torn. I mean, sure, China did some inappropriate

258

things. But Hannah was only getting revenge for being disciplined. And I told the old man that when he was sitting on the couch in my mother's living room.

"Pinkerton's Family Drug," he said, "does not condone sexual harassment, no matter the reason for its being reported."

He was a very formal sort of man. He told me to tell him of any instances in which China made me feel uncomfortable. Any at all, he said. He would determine if they were relevant or not. So I told him.

I told him that it always happened in the back room, when I was pricing stock. On the floor, China was a typical boss. She treated me like garbage and useful only to get work done. But in the back room, we were friends. She'd tell jokes and laugh at my stories about going out to the bars and meeting jerks. She'd give me advice on men, and order lunch in and pay for it herself. It's stupid, really, but I didn't realize she was like that with all of us. I thought I was special. But it did puzzle me when she'd look right past me on the floor or yell at me if I did something wrong–like that time I gave a man change for a ten instead of a twenty–as if she didn't like me at all. But back in the stock room, we were friends again.

"There was this one time," I said. "We were working in the stock room and I told her I needed to use the restroom. She said I could, if I gave her a kiss first. I laughed. She was only joking."

"We at Pinkerton's Family Drug do not condone that sort of joking, Miss MacMillan."

Well, sure, I guess. And I reiterated that this was all happening because Hannah got into trouble–we don't condone blah blah. I suppose I had to see his point.

And then there was the other time. I wasn't sure I could tell the old man about it. I mean, it would be like talking dirty to my grandfather. But I did. I said, "And then there was the time that I was telling her about a problem I had with men. I'm not fond of them, you might say. And I guess that made her think, maybe, I don't know. She said have you ever been with a woman, and I said no. I said I had no more interest in women than I did in men. And she laughed. And then she said, once you've been with a woman, you'll never go back to men."

And I sat staring at the old man as he wrote notes in his book. He didn't flinch. Didn't blush. Didn't smirk or anything. He must have heard it all. And then I could see it. Pinkerton's Family Drug was a mosh pit of orgiastic sexual and criminal elements and this poor man had the job of documenting it all.

China was sent to another store in some podunk Georgia town with a reprimand and a warning. Hannah was radiant for several days and though she wasn't allowed to discuss it, she knew that I, at least, knew it was all her doing. She was the one to take down the witch. The Friday after China's last day at the store, we went out. I drove because Hannah said my little Datsun was the cutest things she'd ever seen, much better for partying than her monster Chevy. I think she was just upset, because she got drunk at The Sandbar and started crying.

"Would you do me a favor and drive me somewhere?"

Of course, I said, and I drove her into the neighborhood back behind the house I grew up in, back when we were a family. I was all sentimental and basking in reverie about my poor childhood–remembering the nights all the neighborhood kids hung out under streetlight and played jailbreak–when she had me pull up at this particular little house with jalousie windows and a carport instead of a garage.

"Wait for me," she said. "I'll be right back."

I watched her walk up the drive and up to the tiny front porch, standing in the glow of the little porch light. She knocked on the door and what the hell but China was standing there. She came outside and they were arguing. Hannah turned back to the car, but China reached out for her, grabbed her, and before I knew what the hell was going on they were kissing like mad.

Holy shit. Hannah gave her notice and left Pinkerton's a week later and the rumor was that she'd gone to Georgia to be with China. You never really know about people. I got a call from Alice at the bookstore and quit without notice to start the next day. Working there was going to change my life–I just knew it.

# 23.

*Dear Camelia, There are times when the darkness overcomes me and I can't breathe; I claw and scratch at the world, trying to tear a hole and scream; someone will hear me—find me. But the world isn't changed and nobody knows I'm here and there is only darkness.*

I'm a bad person. Some things you just know. I have to wonder at my mother, for expecting so much of me. I was never good. Why was I supposed to suddenly become good when I learned to drive a car and go to bars? Suddenly I'm supposed to follow the rules, be in on time, not come home drunk or stoned, and certainly not stay out all night. Parents are stupid like that. They spend your childhood screaming at you to clean your room and do the dishes and walk the fucking dog and stop puking on the carpet and you never listen. They tell you again and again that you're no good and yet, boom, you graduate high school and suddenly they expect a responsible adult will poof into existence inside your body. And they're so disappointed until boom, you get a job or go to college and there they are, looking at you like you're grown up and this time it's for real. But it's not. It never is. Because you're just no good.

My mother stood in her tiny kitchen on Willow Branch Road with her hand on her hips smirking at me. "So, you're going to act responsible now?" Working at the bookstore was equal to adult for her. Only good people, reliable people, are allowed to work there.

The bookstore was like heaven. If heaven is muted and dusty and always at the outer edge of organized. We booksellers, as we were called, spent most of our time cleaning up and rearranging after customers. The register process was just to hurry them out the door so we could get back to cleaning up after them. But it was a glorious clean up. Books everywhere. There was no more joyous task than reordering all the books in a section by author. Especially true crime. True crime readers were the most disorderly and least respectful of all, if you don't count the masturbators. Maybe true crime readers were criminals at heart.

When my father left us, he moved out of the house discreetly. I didn't even know he'd gone, really, until a week or so later when he called me and asked to meet me at the dime store in the mall. I sat in a booth, in that dumpy restaurant, watching people walk past and hoping nobody would notice me. There's just something not right about sitting across from your father while he tells you he never loved your mother—it was really that he took out his wallet, pulled a fifty from it, laid it on the table in front of him and slid it across to me...like he was offering me a bribe or something. I took it. Then he went off on some rant about how, when you think about it, there has to be a god. And if you think about it some more, you'll realize that there can only be one. Logical thinking wasn't a strong suit in the MacMillan clan. This was the same guy, after all, who made a pyramid out of popsicle sticks and wore it like a hat as a talisman to ward off ill-health and disharmony. Now I was supposed to believe he'd found God–the one and only.

Gods and universes; I couldn't tell the difference. Both aloof–and really, really big. Some scientists think there are multiple universes and, given infinity and all, there are multiple Aprils. So, maybe I jumped off the roof of Three River Terrace. And maybe the fake Ron Brigham murdered me and dumped my body in the woods. And maybe a train came along and sliced off my head. In those other universes. There's a fatalism to it–it's not enough to end your life in one universe. You've got to keep doing it through infinite universes and it'll never work. You're like a hydra–you cut off one life and two more go on living. Maybe you finally get to a place where you just give up and live already. Maybe I was at that place.

That first Sunday, I celebrated my new respectable job as a bookseller by stopping off at one of my usual stores and picking up a six-pack of talls. I drank four of them–my mother taking two and hiding them from me in her room. But it didn't matter. By ten that night I was ready to go out. I got all dolled up with my big hair and plastered-on face and leggings and one of those really long, oversized button-up shirts with the shoulder pads. I stomped my high heels up to the door of Spike's Pub, and a few girls coming up the walk let me know just how stupid I looked.

"Oh my god," one of them said. And they laughed. They were wearing jeans and t-shirts. Always a wise choice.

I sat at the bar and let guys buy me drinks until closing, and then drove up past the county line to Harold's to get more drunk. The next morning I woke at eleven and had to be at work by twelve-thirty for my first full shift. Nobody noticed that I was hung over. Shit, I was probably still drunk. The assistant manager, William, was working that day. He didn't like me; I could tell. William was one of those people who was mature and let everyone know it. Two old women worked at the bookstore too, Barbara and Elaine, and William acted like he was older than they were, even though he was younger than us all.

That afternoon, I trained on the register some more, with Alice, and this guy came through the doorway, walked right up to us, looked at me and said, "Hi."

"Hi," I said. I'm nice like that.

"How are you?" He said.

"Fine."

Then he said, "You don't remember me, do you?"

And I'm thinking, what kind of come-on line is that? "Sure I do."

Because by that time I started to think maybe I'd met him somewhere before. Probably when I was drunk. Why do people think you'll remember them? You're in a bar. You're plastered. You're probably laughing way too loud at their stupid jokes. You dance with them and let them kiss you, and maybe they even take you home, or to their cars and have sex with you. But why do they think you'd remember them?

"Last night," he said.

I balked. But I was standing next to my brand new boss and mother-slash-sister figure, so I smiled at him and nodded slightly in Alice's direction, trying to give him the don't-let-my-boss-know-I-pick-up-strange-guys-at-bars look. He didn't catch on. Naturally the sorts of guys I would pick up in bars would be the types who think I'll remember them the next morning and want them to come visit me at work. Rude beyond belief.

"Oh, sure," I said. "I remember you."

He looked at Alice and back to me, then turned around and walked out. I was pretty pissed off. I mean, he was really cute. Why would he do that to me? You don't just show up at a girl's place of business after you've spent the night with her in a bar. What was he thinking?

"Who was that?" Alice asked me.

"I have no idea."

She laughed and I laughed with her, pretending it was all a big joke and I was so popular that guys followed me around acting like they knew me. That night I got off work at ten and headed back to Spike's Pub until two and then back over to Harold's. And there he was. Cute little prick sitting at the bar. And what do you know? I remembered everything.

"Now I remember you," I said with a laugh. And I did think it was funny. No clue when I was semi-sober. But drunk, it all came back. And I remembered bragging about how I worked at the bookstore in the mall and telling him he should come and visit me there. It made me wonder which was real and which was delusion. Like dreams. Some people actually think that the dream world is the real world and this world is a dream. They only think that because this world is shit and dreaming is better. I guess. I imagine they must be the kind of people who dream about flying, and cake, and bliss. I dream about clowns and needles and running toward people I don't know screaming. Still, I think I'd take dreaming. I'd take sleep. Death would be even better. No dreams at all.

"Thanks," he said and slid off the bar stool, never to speak to me again.

Right. Like he's got morals. He's sitting in a bar at three in the morning picking up plastered girls and thinking he's going to have a real relationship. Please.

The first week at the bookstore flew by and I was pretty sure I impressed Alice with my ability to learn the title and author of nearly every book we stocked while still drunk or hung over. Who wouldn't be impressed? Friday night was Halloween. I was in the back of the store, in the automotive section, searching for semen-saturated girlie magazines when I realized someone was standing in the aisle staring at me. I nearly jumped out of my skin.

"Paulie," I said. "You scared the shit out of me. What the hell are you doing here?"

He smiled that weird kid smile of his, like he was in trouble but he didn't care. "I came to see you."

"How did you know I worked here?"

"I got sources."

"What kind of sources?"

"I know people, that's all. And people know you."

I didn't believe him, of course. "Well, what do you want?"

"You don't have to be mean about it."

"I'm not being mean. I'm working."

"So when do you get a break?"

"I've already had my break. Paulie, what do you want?"

"Sue's dead." He was still smiling. Like he'd brought good news.

"Stop joking with me; I'm busy."

"I'm not joking. The obit was in the paper this morning. Funeral's tomorrow." He dug a crumpled clipping of news print from his front pocket and gave it to me. It was damp and warm. "See for yourself."

Sure enough. There was a picture of the anorexic in the obit section. Sue Munns Tipford, thirty-one, was dead. "Holy shit." I looked up at him.

"I know," he said. "She did it."

"Are you sure?" I read the obit a couple of times with him peering over my shoulder. "It doesn't say what happened. It could have been a car crash or something."

He laughed loud and I shushed him.

"No. She did it," he said. "Slashed her wrists. That's what I heard."

"Where did you hear that?"

"I have my sources."

Maybe Paulie was a ninja addict, or a psychic. Whatever it was, this time I believed him. And anyway, what were the chances that an undiagnosed anorexic who'd already tried to slash her wrists at least once, had died in a car wreck?

"So, you want to come with me to the funeral?"

"What? You mean like a date? A date to a funeral?"

"You said date, not me."

I shook my head. "You're going to the funeral?"

"Well, yeah. Aren't you?"

"I don't know. Why?"

"We all spent, what...three days together at Lakeview Psychiatric. That practically makes us family."

"I don't think I'd feel right. I wasn't invited."

"You don't get invited to a funeral. It's an open event. That's why they put the information in the paper."

"Maybe."

"Well, here," he pulled another slip of paper out of his other pocket. "My number. If you decide to go, call me. I can come get you, or I'll just see you there."

I shrugged.

"So, what's up? You want to go out with me tonight? Since I'm up this way I thought I'd check out your fine drinking establishments–see what's new."

"When did you get out of Lakeview?"

"A couple of months ago, why?"

"And you're drinking already?"

"How long before you started up again?"

"What makes you so sure I have?"

He smiled a goofy kid smile and I had to laugh.

"What does Lakeview have to do with alcohol, anyway?" He said. "And I'm not the one who got drunk and tried to jump off a building."

"I didn't try to jump."

"Right. And I didn't shoot up to kill myself. So, you want to go out or what?"

He was probably right. We were just victims of circumstance. Killing ourselves didn't have anything to do with drinking or heroin. I heard Alice cough. I thought that was nice of her. That's what polite people do. They don't just barge in on your conversation and tell you to get back to work. That was Mr. Toby's style. You could be in the utility closet with someone and he'd know full well you were in the middle of something, but he'd pull the door open and start yelling.

"You have to leave now." I told Paulie.

"So, what about it?"

"No."

"Aw, come on. Why not?"

"It's not a good idea for two drunks to go out together. Trust me. I know."

"But you're the drunk, not me."

I pushed him forward, toward the front of the store shushing him and telling him he had to go. It was all a big joke to Paulie and sure I was laughing too, but I didn't want to get fired. Alice was back at the register by the time we passed it and Paulie had the nerve to wave good-bye to her.

"One down," Paulie said, smiling at me. "Who's next?" And then his happy kid face disappeared into the mall.

Alice raised an eyebrow at me but didn't say anything so I got myself back to work. We switched off later and I was up at the register while she tackled some returns. A lady wearing a scarf over her head and wrapped around her neck, and sunglasses, came to the counter. I stared at her a little too long but I couldn't help it. I was sure the sun had gone down by then and anyway, we were inside. Who wears sunglasses indoors? She looked bruised.

"You have a book for me," she whispered, her voice hoarse and crisp. "Dougherty."

I was glad I could turn my back to her while I bent to find her name among the books we'd ordered in. It had to be her–the elusive Mrs. Dougherty from Hope House. I found her book, pulled the order form and rubber band from it and rang it up. It was *The Burning Bed*. I didn't even know it had been a book before it was a movie.

When I took Mrs. Dougherty's money, I tried to smile a bit, but as far as I could tell she wasn't looking at my face. She was thin, and pale, except for the bruises, and her lips were set rigid and un-glossed. I put the book in a plastic bag and handed it to her. She didn't say thank you–just turned and left. Have you ever wanted to do something, but you knew it wouldn't make any difference?

An hour later, when it was time to close and lock the front door, Alice stood at the register ready to close it out and asked me, "Are you going to have different guys come in a lot?"

"Well, it's the mall," I said. "What can you do?"

I went in early the next morning and Alice freaked out right away because I was wearing a black dress and black shoes and black stockings.

"What is this, a funeral?"

"Actually," I said. "I was hoping you'd let me leave early and go to one over on Merritt Island. I'll come back and work this evening, to make up for it. And I'll work right through lunch."

She said I could go. It was the black outfit. I was already dressed and ready, right? What was she going to do? I got more respect that day than earlier in the week. I think people thought I was the boss instead of Alice. I remembered that book in the business section: *Dress for Success* by Molloy. That's when I really understood what those girls were laughing about. When I was all decked out in my shirt dress with the shoulder pads and my hair teased up high. It's not what I was wearing, but where I was wearing it. You have to dress the part wherever you are. Which totally explains crazy people taking off their clothes, don't you think?

Alice insisted that I take lunch. There's some kind of stupid law or something, so there I was standing in line at the Orange Julius waiting to order a chili, cheese, and onions in my funeral dress. This was not success, really. But it did attract attention and Bond was walking past when he saw me. At least, that's the story he gave me. Just happened to be at the mall this weekend. But it was Sandy Point, after all. It's not like there was anywhere else to go. He paid for my lunch and we sat together in a booth. He leaned back, locked his elbows around the back of his bench and smiled.

"So," he said. "Are you going to explain the black?"

"I'm going to a funeral later."

He laughed. "You don't have to be so happy about it."

"I'm not really. But...I'm not sad either."

It was more of a relief. Sue's tension left my body just as I realized I'd been keeping it for her. From the first moment I laid eyes on her, I knew she was killing herself.

273

Reveling in it. Taking her own damn time about it–she wanted it that way. Death was sacrosanct, a pleasure, foreplay to nonexistence. Why shouldn't it be enjoyed? And I was relieved for her that it was finally over, because, let's face it, I never found foreplay something I wanted to last very long. I'm more of a results kind of girl. It's not the journey at all. It *is* the destination. And don't let anyone tell you different.

Naturally, Bond decided he was going to go home, deck himself out in black, and take me. And I let him. I let him because I didn't want to drive to Merritt Island, try to find a cemetery I'd never heard of with an unfamiliar address, walk into a group of people I didn't know, have to act like Paulie was with me, and try to cry, all alone. All those things would be so much easier if Bond was there.

The ceremony at the grave was held under a tent; its edges flapped in the hot breeze. Sue would have liked the comfortable, folding chairs–lots of padding. But then, she was bony, so, of course. Paulie was pissed off that I wasn't alone and, after giving me a dirty look, ignored me. But I was glad. He was wearing his jeans, frayed at the hems, and a t-shirt with a big stain on it that looked like a penis. Maybe Dr. Crazy would say that I'd see penises in a Rorschach, so who knows?

Sue's coffin hovered over a hole in the ground. Her husband was crying in the front row, with an older woman draped across his right side, her left hand rubbing and patting his back. Two children, maybe six and eight, perched in seats on his left. They stared straight ahead, at the coffin, like little ventriloquist dummies, like someone told them to sit still and stay quiet. Or maybe someone punched the air out of them and they couldn't breathe.

A woman behind me sobbed and muttered, "How could she?" Over and over again. "Poor children," she said.

I suppose that's when I first thought Sue was really sick. It didn't occur to me before that she wasn't in her right mind. She wasn't thinking straight. Then again, maybe she was just a sanctimonious, self-centered, vengeful witch who got the final word in her marriage. Suicide is the ultimate final word. Maybe living without her would be the best thing that ever happened to those kids. I don't know. Kind of takes the joy out of suicide, when you think about it.

I used to lie awake at night and cry and cry. I don't remember what I was crying about. I loved it when I'd cry myself to sleep and wake up with my eyelids stuck together with puss-caked, crusty tears. You can't make that happen, I've tried. It has to *just happen*. But as you get older and older, you stop enjoying crying yourself to sleep. You feel silly; and it gives you headaches. That's when you discover alcohol, or drugs, or sex, or food, or whatever it is you need to get your mind off the absolute horror of living. Anyway, I'd lie there crying and imagining I was sick with cancer and dying. My parents would come in and sit by my hospital bed and they'd cry too. And I was so glad to finally be getting my revenge for them not loving me. Wouldn't they be sorry? It makes sense when you're ten.

But the truth is, I'd only be leaving them with guilt, over being ever so slightly–though they could never admit it, especially to themselves—*glad* that I was dead. Would that make it worth the dying? Hard to say, really. Not that I would care; I'd be dead and wouldn't have to deal with it anymore.

When the priest said something very Catholic, like ashes to ashes and dust to dust, which I personally found comforting and poetic, almost like an invitation, Bond reached over and put his hot, clammy, left hand on top of my right hand. It's okay, I thought. The funeral's almost over. But it went on. And on. And my hand under his grew hotter and hotter and damper and damper until it started to burn. I ran a dialogue in my head—telling myself it would be over soon and he'd lift his hand and it would be okay. There wouldn't be burn marks. It was my imagination. I folded my fingers in under my palm, trying to get him to move his hand away, but he must have mistook that for emotion and squeezed my hand tighter. He held it that way, grasping, for several seconds that felt like minutes and then let up slightly. I don't know why I didn't move my hand. Lift your damn hand, I kept telling myself. Just pick it up and do something with it. Scratch something. Smooth out your hair. Something. Why was I sitting there letting him give my hand contact blisters? Because I'd have them. They were breaking out quickly, some spots burning hotter than others. If he didn't move his hand from mine soon, I'd have bed sores. On my hand. How stupid would that be? Move your god-damned hand Bondurant. *Get your fucking hand off me.*

Finally, the service was over and Bond lifted his hand off mine to stand up. I sat dazed, wondering what I'd missed, trying to stop my chest from pulsating with erratic breaths. I looked down at my hand and it was inflamed. I turned it over–my palm was red and clammy as well, having been forced to press itself against the polyester of my black skirt for what felt like an eternity. What if death is not nonexistence? What if it's nothing more than an eternal rotting of your body while you consciously experience it?

"Are you okay?" Bond said, taking my elbow and helping me to stand.

"Fine," I said. Sure, fine. I'd just had the ultimate revelation about the origins of religion. How could anybody be fine after that?

# 24.

I had a great, great uncle who stepped on a piece of glass and he died. I've seen movies where glass ceilings collapse on people and they keep fighting the bad guys. And I've seen movies where bad guys are thrown through glass doors, and they get up, brush the glass of them and go about their criminal escapades. But my great uncle stepped on a sliver of glass in his kitchen and died.

He didn't die instantly, of course. The glass was embedded in his big toe and it got infected and left untreated, he ended up with an infection in his heart and his brain and he died. Nobody in the family knows if this story is true. Why should they care? It's a great story that gives them profound morals to live by. Little things can mean a lot, they say. Pay attention to minor irritations before they lay you flat. The moral I get from the story is to never walk around the house barefoot. Still, I took off my high heels as soon as I got back to work. Bond walked me into the bookstore and met Alice. She gave me a look before she said hello to him. A look that said, another one? I told her I was popular, what more did she want?

I worked a few more hours and Alice let me leave at nine, before they closed. I decided to hell with the hose, and once in the back room to sign out, I took them off. I had to have the shoes on to walk in the mall, but as soon as I got out, against my better judgment mind you, I took them off again and walked across the parking lot, glass bits and all, to my car. The moral of this story is, keep your eyes off the ground when walking in a parking lot at night. Not that I could have done anything about it if I'd seen Paulie there earlier. He was leaning against my car, his arms folded across his chest, smiling at me.

"What are you doing here?" I said.

"Who was that guy you were with?"

"How do you know my car?"

"Was he your brother?"

"My boyfriend."

"You didn't tell me you had a boyfriend."

I stood for a few seconds gaping at him. I'd never met anyone so infuriating–like a child who won't shut up. He was smiling at me, not in a sinister way, but like he needed me to parent him. "Paulie," I said, preparing the tough love. "You're some guy I met in the loony bin a few months ago. You're not the person I call when I start dating someone new."

He frowned, but there was still a grin at the edges; I'm not sure Paulie was ever completely without a smile somewhere in his face. "You should have told me when I asked you to the funeral," he said.

"So you thought it was a date? That's creepy."

"It wasn't a date. I was asking as a friend."

"Then I didn't need to tell you about my boyfriend."

"Well, you should have told me anyway."

"Why are you here?"

He shrugged. "I thought we could go out."

"I can't go out. I have a boyfriend."

"You can't go out with a friend?"

"That's right. He's very jealous."

"If he cares so much, where is he?"

"I'm going to meet him right now."

I moved toward him, with my keys out. But he just stood there. "I need to get in my car," I said.

"We just lost Sue. Don't you want to be around someone who understands?"

"She wasn't our friend, Paulie. We barely knew her. She was a sick anorexic who managed to kill herself. I don't need to commiserate with anyone about it."

"Like you're not trying to kill yourself."

I took a step back and glared at him.

"We were both at Lakeview," he said.

"I was just drunk."

"Just drunk. Trying to jump off a building."

I became very aware, at that point, of Three River Terrace watching me from across US1. I forced myself not to look at it, not to let Paulie know more than he should. "I wasn't going to jump. I don't have to talk to you about this; you're not my therapist."

"You have a therapist?"

"Please let me get in my car."

He stood for some time, staring at me. I stared right back at him and it was weird for a few seconds. Not creepy weird, but reassuring weird.

"Do you think we have an obligation to keep going?" He said. "I mean, for other people?"

I let out a breath—a resigned sort of thing.

"You think," he said. "She should have kept going?"

"I don't know." I turned around and leaned against the car beside him, close enough for our shoulders to touch, and it was like we were bonded, and I said, "I really don't know."

"Do you think we owe it to our parents?"

"No."

"Then why anyone else?"

"I said I don't know. Maybe Sue didn't owe anybody. I don't feel like I should owe anybody."

"But you don't have kids."

"Exactly."

"So, to keep our options open, we should—"

"Never have kids," I said.

"Do you think we owe it to, I don't know...the universe or something?"

"Now you're just being silly."

"No, I mean it. What if there's some kind of universal being and we're just part of it, like ants are part of a colony. A single ant, it's nothing by itself. But it helps keep the colony going. The colony is really just made up of individual ants."

"Come to the point, please."

"Maybe the universe exists as us. And we're killing it by killing us."

I stood up and turned to him. "People die every day. What difference does it make to the universe how we go, or when?"

He looked this way and that, all around the parking lot and finally back to me. "None," he said.

"Sue told me something about being lost," I said. "It's making more sense, the more I think about it. She said once you let yourself get lost, there's only a certain amount of time for someone to save you, before it's too late."

"So it was too late for her. Nothing anybody could do. You think that's what she was saying?"

I nodded.

"You think that's true? There's a window of opportunity and once it closes, there's nothing we can do to be found?"

"Maybe."

"And it's too late."

We stood there, looking around at the people leaving the mall. A cool, damp, salty breeze rushed across the parking lot from the lagoon and sea gulls crisscrossed the sky overhead in the dark. There was something surreal about the air. It carried an omen. And Three River Terrace was across the street, waiting for both of us. Finally, he pushed himself off my car and started to walk away.

"I'll come by again some other time," he said.

"I have your number. I'll call you if I need you."

He didn't answer. Just shoved his hands in his pants pockets, looked at the ground, and walked off toward the cafeteria at the corner of the mall parking lot.

"Where is your car?" I said.

"None of your business," he called without turning back.

I could see having to deal with this if you meet some jerk in a bar. When you meet them in bars, and flirt with them, or have sex with them, they think they have permission to come visit you and see what else they can get from you. But I met Paulie in a loony bin. Where did he get off thinking we were friends?

*Dear Camelia, I just now realized that you're still a little girl. I grew up and you didn't. Is that the way it is with invisible friends? Dr. Crazy would say that you represent the child in me. That something happened to me when I was eight that stopped me from growing and the part of me that stopped is represented in you. Why can't an invisible friend just be an invisible friend? And why are you sleeping?*

# 25.

On Thanksgiving, Sausage drove me, our mother, our aunt Aubrey, and his new girl-friend Patricia, to Orlando–to our grand-mother's house. As soon as I met Patricia, I knew I'd call her Patty. She held out her hand and repeated her name, Patricia, as if to ward off the Patty right away. I decided that if they got married, they'd be Sausage Patty. And any children that happened along would be Links. I liked to imagine that, one day, I'd find someone to let in on my joke. Maybe one of their kidlings would have a good nature. They probably would, as a defense mechanism against their mother who was clearly a younger version of mine. Women marry their fathers, so they say. So, men must marry their mothers.

Sausage Patty were up front. Sausage was telling another story–one that would run into a second and a third and before we knew what he'd said we'd be there. My mother and I were in back, with Aunt Aubrey in the middle. My mother always insisted that she had to sit by the window. Said she'd get nauseated. And Aunt Aubrey then insisted that I also have a window seat. My mother thought Aunt Aubrey was just trying to be nicer than everyone else. Nobody ought to do that; it just makes the rest of us look bad. I thought it was so she could choose which one of us to vomit on if she got car sick.

My grandmother lived in a ritzy neighborhood over in Winter Park. I always liked the name of the place, but it's really stupid, when you think about it. It's in the middle of Florida. Do you have any idea how close to the equator we are? There's no winter park here. There's not even an autumn park. It's summer all year long. But in her neighborhood they hired lawn companies to tend to the grass to make it green and lush and so deep you sunk down to your ankles when you walked on it. Her yard had so much shade it made you want to sit outside and eat under the trees. Crazy.

The house was full of cousins who all looked like Sausage. Square faces, browns and deeper browns in curly, thick, luscious hair. Tans. And wide-mouthed smiles with straight teeth—two really big ones in the front that would only look bad if they weren't otherwise perfect—the mouths of singers and cheerleaders. Lean bodies and almond curved eyes. I was odd man out. I was my father who was no longer representing himself at these affairs. Probably the real reason he left us—he didn't sign up for that. Could I blame him?

If I looked like anyone, it was Grace's boyfriend, The Pudge. Grace being my grandmother, who wasn't really Grace and everyone knew it. But names stick, when you start young. The only people who ever called her Gert were dead, including our grandfather, Pop Willie, the *I-*

talian, as they called him, so she was free and clear. And I thought sometimes about how long would it take until my parents and my brother and all of my aunts and uncles and cousins were dead and I could finally *be* April.

We were not allowed to call Grace our grandmother. Her children were not allowed to call her Mother. She was Grace. And her boyfriend was Lenny, The Pudge. What a shyster he was. Pale and clammy with an oval egghead and freckled face. Beer gut. Rumor had it Grace wouldn't marry him. And he was happy enough to live off her money without the promise of a future in her will.

There was the moment when everyone stood around looking at each other–our way of greeting, during which we all pretended to like one another. The introduction of Patricia, to one Sausage look-alike after another, broke the awkward hello phase until it was time for her to meet the Grace.

"Another one?" She said, taking Patricia's hand and squeezing it too tight. You could tell because once Grace let go, Patricia couldn't help herself rubbing at it. "You bring us a new one every year." Grace sang more than talked, in a high-pitched, Southern sweet way. And she let out that raucous laugh of hers. There's something bewitching in the Southern manner. Everyone laughed along with her even when it wasn't funny–even when it was sick and twisted.

The Pudge gave Patty a big lecherous hug that the poor girl wouldn't be able to shake off until morning. "Maybe this one will last until Christmas," he said and he and Grace laughed and laughed.

Patricia smiled–something like a sneer. This one, I

thought, will last. Unlike Sausage's other girlfriends, it was clear that Patty thought she was better than Grace. You had to think that if you were going to get past her. You had to be able to look down your nose at her or she'd eat you alive.

Grace was one of those old-fashioned rich people who thought it was just fine to wear clear plastic mules with feathers at the toes around the house when she had guests. She wore silk moo-moos and earrings that tinkled when she moved her head. She'd hired in someone to cook the turkey and dressing while the rest of us were expected to bring along home-cooked sides. Nobody ever said anything about it.

The way I'd heard the story, they complained some years ago and Grace said, fine, I'll cook a turkey and she burned it all to holy hell. Coming up the drive to the house, my mother said, they smelled the bird on fire in the kitchen. And Grace dusted herself with flour and spilled red wine on her apron and carried the bird in, black and smoking, and dumped it in the middle of the big table in the dining room.

"There's your god-damned home-cooked turkey," she'd said.

So now we had cold, pre-cooked, pre-sliced turkey– never enough–on a hard foil platter. I thought for the first seventeen years of my life that was how turkey was done. That's just the way it came. You ate it cold.

"Cranberry sauce is cold," Grace said once. "So naturally the turkey ought to be."

It's funny the things you think are true because you don't know any better.

The cousins ventured off into the fancy living room and talked as if we hadn't seen one another in years. Every holiday we remembered the few previous good times we'd shared. The time we laid out plastic tablecloths all in a row in the back yard under the sprinklers and ran hard and fell onto them to slide and Shirley nearly broke her neck. The time we ran around the neighborhood ringing doorbells and running and how Grace came after us with a switch later in the day. The time we found the dead dog in the road. And the time we moved all the furniture to the walls, partnered up and danced disco until Sausage dropped Cloris trying to lift her over his head.

I sat there for a while listening and wondering how many times a topic could be passed through a group of people before they all came to realize they'd already been over it, thoroughly, several times. I wasn't in the mood to find out, so I got up and wandered through the family room toward the kitchen.

My mother was telling someone, "She's a drunk, that's what." I stopped, and eased myself up a bit, to peek in. She was talking to Grace and my Aunt Keety. "All the time. Every day."

"Well, we all drink every day," Aunt Keety sang and giggled.

"Not like this," Mom said. "Sure you have a drink or two after dinner, but she's sloshed all the time and stays out all night doing god knows what."

"Do you think she has a boyfriend?" Grace said.

"Are you kidding me?" Mom said. "She's a slut. That's what she is. And I told her the first time she brought some stranger home to spend the night, she'd be out on the curb."

My mother was often the super hero of her own imagination. Fighting against the barbarian Eunice and her drunken crimes. Then Keety called us all to eat.

The buffet was spread all over the kitchen and the eating tables, and we formed several chaotic lines filling our plates. Turkey, stuffing, mashed potatoes, sweet potatoes, macaroni and cheese, green bean casserole with those crunchy fried onions on top, corn, peas with little pearl onions, broccoli, Waldorf salad, and something congealed. Finally we all sat. The grownups—my mother who never smiled at these family things; Aunt Aubrey who couldn't stop; Aunt Keety and her husband Uncle Frank, the authoritarians; Uncle Bull, whose name was actually Oxford, another family name, with his wife Aunt Helen, the old hippies; Pudge, the shyster; and Grace— were in the dining room with the good China. We kids were all in our twenties then but were still the children, and were put out of the grand dining room and scattered at kids' tables in other rooms. Sausage would marry first and have kids and then what would happen? It was as if we were frozen in time like that, and none of us would be allowed to reproduce because it would alter the order of things and Grace was for damn sure not going to purchase two turkeys.

Grace called out, "Prayer."

Everyone quieted down; we all bowed our heads and The Pudge said the grace. He was never very good at it and it always took too long, but as I recall no one else wanted to do it. On and on he'd go, about what we all ought to be thankful for. America. The flag. Baby Jesus.

Our freedoms. Our guns, trucks, and two-by-fours. President Reagan, The Gipper. Pat Robertson. Wilkinson, old Pudge's dog. And then he'd rattle on some names of his family and friends that none of us ever knew. Amen. And we started shoveling the food in.

I'd promised myself I would take it easy that year. I was getting fatter. Beer has a way of doing that to you. But there I was with my plate piled high and I looked across the table to my cousin Shirley, and Patricia–the little snots had no mashed potatoes on their plates and the tiniest bits of stuffing. One finger's length of turkey and a mound of broccoli.

"I don't think I can eat all of this," Shirley said in her high-pitched little lilt of a voice.

For Christ's sake, just eat. It won't kill you to eat on a holiday. And that was cue for me to do so. For spite. That's right. I would eat too much for spite.

"Eunice. Eunice dear," Grace called from the dining room. "Tell us all about the psychiatric center."

She was around a corner, in another room, but clear in my mind. One elbow on the table, a dainty, manicured hand near her face, an index finger gently petting her pale, face-lift-taut cheek, she was snickering at Aunt Aubrey, maybe tossing my mother one of those you-poor-dear smirks.

I froze. Naturally. Everybody at my table stared at me. My cousin Winnie laughed and nearly spit out her potatoes. "It was great," I said as loud as I could manage. "Lots of fun."

"You tried to jump off a building?" She said.

"How high?" Pudge asked.

Giggling erupted but I didn't look around. My gaze was on my plate at the enormous lumps of potatoes–sweet and white–loaded with butter, the huge mountain of stuffing covered in gravy, the half-pound of turkey, and the mush of green bean casserole with the extra onions I'd poured out of a can I'd found by the sink. I wondered if Grace kept beer in the house.

"Well?" Grace said. "How high was it?"

I pushed my chair back, nearly in tears by that time, let my napkin drop to the floor and walked to the back door and out. I walked all the way down Grace's street to a park and sat on the swings and waited for someone to come after me, to find me and tell me to come back, that everyone was sorry, that they didn't mean anything, even that I was overreacting. And I knew it was stupid to do that. I knew it was head games, wanting people to prove to you that they cared about you. It was very much fourth grade, but I couldn't help it. I'd stopped crying by the time I realized no one was going to come for me, that they'd all continued with their meals and now I wouldn't get to eat mine. Even if I went back, there was no way I was going to sit all by myself and eat, reminding everyone that I'd left and no one cared.

I saw Patricia coming yards away; she waved and shoved her hands into her jacket pockets. She seemed a nice enough sort of girl for Sausage–she didn't talk a lot so he could prattle on as much as he wanted; she was smarter than he was, you could tell, but she wasn't the sort to let him know it too often; and she was happy. But I wondered about that. At some point, even Sausage was going to show the signs of an Abernathy upbringing. It seemed to exit the men in the family as scattered outbursts of rage. What was she going to do with that? Finally, she approached, took a swing and started gliding back and forth.

"Sorry," she said.

"For what?"

"I should have left when you did. It wasn't nice. What your grandmother said. But I think we got back at her."

"What do you mean?"

"After you left, Winnie said that a grandmother shouldn't be nasty to her grandchildren and then, I'm not sure how it happened, exactly, but there was a fight."

"A fight?"

She nodded and swung back and forth and back and forth getting higher and higher off the ground. "I guess your grandmother doesn't allow anyone to use the G-word."

I chuckled. "No, she doesn't."

"Well, it ended with some shouting and your aunt, that other one, she was screaming, 'you're a god-damned grandmother, Grace, get over it.' And I'm pretty sure I heard your mother saying something about giving birth automatically making you a mother and there's nothing she could do about it. It was pretty funny."

"You enjoyed it?"

"Well, maybe not while it was happening. And not watching James eat while it was all going on, like it happens all the time. Does it? But I got quite a laugh during my walk here."

"He shouldn't have let you walk out alone. You're not from around here."

"I have a sense of direction."

I supposed I was wrong about Patricia. Maybe Sausage wouldn't end up with his own mother in a younger package. I felt better, lighter somehow, as if finally there was another sane person in the world. Well, one sane person. I'd pretty much decided I was going crazy. When Patricia and I got back to the house, everyone seemed to be over the episode and Grace didn't say any more about me. It's not like she expected an answer to her questions. She was the kind of person that liked to stab at people, make them bleed; she wasn't looking for a fight.

It was dark when we left and I'd decided that I was going to stay home on Christmas. Everyone in the car was quiet and a distinct hum echoed all around us. Mom told Aunt Aubrey she could have a window seat on the way back, by which she meant that I was to sit on the hump between them.

Lights flashed through the car, front to back, like we were passing through a scanner and my mother reached over in the darkness and gave my thigh a little pat before taking her hand back to her huddled lump of a body. I turned to look across Aunt Aubrey to the window and watched the lights pass. She'd told Grace god knows what—certainly that I'd been up on the roof of Three River Terrace and was forced to stay in the psych ward. Did she tell her I went to the halfway house? Was Grace going to ask about that if I hadn't left? And now she thought that a pat on the leg would make it all right. Everything was back to normal, as if she'd given me a card and flowers and we'd made up.

294

Have you ever noticed that they don't make cards for real relationships? They don't make cards that say things like, "I know you don't love me. I don't love you either. So it's all good." Or, "Thanks for not aborting me. Even though you probably should have." Somebody ought to make cards like that. Cards that say, "Thanks for nothing."

It's not like I hadn't tried before—to see if anyone cared about me. There was the time I was about eleven and we were all up in the mountains at Grace's homestead, they called it. It was a little cabin on the side of the road near Asheville and behind it the land sloped down into a valley where an old decrepit barn rotted away the years. There was another fight and I cried. It was probably my fault, but I liked to think I was the victim so it was okay that I was crying, and I ran out of the house and down into the valley and hid in that old barn with the spiders and rats and snakes and forgotten bales of hay. I climbed atop a bale to get away from the things squirming around in the dirt. I wasn't afraid of the animals and bugs; I was afraid no one would come for me.

And no one ever did.

*Dear Camelia. I would come find you.*

# 26.

Back at work on Friday, I found that Alice had been in the day before to hang the holiday decor. Everything was starting to feel like Christmas, especially in the mall where air conditioning felt like autumn and Christmas music played, and would play for the next month. And inside the store we ran a continuous track of our own, when we weren't showing movies on our video monitor advertising all the VHS films we had for sale. We got to play *It's a Wonderful Life* over and over again and only William complained. Alice was too professional to notice, either the movie or William's whining, and I loved it. I could recite the entire film by the end of that season.

Friday was the craziest day at the bookstore. All the employees were there, even Petrie, the little geek girl who might have liked books more than any of us. It was like a high school reunion. Alice was that head cheerleader that liked to smile but she also yelled a lot, even at her friends. William was the nerd you couldn't tell anything to, because he already knew everything and never kissed a girl. Petrie was the girl everybody made fun of because she didn't shave her armpits or wash her hair daily. And then you catch Petrie and William in the back room going at it on break. Not really, but that would happen at a reunion. Barbara and Elaine were there too, but they were old. They'd be the teachers you didn't really like, who came to the reunion uninvited to remind you that you weren't ever going anywhere—you'd never be more important than you were in high school. For most of us, that's really, really sad.

Pizza was delivered so no one actually took a lunch or dinner break. Maybe the law didn't apply to Black Friday. We worked in panic mode all day. I liked it because I didn't have to think. I was on the floor, cleaning up and helping customers when Bond came in and found me. He followed me around, people nudging him to get past, trying to have a conversation with me—it was annoying. But he reached top shelves for me when someone wanted a book down. And once I let him climb the sliding ladder to get a book from over stock. That brought Alice stomping over.

"That ladder is for employees only," she said. She pointed to the yellow tape on each rung that said 'employees only.' Bond apologized. "Is there no end to guys streaming through this store visiting you?" Alice said and turned to leave.

I didn't like the look on Bond's face but there wasn't much I could do about it. It was the middle of Black Friday, in the only bookstore in town, in the only real mall in town. All of Sandy Point was there, crowded into every store, packed around the Orange Julius, trying to get as much shopping done near home before having to make the holiday treks to the mega malls in Orlando and Merritt Island. I didn't have time to explain to Bond that I knew other guys and they came to visit me. Like it was any of his business, anyway.

"I really need to get to work," I told him. "Did you want something?"

He looked like a deflated flesh-colored balloon. "No. I'll see you later." And he was gone, just like that.

When it was finally over and the store was closed and we all worked on straightening, I settled in at the true crime section while William closed out the drawer and Petrie vacuumed.

"I hope I didn't run your boyfriend off," Alice said, stopping by with an armload of books.

"He's not my boyfriend."

"Well, I'm sorry, anyway. I get a little frantic during the holiday season."

"It's okay." I didn't want to tell her that she was pretty scary when she yelled.

"This is your favorite section," she said. "You like a good murder?"

I nodded. I guess I did. The gorier the better. The Black Dahlia, Hollywood crimes, *In Cold Blood*, *Fatal Vision*. But I didn't want to read them. I just liked to look at the crime scene photos and mug shots.

"You should go into police work," she said.

"I just like to look at the pictures," I said. "I don't think I'd want to actually see it...in real life."

"Maybe law then," she said. And then, "Don't make it your life." And she was off to clean her own sections.

She meant the cleaning, of course. That was her motto. Don't make it your life. The mess would still be there tomorrow. No sense making it perfect. It was like making up your bed every morning knowing full well you planned to mess it up again that night. But if you asked me, there was no sense in straightening up the books if you weren't going to make it perfect. It's highly unprofessional to label the shelves 'alphabetical by author' only to have to pull *Helter Skelter* off the bottom shelf with the Ss and give it to a customer with a sheepish grin.

"No wonder you couldn't find it," I'd say. "William is dyslexic, he reads Bs as Ss."

"That's not what dyslexic means."

Like I didn't know what dyslexic meant. What really happened was some freak who liked to read those books, probably to get ideas on killing people, sat down and read one and then, without regard to the booksellers' hard work, shoved it on the bottom shelf and suddenly Bugliosi is in with the Ss.

At least it wasn't back in the automotive section where the wackos masturbated into magazines and left them folded up and stuck together for us to find later. You've got to be pretty sick to jack off in a bookstore. But that's Sandy Point for you. Any other time of the year hours would pass without anyone else being in the store, so you found yourself a little out-of-the-way spot and went at it. No sense trying to steal the magazine after that.

Not that making 'alphabetical by author' sticky labels with one of those plastic label-making guns was professional, anyway. It was tacky. Sandy Point tacky. So maybe Alice had a point.

We got out at ten-thirty and I stopped and got a six-pack of talls on the way home and took four into my room to drink while I got ready to go out. My mother wasn't at home so I could turn my television up as loud as I wanted. I was ready to leave by midnight and she still wasn't there. She wasn't much for going out. She worked in an office and sat at a desk in a little room all day typing, from what I could tell. Someone else answered the phone for her whenever I called. I never understood what a person could be typing all day. She clacked out forms and letters on an enormous typewriter that hummed and dinged. I think it was insurance. Who ever really knows what her parents do all day? Then she'd come home, make some dinner, drink a few beers, sit in bed and read, and go to sleep. She was a complete bore. But I didn't think anything of it. It was Friday night, after all.

I went up north to Harold's and sat at the bar. This guy started talking to me. He was pretty cute, if a bit on the scrawny side. He bought me a couple of beers and we were having a great time when I noticed Paulie sitting across the bar staring at me.

"Holy shit, no way," I said. I must have been really drunk because I don't think it would have bothered me all that much otherwise. Getting drunk is just another way to add drama to a dreary existence, truth be told. Everything is more important when you're loaded. Everybody's better looking. And meaner, too. Or nicer. If someone's nice to you, you think they're in love with you...when you're drunk.

I picked up this guy once at a bar over on the island and followed him home. We spent a great night with his friends at his little house in some dumpy neighborhood that I'd never be able to find sober. We had sex at, like, four in the morning, and I was so drunk and everything had gone so silent from the loudness of the party that I had this long-running hum of static in my ears that I mistook for, I don't know, the music of true love or excellent sex. I got it in my head it was the best sex I'd ever had—the most wild, the most passionate, the most meaningful. And I decided this guy loved me.

A few days later, after he never called me, I got really plastered and found my way back to his house and while he let me in, he and his friends were not at all the way I remembered them. They acted like I shouldn't be there. And when the party was over, I followed the guy into his bedroom and gave him what for. I said, "How dare you treat me like shit. You invite me over here and then ignore me. What's with that?"

"I didn't invite you over here," he said.

I stomped out and went home or to a bar to drink some more. Either it was a fluke and the guy didn't like me as much the second time around, or he didn't like me the first time either, and I was too drunk to notice. Or, the second time I went to some stranger's house, barged in on his pot party, and then demanded he make passionate and wild sex to me. I can't understand, though, in the latter case, why he would have said no. Not that I'm all that much to look at. I just always assumed men never turned down sex. Maybe he was religious. Maybe I'd barged in on a Rastafarian rite or something.

I turned my head and acted like I was hiding from Paulie. Mikey, or Dickie, whatever the guy's name was, said, "What? What is it?" And I told him there was this guy there that I didn't want to see, so he suggested that we all go down south to the The Shack. We being his friend Budge, Dodge, or Rookie, something like that, and his girlfriend Joyce. I didn't normally go to The Shack. It was a nice enough little bar, not much to it, tiny little thing, really. But they had this bitch patrol–about five women who wouldn't let any other girl talk to the regular guys without yanking them out the front door by the hair and throwing them into this shrubbery. At least, that was always my experience.

But Paulie followed us outside and he got in this little green Ford and we climbed in Dickie's black Camero. Paulie followed us down US1 and all the while, Dick and Rookie were talking about it.

"Who is this guy? What's he want?"

And I told them this story about how Paulie tried to rape me one night at a party and he nearly broke my arm. So, Dick turned onto Fiddlewood Highway and drove to Yellow Sands and turned south, into no-man's land where acres and acres of streets wound around, waiting for the housing development that never materialized. He drove and drove and slowed the car. Finally, he pulled off to the side and let Paulie go around, and Paulie did. Then Dick took off and Paulie took off and I was so drunk I wasn't really sure what happened, but if I recall, Joyce was enjoying the ride very much in the back seat. Finally, Paulie stopped, lost in the nowhere of Sandy Point, and started to turn his car around. Dick slammed on his brakes and he and Dodge, or whatever, were out of the car and dragging Paulie out of his, before I knew what was happening.

I screamed at them to stop. Just stop. You're hurting him. You're killing him. And Joyce, whose mouth was much bigger than mine, was screaming, "Kick him in the head! Kick him in the head." I crawled on top of Paulie, and Dick and Killer hit me a few times before they stopped their attack. They all stood staring at Paulie and me on the ground, the guys blowing air out and sucking it back in like they were starving for it, and Joyce still running her mouth about wanting more blood.

"What the hell are you doing?" I said.

Dick started cursing. I didn't know what he was saying but it was something like "freak cock sucking bitch fuck all the mother fucking hell you told me this guy raped you."

And I said, "I never said that. I said he tried. Sort of."

"You said he broke your fucking arm," Joyce said.

"I did not."

Dick raised his arm and slapped me hard across the cheek with the back of his hand knocking me onto Paulie and I was thinking he'd done that before. You could tell he was practiced at hauling off and hitting women. Paulie was lying on his back with his hands raised in the air in surrender, looking dazed and scared. They left us there and I tried to get Paulie to sit up. He finally climbed to standing and wiped his nose off on his t-shirt. He staggered to his car and got in, starting the engine, and I stood, staggered a bit, and watched him.

"Get in," he said.

So I did.

When I woke up the next morning, Paulie was in my bed.

# 27.

I jumped up so fast I fell onto the floor and hobbled across the room and out the door. Don't get me wrong. It's not like I'd never woken up with some weird guy in my bed before. Heck, when I lived in my own apartment it was a regular occurrence. I'd just never been stupid enough to bring one to my mother's house. My head was pulsating with nagging pain and I felt like I was going to vomit. A normal morning.

I peeked into my mother's room but she wasn't there. I searched the whole place, even slid open the back door and got the PPC yapping at me. But my mother wasn't out there. I went to the kitchen and nearly vomited just thinking about food, and the smell of the trash wasn't helping, and looked out the window. Her car was gone. Relief flooded over me. Until I saw the clock. Holy shit I was supposed to go in to work at twelve-thirty and it was already ten o'clock.

I pushed open the door to my room, sucked in some courage, and said, "Hey."

He turned over and nestled his little, blond freak-boy head into my pillow.

"Hey," I said. "You have to leave." And then it hit me. "Oh, shit." I looked out my window and there at the curb was his car. "Shit, shit, shit."

He was waking up now.

"I have to shower," I said, pulling clothes out of my drawers and closet. "And then you'll have to take me up to Harold's to get my car. I need to get to work."

He sat up in bed and as I was leaving I turned to look at him. "What the hell?" His face was red and swollen and blood matted his hair. He was sitting up and pulling on his blood-spattered t-shirt.

"What happened to you?"

He stood and pulled his jeans on, laughing. There was a gaping hole in his mouth. Holy mother of Christ someone knocked out one of his teeth.

"I'll tell you what happened," he said. He walked toward me and the door. "Last night you told some wiry dude and his thug of a friend that I raped you and broke your arm. Remember that?"

A tinkling of a memory came through, but now that he was standing in front of me, taller than I remembered, swollen up like a mutant, whistling a bit when he tried to say Ss, I wasn't sure I was going to admit to it. I glanced over at my bed and noticed he'd left the sheets bloody. I was not happy.

"I don't know what you're talking about," I said. "You bled all over my bed." I laughed a little at the rhyme. It was cute.

He shoved me up against the edge of the door and it

306

rammed against my spine–the impact forced the door to swing to–then he pushed me again and I fell against it slamming it shut.

"Then you watched them beat me to a pulp."

"I made them stop," I said. "I didn't know what they were doing, I swear. They must have misunderstood something I said."

He shoved me again and nearly knocked the air out of my lungs.

"We need to leave," I said when I caught my breath.

"Damn right I need to leave."

"Just let me take a shower."

I had my doubts about the safety of it, but it seemed to me that Paulie couldn't stand me at that point and the last thing he'd want to do was come into the shower and try to mess with me. So, I opened the door and walked across the hall to my mother's room.

"It'll just take a minute," I said.

"You're crazy," he called after me. "You belong in an asylum. Fucking bitch."

*I* was crazy? I wasn't the one stalking me. So what if I told that squirt Dickie and his ogre, Cookie, that Paulie had hurt me? How was I to know they'd beat the shit out of him? A small part of me thought he deserved it. I mean, what was he doing at Harold's staring at me? What was he thinking following us in his car? I could only hope he'd learned his lesson.

"Oh, crap." I was staring into the mirror in my mother's bathroom at a spot on my right cheekbone the color of an apple. My right eye was swollen. No wonder my head felt like it was going to explode.

How exactly do you ask a guy if there was any sex? I mean, what if there was and you were so drunk you didn't remember it? Would he be insulted? I didn't think there was any sex, with Paulie. I hoped there wasn't, not that it really mattered, but I didn't like the feeling of not knowing.

When I got out of the shower and dressed, Paulie had gone. The little shit left me stranded with no way to get back to my car or to work. That was it; I was done with him. Aunt Aubrey drove me up north to Harold's. She chattered the whole way about Jesus, and church the next day, and how the choir had new robes and the women bought hair ribbons to match. She invited me and I said maybe I'd go. All the while she kept peering over at me and I knew she wanted to ask about my face–I'd loaded it with layers of foundation, but there was no hiding that I'd been hit.

"Is this where you do your socializing?" She'd pulled up beside my car behind the bar. "It's got a certain... personality."

If she meant the personality of a drunken whore, sure. I hated to look at my favorite bars during the daytime. It always made me feel sad.

"You know how to get home, right?" I reminded her which way to go, not toward the interstate.

"Is everything all right?" She asked.

I nodded and tried to act like everything was normal. "Of course, why?"

She stared at me for a minute and smiled.

# 28.

I was late to work and a little disheveled with puffy eyes and that sick-like-you're-going-to-vomit look. Alice eyed me suspiciously as I headed to the back room to sign in. William was back there and he told me I smelled like beer.

"Stay here," he said. "Alice needs to talk to you."

I stood there surrounded by stacks of boxes that still needed to be unloaded and the books shelved, touching my face where it hurt. She came in and closed the door and stared hard at me.

"William says you smell like booze."

"He said you wanted to talk to me."

"What's going on? What happened to your face?"

"It's nothing. What did you want?"

"I want to know what's going on with you."

"I had to save my stalker from getting the life kicked out of him last night."

"Tell me."

She stuck her hands on her hips and looked at me as if she had the power to make me tell her. So I told her. I told her about how Paulie was stalking me and how when I saw him at the bar, for some reason I told these guys that he'd raped me and broke my arm. So when he followed us south, they took him to that old neighborhood they started to build and never finished. You know the one off Yellow Sands. She knew the one. And they wound him around and around and finally into a *cul de sac* and he stopped and they dragged him out of his car and beat the living shit out of him. "And I stopped them. But they hit me. The one guy hit me."

She shook her head. "Okay, look," she said. "It's none of my business what you do on your own time, but you have to come in to work sober, and smelling clean—"

"I showered."

"And free of bruises."

"How could I control that? What if I was an abused wife or something?"

"I'd tell you what I'm telling you now. Before you start work, go down to Pinkerton's cosmetics counter and get some heavy-duty makeup to cover that bruise. I can't let you walk around in the store like that. And get some perfume. You reek."

I doubted they had any kind of makeup like that, but I didn't mind not having to start work. I'd already signed in, too. I walked all the way down to the other end of the mall to the drug store and walked in, past the counter where I used to work, and over into the cosmetics department and behind the counter was Hannah.

"What are you doing here?"

She shrugged.

"I thought you were in Georgia."

"I came back."

I wished I was nosier. I had a million questions. Like, are you in love with China? If you were in a psych ward, would you expect to sleep in the men's dorm or the women's?

"Did China come back, too?"

"No," she said. "Don't be stupid. They'll never let her come back here. What happened to your face?"

"I walked into a door."

She froze a bit before looking away, nodding slightly. It was just like the drunks at Hope House, or the loons at Lakeview Psychiatric, when I said something off script—they'd pause, let the glitch pass, and then start again, acting like nothing had happened.

"Alice said you guys might have some makeup to cover it."

She pulled a little tub of cover-up from under the counter and held it up to my face. "This will do. Come on over."

She let me sit in her make-over chair, opened the tub and dabbed the stuff over my bruise with her ring finger; then she dusted it with some powder using this funky, puffy, black brush. "There, see?" She held up a mirror for me and I thought it looked really good. Almost no bruise at all. "It's expensive," she said. "But worth it."

I paid seven-ninety-nine for a little tub of it and let her sell me a set of fancy makeup brushes—so I could have my own puffy one—a tub of silky powder, and a bottle of Chanel No. 5.

"Take my advice," she said as she handed me the bag. "Don't ever let him hit you again. Because he will."

"He won't," I said. "I can't even remember his name."

At dinner time, Bond showed up and I was glad that Alice had already left. William and Barbara were there and I took my break. This time we walked across the mall parking lot over to the Burger King. The burger wasn't as good as the Joint, but at least you always knew exactly what you were going to get.

"You don't look so good," he said sliding into the booth across from me.

"I feel like shit."

"I didn't want to say that word, but that's pretty much how you look. You got hit?"

"Crazy night."

The night was still raspy in my overly smoked throat. The Chanel was wearing off and my underarms stuck to themselves. We ate for a bit, and there was this part of me, nagging at me, mad that Bond hadn't raised holy hell about me getting hit. Like Wallace, or Booger, or whatever that creep's name was who hit me—he was out of his mind thinking about Paulie raping me and breaking my arm. He was so protective that he tried to kill Paulie. I thought that my being hit would get some kind of rise out of Bondurant Kilter, but the other side of me, the practical side, was relieved. Maybe there was a limit to the amount of drama a girl could stand in her life, and I'd backed myself up against it. I was ready for people to not give a damn, ready to sit on the bale of hay and watch the snake eat the rat until it was dark and I could walk back home by myself. And maybe I'd get lucky this time and no one would be there.

"Have you heard from Sylvie?" I asked him.

He nodded. "She's dating some doctor. Didn't she tell you?"

"She never calls me."

"She said you dumped her at the Pool Pit that time."

"I didn't dump her. She went off with some guy."

"That's not how she tells it."

"I don't care how she tells it."

We ate some more. Finally he wadded up his napkin and stuck it in his burger box. "When are you going to stop all of this?" He said.

"Stop what?"

He shook his head, irritated.

"God, you remind me of my mother."

He sat back against the weird, plastic molded booth and looked away.

"I've changed is all," I said. "You keep expecting me to be me from school. But I'm not that person; I don't think I ever was."

"Are you working tomorrow?"

"Yep."

"Well, maybe next weekend. Or sometime. You want to go to downtown with me? Look in some antique shops?"

Antique shops? What was he, fifty? I couldn't figure Bond out; I wasn't sure I wanted to. I imagined he was just lonely. It was clear he didn't like me much; he never asked me to go out, like out–to a bar or a dance club or the movies. If I'd had the courage, I'd be like a girl in a movie and say something like, "What are we doing here? Where are we going with this?" But I wasn't a girl in a movie. And anyway, it's best not to ask questions if you don't really want to know the answers.

When Monday rolled around, I had this whole story concocted for Dr. Crazy. I tried to tell her about it—it involved me being at a wild party, and the only one sober, of course, and trying to make my way through the gyrating throng, only to get smacked in the face accidentally by a guy who was dancing with a tennis racket. It could work. But after the preliminaries—the how many days this week did you drink, how many did you have, how do you feel about that stuff—she said, "Tell me about the bruise."

And I just opened up and spilled it, damn it all. It was as if Dr. Crazy brought out the crazy in me. I told her all about it. About sitting at the bar and feeling weird seeing Paulie. That feeling I couldn't define, exactly. How it got stronger when I told Dickie that Paulie was stalking me, and stronger again when he and his friends took me away, and more and more as I told them the lie about the rape, until I was bursting with it. Like I was in control—a wicked spider weaving a web and watching the flies tangle with it. When they stopped the car, left it almost like magic, in one movement, a swoosh of testosterone, and dragged Paulie from his, I was engorged with it. Elated. Buzzing with it. I couldn't name it; I was afraid to name it.

"When did it leave you?"

When I realized they were going to kill him. "When it was real," I said.

"Can you name it?"

"Power."

"What does it remind you of?"

She was a genie, decked out in a paisley moo moo, her hair a mess on top of her head, four earrings in each ear, all mismatched–pearls and dangles and hoops–chains around her neck falling down her chest, catching between her breasts. She smiled that genie smile and made you say things you didn't know you meant to say. It wasn't psychology; it was wizardry.

"I used to have this dream–well, two dreams really. The first one was always the monkeys. The flying monkeys from *The Wizard of Oz*. They're flying down onto the driveway of the house on Yellow Sands, where I grew up. Sometimes they're carrying me and my mother away. But most often, I'm hiding in the living room, watching through the little slit in those thick, green-print curtains, and they're chasing my mother up the driveway. She falls, and one of them grabs her feet, then he drops her and grabs her by the shoulders and carries her away. And she's screaming." I lit a cigarette and breathed in deep.

"When you remember that dream, how do you feel?"

"Powerful."

"And the other dream?"

I shook my head. "I don't know why I thought of it. It's not related, really. The flying monkeys are more relevant."

"Tell me about it, anyway."

I didn't want to. But she was a genie, after all.

"I'm in a long line and some woman is holding my hand but whenever I look up, I can't see her face. It's not there. I can't see the faces of any of the other people in line. We wind around a building and then go inside. It's a

315

church. We walk up the aisle to the front—to a coffin. I start pulling against the woman's hand, trying to get out of line, to run away. But I can't break her grasp and all the other people are pushing me forward. We finally get to the coffin and I'm lying in it."

Here I choked a bit, which surprised me. Saying that sort of thing out loud is unexpected. You don't want to hear it in your own voice; it makes it real. If I'd read it in a book, I wouldn't have minded. Or heard someone say it in a movie. Because it's fiction, after all. And it is fiction; because it's just a dream. But somehow it was too real.

"I start screaming and I don't stop until the woman grabs me and forces me to stand in front of the coffin, and then I see myself real close. And I apologize. I'm saying, 'I'm so sorry, I'm so sorry.' A mistake had been made. I wasn't supposed to be there." I chuckled. "That's crazy, isn't it?"

She was quiet for a few seconds, then she said, "And how does that dream make you feel?"

I shook my head. "Powerful."

# 29.

I wanted to believe I was no different from anybody else, that other girls wanted their mothers carried away by flying monkeys, and other girls felt like they'd buried part of themselves somewhere along the way, and other girls thought antiques were for the elderly, and that men were always fumbling to get at their breasts, but I was wrong. I stood apart, on the ceiling looking down, and alien. I'm outside the machine, watching.

That Monday night, I found my mother sitting in the kitchen of her little duplex with Aunt Aubrey drinking beers at the little table for two.

"Where've you been?" I tried to act like I was worried, but the truth was I'd forgotten that I hadn't seen her all weekend.

"Your mother has taken a lover," Aunt Aubrey said.

I looked at my mother and she smiled a wicked smile that disappeared as fast as it had arrived. "What happened to your face?" She said.

"And he's young enough to be your brother." Aunt Aubrey threw her hands up into the air and let them fall back into her lap. Aunt Aubrey always had the good sense to run around with older men.

"What's his name?" I said.

"Brock." My mother said, and for the love of god she giggled like a fifteen-year-old girl. My face, a lovely eggplant purplish black by that time, muted by tan cover-up, was forgotten and I suppose I had Aunt Aubrey to thank for it.

"Oh, for Christ's sake," I said.

Brock was the name of a man in one of the romance comic books I used to buy at the convenience store when I was thirteen. I'd walk across the enormous, unused field next to the middle school to Coquina Drive and buy a comic book of love, a grape soda, and candy and sit along the ditch behind the store crying my heart out over Brock, or Derk, or Stone. Nobody really named his son Brock.

I pulled open the fridge door and said, "Will all of my talls be safe in here? Or do I need to hide them?"

"I think your mother has had enough beer this weekend to last her for months."

"They'll be fine," my mother said. "I've got my Pabst."

I couldn't help thinking about the whole good-for-the-goose thing, but the pictures this affair conjured in my brain were all too clear. Nothing that a six-pack of tall beers wouldn't wash away. Parents should not be allowed to have sex. Or at the very least, enjoy it.

When Paulie came into the store again it was nearly Christmas. He blushed right away and gave me a crooked smile. "Hey," he said.

I was working alone for a few hours that Sunday and

318

feeling like a book-selling god. I ruled the store. I knew almost every book by that time and could tell you where to find it. I followed the teens all around the store pestering them with helpful questions and suggested reading until they fled. I left the old and feeble at the front desk while I ran around finding the types of books they'd be interested in so they wouldn't have to do any more walking. And when that man came in and asked me about a book for his wife, the one with a bleeding rock on the cover, that maybe had something about golf in the title, I found *Master of the Game* by Sidney Sheldon for him.

"Hey," I said.

He looked around and I half expected him to ask for a book. But instead he asked me how I was doing and I said I was fine and how was he doing and he was fine, and I stood there for a long time wondering how long it was going to last before he was gone. He'd had a new tooth put in where Dickie knocked one out, and it only looked a little bit cleaner than the rest of them.

"I'm going back into rehab," he said. "I just thought I'd tell you."

"You mean Lakeview?"

"No," he said. "I was in there because of the overdose. My dad thinks I'm trying to kill myself."

"Aren't you?"

He looked to his right foot, scuffing something off the old carpet next to floor stacks of *Elvis and Me* and *The Mammoth Hunters*.

"No, I'm just going back into rehab, over in Tampa where my mom lives. I don't know if I'm coming back."

I wanted to say, so what? I wanted to say, why did you come here? Why should I care? Rover never wrote me letters barking at me. Sue never called before she put the knife to her wrist. Paminaldi never showed up to psychobabble-ize me. We weren't the class of Lakeview Psychiatric 1986. We weren't friends.

"Why rehab?" I said.

He shrugged and looked at me. "I got wasted bad after that night. With those guys, you remember?"

That's not the kind of night you forget. The morning was pretty memorable, too. I had to bum a ride to work with Aunt Aubrey for Christ's sake. "But that wasn't your fault," I said. "Why would you binge out over that?"

He winced and looked around the store, up at the ceiling and those little clips stuck in those metal slats that hold up the ceiling tiles. He glanced behind him at the door. "You get tired sometimes, right?"

I tried to smile. Paulie knew how hard it was to battle the desire to stop fighting. "Yes," I said.

"But we keep going."

I nodded. "We keep going."

"I wanted someone to know, you know. Where I went."

"I'll remember," I said.

I knew exactly what he was saying and it pissed me off–a little bit. Of all the people who would understand Paulie, it would be me. I was cast, like in concrete. Paulie was kindred–we were bound by the world view that made us what we were, and there was no getting around it. He wasn't the mirror I was hoping for.

"So, you'll let me know if you do come back."

"Maybe. If I think I need to."

I'd heard about people who loved each other, but never spoke or got together. They each knew the other was alive, out in the world, and were keepers of the other's heart and soul; that was enough. I was the keeper of Paulie's being. His placeholder. His bookmark. Ah, I'd made a bookstore pun, and I laughed about it after he left the store.

# 30.

We got to meet the young lover on Christmas Day. It was god-awful. He was in the duplex when I got up, hung over, as usual. He stood in the little kitchen making eggs and bacon and grits and that would have been enough to turn my stomach. But he was wearing real pajamas, a button up shirt and long pants, and slippers. I shit you not, man slippers. He'd tied my mother's apron around his waist.

He stood on twig legs–you could tell by the ankles poking out under his too-short jammies–and everything was reed thin except for his beer gut which made him look like an abnormally tall, starving white kid, like those bloated children they show on television. His face was sweet enough, especially with the dark morning stubble. Eyes so black they twinkled when he smiled and he set a plate of food in front of me.

"I know just what you need." His voice was not nearly deep enough for his jaw line and he poured me a tiny glass of tomato juice.

I was thinking, there's an alien in the kitchen and

what is he doing dating my mother? Was he looking at her like some kind of Mrs. Robinson? Was my mother the experienced sex goddess to this guy's nerd? Was I missing something when I looked at her? Was I programmed to see my mother as a soft, pudgy, shrill of a human because, well, because maybe we're not supposed to see our parents as sexual beings? When she staggered into the kitchen, that sour look on her face, and made for the coffee pot, I still saw the short, fat, wicked woman I'd always seen.

Brock drove all of us over to Winter Park in his Lincoln Continental, which made him look much older than when I first saw him in the kitchen. What he was, as it turned out, was an attorney.

It wasn't really *as usual*—the hangover I mean. I'd actually managed to go a few days between wild drunken rampages several times. And I was sure I was going to register for classes as soon as the new year started. A few days sober here and there would be all I'd need.

Christmas was the best holiday to visit Grace and the family. It was cooler outside, for one thing, so when you wanted to leave, to breathe or scream or get away from the insanity, you didn't have to come back to the cold house with a sweaty bra. And everyone was dressed up so nice. My cousins, the dark-haired models, even made jeans look dressy. All the girls painted their nails in Christmas colors. You know how women who paint their nails hold their hands as if they're art? My cousins all did that. Always made me want to hide my hands. It's not like I had bad nails, but I was never good at painting them. I couldn't manage to let them dry long enough so they

324

always smudged. My cousins, I imagined, were good at sitting around with their hands in the air and cotton between their toes for hours yakking at one another. And somehow I was the weird one.

Grace was livid about Brock when she met him. She took my mother aside and accused her of hiring him as an escort. My mother was so shocked she said nothing, and the rest of the day Grace called him a hired man.

"Is your hired man getting enough to drink?"

"Would your hired man like another roll?"

"Can we get your hired man another piece of pie."

Of course it was going to erupt. It was about the time we were all ready to leave, leastwise Sausage Patty were gathering up their things and Sausage was looking at me hopefully. We were standing in the family room at the back of the house when we heard the screaming in the living room. It was something about jealousy and bitches. Finally we were able to make sense of it, as we fought through the crowd of cousins at the doorway to watch.

Grace and my mother were standing in front of the coffee table. Aunt Aubrey and Aunt Keety were sitting behind them on the sofa looking at the ground with smiles on their faces.

"You're a disgrace," Grace was yelling.

"You're just jealous," my mother screamed and everybody turned to someone else with their mouths open. "Because Brock is younger and better looking than your fat slob."

"At least I have the good sense to have a man and not a boy."

"Oh, please, we all know he's incapable. That's the

only reason you have him around. You couldn't handle a performing man. You don't even want one."

At this point, Grace swung at my mother, but my mother dodged her and screamed, "Frigid."

"At least I had sense enough not to keep a man around my children. You've already got Eunice bringing strangers over for the night."

A million emotions crossed over my mother's face and she ended up settling on confusion.

"That's right," Grace said, "And he beat the shit out of her too, from what I hear. Your own daughter is in a sexually abusive relationship and you're off screwing around with a man half your age. You should be ashamed of yourself."

My mother stared, open mouthed, first at Grace, then around at the rest of us. But my cousins were all staring at me and I was frozen, watching my mother begin to cower in front of Grace. Shame washed over her. She had no defense now; mothers have great power.

"You're no better than a slut," Grace said, nearly spitting.

For the tiniest second, I thought my mother might slap her. I wanted her to. But she turned her back on Grace and stomped out of the room, pushing us all aside. Sausage Patty and I followed her out of the house and found The Pudge and Brock in the driveway.

"Is it over yet?" Pudge called out. He smiled and waved. "I took the liberty of removing Brock from the fury."

He was expecting someone to laugh, but my mother pushed past him to the street toward Brock's car and

Brock followed like a toddler chasing after his neglectful mother. We all piled in and sat waiting for Aunt Aubrey. We waited and waited and my mother got madder and madder. She was next to me in the front seat, in the middle trying not to let her leg touch Brock's, vile energy pulsating off her. Brock reached out and put his hand on her leg and she shoved it off. We Abernathy women don't like to be touched when we're angry. Some of us don't care much for it at all. Finally, blissful Aunt Aubrey came smiling across the front lawn, turned back to the house and waved.

I heard her shout, "Merry Christmas, Christ is lord."

She got in the back seat behind Brock and as soon as Brock pulled away from the curb my mother looked to me and said, "What the hell was that all about?"

"No need for that language," Aunt Aubrey said.

"You keep out of it." My mother told her without looking back.

"Why are you asking me?" I said.

"When did you have a boy over?"

"A boy?" I almost laughed. It was like I was twelve and got caught smoking.

"You had someone spend the night while I was away."

"How do you know?"

"How did Grace know?" Shame flared up in her cheeks.

I twisted in my seat and glared at Aunt Aubrey. She was looking out the window, trying to pretend she didn't hear us. Sly bitch.

"How dare you have sex in my house." My mother

wailed and the tears started.

I was pretty sure I hadn't had sex with Paulie, but somehow I didn't think my mother wanted to hear about that.

Aunt Aubrey cleared her throat and said, "Aren't you going to ask your daughter about the bruises?"

"What bruises?"

"On her face that day. After she had the boy over."

"Serves her right."

Cosmic justice–my mother was in tune with it and liked to inform its sufferers. We endured a long bout of fuming silence until Sausage leaned forward, slapped his left hand on Brock's shoulder and said, "Welcome to the family."

It started with me giggling, I think. At some point we were all laughing and passing the tissue box. The only one stony and quiet was Brock.

I let Bondurant take me out to a party on New Year's Eve, against my better judgment. It was out in Beacon Hills at the home of his boss. I was going to tell him he was out of his mind taking a known drunken whore to a fancy party in front of his coworkers. But as it turned out, he worked with some wild drunken whores himself. No one would have noticed if I'd got drunk and had sex on the dining room table with half the people there. Maybe I'm exaggerating a little bit.

"Did I tell you how nice you look?" He yelled over the music while we were dancing.

He meant I looked respectable. I'd put on a dress and hose and high heels and everything. I thought I was going to a party of nerds who were going to talk philosophy and drink champagne, so I had to look the part. And I'd psyched myself up to have only two drinks the whole night. Instead I was on my fourth, still pretty tame for my standards, had pulled the scarf from around my neck, yanked out my shoulder pads and tossed them at one of the drunk engineers dancing on a coffee table, and stepped out of the hose. I'm not sure where they ended up, but I did see someone wearing hose on his head.

"Resolutions?" Bond said.

The music stopped and we walked into another room filled with drunk people talking about things they thought were very important but would turn out to be meaningless in the morning. Outside on a balcony overlooking the back yard and pool, a piano player–I couldn't tell if he was a guest or hired in–tinkled out all the songs from *Annie*. We stood at the railing, watching people dance and play down below.

"I don't do resolutions," I told him.

"Why not?"

"Why bother?"

"It's a fresh start, don't you think? Every new year, a new beginning."

"Oh my god, Bond, don't start talking like a motivational poster."

He laughed. "Why do we make a big deal out of it, if it doesn't mean anything?"

"You don't know people at all, do you?"

"And you do?"

I rolled my eyes and shook my head and drank some more of my rum and coke. "It's all just excuses to have a party," I said. "Birthdays, holidays, the races, football games. Just reasons for people to get drunk and make asses of themselves. Sometimes on tv."

"You're a cynic, aren't you?"

"I'm a realist," I said.

They started shouting out the countdown and I turned to look back into the house. I had a look on my face that shouldn't be there but I wasn't sure I could wipe it away. I knew this kid once, back in sixth grade. I'd never kissed anyone before but everybody thought that was a big lie, and Peter Bollinger told me so. He said everybody in school said I was already screwing around and he didn't believe me when I told him I was scared to kiss him. I fought him for a while, until I started to cry, and he said, "Okay, okay, I believe you. Do you want to kiss or not?"

"Yes,"

"Why do you keep pushing me off you?"

"I want to do it; but I'm scared."

"Just breathe," he said.

I sucked in a few gulps of air and wiped the tears from my face.

"There's nothing to it," he said. "Let me do all the work."

He kissed me and it turned out not to be too awful. But then he went in for more and I couldn't breathe without his nose breath getting mixed in and I gagged and pulled myself out of his grasp.

"Don't make a face like that after you kiss somebody," he said. "They won't want to do it again."

So, I put on a nice face, that smile with the bedroomy feel to it that I'd rehearsed plenty, and turned back

330

to Bond. He had to kiss me. It was like a law or something. I didn't care if he didn't, but I didn't want him to think I didn't want to—if he wanted to. And I figured he knew the rules and would do it whether he wanted to or not. It wasn't awful. A little soft. Timid. Lasted a bit too long, but, it was New Year's and there were fewer expectations.

# 31.

Things settled down at the bookstore and I didn't have to work as much, and I thought about going back to school. But it didn't feel right. So I let the deadline slip by. I was starting to feel like a normal person, though. Like a person who works and lives and doesn't get drunk every day or fight the real world all the time; and the screaming was fading away. And I thought about Paulie, and the shields. Maybe I was building a shield and one day I'd be normal like everybody else.

Bond came by a few times a week to take me on break and one Saturday afternoon in mid-January, when we came back to the store from the Orange Julius, he kissed me before he left. Alice and Barbara, one of the old biddies, were giggling and giving me weird looks from behind the counter.

"How's it going with the boyfriend?" Alice said.

"He's not my boyfriend."

"He kissed you," Barbara said.

"That doesn't make him my boyfriend."

"It makes him think he's your boyfriend."

I shook my head and leaned against the counter in front of them. "Kissing doesn't make a relationship," I said. "Sex, maybe." Of course, I knew damn well that wasn't true.

"Have you had sex with him?" Alice said.

"Don't even go there."

"What?" Barbara said. "He's cute enough."

"Not interested."

"In him?" Alice said. "Why not?"

"In sex."

They acted like I'd broken the first rule of womanhood and gasped, and then laughed.

"You can't be serious," Barbara said.

I thought at least Barbara would understand. She was old—in her fifties. Did people have sex in their fifties? I certainly didn't want to imagine that. Sex was for young people. Young reckless people with the hormones of rabbits. Never mind my mother—Brock was an aberration.

"Don't jump on her," Alice said. "Maybe she's gay."

They both turned to me and Barbara said, "Are you gay, honey?"

"I don't think so."

"You don't think so?" Alice said. "Shouldn't you know?"

"I'm pretty sure I'm not gay."

Barbara sang out, "Pretty sure, ain't sure."

"I'm pretty sure," I said, staring hard at her, "that I'm not interested in sex. At all. With anybody."

"That's impossible," Alice said. "Everybody is interested in sex."

"Maybe I'll be interested later," I said. "Don't you

have something for me to do?"

She let out a disappointed sigh. "Straighten, I guess."

The next day Bond and I went downtown. I'd never really been downtown for fun before; it was just a bunch of second-hand stores. Bond liked to go in the antique shops and touch things. He bought trinkets all the time—old picture frames and old clocks; lockets and tie clips; the occasional odd chair. He told me I should come over to his place sometime and see his collection and I imagined his house was stuffy and dusty and filled with old things. Bond was an old thing, when I thought about it. He was my age, but had somehow seen more, done more. I'm sure I had actually seen and done more, but doing and seeing things drunk doesn't give you that experienced air about you that Bond had.

"You'll like this," he said and took me to a used bookstore.

As soon as we walked in, the urge to start organizing fell over me. "It's amazing," I said.

We walked the crowded maze of bookshelves half-heartedly sorted by category and I ran my hands along the spines. It smelled of mold and mildew and dust and paper. Back in the back the sound was muted—even when someone walked into the shop and the little bell above the door tinkled, it was far away, like in another time.

Bond and I spent every weekend downtown after that; I bought old books, stacked them in my room at the duplex and read them at night. At first, I'd take a six-pack of talls and set it on the bed beside me while I read. But I couldn't read drunk—the words blurred and I ended up reading paragraphs over again. Within a week, I was reading without any booze at all. And I thought that was odd–that books would be my cure.

One Sunday as we walked along the sidewalk downtown, I asked him, "So, when am I going to get to see your place?"

He stopped and turned to me. "Would you like to?"

I nodded. And we walked again. He pulled the door to the bookshop open and the bell tinkled.

"It's not a big place," he said. "Not like my boss's house."

"Of course not." I headed straight for the true crime section and started sorting books.

"Doug should pay you a salary," he said.

I laughed and we heard Doug laugh, too. "I don't force her to work," he said, his voice muffled and distant like in a dream.

"I do it for pure pleasure," I said. "You live up north, though. In Beacon Hills."

"But not in the big mansion part. In the entrance section. Smaller homes."

"Are you ashamed of having money?"

He shrugged. I pulled books out and put some up higher and some down lower. It was a grand author puzzle, like those cheap plastic squares, with the tiles inside that you slid around and around, mixing them up and back, until you finally managed to get them in place and they made a picture. I worked on the true crime section at Doug's once a week and still hadn't made it work.

"Maybe a little," he said.

"Why?"

I pulled out a thick, squat hardcover with a red dust

jacket. Large white letters on the front said, *Murder of a Little Girl*, and the I in "girl" was a dagger. I hadn't seen that one before and I turned it over briefly, out of habit, to check out the blurb, and then went to shelve it down lower with the Rs. But something had caught my eye and created a pin prick in my brain; I shivered. Bond was saying something about his parents and his siblings.

"I think they resent me, somehow, but it's not like I didn't work to get through college. Sure my parents helped. And the scholarship."

I couldn't concentrate on what he was saying. Yeah, yeah, he worked hard. Something was not right with that book. I stood there, listening to Bond go on and on and me just looking at the bookshelf. Finally he said, "You know what I mean?"

I looked at him. "I don't have any money. And no one resents me for anything."

He chuckled. "That's not true."

"It's not?"

"Sylvie resents the hell out of you."

I sucked in a breath. "I don't think I've ever heard you curse before. Am I rubbing off on you?"

"Maybe."

I bent down a bit and pulled the red book back off the shelf. "Why would Sylvie resent me?" I turned the book over and there it was: Camelia.

# 32.

I tucked the book under my arm and walked to the front of the store.

"Are you buying that one?" Bond said as I handed it to Doug and pulled my wallet out of my purse. "I didn't think you ever read those."

"I'm reading this one."

I had a hard time concentrating the rest of the afternoon. I let Bond drag me to his antique shops where he got to run his hands on everything and I knew he loved old things the way I loved books.

"About Sylvie," I said.

"What about her?"

"You said she resented me."

"You didn't know?"

"Why would she resent me? She has everything I don't."

"How do you figure that?"

"Well, she's prettier, for one thing."

He chuckled under his breath. "No, she's not."

"She's not?"

"No. And she knows it."

"Is that it, then? She thinks I'm prettier?"

"You really don't know?"

I shook my head. We were standing in the back of Days of Yore where they displayed old China ware and dolls, because apparently a great way to display dolls is to set them on plates. Bond picked up a Madame Alexander and started pulling at the lace collar and the drawstring of the bonnet.

"You always had more than Sylvie. You had more money. Your parents weren't a hundred years old–"

"I wasn't the last of seven children, what did she expect? It's not my fault."

"She didn't blame you."

"Then what is there to resent?"

"There were the guys you dated."

"She never liked any of the guys I dated."

"She liked *all of them*."

"What are you talking about?" I grabbed the doll from him and put it back on its plate. I couldn't stand the way he was holding it. Something about it was just wrong. What kind of guy looks comfortable and cute petting a doll?

"Every single time she'd tell me about her new crush, you'd end up going out with the guy, or at least sleeping with him."

"Who are you talking about? Not Lee Harper."

"Even Lee Harper."

I started walking through the store again, this time I was touching all the trinkets. Ceramic figures and masquerade masks. Old desks and sewing machines. Bond rubbed off on me with every stroke. "I find that hard to believe."

"It's true."

"I didn't sleep with that many guys, you know?"

He laughed again. "Enough to give you a reputation. But you know what Rhett Butler said about that."

"Do you know what Rhett Butler said?" The guy pet dolls and watched *Gone with the Wind.* There was something very wrong with Bondurant Kilter–and something wrong with me for liking it. "Anyway, *you* still kissed me." I stopped and turned to him, my chin up in some kind of romantic defiance.

"Maybe I'll be the only guy Sylvie didn't like, to get you."

I punched him and he laughed and we left the store hand in hand.

"You're very strange, Bond," I told him once we were in the car.

When we got back to the duplex, he finally asked me out on a real date–dinner and a movie. I said no, of course.

"Another time," I told him.

He nodded, his smile droopy, and I got the feeling he didn't mind all that much. I wanted to tell him I couldn't think straight, that I'd found this book that scared me and I couldn't keep my mind on anything else, but it wouldn't make sense to him if I did. I knew the book must be a fluke. A coincidence. So what if I had an invisible friend from childhood named Camelia and now that name was on the back of a true crime book? She might not even be the victim. She could be the killer. Maybe she strangled her mother to death and buried her in the back yard. Who hasn't wanted to do that? But sometimes, there's that thing in your gut that knows more than you do.

The oneness people believe that everything in the universe is connected. They think you can know things that you couldn't possibly know, because those things are imbedded in the universal subconscious. I'm not making this up. When I was about ten, after their Episcopalian phase, my parents took me to a church that was all about this universal consciousness and we practiced tapping into it through meditation. My father even took special meditation lessons from one of the goddesses that ran the church. Private lessons, because apparently you have to be alone to do it right. Naturally, being ten, I imagined the goddess, whose name I think was Peoria or something exotic like that, danced circles around my dad sprinkling him with fairy dust and holy water until he was in a perfect state of subconsciousness and then left the room. What else would a ten year old imagine?

During the summer I was fifteen, this girl Cecily called me out of the blue and asked me if I wanted to go with her and her friends to a KC and the Sunshine Band concert. I was so excited about it I couldn't stop smiling. It would be a long trip, all the way to Miami and back. I wondered why she invited me, but I didn't ask—that would be too risky. I was afraid she'd say, "Oh, Eunice, I'm so sorry. I didn't know that was you. I was calling April Suchandsuch; you know, a cool girl." And that would be the end of my dreams of seeing KC and the Sunshine Band in concert.

As it turned out, she'd won six tickets on some radio show but one of her five best friends couldn't go. Instead of just wasting the ticket, her dad tried to sell it. He found someone who wanted all six of them or none at all. So her dad said she'd either have to find another person to use the ticket, or he'd sell the lot of them to his friend. They called everybody they knew in school and no one could go until they got to my name. That's the way I heard it later, anyway.

That was all fine with me. It's not like Cecily and her friends were gross. They weren't cheerleaders or anything; they were normal girls, but too mature to hang out with me in school. But as I picked out what to wear and miraculously got cash from my father for the trip, something in the back of my mind kept telling me it wasn't going to happen. It was just too good to be true. I couldn't picture myself at a concert at all. I couldn't see lights, a stage, KC up there whining–none of it. It was less than a fuzzy dream that you can't remember when you wake up; it was nonexistent. And as it turned out, it really was. The whole trip was called off. I never got the exact story but it had something to do with Cecily spouting off some selfish shit to her dad, so he decided to sell the tickets after all.

For a while after that, I thought I had real intuition. I thought that if I would just open myself up the universal consciousness I could know things like that–like if something was just not going to happen, and maybe I could even predict the future. Until a year or so later when I had that same feeling about my trip up to Asheville to spend a summer with my father's family. I just knew it would never happen. It was too good to be true. An entire teenage summer without my parents. That time, though, it actually happened. And that's when I started to realize that the universal consciousness was bullshit. More of that rosy kind of hope people try pass off on you to make you think you're more than you are. Of course, I had a lousy time that summer. My cousin spent every day with her boyfriend while I sat and watched them make out.

Still, a small part of me held out hope that I had an intuition. And that's why I knew somehow, that Camelia was the victim. I thought it would be cool that I would have a childhood invisible friend named after a murdered person and I started to imagine that she had come to me as a ghost. Maybe I was so terrified I'd blocked it all out and couldn't remember. Ghosts are terrifying, most of the time. Especially creepy little girl ghosts. What if the forces of nature, or rather, ghostdom, conspired to make me forget that Camelia's ghost came to me and scared me shitless, and now I had this book, and all would be revealed? What if I upset the natural balance of space and time by finding out? I didn't believe any of that, of course, but it's always nice to imagine that there's something else out there.

I grabbed a beer out of the fridge and ignored my mother in the living room, even though she started asking me questions. How was downtown? Did you have a good time? Are you in love? She kept asking until my bedroom door slammed shut. I popped open my beer, sat it on my night stand, crawled into bed with my reading pillow and started with the back of the book.

A couple of hours later I was still trembling, fighting the urge to scream out loud, and sitting on a bar stool at

Harold's up north of town trying to fend off advances from the usual assortment of drunks. Herbert the Pervert was there. He kept sidling up behind me and leaning in to put his face in front of me. He never should have shaved off that handlebar mustache. It was the only thing that gave his face character.

"Why so glum, chum?" He said.

"Are you fucking kidding me?"

"You are so testy when you're drunk."

"Like you've ever seen me sober."

"You were sober when I met you."

"How do you know?"

"It was the end of the school day, don't you remember?"

"How could I forget?"

"Where've you been? I thought you'd given up the booze or something."

It was true. I hadn't been out in weeks. "I've taken up reading," I told him. "It's hard to read when you're plastered."

"How's your friend, Sylvia?" He said her name like it was a snake, drawing out the last two syllables like shed skin.

"Sylvie," I said. "I don't hear from her."

"But you two are best friends." He finally managed to get the guy in the stool next to me to give it up to him. He rested his elbows on the bar and ran his hands through his greasy dark hair.

"What do you know about it?" I said.

"In school, you were always together."

"We haven't been friends since then."

"Really?"

He bought me a few more beers and I drank until everything was blurry.

"I think I finally get it," I told the Perv. "I understand you drunks."

"You don't include yourself in that?"

I shook my head. "Nope. I've always known why I drink. But you people—" I waved my beer in the air. "I've often wondered what drove you to inebriation."

"And what is that?"

I slid off the stool. "You're trying to forget something. What are you trying to forget?"

He stared at me and I could tell neither one of us could see exactly straight. "Why do you drink, if not to forget?" He said.

I couldn't manage to climb back onto my stool, so I leaned against the bar. "I drink to get numb," I said. "Numb is the only way I can feel anything."

"That doesn't make any sense."

"You think I don't know that?"

"Let me drive you home," he said.

I laughed and left the bar with him following me. I got as far away from the front door as possible, to the middle of the dirt parking lot, before I vomited. That was the first time I vomited during the night and not the next day since that time I got trapped in a bathroom stall at The Sandbar, and some girl was kind enough to pick me up off the seat and turn me around so I could puke on my own pee. It was not pleasant. Not so much this time either; there was only the Perv to hold onto and when I fell to my knees, I got vomit on my pants.

346

I had a meeting with Dr. Crazy in the morning but it was difficult to get out of bed. I lay there for a long time staring at the red book on my dresser. I'd only managed to read the first chapter the night before and panicked, like I couldn't breathe, like my room was suddenly darkening and if I didn't get up and get out, it would go completely black and I'd be blinded and unable to move.

I trudged into the kitchen to get a big glass of water and downed it in one long glorious gulping session then nodded a hello to my mother, who was sitting on the sofa crying, on my way to the shower. After I got dressed, I found myself standing in the little living room for a bit watching her sobbing on the couch. I went over and sat down on the other end. She was hunched over just a bit with a beer can between her legs and wadded tissues scattered about.

"It's only ten o'clock," I said.

She looked over at me like I didn't make any sense. And maybe I didn't. Technically, I was still drunk from the night before, so who was I to criticize?

"What's wrong?" I asked her.

She shook her head and made the ugly crying face at me, but she managed to drink a few gulps of beer. I could see it then. My dream–standing in line at the church; the missing face–but it was real. And it was my mother. She was leading me up the aisle to the casket. Camelia was in the coffin, not me. And my mother stood behind me while I tried to get away, holding my shoulders tight against her belly. "See here?" She said. "This is what happens to little girls who don't obey their mothers."

"What's wrong?" I asked her again. "Is it Brock?" I

wiped tears from my face.

She nodded.

"I have to go to my session."

I got up to get my purse out of my bedroom and she followed me. I took it from off the back of my desk chair and turned to leave only to find her there staring at me all red in the face with a stream of snot on her upper lip.

"He broke up with me," she said.

Before I knew what was happening, she'd grabbed me, pulled me into this tight squeeze and was sobbing hard, shaking both of us. I froze. Motionless. My left hand extended beyond us to save my purse from the horror. After a few seconds I managed to extricate my-self; I knew it was an awful thing to do. I was supposed to hug her back, to hold her close and pat her and tell her everything would be okay, but it was alien to me and I couldn't do it. The best I could do was lead her, sobbing, out of the bedroom and back to the couch and tell her to drink more beer.

"It'll be okay," I told her.

I was lying. Things get back to semi-normal, but they're never the same again. The world shifts. Scar tissue forms; we harden. Things are never okay again. But we try to pretend they're better than ever.

# 33.

*Dear Camelia, Things are always dark, now. Muted. I remember sunshine; I can almost feel it when I think of it. But the sun doesn't shine like that anymore. I can look back, to a time when I was young, like you, and I see myself frowning; I'm not happy. I've tried to bury it, but it won't go away. Dulling the brightness of it didn't help. Not at all.*

I brought the book with me to see Dr. Crazy, but left it in the car at the last minute. I knew I needed somebody to read all of it and tell me if it was okay or not. I needed a buffer between myself and the reality of it. But it couldn't be Dr. Crazy.

I told her that I'd been drinking less—no need to go into the night before—that work was going well, that I thought I might be ready to go back to school next fall, and that my mother hugged me.

"She hugged you?"

I nodded.

"Is that significant?"

"Significant to what?"

"To you," she said. "Do you want to talk about it?"

I looked around the little office. It smelled like cigarettes and I figured that was why I always lit up, even though I was getting pretty good at quitting everywhere else. I felt like I'd gone backwards, but I couldn't put my finger on why. It seemed that there was forward movement, a life working itself out, but just then I thought, no. It's falling away.

"About what?"

"The hug."

Oh, the hug. "It was very uncomfortable."

"Why is that?"

"We're not a hugging family."

Debbie Clark lived in the neighborhood back behind my house when I was growing up, in that house where we were a family. Debbie had enough imagination for both of us. Once at P.E. the sky was filled with gray clouds and there was a hole in them where rays of sun blistered through to the ground and Debbie told me that God was talking to someone.

I thought she was insane. One day, she and I walked home from school together. We didn't get to do it very often because her mother picked her up most days and took her off somewhere. We stood in her driveway chatting and her father came out of the house with a suitcase, his suit jacket slung over his arm.

"Are you leaving again?" She asked him.

They hugged and he said he was sorry; and then he kissed her on the lips. I was grossed out and it must have been on my face because she said, "What? What is it?"

"You kissed him on the lips," I said after we'd

watched him drive away. It was the oddest thing I'd ever seen.

She just shrugged and said, "So?"

I guess I knew people hugged their parents. And I suppose I knew that their parents kissed them on the cheeks. But to kiss on the lips was one bit of intimacy too much for me.

"So, how did it feel?" Dr. Crazy asked me.

"Uncomfortable."

"You said that. Why?"

"It ought to be uncomfortable to hug someone that you aren't used to hugging."

"You think so?"

I nodded. But I didn't think so. Not really.

"What sort of uncomfortable was it?"

What kind of uncomfortable was it? How was I supposed to answer that? The truth was that it was like a horror movie. You know the kind where a crazy person is crying and follows the girl into a room and just stands there, weepy like, hunched over, like a psycho axe murderer and then she shuffles forward and hugs the girl. Like that. Scary stuff.

"I just didn't like it," I said. And I wasn't going to talk more about it.

"Remember the dreams?" She said. "And how you felt powerful watching your mother being carried away by monkeys?"

"The flying monkeys. From *The Wizard of Oz*."

"Right. Did it feel like the opposite of that?"

"Not exactly." She leaned forward slightly which meant I was supposed to keep going. "When I felt powerful in the dreams, I was still really scared. And pretty disgusted, too. And I felt like that when she hugged me. Scared. Disgusted. But not powerful."

"Weak?"

"No. Not weak. But...helpless."

How was therapy supposed to help when the therapist never tells you the answers or the results? So, what did it mean? That was for me to figure out. But I wasn't going to spend my time trying to figure out riddles like why I felt powerful watching my mother be torn apart by flying monkeys, or staring at myself in a coffin, but helpless when my mother hugged me. Maybe if I told Dr. Crazy that I knew now that it wasn't me in the coffin, after all, she'd tell me what it meant. But I knew exactly what she'd say. She'd say it was me in the coffin in the dream, and that was all that really mattered.

None of it meant anything and therapy was just me talking to myself. Dr. Crazy never acted like a mother figure, or a sister figure, or a therapist figure ought to. She never said go to school, express your feelings, or stop hating your mother. Don't get drunk all the time. Don't jump off the roof of Three River Terrace. None of that. How hard could it be?

# 34.

It was almost Valentine's Day before I talked to Bond again. He ambushed me outside work one evening at six and demanded to know why I was avoiding him. The parking lot was full of people, going in and coming out, not a good place for a confrontation.

"It's not just you," I said. He looked at me like I was crazy. "I'm avoiding everyone."

I thought that would make it okay. It was a few weeks after I vomited out front of Harold's and I hadn't been out since. I stayed in my room most of the time, trying to avoid my mother and Aunt Aubrey. It wasn't easy. And I carried the red book around with me in my huge floppy purse that rarely matched my outfit. I thought that at some point, I'd find the courage to read beyond the first chapter.

"Why?"

I shrugged but said nothing.

"Tell me."

I stared at him. I opened my mouth. I was going to say something but I didn't know what, and I couldn't make anything up quick enough. I was thinking along the lines of, "Jesus H. Christ, Bond, it's only been a few weeks." Instead I started crying. Right out of the blue. Like I'd been bottling it up–but I hadn't been. And there was that pain in my chest; I hadn't noticed it before, but maybe it had been there for a while. It felt like someone wrapped a rubber band around me and was tightening it with a garrote. Turning and turning, suffocating me.

Bond grabbed me and held me close, rubbing my back, and I let him for just a little while before pulling away.

"Please tell me what's wrong."

"I'll show you." I pulled open my big floppy purse and took out the book.

"It's that book you bought–your first true crime." He took it and started flipping through the pages.

"She was my childhood invisible friend." It sounded ridiculous saying it out loud. Lies can sound ridiculous; the truth is supposed to sound reasonable. "I used to write her letters; I was such a weird kid. My invisible friend was a real little girl, and she was murdered. How strange is that?"

"Over in Ocoee," he said.

"She was only eight. And I was eight. I must have heard about it on the news." I couldn't tell him about the viewing–that my mother drove me all the way over to Orlando to look at a dead girl. Who does that?

"And you wrote her letters?"

I nodded.

"Did you save them?"

"Yes. But I lost them."

"Wouldn't it be cool to read them now?"

His face was all lit up with excitement and I remembered how much he loved old stuff so I nodded and said, "Maybe I'll look for them."

"You don't think it would be neat to read them?"

"I don't know. I might be too afraid."

"Of what? It's your invisible friend from childhood. They'll be embarrassing, sure, but you were young, right?"

"Bond, you're being a little bit creepy. She was a real little girl."

"But your invisible friend wasn't."

He stared at me, his face still frozen in excitement about old letters and creepy ghost stories. Why was language so fluid? Why couldn't words carry your meaning with them over into another person's head. Then we wouldn't have to explain things so much. We could say one or two words and the other person would understand.

"Yes, she was," I told him. "I was writing to *her*. My invisible friend from childhood was invisible because she was dead."

"Why would you do that?"

"Because I'm crazy insane."

"You are not."

"I am. I really am."

"I think you want to be crazy."

"Why would anyone want to be crazy?"

"You're not crazy. You're just...I don't know. Sensitive."

I waited a bit, just staring at him, before I said, "You really do sound just like my mother."

# 35.

Valentine's Day was Saturday and Bond wanted to go out on a date. I told him that Valentine's Day was heavy with expectations and wasn't it enough that we did the New Year's Eve thing? But he insisted we act like a couple.

The old biddies worked the evening shift so the young people could enjoy the biggest date night of the year. William found a girlfriend who no doubt followed all the rules and guidelines of dating and wore comfortable shoes. Petrie was spending the evening playing *Dungeons & Dragons* with her horde of fellow questers. They were all going to eat chocolates and battle demons in a field of roses to mark the occasion. Alice had a date night with her husband, which I found a little gross. And Bond and I went to the movies. He brought me a box of chocolates in the shape of a heart that I left with my mother knowing she'd eat all the good ones and pinch open the fruit-filled ones for a taste. We saw *Mannequin*. And then afterward we laughed about how we should have gone for the Stallone flick instead. I let him kiss me good night. I went to bed thinking it must be that simple—you just ended up with the person that liked you enough to bother.

A few days later, I was sitting on my bed staring at the red book about Camelia. I opened it up and turned to the bookmark at the second chapter but as soon as I saw the first few words I snapped the book shut and went out into the living room. The police lieutenant was uncovering the body. They'd already found the dog, its head bashed in, and they'd shuffled Camelia's father away from the scene. Samuel Roen, the guy who wrote the book, was too good at description for my taste. For a novel, sure, like *The Shining*. It's fine to feel like you are that little kid staying at an enormously spooky, empty hotel. And you're being chased by shrubberies. But if it's real, no thank you. I don't want to feel like I'm there, brushing the Florida sand away from a little girl's body. What was he thinking? But I finally understood the weirdos who spent all their time in the true crime section. It was just as I'd suspected; they were barely a few maternal confrontations away from going on murderous rampages.

"The mental health center called again," my mother said as she took her seat on the sofa with Aunt Aubrey. I was in the big rocking chair. They were watching Sally Jessie Raphael on the television. Princess Patty Cakes was outside scratching at the sliding glass door; my mother squawked at her—this shrieking noise that she made whenever she wanted a person—or a dog—to stop annoying her. It was something like a snort and a scream at the same time. The PPC startled and ran off to the back fence to bark at the ditch. I hadn't seen Fat Orange Jack in about a year and now he was out there digging stuff out of the pond. Mom and Aunt Aubrey didn't talk to him anymore, not since he married a girl about my age and trotted her out now and then to play in their above-ground pool.

"So?" I said.

"So, why aren't you going to your appointments? They said you haven't been there for a few weeks."

"I don't think they're allowed to give you that information."

"I'm paying for it, so I guess I'm entitled."

"I thought Dad was paying for it."

"Your father? Since when has he ever done anything for you?"

"Aside from the sperm donation, you mean?"

"What's gotten into you?"

"Aunt Aubrey told me Dad was paying for it."

"He paid for the first few visits and then told me if you kept going, I had to pay. He said there wasn't anything wrong with you."

"Is that true?" I asked Aunt Aubrey.

"Of course there's something wrong with you," she said.

I knew she meant well. Aunt Aubrey always meant well. You could tell by the way she was always smiling. And anyway, there *was* something wrong with me. It wasn't like she was lying; and it couldn't be an insult if it was the truth.

"Not that," I said. "Is it true that my dad quit paying?"

She shrugged and looked down at her lap.

"How the hell would Aubrey know?"

"She talks to him."

Aunt Aubrey looked up at me, her eyes wide like I'd called her a slut.

"Well, you do," I said.

"Is that true?" My mother turned on her.

"He calls me to find out what's going on. He said you won't let him talk to the kids."

"That's not true."

"He says you hang up on him when asks for Eunice."

"Well, that's true."

"Where are my letters to Camelia?" It just popped out. I was sure I hadn't even been thinking about it. But there it was. They both looked at me like I was from Mars. "Where are they?"

"What the hell are you talking about?" My mother turned her attention back to Sally, who was interviewing a panel of prostitutes or something.

"The letters I wrote to Camelia, my invisible friend."

"Oh, for Christ's sake, *that*. Jesus, you were odd, weren't you?"

"Where are they?"

"How the hell should I know?"

"You stole them from me."

"I did no such thing. Princess Patty Cakes stop all that barking or I'll give you something to bark about. I did no such thing."

"You did. You found them in my closet that time and took them from me."

"Oh, that," she got up to open the sliding door, screamed at the PPC again, and then returned to the sofa, letting herself drop hard enough to bounce Aunt Aubrey. "I remember."

"What did you do with them?"

"I wanted to burn them. I figured if I put them in the trash you'd dig them back out again. But I didn't know where to light a fire, so I put them up in the closet."

"Are they still there?" I started to get up.

"Don't be stupid, of course not. That was at the Yellow Sands house. I don't have room for them here. If I still had them, they'd be in storage."

"Storage?"

"Well, yes. Don't look at me like I'm insane. I'm not the crazy one." She laughed and Aunt Aubrey giggled with her.

"You have a storage unit?"

She rolled her eyes and got up to dig through her purse. She pulled a key off her key ring and handed it to me. "Baker's. Way up on US1. On the left. Why do you want them anyway? Are you going to throw them away?"

"Why didn't you want me to write to Camelia?"

"Because it was weird." She plopped back down on the sofa.

"You knew she was a real little girl?"

"Your invisible friend? Don't be absurd, she was imaginary. But you named her after that girl who died. That was weird."

"Why did you try to get Puddles to go to school with me after you took me to the funeral?"

She stared at me with this look on her face, like she was realizing for the first time that I really, really was insane. But when she spoke, it wasn't usual. It was quiet.

"What the hell are you going on about now?" And she shook her head, like something was rattling around in there and she had to pop it back into place.

"You took me to see a dead girl in a coffin. A little girl who walked to school alone with her little dog and was kidnaped and murdered. And then you told me to go to school. All alone. With my dog." I shuddered.

"*Your* dog?" She threw me one of those harrumph snorts and started watching Sally again. After a second or two, she mumbled, "Can't leave anything in the past."

"Mom, you pushed me up to her, in the coffin, a dead girl, and you told me it would happen to me if I disobeyed you again."

The color drained from her face and her eyes were round and she trembled. "I did not. I never said such a thing."

"I remember it."

"How the hell can you remember anything? You spend all your time drunk."

"That doesn't mean I wouldn't remember what you did when I was eight."

"I remember it." Aunt Aubrey said. "I remember when you both came home. You'd have thought you took her to a war zone. You scared the shit out of her, Darlene."

"I did not. There were other kids there, you know, and it wasn't like the child was bloody or anything."

"But you threatened me," I said.

"I did no such thing. I told you all about talking to strangers. It was a lesson, that's all. A lesson any good mother would teach her child."

362

"In front of a dead body?" Aubrey said.

"You keep out of it."

"You were so upset," Aunt Aubrey said to me. "You cried for days while they ran the news story." She turned to my mother. "And you kept letting her watch it. And then you had the gall to take her to the viewing–and on the day after her birthday. What were you thinking?"

"She didn't cry over the news."

"Maybe not while she watched it; but all the time after."

"Hell, Aubrey, that's just it. She cried *all the time*. Every little thing made her cry."

"So you took her to see a corpse."

"Maybe I did." And here my mother turned to me. "But I wanted to go. And I thought it would help you get over it."

"And then she couldn't get you to go back to school." Aunt Aubrey said, smiling as usual. "You stayed home the rest of the week. Every time she tried to get you out the door you screamed your head off and she thought the police would come and lock her up."

"How did she get me to go back?"

"Don't you dare," my mother pointed a finger at Aunt Aubrey.

"Tell me."

Aunt Aubrey's smile faded and she raised her chin, offering my mother a wicked sneer. "She beat the hell out of you."

I looked at my mother and wondered why I wasn't angry, why I just felt sad and like I ought to cry, but I was too sad even for that. "And then you told me to go to school and not be afraid. You're no sissy, you said. And here, take your little dog with you. Just like Camelia did. Just like Camelia."

They both stared at me with their mouths open and Sally was on the television talking about sex or love or some god-awful thing.

"I didn't think it would be that big of a deal. My god, how many years ago now? And you're still upset about it."

"I thought you were trying to have me killed."

"Don't be ridiculous. You are so god-damned sensitive about every god-damned thing."

"You wanted me to die; just like Camelia."

"I did not." Her hoarse yell echoed in the small room. "All I knew was that you refused to go to school for a week. And when I finally got you to go back you came home crying every god-forsaken day. And then that woman brought you home and said you were running around the neighborhood screaming at people. I swear you've been crazy all your life."

"Darlene, stop saying that," Aunt Aubrey said. "It's not nice."

"Why didn't you talk to me about it?" I said.

"Lord have mercy." Her neck veins flared and pulsated. That was when you were supposed to run—when the veins popped out. They signaled an oncoming slap. But I didn't think she'd expend the energy necessary to get across the room to hit me. "You think I didn't try?" She flung her arms in the air as if only God knew her pain. "But you wouldn't talk to me. You were so god-damned sensitive about everything. Nobody could talk to you. How was I supposed to know it was about that little girl. You cried when squirrels were dead in the road. You cried when you saw soap operas. Jesus Christ, Eunice, you cried all the damn time. You're still crying."

We all sat trying not to look at one another and I struggled to stop the tears. I half expected my mother to jump up and tell me to go to my room or she'd give me something to cry about.

"It wasn't my fault." She burst out sobbing and wailing. "I did my best. I wish you could appreciate the things I've done for you."

In the movies, and in books, characters have these grand epiphanies that hit them in one fell swoop. Something triggers a memory or a bit of knowledge and bam, they figure it all out and soon after that, the story is done. But that's not how it works in real life. Grand revelations come at you in snippets of insight that you sometimes catch hold of only for a split second, and they're gone. And then you spend the rest of your lifetime realizing them again and again until you finally become fully conscious of what they were trying to show you.

As I watched my mother's shoulders shudder with sobs, and as I watched her fight back the choking and blubbering long enough to drink her beer, I realized two things. First I understood, finally, that my life was my life and I was stuck with it. I couldn't go back and make my childhood Camelia's. I couldn't do it when I was eight and I couldn't do it now; and that was probably why I was on the roof of Three River Terrace. Not because of sex, or booze, or just that this place sucks balls, but because I would never get to have the life that Camelia could have had. Neither of us got it. And only one of us deserved it. And second, I would never be free of my mother until I was dead. Even if she walked out of the house at that moment and into the path of a garbage truck, she would haunt my thoughts, my psyche, and my dreams of flying monkeys for the rest of my fucking life. Those are heavy philosophical things to ponder. It was best that I didn't think much more on them at the time.

"Whatever all this is," my mother said. She wiped the tears from her face and guzzled beer from her can. "You get it all worked out by the twentieth of June."

Aunt Aubrey and I stared at her, trying to figure out what the hell she was talking about.

"What are you talking about?" Aunt Aubrey said.

"I'm talking about June. Jimmy and Patricia's wedding." She turned to me. "You get back to therapy and get this nonsense out of your system. I can't handle your theatrics on a normal day; how can I get through a wedding? Not everything is about you, you know."

What is a fell swoop, anyway?

# 36.

I was still digesting my childhood and my epiphanies, and forcing all the puzzles into one stunted life, over the next week. Bond was kind enough to give me a bit more space. But it was Saturday again; I was at work, and it was habit for me to look for him around lunch time. I looked once or twice toward the front of the store but made myself go to the back and shelve books where I wouldn't notice if he decided not to come. I was walking around in a fog, I knew. But luckily I'd worked out all the details of the job by then and could do it all brain dead. The phone rang and I thought for a few hopeful seconds it might be Bond, and when Alice found me, I was sure of it. She pulled me into the back room.

"A man called for you earlier," she said, closing the door behind us. "Before you got here. I told him to call back and he's on the line now. You need to talk to him."

"Who is it?"

She shook her head. "Just pick up the phone." She stood there and waited, watching me, and that scared me.

My first thought was the FBI and I'd somehow fallen

into a drug ring or a baby stealing ring. I always imagined these things could happen when you spent a lot of your time plastered. I liked to think I remembered everything I ever did, drunk or sober, but if I was being questioned by the cops, I'd cave and admit I was wasted and didn't know a thing.

I picked up the phone and said, "Hello."

"Is this April MacMillan?"

I nodded, which, I knew, was stupid. Alice left and pulled the door closed very quietly, which only scared me more. "Yes," I said.

"You knew my son, Paul Brown?"

"Yes." I'd already started tearing up and my mouth was curling into that ugly cry frown.

"Did you know that he passed away last week?"

"No, sir."

"He left you a note. A letter. If you give me your address, I'll send it to you."

"I thought he was in rehab?" I said, as if no one ever died in rehab. But seriously, has anyone ever died in rehab?

"There was a waiting list," he said. "He was going in, in a few days, before he..."

"I'm sorry."

"I just wondered," he said. "Would it be all right–do you mind? Could I read it?"

"Read it to me," I said. "Over the phone."

"You're sure he wouldn't mind?"

Why do people do that? Why do they convince themselves that the dead remember? That they hover and watch? Why wasn't that creepy instead of comforting?

"He wouldn't mind," I said.

I heard him tear open an envelope and there was a pause and then he breathed a jagged sigh and I knew he was crying.

"Dear April," he read. "It's just like Sue said. I let myself get lost and every time they tried to find me, I pushed myself farther and farther away until I was too far and it was too late. And you were right, too, about the universe. We have no obligation to time." Another ragged breath and something of a whine escaped him. "And I want you to know that I know it's not a game and I'm real sorry that I said that about Sue being one down. Nobody's counting."

And then I heard him weeping.

"Mr. Brown?"

"I'm sorry. Sorry. Thank you for letting me read it."

Now I was sobbing, too. "Can you go ahead and send it to me? You can make a copy if you want, but...can you?"

"Of course, of course."

I gave him the address at my mother's duplex.

"Thank you," he said.

"For what?"

"Paulie left me a letter. He said that nobody under-stood him, until you. But he said," he sobbed. "He said it wasn't enough and it's not your fault. And not my fault."

"Of course not. Trust me," I adjusted the phone into my shoulder so I could use both hands to wipe my face. "It's not about us."

"What is it about then?"

"Didn't he give you a reason?"

"He said there was too much pain everywhere. He couldn't live with it. Was he in pain? He was always a happy kid, maybe a little sensitive. I don't understand."

"I know." I said. "And I know you want me to help you, but I don't think I can." He shuddered and cried and it only made me cry more. I wished he understood about Paulie and me. If he understood he wouldn't be doing that. "It's like," I said. "It's like a nightmare that you can't wake from and when you try to tell people about it, they don't see that it's scary–like, they don't see the shadows that you see. It's like being at a party where the furniture is corpses but people are sitting on them and putting drinks on them."

Mr. Brown was probably realizing that I was crazy, like Paulie, and maybe that was a good thing. Paulie and I, and Sue, we knew we couldn't explain it to anyone. They'd think we were nuts. And maybe we were. If that made Paulie's dad feel any better, fine by me.

"There's pain everywhere, Mr. Brown, and Paulie didn't know how to look away."

"I think I understand," he said.

"I'm really sorry."

"Me, too."

I could hear him already licking his wounds, repairing that opening in the wall.

Everybody's walking around wrapped tight in a cocoon. Pinpricks of light bring the real world through the barrier–sometimes it's good stuff, like warmth and love and hope. But too often it's horrific–pain, genocide, lemmings throwing themselves off a cliff. Most people spend an inordinate amount of energy every day patching the holes that make them want to scream, ridding themselves of the reality they'd rather not know. And it works well enough; if you can call what the human race enjoys mental health.

Sue was the type of person who, in her frantic race to blot out the ugly, patches up the good holes and the bad, and turns herself away from all of it—she closes herself up into herself and can't see outside anymore and the sadness, loneliness, and desperation of it drives her insane. Paulie—he was like me. A glint of light scared him and instead of covering it up, he had to see...he ripped a wide gash in the cocoon and once the real world was exposed he spent the rest of his life trying to turn away. But the cocoon had wilted all around him. The cocoon couldn't protect him anymore.

"I don't know if I should ask." I didn't know if I should know. "But, how did he do it?"

He sobbed and coughed and sobbed some more. "He jumped off the roof of his mother's apartment building."

That little addict stole my idea. I could see him standing there, on the roof, looking off over the bay, the wind whipping at his hair. And he'd smile, remembering how I hate that sort of thing. And then he'd think of peace and darkness and nothing, and step off. I'd never be able to jump from the roof of Three River Terrace after that; it would look like I was copying. I was willing to bet that Paulie did that on purpose. Maybe it was his way of trying to find me.

# 37.

Bond lifted the garage door of my mother's storage unit and we peered in. We were up on US1, north of town where the only things a person expects to see are seedy motels and storage facilities. This was the kind of place you stored dead bodies or locked trunks, with secrets you hoped no one would find until after you died. Nobody would keep anything of real value there. It was musty and dirty and dusty and Bond and I stood there staring, gawking really, at the stacks of boxes my mother had stuffed in the tiny unit.

"What are we looking for, exactly?" He asked.

"Letters."

"Don't be facetious. Were they in a box or an album? In envelopes, even?"

I wanted to ask him what facetious meant, but I didn't. Sometimes I thought Bond didn't believe anything that he didn't want to. Life was, for him, however he imagined it to be. In his world, I wasn't crazy, just a bit sensitive. I didn't have a drinking problem, really; all I needed was a dose of good sense. And I wasn't stupid in the least; I could probably be a rocket scientist if I wanted. And while I supposed if it was just a matter of reading more books and learning more words, I might could do anything. But there was a modicum of self-respect a person needed to take it all in, and some of us didn't have the shields necessary for focusing on building it.

"I put each one in its own envelope and I wrote Camelia on the front. But I don't know if my mother took them out of the envelopes or not. And I kept them in a shoe box, but I don't know if that's still with them, either."

"So, letters. Okay then."

"I was right the first time, see?"

He laughed and started pulling boxes out of the unit, organizing them in the parking lot. Anything we'd looked through went on one side and anything he wanted me to check on the other. He said he didn't feel right going through personal papers and anyway, I should be the one to find the letters. He found two boxes full of pornography on VHS, boxes of sports stuff, knee pads and gloves, boxes of records, and boxes of men's clothing.

"This is my father's stuff," I said, finally figuring it all out.

"Why would your letters be in here, then?"

"She said she put them up in the closet with the photo albums."

"Were they your father's, too?"

"Well, he was in them."

It was family memorabilia–anything that reminded her of him, and what we once were. The China they got after they were married; the family silver; his college fraternity junk; even her wedding gown. All stuffed into a five-foot dump. And finally, in the back right corner, we found two boxes full of photo albums. Bond took them out into the bright spring sunlight for me and started packing the other boxes back into the unit as I went through them.

"Look, look," I said. "Pictures of my brother and I when we were babies and little people."

"You were cute as punch," he said.

Who says that? Who says cute as punch? And what does it mean? Does it mean spiked punch? I was as cute as a girl can be after you've drunk a lot of spiked punch? That's what I decided it meant. One time I was at Harold's and this guy was buying me beers and I left with him. He took me out to the marina on the lagoon and we got on this boat and lowered a little dinghy from the side of it. He said it was his friend's boat, but I didn't believe him. He rowed us out into the river to a tiny island where we had sex on sand and sharp bits of shell, and among the crabs. Then he rowed us back as the sun was rising and I remember thinking how odd that all was. How odd that this guy should want to take me out to an island when we could have just done it in the back of his car; and how odd that he hadn't taken the opportunity to slit my throat and leave me there. I mean, it could have been months before anyone found my body–he'd have plenty of time to skip town or come up with an alibi.

Unless that was his go-to island for sex. Like he had a fetish where he couldn't perform unless he was on that little island with the odor of rotting fish and seaweed all around and the gulls up in the palms watching us, waiting for morning, and imagining we were shipwrecked and had to start a new society. But I didn't see how that would matter. I mean, sure, maybe he was squeamish and wouldn't want to bring another girl there knowing my body was rotting somewhere under a bunch of sea grapes. But he could be a serial killer and just kill every girl he brought there. Maybe that wasn't part of his castaway fantasy.

Anyway, as we were rowing back to his friend's boat, he said, "You look different in the light." And I was thinking I should ask him what he meant. Different, better? Or different, worse? I was pretty sure he meant worse. That's what happens when you pick up girls at bars wasted out of your mind. Everyone knows we look better as the night moves along and the more you drink–I mean, come on, I was alone in a bar at three in the morning, you think I'm going to be prom queen material?

"Do you want kids?" Bond said.

"What kind of question is that?"

"I'm not offering," he said and laughed. "I just wondered. Making conversation, you know. We saw cute little kids."

"Well, no."

"No, you don't want to have the conversation?"

"No, I don't want to have kids."

"Who doesn't want to have kids? Everybody wants kids."

"Then why did you ask me?"

"I told you, I was just making conversation. You really don't want any?"

"No."

"But why?"

I dug out another photo album. "I don't know. I just don't."

"Okay. So, you'll consider it."

I laughed and I guess he took that to mean I *would* consider it. "No, I don't think I will."

"But why not?"

He stopped moving boxes and came over to sit down on the asphalt next to me. I knew somehow that this wasn't about getting married and having kids. I didn't think Bond was any more interested in reproducing with me than I was with him. I knew it was deeper than that.

Bond wanted kids. He wanted that joy of watching a creature he'd created smile and laugh, and burp and eat, and he wanted to hear the word "daddy," and he wanted to feel tiny little kid hugs. He wanted to be a kid again, play on the floor, read *Green Eggs and Ham* fifty times, wear towels as capes, play in the tub. He wanted that joy and he couldn't fathom how anyone else would not want that. But he didn't understand—hardly anyone did—that with that joy comes unbelievable pain.

I turned away from him, put my face in the sun and squinted. "I have this weird family, you know? They don't feel like other people. They're...stagnant, maybe is the word. You'd see if I ever brought you over, for like, Christmas or something. *I know.* I've gone with other people, to meet their families. I spent the night with Cricket Swanson, in middle school, and I saw how her family hugged one another, for no earthly reason at all. You come into a room, you get a hug; you say something funny, you get a hug; you thank someone for a gift, hug. They hugged all the god-damned time. It was seriously weird. And I spent the night with Debbie Clark, and even with Claire Lindsay. All smiles. Kind words, and how sweet you are and how clever you are, and how great that dinner was and wow, mom, what a fabulous dessert, and mom and dad were twinkling in the eyes when they looked at their families. That's how I knew that love existed. That's probably what freaked me out about Janet Kingston when I went to stay with her family that time and cried so hard they sent me home. She just wanted to touch me all the time because, apparently, that's what people do."

He stared at me with a smile on his face.

"What?" I said.

"That's more than you've said to me in your entire life."

"I said all that out loud?"

He laughed and fell over on the ground. Bond was always a good exaggerated laugher. I kicked at him and he finally sat back up and went back to smiling.

"So you don't want to have kids because you think you'll be like your family. I get that. But just the fact that you recognize that–"

"No, that's not it. That's not it."

"Then what?"

"I don't know if I can explain it. I guess you're part right. I'm too much like my family. But, I'm also different from them. Not different in wanting to touch people, or wanting to say nice things. Just…I feel different."

He tilted his head and squinched his mouth. "That

doesn't make much sense."

"It's like, honestly, it's like all the thwarted and shunned emotion of the Abernathy family has finally found a place inside me. And it's too much."

He stared at me. This was why I didn't like talking. Connections can be imagined, and usually are. You tried, but it was fake. No one understood what you were getting at. No one could get into your head or your heart and really feel you. My family made more sense to me than all the others hugging and smiling and making nice. Because the world was not a place that deserved that.

"I don't want to have children," I said. "Because I wouldn't be able to stand the pain."

"They have drugs."

"No Bond," I started digging into the box again, pulling out photo albums and rubber banded clumps of papers. I wished now that Bond was gone. "Not physical pain. I mean–just imagine it. Imagine when your child is hurting, or worse, dying. Imagine living knowing your child isn't happy. Imagine when he cries, when someone hurts him, when no one likes him, when he struggles. I don't think I could live with that constant, unforgiving pain and fear, tearing at my heart."

I dropped everything back into the box and turned to him. I'd hurt him, connected him with those parts that no one wanted to touch. I'd ruined that perfect picture of a little family, all smiling and happy, because no one was like that. And even if they were, they weren't the kind of people I would be, not even the kind of people I'd want to know. Maybe Bond was seeing that now. Maybe he was understanding me and would stop coming around.

"Okay," he said. He got up and started packing boxes in again. "I think I get it."

I reached in the box and pulled out a bunch of envelopes. Scrawled on the first one, in childish print, was the name Camelia.

# 38.

I read chapter two of the red book with the knife on the cover and left all of my opened letters to Camelia on the bed. I drove over to the Pool Pit and took a seat at the bar, ordered a pitcher and the bartender didn't even blink. I was on my second when the bar was full and noisy and Herbert the Pervert took a seat beside me.

"You all right?"

I nodded. We drank together for a while and he swiveled in his chair to look at me.

"The only reason I asked you about your friend last time I saw you," he said. "I was just making conversation. That's all."

"So?"

"You remember that time we went out and, you know?"

"I know."

"My wife left me. That same day. She took the kids and went off to Montana and I never saw them again."

"Why are you telling me?"

"I thought you should know. I wasn't just, you know,

making you. I was trying to forget." He raised his glass with a sheepish little grin and we clinked together. "I know you and Sylvia call me a pervert."

"It was you picking up that girl at school. We figured you liked them real young."

"She was my niece."

I nodded and laughed at him. "Your niece, Lolita."

He thought for a second and then he bowed his head and chuckled. "I guess I thought that would impress you."

"See. You were a pervert."

He worked hard to catch up with my drunk, and he let me not talk. When the bar closed at two, everyone filed outside planning what to do next. Harold's was just over the county line and open late and most of us would end up there. But I started walking along the plaza and Herb followed me.

"Where you going?"

"Out back."

"You got to pee?"

"Nope."

He came along and we walked down the alleyway and across the asphalt where the trucks unloaded into the stores and through the broken fence and leftover bits of yellow police tape. We sat against the hill that led up to the tracks and when I lay back that was his cue–the Perv was all over me.

I couldn't get the picture of Camelia's battered, mutilated body out of my head, or the thought of the pervert who had done it to her. I never should have read the second chapter and I knew I'd never read the rest.

When Herb put his hand up inside my bra, all I could see were the letters, strewn across my bed. I heard the train in the distance. I was just a little girl.

"Get the fuck off me." I pushed him away.

He stood up and looked down at me. "Sorry," he said.

I kicked at him and he turned to leave. I watched him walk away and heard the signal at the intersection down the way. It was the two-thirty train–the one that took off Bryan Cleaver's head. I laughed. His name couldn't have been Cleaver. The train roared closer, louder now, and I climbed the hill and onto the tracks. There in the distance, a white hot star, searching for me. I started screaming. My screams matched the screeching breaks. I screamed until my throat was raw and the tracks were vibrating–the little white rocks in among the ties danced and bobbed. The earth was going to open and swallow me before the train got the chance to hit. The horn sounded and sounded and didn't stop and the breaks ripped at the night and I screamed against the light that turned the night around me into heaven. When I thought the air in front of the train was sucked into a void, someone enveloped me, tore me off the tracks and pulled me down the hill; we rolled together and landed against the fence at the bottom while the train continued its shrieking halt and the earth trembled.

"I just saved your life," the Perv said, still holding onto me.

"Did you?" I said. "Are you sure?"

I woke up in the morning light, sitting in the Perv's car, the front seats tilted back. We were in the parking lot at the Pool Pit. I pulled at the lever and my seat popped upright and Herb woke beside me. He rubbed his face and sat up.

"Did I sleep all night in your car?" My voice quaked and little sound made it into the air, but I figured I made enough sense.

Herb nodded. "You remember last night?"

"I think so."

"I dragged you away and you passed out so I put you in here."

"Why didn't you leave me lying somewhere so you could go home?"

He squinched up his face. "Are you crazy?"

Well, yes, I wanted to say. But isn't that what a guy does when a girl passes out? It's the perfect excuse. He has no responsibility and she wouldn't remember who left her there...most likely.

"Did you pull me off the tracks?"

"You were screaming."

"My throat feels like it."

"You passed out. The train was stopping; the guy would come out to investigate. We could get charged with trespassing...even now."

"What was I saying?"

"Huh?"

"When I was screaming. What did I say?"

He shrugged. "Fucking bitch. Fucking whore. Slut. God-damned fucking freak. That sort of thing. Were you talking to the train, you think?"

"I don't think so."

We sat for a few minutes until I realized that I didn't

384

know what day it was, or what time, or if I had to work or not.

"Thanks," I said and got out of his car. As I made my way over to mine, the only other car in the parking lot, I heard him opening his door. Jesus, I thought. He needed more. You can't stare down a train and be saved like that and just give the guy a thanks. But what was I supposed to do? I wasn't all that sure I was happy about being saved, anyway. Does a person have to thank a hero if she wasn't happy with the service?

"Hey," he said when he caught up to me at my car. "You're not a freak. You're not any of those things."

I pulled open the door and tossed my purse inside. "What do you know about it?"

"It's like you said. We're all just trying to forget. There's no shame in it."

I got in and looked up to him, hoping he'd move so I could close the door.

"Don't let something outside you tell you who you are," he said.

When did Herbert the Pervert get all psychological? "You don't write inspirational posters for a living, do you?"

He looked at me weird, worried-like. "I'm in construction."

"Of course you are. How old are you, anyway?"

"Thirty-six."

I nodded. Pervert.

# 39.

Dr. Crazy was able to fit me in at the last minute. Alice was nice enough to give me some time off. She'd cornered me in the back room when I got in that morning, still dazed and hoarse from my meeting with the train, and asked what was wrong with me.

"Are you pregnant? Do you have cancer? AIDS? Did someone die?"

I must have looked stunned. "It's nothing as cool as any of that."

I told her about being something of an addict. She said, well I knew that much, and asked me if I was going to AA and I told her I didn't buy into any of that twelve-step stuff. To my surprise she said, good for you. But it's hard to tell sometimes if people mean they agree with you or they think it's cool that you're bucking trends.

"I can't talk about it, really," I told her. "Maybe in a few months, or years. But I need to get to my therapist."

She told me to just let her know when, so there I was, sitting in Dr. Crazy's office apologizing for canceling all those times. I suppose I thought she would be offended by my ditching her. It was hard to think of Dr. Crazy seeing other patients. Sitting in that chair across from the couch doodling in her notebook when they talked, leaning forward slightly when they said something particularly insane, nodding knowingly and expectantly with her earrings chiming...all for other people. You wonder things like that. Like, am I her weirdest client? Am I the craziest one? Does she think I'm interesting enough to write a case study about?

She read through my letters to Camelia and when she finished she got up and went to her desk, sat down and started writing stuff. I told her about the dream–that it really happened. Camelia was lying in the coffin and my mother took me there. "She told me that if I didn't straighten up and be good, the same thing would happen to me," I said. She kept writing. "Is that weird, or what?"

She closed her notebook and got up to hand me my letters. Then she took her seat in the comfortable chair across from me. "How do you feel about all of this?"

How was I supposed to feel? I wrote to a dead girl when I was eight years old and told her that it should have been me. I told her how sorry I was that she was good and I was not, and that if I died maybe she could live. Even my mother knew that. And I tried so hard to be good–for Camelia. To make it up to the world, or the universe, or God–make up for her dying instead of me. God failed me. And I failed Camelia.

"I guess I couldn't handle the pressure–you know, of trying to make life into something special. It's not, you know? It's not anything special. It's just life."

There was this question on her face that Dr. Crazy didn't ask. I always thought it was, "How do you think Camelia would feel about that?"

# 40.

It was April. Hot and muggy already and I couldn't stand to think about the suffocation of the coming months. At least I finally understood why April plunged me into depression every year. Too much happened all at once when I was eight and it shifted that thing inside that kids are supposed to have–that resilience that keeps you innocent, keeps you shielded. It's that thing that makes it so you can read stupid motivational posters and think they mean something. Some of us lose that and I finally knew there was no one to blame.

Bond brought me flowers even though it wasn't my birthday yet and told me he wanted to take me somewhere–a weekend trip away. "Can you do it?"

"I don't know if I can get off work."

"You really should try."

"Where are we going?"

"To see Camelia."

We left Sandy Point at about six-thirty, before sunrise, the weekend after my birthday, and I wanted to tell my mother I wouldn't be coming back. But instead I left a note telling her I was off for a weekend away with Bond. She'd think we were in love and maybe she'd imagine we'd return married. I liked the feeling of disappointing her.

"How did you find it?" I asked Bond as he drove us north through Florida.

The middle of the state is unlike the rest of it: hilly, green, shady. It was like another world. And driving through it, I imagined Alabama was going to be the same. And Camelia would be entombed in a hilly, moss-hung, oak-filled, cool spot. Statues of angels, their faces tear-stained, or hidden in their hands, would watch over her. There would be one of those permanent vases you stick in the ground just in front of her tombstone and someone would always fill it with camellias, pink and white.

"I read the book, for one thing," he told me.

I shuddered. I couldn't finish the thing. I had all the information I could stand. I'd given it to him and told him he'd have to read it for me—he'd have to be my shield. And instead of asking some dumb question, he nodded, like he understood me.

"And the cemetery was in there?"

"No. But Roen said her parents went back to Alabama. I called a research librarian up there and she found the cemetery. She's into genealogy."

"What does that have to do with cemeteries?"

He laughed. "Everything. Genealogy is the study of the dead."

I liked that right away. A study of the dead. The dead weren't forgotten really, and lived as much, or more, once they were gone. Maybe they lived in the charts, or in the

mysteries they left behind. I felt the yearning–that emptiness that calls you someplace you'd rather be and I knew
I'd be comfortable with mystery. Something was nagging
at me. There in the car, watching the road disappear
underneath the tires, I understood. I couldn't imagine a
future. I couldn't picture myself older, married, with
children, and one of those minivans. I couldn't see it at
all. It was less than a fuzzy dream that you can't remember when you wake up; it was nonexistent. And no matter
how much I tried to tell myself it didn't mean anything, it
frightened me.

As we got farther north the world started looking like
the east coast–flat and barren and my heart sank thinking
that no matter where you go, you always end up home
again. Alabama, as it turned out, was little different from
what I'd left behind.

"Do you believe in God?" I asked him.

He made that face, half smiling half balking, and
shrugged. "I don't know."

"What do you mean, you don't know? You either
believe in a god or you don't."

"I guess I do, then."

"You didn't want to admit it."

"Maybe not."

"Why not?"

"I've been thinking about what you said the other
day–at the storage unit. About the pain."

"What does that have to do with God?"

"Everything."

We were silent for a while and I looked at the map,
tracing our pathway with my finger. There wasn't any-

thing out there but land. Occasionally we'd pass through something like a town with a few old buildings, an abandoned bar or strip club, and then back into land again.

"I guess I figured that you didn't." He said.

"Didn't what?"

"Believe in God."

"I read the Bible," I said.

"When did you do that?"

"I told you, remember? Before Sylvie showed up at the Orange Julius that time."

"The whole thing?"

"Up to Corinthians."

"How do you like it?"

"It's got some pretty awful stuff in it."

He nodded.

"It just seemed," I said. "Really human."

"And you expected it to be different."

"I expected it to be holy and divine—above all this."

We checked into a hotel in Dothan and then drove out of town. I rattled off Bond's scribbled directions as he made the few turns. We were lost in the country where nothing was big or shiny. Just tiny roads and land and little houses. I saw the cemetery on the left as we came upon it. It was a sad and dumpy place; a lot like the cemeteries back home. Bond took a parking spot at the little red-brick Baptist church on the other side of the two-lane road. The cemetery was enclosed in a wrought iron fence with an arched opening.

The late afternoon sun burned bright and hot and my heart sank deeper and deeper into my chest as we walked across the street. There were maybe two trees, over on the left, against a fence. Bits of weedy grass grew between the graves. Some family plots were raised, edged in granite borders. Statues were tipped, weeds sprung up at every opportunity, concrete and granite were crumbling and loosened. I couldn't stand the thought of Camelia being there, in that barren wasteland of ignominy. Bond stood by me at the entrance and we stared about us in disgust.

"Well," he said. "I'll look in the back. You take the front."

I watched him walk down the main dirt road and then turned to my left. I saw it–a small headstone, behind and to the left of a larger one. I walked through the plots, catching glimpses of the dead. Children who died too young. Some stones set in the ground and unreadable. Slabs of concrete covered most of the graves. I'd never seen such a thing. Were they overrun with grave robbers? Were there wild animals digging up bodies? A local Frankenstein?

Her name was on the tiny stone, so much smaller than I imagined it would be. She was behind what must have been her grandfather's grave, still awaiting the death of his wife. Their little family plot was set off by four cubes of granite each carved with the letter B.

I stood at her feet–the sun cast a shadow across her slab. Have mercy, the stone said. Between the two words was a cartoon Jesus on a cartoon cross. I thought I would feel peace; I thought I would heal. Bond thought so too or he wouldn't have brought me, but my fingernails dug into my palms and the tombstone blurred through my tears. Two cars sped past on the little road out front.

People went on living, pretending everything was okay. We were all walking around like zombies convincing ourselves everything was going to turn out all right. But that possibility was already lost.

Bond was crossing the cemetery, coming toward me, when I remembered the homeless man by the soda machine in the dark. I handed him the bottle of water, and that weird tiny loaf of brown bread I'd found at the liquor store. I remember thinking how cute it was. How ridiculously vulgar and trivial, and how it was the only thing I found on the shelves to nourish a starving man that I could afford. And the beer. I handed him a beer.

"I don't know," I said. "I thought it might help."

He took the stuff from me, said thank you, and then as I was starting to turn away, he reached out again, pawing the air like he wanted to pet me and I grabbed his hand. His fingers wrapped around mine and he said, "You're dancing in the light. I'm asleep in shadows."

I nodded. The guy was losing his mind, from starvation or drugs or something, and I'd just given him a beer.

"What's that from?" He said. "Was that right? What song is that from?"

Before Bondurant sidled up beside me at Camelia's plot, I whispered to her, "So there you are." All my life, she was a fiction and I was concrete. Now she was real and I was not. It had always been that way, but I'd been numb and unaware. My life was only fragments, stills in the sunlight, pieces of emotion that never connected–a puzzle without meaning. There was no story there. Looking forward, into that oblivion, I feared I couldn't make one out of what I'd been left with.

I was trembling and made an effort to stop; I didn't want Bond to think he shouldn't have brought me. I knew he thought this was a good thing to see and maybe it was. But not the way he intended. He stared at the tombstone with me and then read aloud, "God gave, he took, he will restore, he doeth all things well."

I stifled an angry chuckle and shame washed through me, imagining Camelia's mother kneeling there, weeping and tracing those words with her fingers. It was hope; it was all that was left to her. I turned my face away so Bond couldn't see me wiping the tears.

"This is an awful place," I said. My only comfort was the familiar screaming, in my gut, in my ears.

Bond followed my gaze to the tilted stones and wild flowers; he shoved his hands in his pockets, and said, "Definitely needs some work."

We are encapsulated. Contained. Trapped inside our own heads and it made sense to me, finally, why people talk all the time. Why they get together and just gab and gab and yammer about how they feel about every god-damned thing going on in the world. It keeps them sane—keeps them each dissociated with the vast empty hole that is his consciousness. It made sense. But it didn't mean I could reach it.

"I don't know how much longer I can stay here," I said. But Bond didn't understand.

It was as if the world lie across the gaping hole of the Grand Canyon and people like me and Paulie, we were standing alone on one side watching them go on about their lives on the other. Some of them tossed us ropes.

Twenty-foot ropes. They thought they could span the Grand Canyon and reach us. Why were they so stupid? Couldn't they see the enormous pit? Did Paulie and Sue and Rover and I even want to cross?

"Take your time; let me know when you're ready," Bond said and walked away to explore the cemetery.

I wondered how to make it right–her death, my life, what we'd both lost. Bond thought I could find the answers by being there, but I was worn raw. I looked down again at Camelia's name on the stone. "I'm sorry, I'm sorry, I'm sorry," I said.

When my mother brought me home from Camelia's viewing that Monday evening in 1969, Aunt Aubrey was at our house on Yellow Sands. She was there to tend to Sausage when he got home from school. She smiled and patted me on the head and sent my mother off to the store for dinner supplies, then took me to my bedroom.

"You look awful, honey," she said. She got down on her knees at my bed and pulled me down beside her. She prayed and prayed with her arm across my shoulders making sure I didn't try to get away. "Dear merciful Jesus," she said. "Purifying Jesus, keep Eunice in your holy bosom; keep her from the world; shield her from your wrath; bring her an angel."

She gave me a pad of stationery that she said she'd bought specially for me. It was peach, never a favorite color of mine, and lined, with a small stack of peach envelopes to go with it. She told me I should write to my angel.

"It'll make you feel better," she said. "You can write whatever you want."

When she left the room, I took the stationery to my little corner desk, got out a pencil and wrote on the top page. *Dear Camelia. I'm sorry. I'm sorry. I'm sorry.*

As we walked back through the wrought-iron arch, regret tugged at my mind–I should have said something more, commemorated the moment somehow; I should have left flowers. Paulie's verse came to me then; I'd read it a few days before in the Bible *Thee* Reverend Billy Davies gave me. When I was a child, I understood as a child, but when I grew up, I put away childish things. Paulie said it better, that day at the psychiatric center. It was like Paulie to understand it all–to know what to say when it needed to be said.

I saw the school bus, as we approached the street, but I didn't stop walking. It wasn't deliberate. Stopping would have been deliberate. Bond's hands grabbed me at the elbows and pulled me back from it just as it passed. My hair flew about my head and face as diesel exhaust clogged our lungs.

"I just saved your life," Bond said. He was panting, his face splotchy red, and his hands jittery, but still grasping one of my arms.

"Did you?"

# Books by Dianna Dann Narciso

Mainstream/Literary Fiction by Dianna Dann
*Camelia*
*Always Magnolia*
*Bury Me*

Romantic Comedy by Dianna Dann
*Bookish Meets Boy*

Fantasy by Dana Trantham
*Children of Path: The Kell Stone Prophecy Book One*
*The Wretched: The Kell Stone Prophecy Book Two*
*Mark of the Faire: The Kell Stone Prophecy Book Three*

*The Kell Stone Prophecy: Complete Trilogy*

*Story Runners: Awakening*
*Shards of Kholkari (2018)*

Paranormal Humor by D.D. Charles
*Zombie Revolution*

Children's Fiction by Dana Trantham
*Wayward Cat Finds a Home*
*Zombie Cats*

For more, visit
waywardcatpublishing.com